ALSO BY ROY BLOUNT, JR.:

About Three Bricks Shy of a Load
Crackers
One Fell Soup
What Men Don't Tell Women
It Grows on You
Webster's Ark & Soup Songs
Not Exactly What I Had in Mind
Now, Where Were We?
About Three Bricks Shy . . . And the
  Load Filled Up

First Hubby

FOR ESTHER NEWBERG,
A GREAT AMERICAN

Published in the United States by Villard Books, a division of
Random House, Inc., New York, and simultaneously in Canada
by Random House of Canada Limited, Toronto.

Library of Congress Cataloging-in-Publication Data

Blount, Roy.
    First Hubby / Roy Blount, Jr.
        p.   cm.
    ISBN 0-394-57420-6
    I. Title.
  PS3552.L687F5   1990
  813'.54—dc20   89-40197

Book design by Iris Weinstein
9 8 7 6 5 4 3 2
First Edition

ROY BLOUNT, JR.

First Hubby

VILLARD BOOKS NEW YORK 1990

"My God, I'm not going to preach morals. But yet respect is due to a husband, else nobody would want to be one. Do not oppress the vocation too much, it is necessary in the world."   —ALEKSANDR PUSHKIN, in a letter to one of his mistresses, who had proposed leaving her spouse

"Men are not against you; they are merely for themselves."   —GENE FOWLER

"If a man be not irritable, he is *no poet.*"
—EDGAR ALLAN POE

ACKNOWLEDGMENTS

Aside from that great American Esther Newberg, my literary agent, the following people should not go unacknowledged:

Peter Gethers, my always gratifyingly enthusiastic editor, who showed admirable restraint when I was lying like a dog about how close I was to finishing this book, and who, after I finally did finish it, pushed me to finish it one more damn time, thank goodness. Vereen Bell, Pauline Kael, Veronica Geng, Sarah Ballard, and Kathy Pohl, early readers whose approval I wish I warranted more and whose suggestions I wish I had done more justice to. Lamar and Honey Alexander, who are *by no means* to be identified with any of the political sentiments herein, but who do deserve credit for, among other things, the presence (in this book) of the Wall of China. Dr. John Sergent, spermatological source. Ruff and Barbara Fant, Washington hosts and providers of tidbits they will recognize. (Other old friends—Slick Lawson, for instance—may also note that I was listening, over the years, when they made remarks of particular literary quality.) Christabel King, who was in on the conception and a number of germane discussions. Greg and Madeline Jaynes, with whom I dined on the night I reached the end, and on many other good nights as well. The children, sister, and spouses of my life, who are not to be confused with the children, sisters, and spouses in this book but who have given me things that no one else could have. And a rose for Anita Varoom.

First Hubby

THE FIRST TIME I saw her she was naked, except for pearls and the look in her eyes. My thoughts, as best I can reconstruct them, were: "What? Hm. *Well.*" It did not occur to me that some day this woman would make me the first male First Lady of the Land.

Aside from having no clothes on, Clementine was running from dogs at the time. No doubt Abe Lincoln was doing something more indicative of his prospects when Mary Todd first laid eyes on him, but even so, I doubt Mary's reaction was, "My, he's striking—why do I have the feeling that someday my portrait will hang in the White House looking crazy as a road lizard?"

They all do, you know, there's a hallway in the White House where the First Ladies' portraits hang, and they all look abused, taken advantage of, driven to distraction; and I don't blame them. Abigail Powers Fillmore looks like she has just been induced, for the good of the nation, to eat a dozen mud pies. Jane Means Appleton Pierce looks like she was required to spend the previous night in bed with three dead strangers. Eliza McCardle Johnson looks like she is sitting, out of the frame, in a tub of coffee grounds. Julia Dent Grant looks like somebody just sapped her over the head several times in order to obtain her consent to pose. Frances Folsom Cleveland looks like she has seen things that nobody who bathes daily should ever have to see. And all of those are my sentiments exactly.

Except, no they're not. My sentiments are that I have not been myself since I beheld that streaking vision one April afternoon in 1969. Nobody knows this story, and maybe the nation shouldn't, but there the future forty-third president was at first sight: naked, unruffled-looking and running, with her own odd almost-hitchy litheness, from certain forces of dumb-ass order. She did have a pearl necklace on. The pearls were bouncing, and so was her hair in a loose jet-black plait.

Our eyes met. Maybe the face comes first in a person, and the character follows or tries to. I know that some people have faces

they can't live up to, and in time their faces give in. The thing about
Clementine's face is, it makes us want to support her living up to
it. It looks like a face that has taken things on board that it doesn't
know what to make of, *yet*. A face that wants to laugh but can't quite,
for reasons you secretly almost know. If you could help her face up
to those reasons . . . So I pulled her into some bushes, the first time
I saw her, and offered her what I had, my dirty laundry.

She was nineteen and looked fifteen to twenty-eight. She has
always looked older and younger than her age at the same time,
more mature yet fresher. She regarded me levelly, conspiratorially
up to a point (just as she did in a couple of quick glances twenty-
four years later on the Wall of China, when we suddenly realized
she was going to be Leader of the Free World). She swallowed, as
she sometimes does now during a speech. In most cases that would
suggest nervous weakness, but in her case it softens, without under-
mining, her poise. Her hand went to her pearls, which were yellow-
ish against her coloring in the late-afternoon shrub-filtered light.
I don't notice that sort of thing usually, but I did then. And she said,
"Tell me your name."

Just that. Then waited for an answer.

Her face was almost too amazing. There may be a sense in which
it *works* better on television, but in person it is more amazing,
unsettling. For your own relief, you want to do something to help
tune in that level look of hers that says, "Right. We'll go with this."

Remarkably, under the circumstances, she was close to that look
then. Comfortable in her own skin, as they say. But not content in
it—still off balance enough to take the offensive. Not "Thanks," on
the one hand. Nor, on the other hand, "Who are you to intervene
in my confrontation of the system?" Just: "Tell me your name."

It nonplussed me. I was concentrating on trying to find something in my laundry bag that wasn't too unsuitable for her to wear.
Though she was in no position to be choosy—security men with
dogs running around a few feet away, chewing on clothes (the dogs
were) and salivating after nakedness. She was in no position to be
taking anybody's name, either, but then who the hell has ever been
able to tell Clementine what position she is in?

And then I thought she might be going to cry. *Her.* (Already I was
thinking of her as *her*. Her Secret Service code name is Herself.
Mine, Hubby.) That is part of her power. The country doesn't want

her to melt into tears. Even at that moment three months ago when the nation had just witnessed its President killed by a fish; and, well, "not knowing what to make of it" would have been putting it lightly; and C's face, the suddenly new President Clementine Fox's, filled the TV screen—one reason the succession was so smooth, under the circumstances, is that the nation's heart cried out to her, "Don't cry!" And then, of course, she didn't cry. By any means. Nor did she cry there behind that bush that evening twenty-four years ago, as she eyed me alone.

"Guy," I said, it (the sixties) being an informal decade.

She took that under advisement. Whatever kind of bush we were behind, it was soft for a bush. A spray of it lay across her forehead and she brushed it off. She had dark, sad, almost too-steady eyes. They glistened, or glinted. You can't be quick to characterize what Clementine's eyes are doing. It seemed that all I could find was socks and then a jockstrap, which I stuffed back quickly. She took that in too.

"Guy Fox," I said.

A dog arrived. I saw it coming. And I saw her shrink back, stiffen. I didn't want to see that. I stuffed some bush in the dog's face and punched it in the throat—the only time I've ever hit a dog—and it went "SNUNK-kyak" and ran after some other protester. I love dogs. I'd always been able to look a barking dog in the eye and ask it what the problem was, before. But I was evidently willing to hit a dog for her.

"I'm Clementine Searcy," she said. "You don't look like you go here."

"Hell no," I told her, still digging and coming up with the same things. She must have thought I went through half a dozen jock-straps a day. "I don't know why anybody in their right mind would."

"Would go here? Or would look like it?" She didn't crack a smile or give away a nickel. She was slim, kind of kneesy, even, but graceful—graceful *hunkering under a bush.* She was wearing, as we all know she has continued to wear, bright-red nail polish, fingers and toes. Another violation of the Dingler dress code.

"Either one," I said. "I'm a wri— a reporter."

"A reporter for . . . ?"

"The *Beacon,*" I said.

"Ah," she said levelly. Freckles on her nose. The *Beacon* was about as good a paper as Dingler was a college. A cruder and more defensive nineteen-year-old person would have thrown in some pat tit-for-tat sarcastic phrase, but Clementine just let me fill in the blanks. I'd never had such a shorthand conversation with a woman before, let alone a naked one, and as she talked she gave me something that I felt she'd never given anybody before: a quick candid tour of all that her face had so far learned to bring into play, with hints of what it hadn't. There was commonness and emerging elegance; unblocked sweetness guarded by bite. Fear; and determination to ride fear, not be ridden by it. There was a wistful pretty girl in her face, a girl to be snugly fond of; and there was deep gritty resistance to the lot of a wistful pretty girl. Resistance to something else, too. Resistance extraordinarily developed, but like a muscle, not a wall. Resistance to something in me? That was an open question, but one that seemed more interesting than daunting at the time. As to what I might resist in her, perhaps my look was less forthright in that regard than hers was, because what was uppermost in my eyes, I daresay, was desire. To her surprise, I think, she liked being desired, *by me*—why?

I had always seen in women a confusion—or a jujitsu—of yielding and imposing. In C, I saw the beginnings of something new, more nearly freestanding, less soft, less scary, more productively demanding. I also saw that she saw that I saw it; and that, I believe, is what she saw in me.

I say all that now, as if we realized—even realized we realized—all that at the time. I, at least, was not so acute on my feet as I make myself seem. But I did become more acute as I looked at her. I felt like I had brought down a dove, and was watching the dove browning tastily in the pan, and at the same time the dove was eyeing me and taking wing. Enough to put a man off bird hunting. But not to put me off Clementine. A base element in my makeup sighed, threw up its hands and gave way to something else.

★ JULY 10, 1993

I DON'T KNOW WHY I call it a "base element." If I represented
any kind of oppressed people, I could call it "self-determination."
Or "control over my own life." Or "the sense God gave a goose."

All I know is, now I have this job that I can't quit because I can't
give up my wife.

★ JULY 12, 1993

"I HEARD FROM Orie Ledyard today," I said to C last night.
"You remember Orie Ledyard."

"Mm?"

"We knew him in the country. He would do anything for attention? Drove around with a 'Honk If You Love This Sticker' sticker
on his front bumper and a sticker on his back bumper that said, 'If
You Don't Love This Sticker, Honk'? When you were with him in
a car and drove through a skunk smell he'd say, 'That was me'?"

"Mm."

"Well, he's offering to be my new press secretary."

"Guy . . ."

"No, no, I'm not going to take him up on it. *That's* what I wanted
you to know. So you won't worry."

"Another major headache off my mind."

I went up behind her and put my hands over her eyes and said,
"You nonnnn't want to know." (A family joke.)

She looked back and said, "Why, Hopsie!" (A marital joke.)

"Jean," I said. "Jean, I have been thinking about the Redick
episode, and I'm sorry, I realize now, I was acting like a normal
red-blooded American instead of a person in my position."

"Oh, Hopsie," she said. "Why didn't you take me into your arms that day, why did you let me go, why did we have to go through all this nonsense? Don't you know you're the only man I ever loved, don't you know that I couldn't look at another man, don't you know I've waited all my life for you, you big mug?"

That's the rest of the marital joke. She says it just like Barbara Stanwyck, almost. I mean, you can tell it's Clementine *doing* Barbara Stanwyck, but that makes it even better. I can't do Henry Fonda's voice, but I can get into the scene emotionally. It's the big reunion scene from *The Lady Eve,* our favorite movie. I drew her up out of her chair (which used to be Harry Truman's), and we melted into each other's arms.

Sounds pretty silly, I guess. In fact, I have learned to my astonishment that there are people who feel that *The Lady Eve*—or, anyway, Henry Fonda in *The Lady Eve*—is pretty silly.

Hey, marital jokes are all pretty silly.

And the more they have to cover up, the sillier they get.

★ JULY 13, 1993

I HAVE a press secretary now, but we are not speaking. Which is okay by me, because I'm not doing interviews anymore.

My first press secretary was Redick. Back when I was just Second Hubby, spouse to the veep.

People seem to think that Redick was some kind of stunt on my part. Washington is such a hotbed of intrigue, everybody thinks that everybody is trying to pull something or prove something. Well, I have nothing to pull or prove, now that my irrelevance is, I hope, established. And no, I did not write Redick's statement for him.

Here's exactly what happened. Since my wife was Vice-president, they said, I had to have staff. I didn't *want* staff. Now I have not only staff but *infighting* staff. It's worse than children. Much worse. I hate my staff. (I love my children. Even though they don't call. Sometimes Lucy calls.)

But okay. Staff. I had to pick a press secretary. So I started
interviewing candidates. I had a beer with each one, to see how we
would get on together, and after about eight candidates, I knocked
off and went over to Lafayette Square, across the street from the
White House, and sat down on a bench. I could still do that then.
Trailed by Secret Service, of course, but crowds wouldn't gather.

And Redick sat down next to me. I'd never seen him before in
my life, but he said:

"My head is so bad. *Kaf, kaf.* Do you know how bad my head is?"

"How bad is it?" I asked.

"I can only smell certain farts and green onions."

As he went on and on about his sinuses, about sinuses as the last
environmental frontier ("Our sinuses are where all our chickens
come home to roost, *fnf*"), and about what was wrong with Washington, I became fascinated. Also, I didn't want to interview anybody else.

So I hired him. And oh, the consternation. Even Leonard, whom
I knew back when he was a reporter, when he was digging things
up instead of putting spin on them. "Press secretary is a *profession,*"
he said, "and you bring some guy in off the street."

"Out of the park," I said. "Hey, he says he's an old newspaper-
man. Run a security check on him. If he's subversive, I'll tell him
he won't do. I'll tell you what, though. I don't know whether it's age
or my current eminence, but it isn't any fun getting shitfaced anymore. Anyway, Betty Ford has done alcoholism. I'm going to quit
drinking except every now and then." I have, too, and it's a good
thing, since otherwise I wouldn't believe anything that's happened.

As the new Second Spouse, I had to have a press conference.
Why, I don't know. Redick took the podium to introduce me.

"Assorted inquisitors," he began. "By way of prologue, I would
like to assure you that the stuffiness of my nose, which I have no
doubt you can detect from my speech, *kaf, snk,* has nothing to do
with cocaine. Like most sane Americans, I have had no more than
ten or twelve—*kaf, snrk*—say, two dozen—snorts of cocaine in my
life, and the last was years ago, in the Carter administration. *Snrk.*
By which I do not mean to implicate that administration. Odd as
that administration was, and I should say that I knew no member
of it personally—odd as it was, it was immeasurably preferable, in
my view, to the Reagan one, during which I seldom passed a day

without thinking, often aloud: 'My President is such an asshole!' *Snrk kaf-kaf.* Day in and day out. A president should not be so integral a part of a normal American's life.''

At this point some reporter asked, "Are you *sure* you're Second Hubby's press secretary?" This Hubby stuff started very early on. The male press seemed to get off on it.

"Yes," said Redick, "I am sure, so far as we can be sure of anything in this life—which, incidentally, I believe is the only life: that there is no hereafter, though I am willing to be pleasantly surprised: but not anytime soon, I hope. *Kaf-kaf.*"

"Are you *sure* you're sure you're Hub's press secretary?"

"Ah. I seldom scrutinize my certainties quite to that extent, until they are shaken. *Snnnrk.* Certainties, I might mention, are often more shining than durable—an example:

"From watching a cat, I had worked it out the other evening, from watching, as I say, a cat, *kaf, snrk,* that what separates us from the lower animals is that we are not flexible enough to lick our own genitals. So we seek satisfaction in the arts, the sciences. Money. War. *Kafkaf.* Then, however, I stopped to think. And I realized that cows couldn't either.

"Are there any further questions, before I introduce the Second Spouse?"

Nothing arose from the Fourth Estate except odd—scarcely appreciative—grunts. What has *happened* to the press in this country?

"Well, then, before I do that," Redick went on, "please indulge me in a few remarks about the press. Reporters—I say this, having been one—are like children who say to their parents, 'But you *said* . . .'—picking up every little contradiction. Most people don't care about that. Most people just want to do well. They want a government that will help them do well. Doing well is doing right, to most people; they don't see the conflict. What they want is to be *done right by.* And the terms of our government are: *most people.*

"And most people are inclined to forget or ignore most things. Therefore it has always seemed to me that the media err by not reminding people of what has already been brought to their attention. Certain bits of boilerplate, of established old business, should—in my view—accompany every bit of news. Your audiences might have been less shocked by the sudden demise of the Bush administration, for instance, had you begun your stories during that administration's extended honeymoon as follows: 'President George Bush, who made it plain during the Iran-Contra affair that he tends not to know what is going on around him, announced today . . .'

"And before that, 'President Ronald Reagan, who is so full of shit that his hair won't turn white . . .'

"And yet I do not claim to be an authority on how Washington works. Here is what I think, *kaf*, about every book I have tried to read about how Washington works. Every such book, that I have tried to read, boils down to a well-placed reporter massaging the egos of the sources of his material by reporting how effective these sources are at massaging still other such people's egos. And therefore this is the standard by which a president is judged: not by whether he did the nation any good, *a'hm*, but by whether he massaged egos—egos of solons, egos of reporters, egos of lobbyists, egos of voters—well enough to ensure that Washington continued to regard him as a real ass-kicker.

"And yet the government is not overmellow, as you might think one so caught up in ego rubs might be. On the contrary, it is too mean. By that I do not mean too greedy or too ready for international aggression. I mean too mean. Too mean internally, intrinsically—too mean to do its job. Too much energy goes into cutthroat jockeying for position. It's as if the government were a garden in which the only flowers that succeeded were not the beautiful or the fragrant but the ones that were good at killing off the others. The rank choking out the sweet, for the power to stroke and be stroked."

I could tell that Redick genuinely welcomed this opportunity. He had even stopped coughing and snorting. It made me feel good, to have given the man a forum.

"It has always seemed to me, as well," he went on, "that the press turns out for press conferences too dependably. Had you been delving independently in the governmental garden plot, you might have uncovered the Quayle coup before Mrs. Quayle could get away. I want to assure you that Mr. Fox will neither announce here today, nor admit here today under the most intense handwaving and backup questioning, that he will continue in the Marilyn Quayle tradition. He does not, in fact, intend to overthrow the government. He does not, in fact, even want to be *in* it. Otherwise he has nothing to tell you—so just go away and leave him alone, would be my way of looking at it. I know you have small 'personality' holes to fill, in your various formats, but why not fill them by seeking out persons who are *up to something*?

"And yet, God love you. Because we in officialdom are worse. We always lie. If we can. Relatively—and I am a relativist—you are a wonderful ilk. Under our system you are uniquely empowered to say, though not in so many words, 'bullshit' publicly. Not the most ennobling franchise in the world, but if you don't say it, publicly (everyone says it privately), who will?"

Then with a flourish he turned the podium over to me, and I spent half an hour fielding questions about whether I thought Redick's presentation had been in good taste. I conceded readily that it hadn't been. I affirmed, however, that he had spoken truly in saying that I had nothing much else to say.

That was my last press conference. Before I could be pressured into letting Redick go, he quit to start his own public-radio talk show. He now tends to roast—graciously enough, I think, though groundlessly so far as I can see—my wife's administration.

There's been a lot of water over the dam since that press conference, of course.

★ JULY 14, 1993

I MENTIONED a base element a couple of days ago. The truth is, that base element—self-interest—had not been rooting for her to be in her right mind. That base element felt: (1) that it had not yet gotten from the sixties what it felt entitled to (it never did); and (2) that anybody whose idea of politics was getting naked to demonstrate against imperialism, in loco parentis and the dress code at B. Vaughn Dingler, Jr., Memorial Junior College, of all damn places, might be just the type—however amazing her face was—to take a quick fling at doing something just as ill-considered, but better appreciated, back at my apartment on my foldout couch.

And (3) that that would be that.

But her nearly-levelness, together with the moves her expression made, turned that base element into something finer and harder to live with. It was as if I'd been sitting at my typewriter and the Muse had said to me, "Okay, you want to write that great inspired *whoa-what-is-this* book you've got in you, well this is it, just flip this switch and cut on the juice," only I wasn't sure I wanted to be that carried away yet. I let the level of things slip back a notch.

You know how, when you keep reaching into a mixed bag of stuff, no matter how deep you think you're reaching and stirring, you keep coming up with the same things? I didn't want to dump all my laundry out on the ground. She reached over, took the bag and dumped it all out on the ground.

"But I'm not covering this," I said, more hastily than befitted a man who was fully clothed, who believed absolutely in the First Amendment, who had already worked his way through a good college and who had just rescued her from dog bite and embarrassment. I pulled my voice back down to where I trusted there was timbre.

"I was just on my way to the Wishy-Wash," I said. "If you're still feeling revolutionary . . ." And my voice trailed off. There was a fad then, people would go down to the Wishy-Wash and get into the dryers and go around and around. So I had made a wisecrack. But as soon as I made it I realized it was too strained a wisecrack for anybody to be expected to get, especially a naked person, and if she did get it, it would make me seem reactionary or even the kind of person who would himself ride around in a dryer, which I wasn't.

"Or," I said, "I mean, would you just like to—I would just like to—to talk, or . . . ?" I said. And feeling that I might be looking at her with too-soft eyes I narrowed them a little and smiled at her in a way that I hoped was not unracy yet not insensitive. She looked back at me almost entirely levelly and, fuck it, I forgot about my own eyes and fell, for the first time since childhood, headlong into the eyes of a woman.

This was a big moment. I'd gone a little lame on her, but I'd stuck it out, and she could either chop it off or take it for what it was. She took my maroon-and-gold softball shirt, pulled it over her tanned and brunette head and—I swear this is true—I took a good look at her breasts for the first time. They looked good. Bouncy-soft as young puppies' heads. They disappeared and her face came through. She reached in at the front to slip her pearls out. She bent her head and reached back to flip out her plait at the back. She sniffed at the armpit.

"Yes," she said.

I swear. Maybe it's not surprising—I mean, we all know she is decisive, and this was the sixties, and maybe women generally make decisions that way. But even so. It still surprises me. I see her addressing the nation, and I know it appears, on television, as if she can be seen thinking—seen registering who she is talking to as if she were checking out every American's heart and improvising accordingly. But I see her addressing the nation and I think, "You should have seen her coming through my softball shirt and then *smelling* it, right there. And then giving me this *smile,* from no-where—it was almost a crazy smile, almost too much. . . ."

Even then, I had no inkling that I would someday become the first person in history to carry the Tampax (only when we got off the plane on the first day of her administration, when she didn't have her staff fully organized) of the most powerful person on earth. I had no inkling how far things were going to develop within the next couple of hours, even.

But I knew something was happening. What are you going to say about a smile from a woman's heart when it comes for you and you feel you partly deserve it but can never entirely deserve it and you know, though, that she *could* be happy, she could be happy with you. The greatest thing in the world is a happy woman, but god damn. I wasn't sure I was ready.

★ JULY 15, 1993

MAYBE I CAN do this and put my own stamp on it, I thought at first. Given the circumstances that put us in the White House, I wanted to be helpful.

We were flying back from China feeling stunned. Kismet had descended in the form of a fish. C had risen to the occasion. Then she'd been provisionally sworn in over live TV hookup, since there were no federal judges in China (which raised the legal question of whether there actually was a President of the United States at the moment). C and Leonard and Milam and I were huddled at one end of Air Force Two. Milam—who can organize anything, yet knows nothing of ordinary human understanding—was already well on his way to working out transition and funeral arrangements. C was tired of being told how great she'd been and was going to be. (And it was bothering me—well, this wasn't uppermost in my mind of course; a man had just died. But I had just paid *first class fare plus a dollar,* which the spouse of either vice-president or president is required by law to pay, to accompany my wife all the way to China, and now I was paying it to turn around and accompany her back. To turn around and accompany her back and try to fill the shoes of, like, Eleanor Roosevelt and Nancy Reagan.)

Nobody could think of anything to say.

So I said, "Well this is a fine kettle of fish."

C gave me a look.

Then Leonard said, "Thank God it wasn't a red herring." And we all started giggling, even Milam sort of. The sight of Milam sort of giggling made the rest of us giggle harder.

"If only it had been a Chinese fish," Milam said.

"Yes?" said Leonard.

"Twenty minutes later, he'd've . . ."

"Yes?"

"You know, he'd've . . . Like Chinese food. You're hungry again. He'd've . . ." Milam's face got tighter and tighter as we watched him, in the comedic sense, die.

"Yes, Milam, thank you for sharing that, Milam," we said finally.

And then Leonard said, "Uh-oh. Eggroll."

"I don't get it," I said.

"It's Saturday now in the States, tomorrow is Easter, which means Monday is . . . eggroll day."

"What?"

"Kids on the South Lawn, rolling eggs. Should we cancel eggroll day?"

C finally began to get teary then, which I hated to see.

"No," I said. "I can do that kind of thing, kids, eggs—what are the rules of eggroll? Never mind, we'll make them up as we go along."

I took charge. We dedicated the event to the not-yet-buried president, and we invited his six kids to help Lucy and Jackson and me hide eggs the night before.

It was good to have Lucy and Jackson around again, rallying behind their mother in her hour of need, and the nation's, and temporarily relieving my empty-nest syndrome.

The two representatives of the DaSilva brood who helped us with the eggs, however, only confirmed Lucy and Jackson in their resolve not to be First Offspring in Residence, or even in Evidence. The DaSilva kids were still very much into their roles.

"Dad," Lucy told me, "if you got killed by a fish I would be very sad. But I wouldn't express concern about your place in *history.*" Jackson got into an argument with Scott DaSilva about fiscal policy—I'll have to admit that Scott did act a bit much like an insider, for fifteen. "Scott *likes* having the Secret Service around," Jackson said. Jackson doesn't. Lucy doesn't. I don't. They have refused Secret Service protection, which worries me, but I sympathize. I *have* to have it, for the rest of my life.

Anyway, the eggroll came off well, I thought. We canceled the regular thirty-thousand-moppet gala, but C's old WOT buddies rounded up three or four of every kind of American under nine. At first the guests were worried about how to act, but then they started to find eggs. And then they took them up on a hill and rolled them. You'd be surprised how far a hard-boiled egg will roll. It was nice. Undertones of Humpty-Dumpty, maybe, but nice. Nobody made any speeches or led any prayers, we didn't say anything about the moment, we just played with the little kids. There were spots on the evening news—reassuring continuity sort of thing. A couple of reporters asked me to comment and I quoted Clarence Day:

> *"Who that ever lived and loved*
> *Can look upon an egg unmoved?"*

My sweet weird daughter, Lucy, on the other hand, came away from the occasion with a song, which she's never sung in public because she steers clear, in public, of the autobiographical:

> *Two of the children began to fight,*
> *I made them stop and think all right.*

Said, "Hey little children, the Pres-i-dent
Been killed by a fish—was a ac-ci-dent.
Anything can hap-pen . . .
Anything can hap-pen . . .
These're Easter eggs, for a man of peace!
Why don't you cease
Being cross, little children,
Why don't you cease being cross?

I didn't see any children fighting myself, but I couldn't be every-where.

Lucy is going to put *her* own stamp on things.

I, obviously, haven't been able to. An eggroll is one thing. But a state dinner? The First Lady plans state dinners. I'm used to kitchen-table kinds of affairs. The first state dinner of my Hubby-ship was a couple of weeks after our accession. "Hell, I don't know," I said. "We ought to have place cards, I guess. Hey, let's try it *without* place cards." People stopped consulting me about the things they traditionally consult First Ladies about. Redecoration, for instance. I hate redecoration. To me, any wallpaper that's al-ready on is better than any wallpaper that isn't. "Looks fine to me the way it is," I said. I also declined to do drop-bys. A drop-by is when it says on your schedule, "1:03, arrive in hotel lobby, take elevator to mezzanine, get off, left to Grand Ballroom, 1:06 talk to audience, 1:12 leave Grand Ballroom." They also stopped asking me to spend a couple of hours a day autographing pictures for schoolchildren who write in at their teacher's behest. "What?" I said when it was pointed out to me that this mindless catering to the least creative of school projects was part of my function. "Tell the schoolchildren to go climb a tree. That's what I was doing when I was their age."

After all (as I believe Marilyn Quayle was the first political spouse to mention pointedly), I am not getting paid.

N O W I A M in demand as an author. Now, after all those years of cranking out:

One nonhumorous book. *The World's Wurst: Sausages of Many Lands.* The advance for which was too small to permit any very lavish sausage indulgence, let alone any travel, even if I could have gotten away.

Three humorous books. *Have You Seen My Lizards, Daddy? Bury Me in the Compost Heap and I Will Turnip Soon.* And *Our Tree Surgeon Doesn't Make House Calls.*

Three million ain't-life-in-the-country-a-hoot magazine columns.

And (as ghost) *Oh, Nekkid, Nekkid, Nekkid: The Unadorned Life of Pudding DuJour.* There was a writing experience: C got jealous and would only let Pudding and me work at our house, where she could pop in on us. Pudding decided Clementine Fox was the classiest woman she had ever come in contact with, which only intensified Pudding's insistence on playing down her life as a stripper, which was of course what the book was supposed to be about. We don't include that book in my official bio material. Although it actually turned out to be a pretty good book. Even if it didn't sell. The title came from a story Pudding told about her seventh-grade teacher, who was the classiest woman Pudding had ever come in contact with until Clementine. One day the word *naked* came up in a story the class was reading aloud, and giggling spread throughout the class until this teacher put her book down and said, "Oh, nekkid, nekkid, nekkid," and dispelled the prurient interest. Unfortunately for my bankability, Pudding took that lesson too much to heart.

Now classy publishers are courting me. Now they want me to write a book for which there is an allegedly large audience (the grown-up equivalent, perhaps, of those picture-seeking school kids). Now, *First Hubby.* A lighthearted, affectionate account of life in the White House under—that is to say, with—Clementine Fox,

the first woman president, the woman who won America's heart.
My wife.

My wife and times.

There's a book in it. But not the book they think they want.

Oh, there are doubtless some readers who would like a kiss-and-
tell. But what kind of guy do you think I am?

I never laid lip nor hand on Pudding DuJour, by the way, except
friendly-like, although I confess that when that project arose I
thought, "Wangawangawanga." The truth is, I don't think Pudding
ever had a feeling of Wangawangawanga about sex. That's why she
was so uninhibited about it. She and a New Orleans scion were in
love once, and of course his crowd was appalled, but he prevailed
upon some of them to come meet Pudding at the club where she
danced. (Her real name, incidentally, was Corinne Lemly.) And
sure enough she was intelligent and poised and likable, sitting at
the table there chatting in the black velvet gown she always started
out in, and the scion's people were actually coming round to her
until she got a signal from backstage and stood up and said,
" 'Scuse me for a little while, y'all, I got to go show 'em my
monkey."

I liked the way C got jealous. It wasn't weak, mean jealous. It was
warm, practical jealous. I have talked about this to other men.
Guardedly. (It's not true, as women allege, that men never talk to
each other about intimate-feeling things, although it is true that
men do so with a whole lot more discretion than women do, from
what I understand.) None of the men I have talked to about this
have ever known a woman to be jealous in a warm way. I think C
had to steel herself to come up with a jealousy that came off salubri-
ous. Or play herself like playing a violin. I didn't want to do anything to throw her out of tune.

"Guy," she said, "does she *look* like a Pudding?"

"Well, I don't know, you know; I guess."

The thing was, she did. She looked kind of butterscotch. In a
black velvet gown. And Pudding would've been happy to turn me
loose on herself, I'll bet, just because we liked each other and she
wanted me to feel good; she'd've written with me naked; but that
would have been disconcerting; what would that have been like,
writing with a naked woman? Both of us. Her in my lap at the
keyboard?

She would have, I mean, before Clementine came into the picture.

"Guy? You know when you were a boy and you had a new friend, and your parents wanted you to bring him home so they could meet him? I want to meet Pudding."

She smiled and looked me square in the eye. In her eye there was something going *jit j'jit j'jit,* like electricity jumping. It turned me on. It was better than Pudding. I don't think it's all natural easiness, that way that Clementine has about her. I think she wills it.

I'll tell you something that surprises me still. She can slip behind me, I don't hear her . . .

When I'm writing I'm always a mixture of disgruntled and fascinated, and I hate for anybody to interrupt me—probably because I *want* somebody to interrupt me and I hate to admit it. God knows I've snapped at the kids, god damn me. And if Clementine were to *say* anything to me when she slips up—but she doesn't, it's like in a dream. C feels so great to me that she can slip up behind me at my writing machine and touch me with her cheek and hands next to my ear and her arms around my shoulders, just for a couple of beats, then she's gone, and not only do I not feel interrupted (although I am interrupted), I am ready at that moment to sign up for another several years of whatever the hell she is up to. She is the perfect size, texture and consistency for me. Not exactly the same as when she was younger, but what am I looking for, baby fat? Where else am I going to feel the sum of twenty-four years of mostly trustful holding?

We're also talking about the mother of my children. It's the only thing that makes me feel all of a piece, holding her. Okay, I do wish I'd had some Pudding. It's *crazy* I was in a room, alone, with Pudding, all that time, and yet no consummation. But it wouldn't have been nuclear like Clementine, the secrets of the atom.

She never comes up behind me when I'm working now, though.

So. I guess I can finally get down to some real writing.

★ **JULY 17, 1993**

THE DOGS AND security men were gone. We stuffed my clothes back into the bag. Hers had been taken in evidence. My shirt on her was almost as big as a dress. We just started walking, and reached the Toddle House. We were sitting there having a piece of pie and feeling crazy—I was anyway—when my fellow reporter Leonard Shore came in.

Leonard was good. Some people, when they see two people sitting there kind of stunned eating the same piece of pie the way we were, will start to poke fun, but Leonard was a serious guy. He took us in with one look and started to talk about himself.

"I moved down here from Chicago," he said, "because you know why? Because there aren't any psychiatrists here. I came down here to break my habit. I've been going to psychiatrists since I was fifteen, one after another, because I keep hoping just one will interrupt me in a voice full of emotion and say:"

And Leonard went into this great voice—not your predictable Viennese accent, but this great suddenly-touched-authoritarian's voice, maybe a voice we always wanted to hear from our parents.

" 'Leonard,' " Leonard said in this voice, " 'let me tell you something! In all the years I have been in this business. All the people I have listened to pour out their stories. You are the first time I have wanted to say: "Here is a good person." Leonard, you are decent. That is your burden. Your problems are not your problems, they are the world's problems. Of course you are frustrated. Of course you feel bad. Because others do not appreciate. Others take advantage. Others do not value a man who deals from decency. Leonard, my advice to you, don't push the decency so hard. You've got plenty of it, just ingrained. Go ahead and pursue pleasures. Aggrandizement. Ease. Others do who don't deserve to. Why not you, who do? Leonard, life owes you. Coast.

" 'And I am not one of these feel-good shrinks, either. I am usually stern. "Of course you feel guilty," I tell them. "Look at what you did. The trouble with you is you don't feel guilty *enough.* If I were you I'd feel *more* insecure.''

" 'But Leonard,' " Leonard went on, " 'you're different. Get out of my office, before I get maudlin. You don't owe me a nickel.' "

In his own voice, Leonard sighed. "Just *once,*" he said.

I had heard him do this before. "Leonard," I said, "I'll tell you what you *need.*" And then I thought, "What am I going to say, exactly?" I was trying to find some apt way of putting it when Leonard said, "A relationship."

Which was helpful because anything I could say was going to be romantic in comparison to that, and I have trouble making romantic statements—I take romantic sentiments too seriously, I think is the problem. I don't want to *lie.* I relaxed a little. Clementine put her hand on my arm.

It triangulated us in a good way. I could tell that Clementine liked Leonard and liked it that I had this intellectual friend from New York. Which Leonard definitely liked. I liked Clementine's hand on my arm.

Leonard took the fork that had just been set in front of him, cut a piece of our pie and held it up like a toast. "Life," he said. C and I forked the last two bites and said, "Life," back.

To this day I get a hard-on when I even see a slice of banana ice-box pie.

★ JULY 19, 1993

I CAN'T WRITE in the First Lady's office in the East Wing. My staff is there. My god damn staff, they discomfit me. I gather that West Wing presidential staff is always snotty to East Wing First Lady staff, and with me as First Lady it's worse. My staff devotes a good deal of its energy to letting me know that. Also, I feel self-conscious chewing tobacco in the First Lady's office. There is a long tradition of tobacco-chewing in the White House (Warren Harding used to pop whole cigarettes into his mouth and chew them, and Andrew Johnson once mistook Senator Sumner's hat for a spittoon), but not lately, and not in the East Wing. But chewing helps me concentrate.

So I've got this little room fixed up here in the family chambers. On the wall I have a big photograph that I found in the White House warehouse over across the Potomac, of Grover Cleveland in a bathing costume. There is a lot of great stuff in that warehouse— dingbats going back to Chester A. Arthur, at least. I have this great paperweight or something, bronze, in the shape of the front half of a bare foot, engraved "To President Chester A. Arthur From the Iroquah [sic] Confederacy." Hell, it may be a *bronzed* half a foot, there may be half of somebody's foot in there. I have it on my desk. One of the precious few consolations of office.

There is another consolation that nobody wants me to take advantage of. I still have to balance the checkbook in this household, and I noticed the other day that half of the checks I wrote in May were still outstanding. I grumbled about it to an aide. I don't know what her title is, I have too many things to think of without learning my aides' titles. "We can clear that up," she said, "if you put my name on your account and I sign your checks."

"What?" I said.

"What happens," she said, "is that people will save your checks for the autograph instead of cashing them. So if I sign them—"

"They *will?"* I said. "That's *great.* It won't make up for all those first-class fares plus a dollar—do you realize how much it cost me to fly first class to China and back without even getting any Chinese food? But it's something. How big a check does it have to be, do you think, before it becomes worth more than my autograph? Here's one for $79.38 to the shoe store. Here's one for *$129.40.* This is a gold mine!"

The aide looked at me as if I had said something monstrous. Now C herself is trying to talk me into putting a stranger—a stranger who doesn't like me—on our checking account. Also, somebody in the presidential counsel's office has advised me never again to mention publicly that presidential access to films is no big deal to 'C and me because we still prefer to watch and rewatch our library of copied videotapes—movies of the thirties and forties, mainly—in bed. Every one of those copied videos, this lawyer reminded me, was a violation of federal law. I never dreamed I would find myself in such a chickenshit situation.

An aide called me up here this morning. To give me some changes in my schedule, which included:

Presenting awards to the mayors of towns that have brought off the most exemplary solid-waste disposal campaigns.

Getting a haircut. (Because I can't look seedy anymore even if I don't go anywhere, because it's bad for staff morale.)

Going over plans for the Comedic Talents of America banquet. (Which I don't want to attend much less give a welcoming address to.)

Meeting with my chief of staff, who wants to tell me about staff morale.

"I tell you what you do," I told this aide. "Cancel my schedule. And cancel tomorrow's schedule."

She started to cry.

"Aw, okay," I said. . . . But then my resolve stiffened. "No. Do it. I hate my schedule. Cancel today's and cancel tomorrow's. In fact, cancel my schedule until further notice."

Hey, Letitia Tyler stayed in her bedroom throughout her husband's administration, running the household "so quietly that you can't tell when she does it," according to her daughter-in-law. Mrs. Franklin Pierce was opposed to her husband's candidacy and wouldn't move into the White House for weeks after his inauguration because she thought the death of their child was some kind of judgment. Ida Saxton McKinley was childish and irritable and had epileptic seizures at state functions, which her husband dealt with by covering her face with a napkin. She spent most of her time in bed looking ghastly and knitting more than thirty-five hundred pairs of slippers.

I think I will be First Hubby in writing, primarily. They think I'm writing a book, so maybe they'll leave me alone. What I am actually writing is this. But what the hell. Now that my wife is making $250,000 a year, plus perks, I no longer need to be commercial. I can cast aside the cap and bells, or at least jingle the shit out of them. Some writing of my own, as they say. Here's something I've been working on.

So You Have a New Child

Please, please, please. There are no new children. To bring a human being into the world at a time like this has been done.

Repeatedly. On television. And the child will have to have a home.

You didn't think about that, did you? It is all very well for you to live in your classic '58 T-bird, but a child can't drive, and can barely see out. And has to go to the bathroom. A home today costs $760,000.

The child will also have to have parents. Whom the child will eventually see through. But not before the parents have invested $6.3 million in the child's care and education. The care will have been impeachable, the education spotty. And what you have had to do to scrape together the $6.3 million will contribute enormously to your being seen through.

It is not all that enlightening to be seen through. On the one hand it seems apt enough, but on the other hand it doesn't help. If one could have done it oneself, it would have been one thing. In fact one may have thought that one had done it oneself, already. But no. Nothing penetrates like the innocent wonder of a child.

Don't give in to them, experts advise. And so do parents advise other parents. Do parents take the advice of experts and other parents? Let me answer that question with another question: do children—the children of experts, even—take the advice of their parents?

It is important that parents maintain a spurious sense of themselves to fall back on, for purposes of holding the home together, when the child has seen through the authentic one. In fact it is wise to keep the spurious one up front, in hopes that the child will go for it; but the child won't. Do wolves go for a spurious throat?

Don't praise children. They see what you are up to, and develop qualities opposite from the ones praised. Think you can trick them by praising those qualities that you wish they would drop? No. They will hold to those qualities *and* remind you that you praised them.

Don't ever think you can beat children. By this I mean both don't ever think you can hit them—which you are *capable* of, as long as they are small, but which would be wrong—and also don't ever think you can get ahead of them, which you are so far from being capable of that neither right nor wrong enters in. You can never get ahead of children because they are growing, in every way; and if they aren't it's your fault.

Children are like the press. To intimidate or deceive them is wrong, in an open society, and to be thoroughly open with them would be so unselfishly self-defeating that there is no point even in flattering yourself that there is any real likelihood of that. They wouldn't like it anyway.

When questions and doubts besiege you, as you get deeper and deeper into child-rearing, just remember this: you were a child once (and will never be again); and remember what your parents were like?; and now you are parents. And if you try to finesse this deal in some way, everyone will be sorry in the long run.

Just try to be natural. And remember that no one wants to hear about it from your point of view.

How is that for making the world a better place? I should be shot. I should be First Lady of Albania. Now I might as well write a poem. Something for the banquet (incidentally, nobody ever invited me to *join* the Comedic Talents of America until I attained my current marital eminence):

Jackanapes's Lament
(What Actually Goes Through the Comedic Mind)

Sure, my gift affords intense delight
To the temporarily *gloomy, whom it cheers.*
My tongue's tucked firmly in my cheek, all right.
It's the only way to keep from tasting tears.

Do you ever, while you're rolling in the aisles,
Stop to think that I might be distraught?
For you it's all a lot of hoots and smiles.
Do you ever give my fear of crowds a thought?

You think that when I leave you limp with mirth
It must be lots of fun for me—and yet
I'm not getting paid what I am worth
And as I speak my shoes are full of sweat.

And the real kicker is, if I should share
My true feelings with you, you'd demand
Your money back, on grounds that who could care?
Although I don't know where my wife is, and . . .

Let's just say my presence here tonight
Is not (no more than this) what it appears.
My tongue's tucked firmly in my cheek, all right.
It's the only way to keep from tasting tears.

The truth is they'll probably go for that. Jack-offs. I *don't* know where my wife is. The phone rang before dawn and I covered my head with the pillow, and when I woke up she wasn't there. I don't suppose it's war, or I'd have heard.

Lucy is doing her music. Jackson is pursuing his money studies. Their Aunt Dancy is going right on ahead being a Christian performance artist. "Some say I am not a Christian and some say I am not an artist, but nobody will ever say I won't perform," she says, as she has always said, and then she sings, for instance:

> *"My God is real, so are my boozums.*
> *And here is how he'd have me use 'em."*

She also does this not only funny but strangely affecting takeoff of a stoned hippie singing "Show Me the Way to Go *Om.*"

Old Dancy. I wish Dancy and I were close. She and C aren't, really. She doesn't look much like C, but there's something about the two of them that goes together. And Lucy obviously takes after her aunt to a degree. Dancy would never be with a musical group that calls itself Smell a Rat, as Lucy has been (her group keeps changing its name), but Dancy was once billed as Brook Burbling (and the Eddies), back before she got into Christian content so forthrightly.

I am a little sensitive on this point of why presidents, so often, have crazy relatives. My position is this: hey, a president's *relatives* have crazy relatives too, and one of them is the president. What if Donald Nixon had been president? People would have been talking about his peculiar brother Richard.

Still, I wonder why C has promised Dancy a White House wedding. But, then, I also wonder how it came to be that C's father and the Reverend Dingler are backing her wild defense budget–cutting ideas. C brings people together. She just does.

Anyway, if Dancy can do her thing, why can't I, if I'm discreet about it? What I am going to do is, I am going to write what I want to write every day until Dancy gets married in the Rose Garden September 5. If the Republic is still standing after Dancy's wedding, then I will adopt a more statesmanlike posture and hack out something breezy.

★ JULY 20, 1993

WELL, I FOUND OUT what C was doing. She was responding
to a crisis. The Avery Milt affair. Apparently Milt was, as he claimed
to be, no more than a jet-lagged vacationing Baptist high school
teacher who got on a plane in Frankfurt thinking it was bound for
the Holy Land and wound up in Beirut, where he was kidnapped
from an airport men's room stall—where he was hiding, "trying to
think," as he put it, and loudly reciting the Lord's Prayer—by an
Islamic group that claimed he was CIA. And Clementine got him
out. Within hours.

Last night in bed she even told me how she did it. Sometimes—
when she thinks telling me something will make me feel more
sanguine about human nature whether I like it or not—she can't
resist.

She got on the horn to Qaddafi.

"And promised him what?"

"Promised him nothing. Just told him the truth—which he believed, because I have told him the truth about some other things.
Also, I asked him if he actually thought that agents of this government, of any government, were *that* flaky. Then I asked him
whether he actually thought the United States was likely to make
any concessions to obtain the release of a person who was that flaky.

" 'Flaky,' Qaddafi said. 'He is *flaky?*' He caught the allusion to
what Reagan had called him years ago. He chuckled."

"Qaddafi chuckles?"

"Guy, all God's children chuckle."

"Garbo laughs. Qaddafi chuckles. Jesus," I added, "wept."

"I just answered yes, flaky. A flaky Baptist. Then, while Qaddafi
was chuckling, I asked him whether any Islamic group was going
to want to have Avery Milt around for long. Avery Milt, in any tight
situation, is a nervous prayer. He can't help it, poor soul, he can't
stop praying. He doesn't even realize he's doing it. Prays louder
and louder. He has been known to do it in the classroom. I had
called his principal and found that out. Woke him up at five in the

morning. I could hear him saying to his wife, 'It's . . . the President, sugar. Calling about Avery Milt.' And I could hear her saying, *'Whuuuuhnf?'* And then, after she'd had time to blink, 'Who *is* that woman?' "

"Didn't Qaddafi try to say that you were appealing to the wrong guy?"

"He wouldn't like to say that to me."

She's a pippin.

"Okay," I said, "if Qaddafi can get Avery Milt out, then why can't you get him to send back Marilyn Quayle?"

"Art of the possible, Guy. Take what they give you. Keep plugging away."

"Like marriage," I said after a minute. But I didn't say it audibly, because I knew I was saying it unpleasantly—something inexcusable gets into my voice that I can't help sometimes; I don't quite feel it but I have learned, from the reactions of others, that it's there.

And C was asleep, spooned snugly against me.

The Comedics applauded my poem. There were in fact, I believe, several wet eyes in the house.

★ **JULY 21, 1993**

''THREE THINGS, QUICKLY,'' I said this morning. She was giving a couple of licks to her hair. One thing we agree on is that the first requisite for a woman president is great hair. Clementine has great hair. It was great when it was longer and wilder and it's great now, presidential. Give it a couple of licks with a brush and it's ready to go. Which means I don't wake up every morning to the entrance of a hairdresser, for which I am grateful.

Great-luxurious, great-orderly. Hair that I can go stick my face in and go *wuff-wuff-wuff,* hair that is, hey, no problem, let's go. Ride in a motorcade? Try on a cowboy hat? You got it. Great hair. Just graying now in a way that on her, of course, looks good.

"One," I said. "I didn't get a genius grant."

"Aw," she said perfunctorily. Thinking of the moon, I expect. The moon, which we must either go ahead and stop futzing around

and land some more men—persons—on, or not. By *we* I mean
America.

"Not that I thought I probably would get one, anyway. Not that
I *would have,* necessarily, if I weren't married to the President. I
probably wasn't even *up* for one. But I'm just saying—hey, it's
nothing for you to *take to heart,* but *of course* no one would get a
genius grant who is married to the President. It wouldn't look right.
The list is in the paper today. I didn't get one. A twenty-six-year-old
entomologist, who studies weevils, did." I held up my hand. "No
need to respond."

She looked at me. She did. She does. She looks at me. Always has.
Pat Nixon, I'm not.

"Two," I said. "It says in the Science section that 'putting on a
sad face or a smile directly produces the feelings that the expression represents, according to a new theory of how emotions are
produced.'"

"Guy . . ." she said.

"Okay, hey, the President doesn't need to know this, I guess. The
President, I realize, will be handed a news digest momentarily
which will tell her all she needs to know. But let me just encapsule
this down for you. According to this article, as I understand it, you
can get happy by going through the motions of smiling, which
causes the tightening of certain muscles, which lowers the tempera-
ture of blood flowing through the hypothalamus, which regulates
emotion. Cool blood, warm heart."

She looked at me, and smiled.

"I, myself, would call this *fooling the hypothalamus,*" I said.

"You, yourself, would," she said. She looked at the middle of my
face and her eyes narrowed. Every now and then some kind of thing
starts growing out of one of the pores on the tip of my nose—not
a pimple, or a wart, I don't know what it is. She took her fingernail
and scraped at the tip of my nose, as if it were her own. I like that.

"My nose growing again?" I said.

"Mm," she said, absorbed in her handiwork.

"Sir Laurence Olivier, you know, worked from the outside. First
he got the nose right, and from there the character."

"I think I've got your nose right," she said. And off she went to
figure the next phase of the moon.

"Three," I hollered after her. But she was gone.

AFTER WE LEFT the Toddle House, Clementine and I went to
the Wishy-Wash and did my laundry, except for the shirt she was
wearing, and I told her I liked her pearls. I had never congratulated
anyone on her jewelry before, but those pearls did look good.
"They're opera length," she said. "I'm wearing them looped
around twice. They're real. Individually knotted on. I have earrings
that go with them. They were my mother's. She didn't have a lot
of beautiful things. But these. She died when I was nine."

"Mine died when I was eighteen," I said. "She would sing sad
hymns while she did the housework."

And C started singing softly, "I love to tell the story, of Jesus and
his glory," and I joined in with her all the way through three verses.

A one-armed woman came in and said, "Is that y'all's clothes
hanger there? Well I reckon somebody's left it, then; I'll just take
it." She had locked her keys in the car. "I bet I do it twice a week,"
she said. "Sometimes I think I'm not all right in the head." We bent
a loop into the end of the hanger for her and went out with her to
her car, but she insisted on flipping up the button herself. It was
a pleasure to watch how adroitly she popped that button up—I
couldn't have done it that fast with two arms—especially since you
could tell she'd been drinking, and the thought occurred to us that
she might be heading right off to the next Laundromat to run
through the whole thing again. In fact, she had Michigan plates on
her car, which didn't prove anything, but what if that were her life,
we wondered: driving across America, alone, showing people what
she knew she could do well.

"I'd like to drive across America with you," I told C. She looked
at me like that might be a good idea. And then a two-armed but
depressed-looking woman came in, slowly, holding a pitiful little
armload of clothes. She dropped them in a chair and said to us:

"Hardly worth the trip, is it? But I like to get out. I don't know
what else to do. My husband used to love that miniature golf, but

it ain't the same without him. I was his peepeye lady. I lost him a year ago."

"Ma'am?" I said.

"Well, I say a year ago. Be a year ago next month. He went to the doctor to have his heart exam—came home smiling and saying, 'Mama, I got no more choresterul in me than a rock-pile snake. Let's have some pie.' So I went and brought out my pecan pie we had had some of the night before. He took a bite and I said, 'Is it good, hon?' And he said, 'Make a puppy pull a freight train. I just want to go on chewing it and chewing it.' And finished his pie and went over to his big chair at the TV and sat down in it like you're sitting in that one. And said, 'Mama, I want to tell you,' and I said, 'What, hon?' and his expression changed, and he said, 'Mama!' and was gone."

"We just don't know," C said. She knew how to talk.

"Peepeye lady?" I said.

"Yessir. He was a photographer. When they'd bring the children in, you know. We didn't have any of our own. But when they'd bring the children in to be photographed, why, I'd be the peepeye lady. They'd be fussing and splaying themselves all around and he'd get the lights just right and he'd call me, 'Hon? We got a little child in here that just *hates* to smile.' And he'd say to the child, 'You ready for the peeeeeepeye lady?' and the child would get just a little curious you know and then I'd stick my head in the door with my hand over my eyes and go: 'Pee-pye.' "

"That's nice work," I said.

"Yes. I don't have the opportunity for it anymore."

I guess I was showing off. I probably wouldn't do this today—well hell, I *couldn't* do it today, I'm famous. Did you know that when an ex-president or spouse goes somewhere today, Secret Service people go ahead and shoo everybody out of every hall they are about to go down?

But I said, "Ma'am? Would you step outside for a moment?"

"Do what, son?"

"Would you step just outside the front door there for a moment while we talk something over?"

"Guy, what in the world?" C said.

"Well, I will, son. I was young myself once." She looked a little bit taken aback, but she went out.

"Guy!" C said, looking at me like she'd misjudged me.

"You be the baby," I said to her, and then I called out, "We got a little child in here that just *hates* to smile!"

And I got down like a photographer and that lady popped in like the pro she was. It was the best peepeye I ever saw, a child's ideal surprise. She lifted her hand to expose eyes that were sort of like Harpo Marx's but more maternal. And then she did it again with them crossed, and again with them rolling around in a way that went right up to the line of being genuinely disturbing but didn't quite cross over. She had three or four different variations. And Clementine smiled and smiled—I wish I had had a camera.

"Well, y'all have cheered me no end," the peepeye lady said, "but while my clothes is awashin' I've got to go get my pep prescription filled."

"Ma'am," C said, "why don't you take up your husband's business. That peepeye is too good to go to waste."

"Nawww, honey, I don't know how to do all the other end of it. Lemme go run to the store."

C sobered up. "I'm not ever going to get caught like that," she said.

Which I liked the sound of. I never have wanted somebody to depend on me for who she was.

I picked up a copy of the *Beacon* that was lying there open to a syndicated health column by a man named Dr. Harris Spruill. "Ah, that's my favorite thing in the paper," C said.

My heart jumped because it was one of mine too. "It's the only thing in it," she said, "besides the funnies and the social notes, that's not hateful."

She was overlooking the fact that I wrote for this paper, or maybe she wasn't, no, she must have been—either way it bothered me a little, but just in the back of my mind and not enough to get me irritated under the circumstances. Anyway, all they'd let me do was wrecks and obits and openings, things you couldn't have a point of view about. This day the headline on Dr. Spruill was HAPHEPHOBIA IS TICKLISHNESS.

I read aloud:

" 'A Puyallup, Wash., man . . .' "

"I want to go to Puyallup, Wash.," she said. "And meet a Puyallup, Washman—not really," she said, looking at me as if she thought she might have hurt my feelings. That struck me as nice. "Puyallup, Wash.," she said.

"Backwards it's Pullayup," I said.

"Mmm," she said. She liked words.

"Rearranged, it's Up, up, y'all," I said, but she wanted to get on with the story. She took over the reading:

"A Puyallup, Wash., man has haphephobia or extreme ticklishness. 'When any person comes up behind me and even brushes me in the ribs,' writes L.D.M., 'I yell, lash out with my arms, and jump.' "

"Vell! He *duss* haphephobia," I said in a kind of Viennese accent, and Clementine laughed. I'd never known a woman who liked puns.

" 'After fifty years of this, I'm more or less used to it, but some of my co-workers and friends are convinced I do it to annoy them.' "

"I don't think he does," I said, though I secretly suspected he did.

"I don't either," Clementine said. "I believe him."

The obvious thing was to tickle her at that point, but there was something too pensive about her.

"Dr. Harris Spruill doesn't tell him what to *do,* " she said.

"Maybe his last couple of paragraphs have been cut," I said. "That's journalism for you."

She looked at me. This afflicted person wasn't just words to her. But we sat close together reading the social notes—"Mr. Dovard Chalk of Beanland checked with a psychiatrist at V.A. Hospital in Spartanburg recently. They have determined he is of sound mind. Anyone wishing to verify this may call" such and such a number.

And the funnies. Her favorite for some reason was "Moon Mullins." My ears perked up.

"Have you ever read anything by the writer Ford Madox Ford?" I said tentatively.

She looked a little shy, or something—sad, actually. I was thinking, "Oh, well, you can't expect . . ."

"The Good Soldier," she said.

I couldn't believe it! I didn't think there were any *ugly* women in Dingler who'd read anything by Ford Madox Ford. *And* were familiar with the characters in "Moon Mullins."

I said, "I read somewhere that a young writer in the twenties said Ford Madox Ford in person made him think of Lord Plushbottom."

She laughed and laughed. I don't think she was laughing at the connection between Ford and Plushbottom, high and low culture, which was what amused me, so much as—maybe she was laughing at how excitedly I was looking at her. I don't know. I almost asked her what she was laughing about, but why mess with it? I just loved to see her laugh so hard. She doesn't laugh that hard very often, but when she does—well, the world has seen her do it on television. It's wonderful. It's like watching a baby break up. Until Clementine, you never thought of presidents laughing. Grinning, but not laughing the way she does. She doesn't laugh at things, she laughs toward them.

I have come to wonder, over the years, whether you ever have any real notion of why she's laughing. I wonder, sometimes, whether she gets things that nobody else does. And conversely, whether there are things she doesn't get that everybody else does.

But I hadn't come to wonder that yet. I said, "I thought I'd have to wait years and years before I could find anybody to tell that to who'd appreciate it. And I *never* thought it would be somebody . . . beautiful." I never had called a woman beautiful, just flat-out like that, to her face, before. You'd have thought you'd need to say something more clever to a woman as cool and unbounded as Clementine seemed to be, but no.

She looked at me so frankly I blushed.

I didn't have anything in the paper myself that day, which was just as well because I didn't have all that much confidence in my style. Maybe it's not a good idea for a man to fall in love with a woman who not only appreciates the same unusual things but appreciates them better than he does. Maybe; maybe; but I couldn't help it.

Then the dryer stopped going womble womble and I walked her back toward her dorm with my arm around her acquaintively, feeling her melony-firm hip through the cotton of my shirt, glancing at the way her loose plait met the nape of her neck; feeling like bulldogs were wrestling in my chest. Well, that's a figure of speech.

I'll tell you how I felt, because it's coming back to me as I write this. I felt dazed, and I also had a hard-on—I've never had such a hard-on—such that there just wasn't any point in being shy about it then nor is there now. I've got a hard-on now.

★ JULY 23-24, 1993

WHAT I'M MOST afraid of is an insane woman, and now I feel like one. In a manner of speaking. No, I know, I can't say that: a man has no idea what it's like to be any kind of woman, can't possibly have, although he ought to. So what can I say?

I didn't much mind being the *Vice*-president's spouse, though I never bargained for that either. Who could have known not only that the Democrats would self-destruct as usual but that the Republicans would too—and in such an unusual way—two weeks before the election. Ah, those crazy Quayles.

But the Vice-president has one of the best houses in Washington, and it's on the same grounds at the Naval Observatory. I would walk over there at night and be free to look through the big telescopes for hours. That didn't last long, though. Thanks to the well-known almost-ineffable act of God.

I do mind being First Lady. It's not so much the gender angle—well, it is the gender angle. But the main thing is that I want to be something that *I* want to be.

I remember the summer I was sixteen, I was working for the campaign of Berry Orr for reelection as mayor of my hometown of Folger, Georgia, and we ran out of *R*'s. If you are trying to put MAYOR BERRY ORR FOR MAYOR up in plastic letters on both sides of one of those signs—one of those signs that are sort of slotted racks that you snap plastic letters into and then you put the rack in the back of a truck and drive it around or park it where the candidate is speaking—you have got to have fourteen *R*'s. There is no getting around it. And we had only nine. So we had to go out and find some more.

The campaign manager—Mabry Packard, a fat man and ex-marine who ate peanuts shell and all and had an ivory hip, he said, from a war wound—found somebody who had a whole pile of these letters stored in a house that this person, whoever it was, owned out off the Federal Highway somewhere. I was dispatched, with my fellow worker Beau Milam, to go sift through them for five more *R*'s.

That's right, Beau Milam. I knew him before C did, although he went on to meet her before I did. He had come from Atlanta proper to outlying Folger to work for Mayor Berry Orr for mayor, and I know good and well they didn't like him in Atlanta either. I was working for Mayor Berry Orr for mayor just to see what went on in my hometown, knowing in advance that I wouldn't be able to believe it. Milam had come there to begin his political career.

Milam wasn't a hard-charging country boy, he was a hard-charging Atlanta boy. His daddy was a big chamber-of-commerce type in Atlanta, and here is the conversation I had with Milam when we met:

"And you're . . . ?"

He had a mouth like a slot. Made you want to put a quarter in it.

"Guy Fox."

"Guy," he said, giving me a looking-you-straight-in-the-eye look without seeing anything. This was when he was young and was still trying to have a personality. "Beau . . . Milam. There is going to be room for us both to do well in this campaign if we understand each other from day one. I grew up in a little different background from you, probably—golf, the country club and what have you. But that is behind me. I am here to learn about politics, pardon my French, at the nut-cuttin' level."

I am sixteen, and he is eighteen. "Pardon my French?" I didn't have much idea of how people who knew what they were talking about talked in downtown Atlanta, but I knew it wasn't like that. It's like when your Sunday school teacher tried to give you a little talk about teenage sex and she used the word *petting.* Nobody uses the word *petting* except people who write Methodist handbooks on how to talk to teenagers about sex.

I decided there would be room for us both in the campaign—I was making $1.25 an hour, he was donating his time—if I never let on anything to him except that he didn't reach my threshold of reality.

That's where C is different. She assumes that everybody who

crosses her path is on the same level of reality she is, and since she assumes it so strongly, it's true, so long as she is dealing with whoever it is face-to-face. Milam would like to be that kind of person, but he never had any level of reality—except the law, after he became a lawyer—that anybody else would acknowledge until he latched onto Clementine's.

But neither of us had met her back then—she was only eleven years old at the time, and she was with her father in Paris, of all places, where he was attached to NATO headquarters and she was learning French, as a matter of fact, and somehow developing that sense of reality of hers against heavy odds.

Anyway, Milam and I were looking for *R*'s. We were given a key to this house out on the highway, and when we finally found the house and unlocked the door I saw the plastic letters in a waist-high pile right in the middle of the living room. I also saw a stick from a candy apple, with red stains and the core still on it, and a little child's scooter and a sprung settee.

Otherwise there wasn't anything. It was a big house, and there was something spooky about it. We had taken so long to find the house that we were in a hurry to get the *R*'s in time, so Milam and I dug into the pile.

You'd think *R*'s would be fairly common, but we dug and dug and spread the pile out wider and wider and it was getting late and we still hadn't found one *R* between us. I was thinking maybe we could go with apostrophes and periods: MAYO' BE'Y O. FO' MAYO'. People in Folger didn't pronounce many *R*'s anyway. But I wasn't sharing this thought with Milam, who was getting tense and saying, "This won't do. This won't do," and throwing letters across the room that looked like *R*'s at first but turned out to be *B*'s or *P*'s—when a woman appeared in the living-room doorway.

She was wearing a raggedy chenille housecoat with dead-chry-santhemum-looking tufts on it, and slippers that were in such bad shape she couldn't pick her feet up very high and still keep them on. I guess she had shuffled down from upstairs. I don't know whether she had heard us come in or not, but she didn't look startled, just wild and detached. She looked at us.

"We just rent," she said. "We don't own."

I said, "Oh, I'm sorry, ma'am, we didn't know anybody was living here; we're looking for some letters." Which sounded lame because it must have looked to her as though we had found a lot more letters than anybody could ever want. But I felt it would be brusque—skipping a step, or something—to say we were looking for *R*'s.

"We never have owned," she said.

Milam looked up and glared at her. He hated the idea of going back *R*-less to Mabry Packard, whose combat experience and ivory hip had left him philosophical. If you didn't do what Mabry Packard wanted you to do, he would fix you with a dreamy but knowing look and launch into one of his anecdotal lectures. Slow lectures. That was the hell of them, the slowness of them. You'd know what the rest of a sentence was going to be two minutes before he got to the end of it. "*O-kay,*" you wanted to say. "*O-kay.*" And the worse thing was that he would get way up close into your face and *while he was talking to you* would pick his nose and roll the booger around in his fingers in complicated ways like he was trying to make origami out of it. People would agree to do things for Mabry Packard because they wanted so bad to get him out of their face. Which is a kind of leadership at a certain level.

The thing is, Milam at the time saw Mabry Packard as a mentor I think. Except for the boogers. Milam was from Atlanta and wore madras Bermuda shorts. I doubt he knew how to make a booger, much less fiddle with one compellingly.

"Did you do something with all the R*'s in here?"* Milam asked the woman. I hit him on the arm because he sounded so cold, but I don't know that what he said had registered with her at all. She didn't respond to it. Except to look at the pile of letters and then down at her feet and sigh.

"This is the kind of life he give me," she said.

That's the way I feel in the White House. I don't want to feel like that. I don't want to feel like anybody has given me any kind of life. Especially one I can't stand. I feel like it's driving me crazy.

The President's responsibility is awesome enough without her having to worry about my sanity. I never have had to worry about hers. I dare say that's a big reason why I take to her so. She has never been a woman who is trying to wrap herself in her craziness and draw me into the endless unbearability of it. Her craziness is always moving on its own.

★   ★   ★

The Mayor Berry Orr for Mayor campaign lost. "Mayor Berry Orr for Mayor" had too complicated a rhythm, and the opposition came up with something better: "Bury Berry." Not only was it catchy, it made him sound like a disease. Yet we were the good-government crowd, emphasizing planning and human services.

Beau Milam worked hard, you had to give him that. He organized youth rallies, wrote speeches, brought in contributions from his daddy's high-dollar friends, canvassed his ass off. I still didn't have any use for him though, and he caused Mabry Packard to wax more and more philosophical.

Then one day Milam thought he had blown the whole campaign wide open. He came to Mabry with the information that Reed Dukehart, our opponent's chief aide, had stolen thirty-six hundred dollars from the city a few years before while he was city treasurer. Milam came breathlessly to Mabry with this information. "Mr. Packard," he said, "this is what we *need*."

Mabry was sitting in the back room of campaign headquarters (a defunct dry cleaner's), leaning back in an old tilt-back chair. He didn't like being told what we needed. "Well," he said. "Now. Noooo, we won't be able to uuuuse that little piece [pausing to get a booger] of in . . . formation."

"We can't *use* it? He *stole money*. I could go to the press. I've got the contacts at the *Journal*, I could—"

"Nooo. Well." Packard inclined slowly in Milam's direction. "Thing is . . . You'd have to know. The people . . . in . . . [rolling the booger pensively] . . . volved."

And if I told the story the way Packard told it, it would take forever, so here it is in a speeded-up version, and meanwhile you can imagine Packard moving almost imperceptibly closer and closer in on Milam, and Milam hanging in there, doing his best not to lean away.

"Mary Gay Dukehart. Reed's wife. A fine woman. Folks knew what she did for Baptist shut-ins. And if you think Baptist shut-ins are a small class of people, well, you ain't been door-to-doorin' as hard as I thought. They are a large class. Baptist shut-ins. And a tiring class. They are a class that will wear you out. *One* of 'em. Alone. Will wear you out. But Mary Gay took 'em all on. The Baptist shut-ins. And then Mary Gay got cancer. Female cancer."

"Oh, right, right—he stole the money to pay for his wife's medical expenses. But that still—"

"Nooo. What he stole it for was . . . another lady. Who shall remain nameless. He stole it so that she *would.* Remain nameless. And not only nameless. Nonexistent. So far as Mary Gay knew. Or ever would know. So that Mary Gay Dukehart could die feeling . . . unrunaround-on."

"He stole it to pay *blackmail*? That's even better!"

"Well, he did. If you want to put it that way. To lend blackmail. You would have to know . . . the people . . . involved. It was a lady who didn't know where else to turn. And felt bad about it. The lady who shall remain nameless. We'll call her. She owed her brother thirty-six hundred dollars. That she had borrowed from him. After her husband died. Because she had trouble with the probate and her lawyer's bills ate up what was left and then she had bills.

"And he had to ask for it back. Her brother, had to. Didn't ask her for any interest. She was his sister. But he did have to ask for the thirty-six hundred. Even though he hated to.

"But he had to ask it back. Because he was about to lose his shoe store. Used to have a parrot in it. Shoe stores, that carried the Poll Parrot line, used to have parrots in them. And they got declared illegal. Back here several years ago. Because of psitt . . . a . . . co . . . sis. Parrot disease. Parrot rickets. Which humans . . . could get.

"And he was slow to get rid of it. The brother. Of the lady. Get rid of the parrot. It was sixty years old. He'd gotten attached to it. And he thought maybe it would just die. Since it was so old. What he told the Poll Parrot people was, it had died.

"They were pushing him about sending them the body. And he was slow to get around to doing something about it. Used to show people all the cor . . . res . . . pon . . . dence. From the Poll Parrot people. They wanted him to dig up the parrot. Send it to them. Insurance reasons. They enclosed instructions. For how it could be done. Hygienically. Through the mail.

"And it bit somebody. The parrot. A customer. Who had heard about the psitt . . . a . . . co . . . sis. The lady's brother had even read aloud to this customer from the Poll Parrot people's letter. In front of witnesses. And lawyers! You talk about lawyers!

"He used old man Red Puryear. Who didn't charge too much. But then Red Puryear *did* die. He was older than the parrot. So that meant more lawyers. For one thing, there was the matter of settling with old man Red Puryear's estate for his work. That he had done before he died. Red Puryear's estate was Red Puryear's daughter.

Who had moved to Memphis. And hired herself a lawyer. Who was a whole lot more expensive than Red Puryear had been. And that got him way in the hole. The brother.

"The parrot did finally die. But then it was too late. By then, the Poll Parrot people wouldn't take it. Insurance reasons. On legal advice. And he'd been losing ground financially ever since then. The lady's brother. Till it just all came down on him. And he had three children. And she had four. The lady. And her brother had to ask her to pay him the thirty-six hundred. He didn't know anywhere else to turn.

"And she didn't know anywhere else to turn but Reed Dukehart. Who she had been seeing after her husband died. And she hated it. Having to turn to him. Reed said he hated it too, and he also said he didn't have the money to lend her. Well. She got frantic. And she hated it more than anything else in the world. But. Her brother was kin. And she didn't see anything she could do but tell Reed that if he didn't find some way to find the money, she was going to have to tell Mary Gay. About herself. The lady.

"And that would just have killed Mary Gay. On top of which, Mary Gay could be *mean* in the face of unrighteousness. Old Reed didn't know what to do. He tried to borrow it himself. But this is a tight-credit town. So he took it. From the town. And the lady who shall remain nameless, well. She paid her brother back.

"And then somebody found out about the missing money. Reed went to the lady who shall remain nameless and said now he had to pay the money back. Somehow. Or he'd go to jail.

"By this time, Mary Gay had died. So the lady had lost her leverage. And the lady's father had died. And she'd sold her parents' home. And moved her mother in with her and the children. So she paid Reed back. And he paid back the city. And Mary Gay never knew a thing."

I was so relieved to get to what might be the end of the story that I started to say something to change the subject, but Milam was staring at Mabry Packard.

Actually, he was staring right at the booger. That Mabry Packard was rolling. (I'm beginning to sound like Mabry Packard.) Which seemed rude. Milam didn't have any sense of delicacy. "Mr. Packard," Milam said, "are you saying that the end justifies the means?"

Mabry Packard looked at Milam. Then he looked down at the

booger. Which was the only time I ever saw him do that. Then he looked back at Milam. And kept on rolling the booger. And said, "I'm saying some of 'em justifies some of 'em sometimes. And if you can get it down to more of a science than that, well."

Mabry Packard paused just long enough for Milam to think scientifically for a moment and then to open his mouth (his timing is better these days). Then Mabry Packard went on.

"You know what they say. A man went to heaven. They took and showed him a big pile of money. And they said, 'That's all the money that ever passed through your hands for any reason one way or another. It meaneth less than nothing.' Then they took him and showed him a big pile of stuff. And he said, 'What is that.' And they said, 'It's all the boogers you ever picked on earth. We just thought you'd be interested to see it. And over here, though, well. If you ever feel cocky about making it up here to heaven, well. Just stick your head in this room. It's where we keep all the hurt you ever caused. That you could see a way out of causing.' They say nobody ever opens that door."

"But Mr. Packard," Milam persisted. "If Mayor Berry gets reelected, it'll be better for the whole town."

"Well, that's what we been tellin' em, ain't it?"

"If it means keeping the right people in power, isn't that worth—"

"If Mary Gay had died earlier, that lady we were talking about's brother would have lost his shoe store. So who is to say which *if* is what. We don't have the big picture. They *say* . . . I don't know. But they *say* that the pile of all the votes you ever helped get. That pile. Is kept in heaven right next to the pile of boogers."

Milam actually leaned toward Packard, till they were nose-to-nose, and put this question to him:

"If you feel like that, why are you a campaign manager?"

Packard managed to find a millimeter of perceived space to move forward into, without turning a hair.

"Well," he said. "There's one other thing. When it was found out that Reed took the money? And it was decided to just let him pay it back? Well. Who do you think was mayor at that time. The toothless yellow bleeding heart son of a bitch that we are campaigning for." And he laughed, *hooooo, hooooo,* and stood up, slapped Milam on the back of his white button-down oxford-cloth shirt with the hand that had the booger in it and walked right through him.

Mabry Packard. The last I heard he was raising chinchillas in his basement, but that was some time ago. I've met worse people at the highest levels.

"You're going to lose," Milam said, and he left the campaign.

★ JULY 25, 1993

THERE WEREN'T a lot of private places between the Toddle House and the Dingler campus, but I did hold Clementine against me for a moment or two, the way you'd share with a fishing companion the biggest trout you'd ever caught, and she liked that too. I brushed my fingertips under my shirt on her, just on the backs of her thighs nicely (on her toes she was nearly as tall as I was, but there was no heaviness to her, I always seemed to be catching her on the rise), and she clove, not cleft yet but clove, but she also shivered, though it was warm out. She said, "I like the way your face goes when we talk to each other, I won't hold back from you, I'm not afraid, I want to talk to you more. Do you want to talk to me more, first?"

"Yes," I said, because I did, there was somehow just enough blood in my brain still that I felt reflective. I wanted to talk, I wanted to make popcorn, I wanted to listen to Ray Charles doing "What'd I Say?" plushbottom plushbottom. I was in no hurry.

She trembled again although it was a nice night out and said, "Walk me back to the dorm, there's a dress I want to wear," but we didn't move. "It's a yellow dress, you'll like it, I never have been in a Laundromat with nothing on my bottom before. Nobody could tell, though, could they? I liked the way you were with the peepeye lady." She pulled back so she could look me right in the eye, in a way that made me feel ill-focused, myself, and said, "You have a way with people."

This was news to me, but I said, "So do you."

"Not with the people I've always been around."

"You must've always been around the wrong people, I guess."

"I don't think most people get this excited about each other, do you?" she said.

I couldn't imagine they did.

"I've always been around people I couldn't tell things to without them looking at me funny. I thought it was something wrong with me. Have you felt like that?"

"Yes," I said.

"Maybe I just haven't met enough people. Do you think I just haven't met enough people?"

"No. I mean . . ."

"You know how in a movie you can tell what's on the main two characters' minds so even though other people don't understand them, or even they don't even understand each other, and you worry about that but you feel it'll be all right in the long run because you do?"

I said I did. We hugged back up again.

"Did anybody ever tell you you look like Henry Fonda?"

Nobody ever had. But I liked Henry Fonda.

"You do. When my father was stationed on Governor's Island, which is just a little ferry ride from Manhattan, he wouldn't ever let me go into Manhattan but sometimes I sneaked onto the ferry, and I loved New York City, Guy. One day I saw in the paper *My Darling Clementine.* At the Thalia theater. I went there. I took the *subway.* I was fourteen. It was a little narrow theater with posts you had to walk around and the floor was sticky and I went in there and I loved it, it was like a little country church. In a way. Only it was so worldly. People were saying things back to the actors in the movie, like they knew them.

"And the best one was Henry Fonda. He was dignified like my father but he was . . . kinder. He was a nice man. He played Wyatt Earp. It didn't have anything to do with the song. But he was in love with Clementine. The scene where they danced! Was he going to the dance, she asked him. 'Yes, ma'am, I'd admire to take you.'

"And you know what the last line of the movie was? People made fun of me because of my name. The last line was Henry Fonda saying, 'Ma'am, I sure like that name Clementine.' "

"I sure like it too," I said. "I never saw that one, but I saw *Fort Apache.*"

"Oh, I didn't like that! He played a colonel who hated the Indians. That wasn't right for him."

"—and I saw *The Grapes of Wrath.*" (I wasn't about to bring up *The Wrong Man.*)

"Tom Joad. Henry Fonda is so good in that."

And did I ever reach back hard for this: ". . . wherever children are hungry, wherever people are fighting for their rights . . ."

She gave me a great look then. I never thought I'd find such a pretty woman I could commune with through old movies. Lord God.

"I don't take drugs. I smoked marijuana once and it made me feel like being touched, but I didn't want the person I was with to touch me. I would smoke marijuana with you but I don't want to take acid because I already feel almost as strange as people say it makes you feel and I don't want to go any further in that direction. I read about it in *Newsweek.*"

"Me too," I said. I pulled on her plait.

She leaned back and looked at me again. "I don't want to change my head," she said. "I don't see anything wrong with my head."

"I don't either," I said. "I don't. At all."

"I want to be in the *real world.* People are afraid of it. People take drugs to get away from it, or they hide in little colleges like Dingler. That's just *ignorant.* People *blame* the world. That's just *silly.* That's just blaming *everybody but them.* People say the world is bad so they can feel good about being mean and little and selfish, *I* think. The world has *everything in the world in it.* I want to *know about it.* People have always tried to save me from things girls ought not to know about. I don't want to be saved from things. I want to save the world from people who want to save me from it. I want to get out into the world and see what I can do."

"Like that one-armed lady," I said, my perversity popping in, which it will do. But I didn't want to hear her speechify. I wanted her to talk to me. Maybe I was already getting a little bit jealous of the world. Maybe that should have warned her off me, I don't know. Her eyes did widen for a moment and—her face: you know how a beauty queen looks, just on campus with other students? Too much, awkward, out of place, part of a different world? It's people like that who succeed in the wide world, but at home they're . . . not quite there. For some reason, maybe because I'm not quite there either, I welcomed that oddness about her. When you welcome the ungainly aspect of somebody, and you feel that it makes the gainly better, is it because it reassures you that she is not too good for you? I like to bring her down to her strange self, the strange self I know how to hold. Maybe that is mean and little and selfish of me.

Anyway, I wanted everything about her so much in such a headlong way that I didn't pause to wonder whether she could want everything about me. I turned her around so her back was to me (with my last name on it and my number, 2) and—thank God, not too fumblingly, but maybe fumblingly enough—began to unplait her hair. It came out all curly.

"Beautiful hair," I said. I'd always been scared of saying anything to a woman about her hair, because you never know how they're going to take it; women know how to talk about hair and men don't. But the obvious truth is you don't have to be apt, you just have to say it's beautiful, even to Clementine.

"Undoing me," she said in a surprised tone. "I am religious," she said. "I hate this college but I believe in the spirit of God."

Uh-oh.

"I wouldn't give anybody at this college the satisfaction of talking about it but I want you to know."

"I . . ." I said, "love the old hymns."

She looked at me and I had a sinking feeling, but then, "I come to the garden alone," she began, and I joined in:

> "While the dew is still on the roses,
> And the voice I hear,
> Falling on my ear,
> The son of God disclo-o-ses.
> And he walks with me,
> And he talks with me,
> And he tells me I am his own.
> And the joy we share,
> As we tar-ry there,
> None other . . .
> Has ever . . .
> Known."

She suppled up close against me and whispered in my ear: "Pagan. Infidel. Let's go get my yellow dress. Guy," she said, "I never have been like this. I'm just like this with you. I never have been in a Toddle House with nothing on my bottom before, either. Or out in the air even. But I'm not going to wear anything under my yellow dress either," she said. "Let's go get my yellow dress." She looked at me again as if she might have hurt my feelings. "I want to always keep your jersey, though."

I said okay huskily. She only wanted my jersey? I was willing to give up *softball* for her.

"Also, I need to get some birth control."

When we got to the parlor of her dorm, a full bird army colonel was waiting for her.

Barefoot in a softball-shirt minidress was better than naked, but it didn't fit the Dingler dress code either. But the colonel smelled more than that. "Sissy," he snapped. For a moment I thought he was adverting to me, but he was glaring at Clementine, who flinched. "You look like a floozy!"

So I hit him.

I say, "so" I hit him. I realize that doesn't cover it. I have trouble re-creating this scene, because I have trouble believing that it happened.

I hadn't hit anybody since the sixth grade. I'd had dreams where I'd hit guys, never quite to my satisfaction. Whereas I hit this colonel such a shot! Big roundhouse right, to the eye, *poom*. And then I hit his aide.

I hit his aide because his aide hit me, also in the eye, and I saw red. I hit the aide in the cheek area with a jerky overhand, *blap*, like knocking on a door.

The three jolts involved, *poom jonk blap*, were not unpleasant, at the time. A little anger dance. Hi ho into the breach.

But why? If I could understand why I hit the colonel, I think I would understand a lot of things that I don't understand.

My blood was up, I had to do *something*.

The colonel's tone was that of a Christian soldier if I ever heard one: piety married fondly to deep-dyed distaste. The tone of a prayer of satisfaction raised over burning gooks or books or witches. It was as if that colonel had been posted there to wait for a woman to show up looking wanton, and Clementine had confirmed his expectations. I hate—and that is the word, too, *hate*—to see a Puritan's prurience gratified.

"Floozy"! In a venomous tone. It's a nice jouncy American word, *floozy*, rhymes with *boozy*, *newsy* (almost), *cooze-y* and *Susie*. What kind of mind, in the Age of Aquarius, would fling *floozy* like a handful of shit at a lovely girl? I love to hear Americans talk! I hate—again, *hate* is the word—to hear juicy American words savored for their capacity to stink.

But I'm just holding forth now, not explaining the moment. There was something about the look that the colonel and Clementine exchanged. It was the flip side of Jesus in the garden with a frustrated older woman and the woman swoons. It was a frustrated older man in the garden with Jezebel and the man spits.

But there was more to it than that. I felt like I was being sucked into some kind of force field that I knew but didn't know.

The colonel seemed to know Clementine. Know her well. I didn't *want* him to know her. I didn't want him to say another word to her, for fear she might take it to heart. For fear I might.

Clementine's abandon had astonished my upbringing. Was she, after all, of GMF? (A term that a Sunday school teacher of mine used to use, standing for Good Moral Fiber.) I *believe* in good moral fiber, sort of. Was Clementine like one of those preachers' daughters I had heard of, who will hump your brains out to get back at God? I did not want to be thinking in these terms. I did not want to be thinking at all.

So I swung. Such a pretty punch, the first one. It's hard to believe that anyone, particularly so inexpert a fighting man as I, could connect so solidly with a Christian soldier unless it was meant to be. Inherent in the situation, as they say. Still it wasn't *like* me. To *feel* like hitting somebody yes, to do it no.

I thought—I sensed, I mean—that Clementine wanted me to. Women have expectations. You feel: *she wants something from me now, and not something I can pause to mull over either.* You do what seems to them patently apropos and they smile so *damn* nice. You get it wrong and they look so *damn* stricken. Such a difference, so often, between women's intuitions and men's. But Clementine is not just any woman. I caught a glimpse of her looking stricken. But also involved.

Security men arrived—count on that at Dingler. A forearm came across my throat from behind, I was swallowing a whole hard gall-flavored apple, Clementine was up against me reaching over my shoulder banging on my unseen throttler and incidentally rubbing up against me, I figured I had done about all I could do for the moment, everything went black and I woke up in jail.

★ JULY 26, 1993

ARE WE IN the same movie anymore? Were we ever? If we are, is there any sense in which I am a leading man?

"What you have to realize," Leonard said to me the other day, "is that the country is in love with your wife. So they wish you were dead." Thanks, Leonard.

I'm not saying I haven't had *some* fun as First Hubby. In the following everything is official except the italics, which I have added to get the tone of voice right:

THE WHITE HOUSE
Office of the Press Secretary

For Immediate Release   May 21, 1993

REMARKS BY THE PRESIDENT
UPON DEPARTURE TO
ANDREWS AIR FORCE BASE

The South Lawn

9:07 A.M. EDT

Q: Ms. President, what about the rumor that you have reached some kind of secret agreement with Qaddafi?

THE PRESIDENT: I won't dignify that rumor by calling it horse-pucky.

Q: *What?* Calling it what?

THE PRESIDENT: I told you, I'm *not* calling it that.

Q: Not calling it *what?*

THE PRESIDENT: Oh, for heaven's sake. *Horse-pucky!*

Q: How do you define that?

THE PRESIDENT: That's not my job. Guy, help me
    out.

THE FIRST HUBBY: It's like bull-hockey.

Q: How do you define *that*?

THE PRESIDENT: No, never mind. Guy might define it
    too pithily.

Q: Oh, come on.

THE FIRST HUBBY: Sorry, I can't help you right now.
    I'm too pithy.

END

9:09 A.M. EDT

I don't think Betty Ford was ever that quick. Dolley Madison,
maybe.

Still. I mean, even that morning—well, for one thing I don't
enjoy getting up and getting dressed appropriately by eight o'clock
in the morning so I can wait around until my wife is ready for me
to go catch a helicopter with her. I've *been* on a helicopter. And my
idea of appropriate dress is pants that still aren't too greasy to wipe
your hands on. And it has never been my dream to have my contributions to history subsumed under "REMARKS BY THE PRESI-
DENT."

I don't even like presidents. I never knew anybody who did,
until my wife became one. Suddenly. I doubt it was as suddenly
for anybody else—suddenly though it was for a couple of billion
people around the world—as it was for me. There I was on the
Great Wall of China thinking things had already been going too
damn suddenly for me and then, bingo. Your proverbial heart-
beat. Which mine skipped, I can tell you that. But who cared
about *my* heart?

Okay, lots of people would feel privileged to have been a part,
however tangential a part, of the most amazing moment in American television if not history. And Clementine was great at that
moment. Everybody knows that. Everybody knows so much about
my wife lately that it's hard for me to keep up, much less add
anything. There are things that I could add. But what kind of hubby
would?

★   ★   ★

One time before I was a part of American history I thought about writing my autobiography, tongue-in-cheek, and calling it *You Had to Be There*. But I never did. It would be a better title for a prison memoir, and I've been in jail only the one time.

★ JULY 27, 1993

YOU ARE SUPPOSED to get a phone call from jail in America, but not in Dingler, South Carolina, in 1969 when you just hit an important military man who is a personal friend of B. Vaughn Dingler, Sr., himself, as well as this military man's aide.

"Well, looka heeyunh," said this overdoing-it black guy with a gold-framed tooth who was the only other person in the cell and who was moving toward me looking at me in a way I didn't like the looks of.

"What would you be in a place like this for?" he asked.

"Civil rights movement," I snapped. Give me that much: I snapped, I didn't whine.

"Ohh, I shoulda guessed it."

He smelled. I don't mean that racially. But I don't like to smell a man.

"Which side?" he said.

"Yours."

"Ohh, good. We winnin'?"

"Well, I mean, it's a long . . ."

He moved in closer. "You the onliest one they could catch?"

I balled up my fist, although it felt like it had an oven mitt on it, and said, "The truth is—*don't fuck with me*! Do not fuck with me! Any other night I would sit here thinking, 'Oh, gee, I don't want this black person to think I'm prejudiced,' but not tonight! I don't care what color you are, I have been through more today than you have, and it is all backed up on me and I am in love."

"Lord Jesus!" the black guy yelled, and he ran to the bars and jumped up and down banging on them. "Let me outa heeyunh. I'm jus' a po' old falsely 'spected breaker and enterer, and you th'ow me in with a mad dog with his goober red! Ain't none of my bizness! Build another cell on this jail!"

It goes to show you that people are often better-humored if you don't hold back with them. But you never know, which is why people hold back so much of the time, or lie, unless they're so drunk or stirred up they just blurt things out, which I was then: stirred up. I woke up in jail stirred up. Stirred up and *tight,* like lots of little wires were trying to lift me by the outermost layer of my skin. I didn't know whether I could live like this.

I felt crazy. It wasn't like me to be so overt, with lies or the truth. Of course I'd never been in jail before, but it was being so full of Clementine that had brought out my barefaced side. Of course I imagine it is always useful with your peers, in jail, if you're genuinely crazier than they are—at least at the moment.

My cellmate turned out to be named E. B. Neighbors, and I think he had just been trying to establish his own intensity with me. Over the next couple of hours, while I sat there gradually feeling a little clearer, he told me how to hot-wire a car, something I'd always felt bad about not learning in high school, and how to clean a turtle. I didn't tell him about how Clementine was dressed when we met but I did tell him about hitting the colonel who'd insulted her.

"My," he said. "What a white boy will do. Where you hit him?"

"Eye."

"The eye. The eye is a strange thing."

My left one was in fact swelling shut.

"I knew a good-looking woman once nobody'd have nothing to do with," E.B. went on. "Wadn't a thing wrong with her—only thing about her wrong, her eyes closed so tight when she smiled, look like she died. She'd open her eyes back up and whoever she was smiling at would be looking at her like she'd gave them the grislies, which she had. You couldn't help it. You'd think a person would smile . . . nice. You'd think that'd be a part of nature. And she didn't have any way of knowing about it. It only happened when her eyes was closed."

"Why didn't anybody tell her?" I was seeing Clementine's eyes in my head and feeling crazy.

"Don't know. How would you start to put it?"

"You know, you talk about eyes," the jailer came over and said through the bars. "When I was in the barber's school I had to learn about the skull, the brain, the mouth, the nose, the eyes, and everything from the neck up. I could've been a doctor, for the head."

I never had felt this way about anybody, never had wanted to. Had Clementine actually said all that stuff she'd said? This was the sixties, but still. I worked to bring her back into focus in my mind.

"My grandaddy wucked for a man one time had a wart on his nose so big," E.B. put in, "that he had a little nose tattooed on the wart."

"But I still can't understand people's *thinking.* The head, yes, but the thinking, no. It's a whole seprit thing. Well, not necessarily a *whole* seprit thing but it's differnt," the jailer said.

★ ★ ★

What was I doing sitting there in jail listening to people talk about eyes and noses and heads? The question was, why had I hit that colonel?

I had been pulled into something, and I don't mean just jail. I had been pulled into Clementine's electricity.

Now, twenty-four years later, I know more about that electricity. But I still don't get it. I don't get why C is President (acts of God aside), what exactly her *charge* is, what has drawn me and America to her. Okay, WOT was an inspired organization and C was its leader. It wasn't just liberal, either, it cut across lines. But how come even the evangelicals and the American Legion seem to go for her? You'd think I would get it, but I don't. Do you think Pat Nixon ever knew exactly what Dick brought to the party? Why do you think she looked so stunned all the time?

Not to compare C with Nixon. But I identify to some extent with Pat. Somebody did a study a while back, tying two monkeys together. Whenever the first monkey did something wrong, they both got a shock. When the first monkey did what it was supposed to, no shock. But what the second monkey did didn't matter. It got shocked or not shocked according to what the first monkey did or didn't do. After a while the first monkey got depressed. The second monkey went crazy.

I identify with the second monkey. But *I don't want to.* I take no comfort from that explanation of my plight. I don't want to bitch at the first monkey. I don't want to get loose of the first monkey. I want the two of us to get at the electric source. I don't see how I can unless I set down everything that occurs to me and see what adds up.

★   ★   ★

I sat there in jail. My hand felt like somebody was tapping it with a hammer over and over and over. My eye was feeling tighter and tighter. I didn't know what to think about Clementine. I told a joke.

Yes, it is the same joke I told the president of the Seychelles or whatever the hell he was at a White House dinner to so much subsequent outrage, and I am going to tell it here again because the press never got it right and the president of the Seychelles didn't either, or his wife:

"Man put his glass eye in his drink, to soak it, and a second man, call him John, mistook this drink for his own and downed it, eye and all. First man was dismayed but John didn't think too much of it until weeks later, when he began experiencing lower-colon trouble. It felt as though there might be an obstruction. He went to a proctologist, who laid him down on a table, put a speculum up his rectum . . ."

"Speculum up his reculum," E.B. said reflectively.

". . . bent down and took a look. Then the doctor straightened up.

" 'Now, John,' he said, 'if you don't trust me, you'd better get another doctor.' "

"I hear *that,* now," E.B. said.

"If God gives you the mind, and you don't use it," the jailer said, "why, then, I feel like that's yo' ship coming in to port."

I looked at my hand and moved my fingers as much as they would. I was worrying whether . . . like when you're a teenager and you go to Bible camp and go up front to the altar and get saved, and you feel like it's an experience that will last but then the next morning you go out and see people and feel sheepish and look away hoping nobody remembers seeing you up there. I didn't want to think about things too much but I was thinking about what Clementine might be thinking.

"Okay, now," E.B. said. "Y'all going to talk about eyes, I'm ona *tell* you 'bout eyes. It starts out with it being two eyes in everybody's head. Hold up your finger. Hold it up."

The jailer wouldn't, but I held up one of mine, which was blue.

"Look at it with one eye closed," E.B. said.

"Okay," I said.

"Okay," he said, "now look at it with the other eye closed."

"Okay," I said.

"Now tell me, *where's your finger at?*

"Is it over there, or is it over here? It's one or the other. Open both eyes and look at it. You know it ain't *there.* That's just a compermise on the other two places you just seen it in with your own two eyes.

"Where is *anything,* if a man don't know where his finger is, in front of his face?"

The jailer shook his head. "Any little thing I've managed to achieve," he said, "I don't take no credit for it. I lay it all at the feet of Jesus Christ."

★ **JULY 28, 1993**

THE FIRST DEMONSTRABLY crazy woman I ever met was Mrs. Beale, who lived down the street from me when I was a little kid. She was Neil Ogle's mother's mother but she lived in a house by herself down the street from the Ogles, and once I saw her standing out in front of her house in her slip screaming "Damn" and "Hell." That's all. In prolonged single-word bursts: "Da-a-a-mmmmn." "Hellllllll." Nobody in my house cursed.

Well, my mother would talk about her *life* being a hell, but that was just being descriptive, she felt. She taught me to read at an early age. We lived with my Uncle Gene and my Aunt Big Sybil.

None of us cursed; so far as I knew nobody in our neighborhood did except Mrs. Beale. But she was hitting notes I already knew. The anguish of women! Brought on by males and children! It scared me, a male child, to death. None of the men on my street scared me, they were all minor-businessman daddies with low resigned voices; they weren't around during the day anyway, except on the weekends, when people were all busy doing yard work. At night when the men were home, the time was taken up by supper and television. It was during the workday when the men were away that things felt untucked, you weren't sure what could happen. That was advantageous in many ways; you could get off on your own more, and get away with more. But when the mothers got together, talking, in breaks from housework, you picked up disturbing intimations. You and the women knew each other better than you and the men did; but the mothers talking together made it clear, while you played nearby and pestered them, that there were ungladsome things they knew, Heaven knew how well they knew, that they shared with each other but not with you. Or rather not quite with you—they knew you could overhear, you were a kind of groundling element over whose heads much but by no means all was passing, and their voices made a certain kind of oblique fun of you, made you guess how innocent they were keeping you. You'd yammer and whine and pull at them to break up their conversations, try to get them to attend to you, and they'd say, to each other, "These children, these children! I declare, sometimes, couldn't you just cheerfully strangle them?" And then there was Mrs. Beale.

When politicians talk among themselves, they make fun of nonpoliticians, including their hovering and pestering spouses, in something like the same way; not ever owning up to it of course— not these days, when it's established that spouses are people in their own right. "Course Guy thinks I ought to just make a clean breast of it," Clementine will say behind the scenes to a gaggle of what used to be called dignitaries, who eat up her double entendres (if she has done nothing else, she has brought to American politics a new mode of saltiness), and she nudges me with her eyes and they all have a chortle—not at my *expense,* oh no; I'm a humorist aren't I? And don't we all know that we need more lighthearted comments in this day and age?

There I go whining. (Which is what humorists really want to do, only we know it won't sell.) The thing is, I remember the early buds of that saltiness. Us laughing in bed. Now she and all these strangers are bedfellows, figuratively of course.

★ JULY 30, 1993

WHEN CLEMENTINE showed up first thing in the morning, which I was relieved to see she had, she was wearing a light-yellow summer dress, all right, but she didn't look at me quite the same, which was understandable but kind of irritated me. I felt like— worse than jet lag, which I don't guess I had ever felt at that point in my life. She had a lawyer with her. I was let up front to see them. "There's this black guy in here who needs legal help more than I do," I said.

"Get serious," said the lawyer.

"I heard that!" said E.B. from the back.

The lawyer was Beauvais Milam. My old Mayor Berry Orr for Mayor buddy. I had heard he was in Dingler and starting to make a name for himself, but we hadn't run into each other or Lord knows sought each other out. Seeing him after ten years, here was my immediate reaction to him, and my abiding one, all the way up into the fullness of his Chieftancy of Staff: fuck him. Whereas Clementine—you wonder, when you're seeing a woman for the second time, whether she is still going to make you feel like you are made up entirely of firecrackers. She still did.

I kissed her, right there in jail, wanted her to know how crazy I felt. Not a long one but right on the mouth untentatively as if it weren't the first time. It was the first time! She liked it, though her eyes narrowed.

"Let me orientate you a little bit, my friend," said Milam, who didn't have the chops for that tone, with me. "Dingler has put in a word with the *Beacon* and you no longer enjoy a position there. I, for my part, will quite likely no longer enjoy a practice here in town, now that I am seeing to it you are sprung. You have Clementine to thank that that is what I am seeing to. Now I recommend we go and eat some breakfast and talk over where things stand."

I didn't want to do that at all. Talk about being sprung, I felt like I was made of springs—springs in my shoulders, springs in my knees.

"You don't have to thank me," I said to Clementine, because I knew even then that a relationship is an Indian wrestle. "But your name really is Clementine, then, hunh? Not Sissy?"

She looked a little hurt, almost a little misty, and I thought oh shit. "Sissy is just what Daddy calls me," she said. "And my sister Dancy. That was my Daddy."

"Ah," I said. Somehow, things seemed a little clearer. And yet . . . not *clear*. Not clear at all. Her *father*?

"Oh, Lord," I said. "Well I'm sor— I mean, see, I don't really know why I . . ." Why did *I* have to explain? It seems to me that I have always had to explain everything, to the generation before me and the generation after me. "Explain yourself, young man," my elders would say. *I* didn't know, I was a kid. And did anybody explain anything to me? Take masturbation. The message I got was, "Your body is a holy temple and it's filthy, don't touch it."

Whereas, when my children came along, I had to come up with a *good* explanation of why they couldn't do it in a restaurant.

And generations aside, I feel like I have to explain things to women. Even though I don't *know*. But, hey, you hit somebody's father and I guess it is incumbent upon you to . . . "I never hit anybody's daddy before," I said.

"My daddy is a hero of the Korean War," she said. "He was in a prison camp." I didn't know what I was supposed to say to that, and it didn't help that Beau Milam was there.

Here came Leonard. "I just heard about it from Brownie," he said. "They not only told him not to write the story, much less me—which, of course, Brownie could give a shit, he's from here— but they fired you. So I quit the paper. I'm going back to Chicago and work someplace real. You want to buy my car?"

(Mine had thrown a rod and was hardly worth what it would cost to fix it.) This was a moment for the right word, the right move from me, but I was off my rhythm. I had hoped that somebody would be making things clearer for me and here I was presumably expected to account for my actions. When something you say makes a woman get almost a little *misty* . . . Not coming-apart misty by any means, but still. It was probably a good thing that a white Cadillac pulled up then, and the window whirred down and this little pink face with a drawn-on-looking mustache came out.

"Young man," it said, "you are fortunate that my friend Colonel Searcy has been summoned to his duties, and based on certain assurances from his daughter, will drop charges. You needn't think you injured him any."

It was of course B. Vaughn Dingler, Sr., himself. Next to him on the backseat was a Chihuahua dog, which you don't see many of anymore, going *"Yarch! Yar!"* and bouncing and losing its footing on the seat cover and scrambling back and going *"Yarch!"* again. The reason you don't see many of them anymore is people have realized that they're mean. Well, come to think of it Leonard has a Chihuahua now named Lupe that cured his asthma. E.B. suggested it. I thought it was an old wives' tale that having a Chihuahua around was good for your asthma, but it did more for Leonard's state of mind than a lifetime of psychotherapy, and Lupe doesn't even *yarch.* I guess it depends on the owner. Actually Leonard was more fun when his state of mind was worse, but that's another story.

"I thought you sprung me," I said to Milam.

"Listen—" Milam said.

"As to you, young man," the little pink face said to Milam in that nationally known radio voice of his. I can't *stand* that voice. Millions of Americans, somehow, find that voice comforting, uplifting. I find it hateful, eerie. It presumes that everyone listening agrees that it has every reason to sound as smugly Saved, and Saving, as it does. And yet it presumes that millions are shut off from its enlightenment. "Don't you think it's about time *we* had a president?" that voice said when Ronald Reagan was running the first time. Now that voice is in Clementine's corner. The pendulum swings. I guess. If I understood why Dingler supports C now, I would understand more than I do.

"I have had four heart operations," Dingler spake unto Milam, "and I do not feature a young man in town who represents disruptive elements. We have been blessed with not having any of that in our town, and we—"

"Yarch!"—bounce. *"Yar—"* scrabble-scrabble.

"Quit that, Angelita, quit it."

"I will represent who I so desire, Dr. Dingler," said Milam. Which is how he got into civil rights work. White people wouldn't hire him. No, I give Milam credit. I just don't have any use for him personally. And it was clear to me who it was he so desired.

"Beau. Dr. Dingler," Clementine said. "Guy and I need to be

together." Hot damn! She had taken my hurt hand in a nice but
semidetached way.

"Now, Sissy"—she flinched at that, I was somehow almost glad
to see, except I know in my heart I'm never glad to see Clementine
flinch—"what you need to do now, sugar, is get in this big lovely
fine car with me and come back to school where you are loved and
among sweet people. I am responsible for you, you are my charge,
and this is ve'y ve'y hateful to my health. And what, pray, are *you*
doing, young man who looks ve'y Jewish?"

"Taking notes," said Leonard. "I don't mean anything by it, it's
a nervous habit, which I thought I could put to good use in local
journalism, but all anyone says to me is, 'Now, Leonard, you know
better than to *repote* this, don't you?' Maybe I'll go into folklore.
Very Jewish?"

"Don't call me Sissy, Dr. Dingler! You don't have the right!
Nobody does. And I think you know what I mean," said Clementine
in a right-down-to-it voice.

Dingler flinched. And swatted at his dog. "Hush, Angelita, I can't
hear myse'f think!" Dingler came out of his flinch looking Clementine right in the eye in a spurious way. You could hear Angelita
*yarch*ing from the floorboard. "Any other Dingler student would
have been unfellowshipped after the behavior you have shown.
But—"

"Dr. Dingler," she said, "I don't want to go to a school where the
founder calls people very Jewish."

"I was going to say," said Leonard.

"May I ask you something about your attitude?" Dingler said. He
wrote something down on a notepad and handed the page to Clementine. I read it over her shoulder.

In a spidery hand, it said, "Does it glorify Christ?"

"Dr. Dingler," Clementine said, "I have read all through the
testaments. And I have never seen it anywhere in there that Christ
liked being glorified. Guy, you don't have a car?"

"Could I just interject at this point," said Milam.

"I do but it threw a rod and it's hardly worth what it would cost
to fix it. But I—"

"Can you afford to buy Leonard's?"

"How much do you want for it?" I asked him.

"I am not going to sit here for this haggling and childishness," said Dingler. "Git down, Angelita. I am fixing just to drive off and—"

"Well," Leonard said, "I paid nine-seventy-five for it, and I don't see how I can take less than seven-fifty. It's just been serviced, and that cost—"

"Come on, Leonard," I said, "I haven't got that kind of money. We've got to have something left to travel on."

"Well, I don't see how I can go any lower than that, though," he said.

"Leonard," Clementine said, "I have just withdrawn all my money from the bank and here is four hundred dollars. Guy, do you have three-fifty?"

We were already buying something together. "Yeah," I said, "and that would leave us enough to go a ways, but I don't think Leonard's car . . ."

"Are you kidding?" Leonard said. "It's a steal at that price."

"I wash my hands. Things can be made to show on people's pummanent reckuds," said Dingler, and his driver drove him off.

I don't know that I have captured the drama of the moment, much of which was internal. We still had to go to the bank and go get the title and insurance changed and get my hand looked at and get rid of Milam and drive Leonard to the airport, so it was nine o'clock that night before I kissed Clementine again. We didn't actually know each other and were tired and too young to be very dexterous, and once I bumped Clementine in the nose with my cast causing us both to *yowtch* and roll on the sofa bed, but what we did, without missing a beat we modulated into two dogs howling, *awoooo-ooo-oooooo,* and took turns imitating Angelita, *yarch, yarch,* and saying Plushbottom and Puyallup and, "I yell, lash out with my arms and jump," like the man in the advice column, and I licked where her nose was bleeding. We had energy and light hearts for one another. You know how Southern women pick up a little baby and say, "Oooooh, I could just eat you up"? Which may sound ethnopsychologically sticky to you, but you can't deny the woman and the baby both like it. Another thing—which did seem sort of advanced—I took her pearls and rolled them all over her slowly; she shuddered and got softer. I eased them inside her and eased them out. By noon we had packed and were driving off in sin.

★ JULY 31–AUG. 1, 1993

EVERY NOW AND THEN I stick my head into my East Wing office. People always seem to be working in there. Doing something. My pet cause is literacy, officially, and what I am doing for literacy, officially, is writing my book. I don't make speeches about literacy anymore because the first time I went to make one I saw to my astonishment that somebody had written a speech for me to make.

"Let me get this straight," I said. "I'm making a speech about literacy that somebody else has written for me? No. I'm going to read something literate that I wrote once about my mother teaching me to read by reading me Uncle Remus stories aloud."

Which I did. Unfortunately I prefaced my reading by saying that I wasn't sure how much I wanted literacy to spread, just from my own selfish point of view, because the only way to attain real best-sellerdom was to tap into the vast nonreading market; I didn't want that market to dry up just as I was in a position to attract its attention. That pleasantry did not go over well. Nor did my tribute to Brer Rabbit. What is the point of literacy without plenty of elbow room?

What I wanted as my pet cause was child abuse. The kids our old WOT friends had rounded up had performed so well for me at my small-scale South Lawn eggroll. I love goofing around with kids (okay, when I am in the mood for it). Yet mine had grown up and left me before I'd had a chance to do right by them. Grown up into obsessions (business administration and weird music) that I could see, now, I could have saved them from (but in fact had no doubt accidentally inclined them toward).

I remembered reading congressional testimony, years ago, from a mother who admitted to battering her little girl: "She cried and cried and that meant she didn't love me so I hit her and she cried harder, so I hit her harder." I never even spanked Lucy or Jackson, and yet I could almost understand where that mother was coming from. I did yell at Lucy and Jackson some, and glared at them fiercely (a huge grown man glaring at barely ambulatory sprites), because they wouldn't *be-have*. Wouldn't *sit still*. Wouldn't *let* me be civil to them. Wouldn't *stop being childish* for just a moment and let me think of something to say that didn't sound like the things I had hated hearing when I was their age. It seems to me almost impossible *not* to abuse children, some.

Even Freud. From what I can see, Freud had a child-abuse problem. First he concluded that an astonishing percentage of his women patients had been molested as children, right? But then he changed his mind, deciding that the women who remembered being molested were fantasizing. So evidently *Freud* was fantasizing when he wrote this amazing letter to his crackpot friend Wilhelm Fleiss. Leonard showed me this letter. Leonard's mother is a Freudian analyst, and he says she refuses to discuss this letter with him. This is the letter Freud wrote:

> I had been meaning to ask you, in connection with the eating of excrement [by] . . . animals, when disgust first appears in small children and whether there exists a period in earliest infancy when these feelings are absent. Why do I not go into the nursery and experiment with Annerl? Because working for 12 and a half hours, I have no time for it, and the womenfolk do not support my researches. The answer would be of theoretical interest. . . . Hysterical headache with sensations of pressure on the top of the head, temples, and so forth, is characteristic of the scenes where the head is held still for the purpose of actions in the mouth. . . . Unfortunately, my own father was one of these perverts and is responsible for the hysteria of my brother . . . and those of several younger sisters. The frequency of this circumstance often makes me wonder.

Now. Maybe Freud was just talking off the top of his head here, in suggesting (1) that he was the type of person who would try to see whether his baby daughter Annerl would eat excrement and (2) that his father was the type of person who would force oral sex on Freud's siblings. (Not on Freud himself, though? How about that cigar?) That seems to be what respectable opinion concludes.

What if someone found that Richard Nixon, for instance, had written such a letter? ("The womenfolk do not support my researches," indeed.) Psychohistorians would close the book on *him* right there.

That wasn't what I wanted to do—close the book on anything. What I wanted to do was to stick my head into the mystery of child abuse in such a way as to raise the question of whether it wasn't something that *everybody*—not just Freud and not just that mother who felt that her baby was hurting her by crying—is in some way involved in. That the horror stories are just one extreme end of a continuum whose other extreme is Mama smile, Papa smile, baby smile.

So. I told Leonard, "You know that Freud letter you showed me? I want to get into that. I want my pet cause to be child abuse."

"Yuck," Leonard said.

"Yuck? What do you think, this is too hot a potato for a country humorist? Because if that is what you think, I am going to hold my breath until you take it back."

"Guy," he said, "talk to the President."

"Leonard," I said. "Please don't call my wife 'The President' to me. I don't call you 'The Press Secretary' to her."

"Guy," he said, "talk to Clementine."

So I did. She recoiled. She didn't want to talk about it.

"Do you think I'll joke about it?" I asked her. "You know I wouldn't joke about child abuse. I don't want to go through life not ever talking about anything that isn't funny."

"Guy . . ." she said. This has become one of her main arguments. "Guy . . ." as if we both know what she thinks and she shouldn't have to tell me.

"Don't you think it's a fascinating thing, child abuse? I mean—"

"Fascinating!" she said.

"Well, you know what I mean. What's wrong with the world? People forcing other people. Exploiting other people. Crushing other people. And people find a way to *justify* doing these things, by appealing to a higher good: religion, national security, social revolution, the market economy. Excuses for turning other people into objects. Right? But there's no conceivable excuse for abusing little children. And yet lots of people do it. It's an *addiction,* child abuse. People who are abused as children grow up to abuse children. It's *human* to do it, evidently. So it needs to be demystified. If somehow people could own up to it and get help

. . . Maybe if somebody who's supposed to be funny talks about
it—"

She gave me a dubious look.

"Okay, forget funny. You know, I think the reason . . . You know
I've told you my mother said her stepmother beat her when she was
a little girl. 'Till the blood ran,' my mother said. She told me that
just one time, and I didn't know what to say back to her. But it's
always stuck with me. And my mother didn't beat me. So she must
have broken the chain, herself. And I think she suffered from the
effort. She suffered from something. You know everybody I guess
wants to try to get at their mothers' suffering. To me it's—"

"Guy," she said, "everybody doesn't." And she looked at me
with scared eyes.

Things that give Clementine scared eyes, the country doesn't
want to hear about, I guess. I guess she knows what the country can
stand.

So. I gave up on child abuse.

But god damn.

★   ★   ★

And here I am ranting along unpublishably and I hear Beau
Milam's voice in my house. The nation's house.

Milam's voice passing in the hall, and he's saying to my wife,
"You know Sturgis," and I know good and well that Milam doesn't
know anybody in the same way Clementine does. Then too I know
good and well that there's a sense in which she knows people—part
of her does—in some way that connects with the way Milam knows
people. Because I hear her say "Mm-hm" in a tone she never uses
with me.

I never even heard of anybody named Sturgis. He's probably
some hot new teenage senator who has something on somebody
and is holding one of Clementine's policies hostage. I probably
don't even know what the policy in question is. I can't keep up with
all of them. Nobody can but Milam.

Once I stuck my head into the Oval Office, saw Milam leaning
across her desk going over some things with her, and I watched as
she reacted: like a pitcher shaking off the catcher's signs, only more
expressively: No. No. You Should Know Me Better Than That.

Nooo. Then: Eyes Light Up. And she was ready to make the pitch, whatever it was. The whole time Milam was talking to her she was fiddling with her pearls, like a pitcher handling the ball, getting a grip, feeling the seams. Those trademark pearls are the ones she was wearing when I first saw her. Now one of the earrings is always off so she can talk on the phone, and she is always leaving it places but she never loses it.

I haven't said enough about my first sight of her. Naked and the dogs after her. Her expression was thoughtful but *gracious.* She looked like she was turning over in her mind what to prepare for a small dinner party on short notice, and her concentration was being broken *slightly* by the fact that she was running naked from dogs. She looked like she might turn and smile at the dogs any minute and say with some indulgence, some asperity, "Excuse me?"

She just tickles me to death.

I made a speech to an international group the other day—a bad idea—and I used that expression, "She just tickles me to death." And I looked around at them, satisfied.

That I had put it just right.

And they looked disconcerted.

"It's an expression," I said. "She . . . delights me." They looked at me like: good for you, get in line. I ended my remarks.

And when I first saw her she wasn't even quite twenty yet, still kind of gangly. She'd never planned a little dinner party in her life. Still hasn't for that matter, unless you count lasagna. She is the only respectable, predominantly Southern mother of two I have ever known who does only lasagna. It's good lasagna. I have always liked it. So have the kids. She does a range of lasagna, from more or less regular to *à la* whatever is about to go bad. She has done lasagna for everybody from the homeless to the Dutchess of Kent, and I have never known anybody to just pick at it. Often they say, "What *is* this"—not having known that there was such a thing as a range of lasagna—but they never look at it askance. As they would if *I* tried to get away with assuming that there was such a thing as a range of lasagna.

Somebody in a family has to cook meat loaf and green beans and one thing and another (me). Otherwise you don't ever have anything that's about to go bad.

Not that cooking is our—my—problem now. Except that now we have a chef, who doesn't like me messing around in the kitchen.

I never even had a secretary before. Well, I did once. When we were living in the country I was always complaining about being distracted from actually writing all the time, and C, who of course has always had plenty of volunteer assistants (none of whom of course ever wanted to do anything for me), kept saying I ought to hire a secretary, so I did. I put an ad in the *Shopper's Guide.* An odd-looking recent college dropout named (she claimed) Miramar was the only person who applied. Miramar. I engaged her to come in a couple of afternoons a week. All she did was handle mail and odds and ends—I don't trust anybody else to do my typing. Certainly not anybody named Miramar. And she would go through the mail—with me casting nervous glances at her—and throw out the wrong things. I would have to go through the wastebasket to see. She'd throw away things like a flyer encouraging me to enroll in meat-packing school.

"See, Miramar," I'd say, "I want to see things like this."

"Things like that," she'd say.

The times she was supposed to come were never the times when I needed any errands run. So she'd sit there. Staring out into space. With her mouth open slightly.

She was an art major. A lapsed art major. "My favorite is somebody like Michelangelo," she told me, "who studied years and years just the human anatomy. I was looking for realistic. For two years I had everything abstract or surreal—not because I wanted it but because it's required. They didn't have a real realistic department."

She focused her eyes for a moment and gave me a look as if to say that I didn't have one either. She made me nervous. She even made C nervous. She had long, languid kind of maroon-colored hair that came down to her breasts in front and shrouded her features. C once referred to her as "that Flemish dullard." It just popped out. I never heard C say anything quite like that before or since. Maybe it was "phlegmish dullard." *Dullard* wasn't exactly fair, but she did *look* like a dullard, except kind of exotic, as in a Flemish painting. I guess that was C's idea; she looked surprised, herself, that the phrase had popped out. I kept praying Miramar would quit, which finally she did. She had to help her mother with her brother Roxie, she said.

"My brother Roxie is twenty-seven and still lives at home. He doesn't know what to make of himself. He is becoming unstable. Last night he burst out finally. We knew he would. By taking a hammer and smashing the johnny in my mother's bathroom into a bunch of little pieces. We shut off the water. But he won't let plumbers in. That's where he is now, trying to glue my mother's johnny back together with epoxy. He tried all morning and it comes apart in his hands. My mother needs help with him."

Well, I almost know how he felt. Now I have a staff of, I don't know how many. Twenty-eight I think. I have a press secretary, a social secretary, a correspondence secretary and a scheduling secretary, and each of *them* has a secretary. None of them is as interesting as Miramar, but each of them is every bit as imposing and unhelpful as she was, in his or her own way, and they all pretty much seem to agree with Miramar's assessment of me. To me, they're the ones who are abstract or surreal. (One of them—I don't know what her job is—calls everybody "Skeeter." Everybody.) But they've got me outnumbered.

And so I come up here and lose myself in illicit reminiscence.

There Clementine came gravely hotfooting it across campus, her pearls and hair bouncing, and I wasn't thinking just, "Yo-ho-to-ho, enter damsel." I was wondering what she had in mind. I was seeing her as I see her today: as a person who, if you saw her falling headfirst off a cliff, you would wonder what she was up to.

And here's what I think about the enduring question of why me. I think, for better or worse, I was the first person (though eventually, as we all know, one of millions) who was curious enough to drift under her, eyes wide and arms outstretched, not trying to judge anything but where she would light.

No, that's not true. First of all, I guess I've never been that wholeheartedly supportive. I just thought I was. I got that impression from doing what I didn't want to do so she could do what she did want to do for twenty-some-odd years.

Second of all, Milam knew her before me, the son of a bitch. Drifting under her (well, not drifting, not Milam). If you want to know the truth (not that anybody does), it may be that I was just the first such person who smelled right to her. A distinction I cherish.

We broke up once though. Not part of her official biography.

It could happen again.

FIFTY MILES down the road it hit me. "Oh, shit. I forgot about E.B."

I told her all that E.B. and the jailer had said about eyes and fingers, which she enjoyed. And not every woman would enjoy talk you picked up in jail. In fact she acted like she wished she'd been the one in jail hearing it firsthand. Then I told her what E.B. had told me later that night when the jailer wasn't listening: that he hadn't been studying any breaking and entering—"well, maybe enterin' "—but had been picked up and charged with it because he was involved in some stuff that was about to come down: politics, demonstrations, in Dingler.

Of course she had to go back and get into some of that.

When I told her I'd forgotten about E.B., for me it was like when you say, "Oh, shit, forgot Mama's birthday, how could I have done that," something that I'd just carry around with me feeling bad about. But for Clementine, she just, click, gave me that look as if I were thinking what she was thinking and said, "You're right. Let's go back."

I'm right, let's what? I thought we were running away, going to take off visiting every motel with a waterbed across America. But how could I say that, with her looking at me like that? Looking back on it I realize it shouldn't have surprised me she became Leader of the Free World.

★   ★   ★

I would like to say this: I think it's harder than people realize, to be living in a damn museum, and the papers are calling you "the least effective first spouse since Bess Truman," and you're going through empty-nest syndrome at the same time.

★   ★   ★

Also, there's a whole area—you know why she had read *The Good Soldier*? She just saw the title in the library, and thought it might help her understand her father.

She told me that once, sort of let it slip, and maybe I leaped on the subject too hard, because she acted as if she'd never brought it up.

★   ★   ★

The story of how White Daughter of War Hero helped pull off the Crowe County Compromise has been told, of course, by reporters at the time and by Clementine herself in her book with Leonard. (Writing it with me would have been awkward, for more than one reason.) As well as in the movie.

Just a footnote to the movement, kind of an anachronism, really, because elsewhere riots and Panthers were the cutting edge, but it was a great six months. Nobody has given credit to E.B. and me for our initial contribution, but E.B.'s upstanding brother, the Reverend Micah Neighbors, was charismatic; Milam outslicked the locals in the courts (where they were most content to be outslicked); Leonard came back and coordinated press. "This is *exactly* what happens to me," he said (C told me—I wasn't around at that point). "Nobody even says to me, 'Leonard, you might think about buying a round-trip ticket, it could save you a hundred dollars.' "

And Clementine was amazing. You think it's easy bringing black Christians and white Christians together on a local level? They don't even sing hymns the same way. Whites go a-soaring as best they are accustomed to soar into "Precious Saviour, Still My Refuge" and look around and feel like penguins in a hurricane. That's when they start putting heavy emphasis on the fact that the blacks' pastor runs a liquor store.

But Clementine did it, brought those folks together.

I don't relish the faith of my fathers, personally. My mother had already died thinking I was literally going to burn in eternity. But we had a hell of a wedding. By the time it was over the organist had thrown off her lavender hat and was playing standing up. And of course when the Three D's were looking for ethnic diversity on their ticket, it didn't hurt to give the number-two spot to a woman who, though white, got married (to me) in a black church.

Then of course there were Clementine's scholarships and her

teaching and organizing and working motherhood and her TV show and the WOT years and playing herself in the movie and onward and upward to the convention and the Wall of China and beyond.

I've skipped ahead of the biggest crisis of *my* life so far. I'm working up to getting back to it.

★ AUG. 4, 1993

THE WOT YEARS. In my defense I would like to say that I loved WOT. WOT was fun. In fact I was invited to sit in on the session, in our living room, when WOT was named. A round dozen women and me.

"Women All Very Exuberant," somebody said.

"WAVE? I don't think so. I believe Nancy Reagan was a WAVE in *Hellcats of the Navy*."

"I kind of like that uniform, though."

"You *do*? Girl, we have got to have a de-retro workshop."

"WE. Women Everywhere."

"Hmm. We here at WE . . ."

"A broad-based coalition," I said.

"Uhhhhh."

"Organization of Hard-nosed Women of the World."

"Well. All right. Give us a little time with this one. OOH-WOT'W?"

"No, OH-WOW. You don't use the *t* or one of the *o*'s. Never mind."

"Great. An acronym with an asterisk."

"I said never mind."

"You'd have to issue a set of instructions: 'How this acronym works.' "

"I *said*, never mind."

"We Owe Men Exactly Nothing."

"Too defensive."

"WOMB!" said Dancy explosively. Dancy never was active in

WOT, but she was paying us a rare visit at the time. "It's wheah we awwlllllll come from," she said, in a kind of weird-sister-cum-Sunday-school-teacher voice. "Couldn't we think of *some* li'l somethin' that spells out WOMB?"

There was an awkward pause. There's something about Dancy—I wanted to back her up. "Women Owe Men *Bupkis,*" I suggested.

Dancy looked at me with something less than fellow-feeling. The others turned on me.

"Oo, gross. I vote Guy leaves."

"No, he's useful, he reminds us of what we're up against."

"Honey, I don't *need* to be reminded. Sitting there talking about *bupkis* and wombs."

"World Organization of Man-Busters," I said. Actually I was beginning to wish that Dancy hadn't gotten this started. I looked to C for help—hey, it was her sister—but she remained above the fray.

"Why are *you* getting so defensive?" someone asked me.

"You realize," I said, "that's the most offensive question you can ask someone."

"I move we give Guy money to go bowling."

"Or we could get him down and tie him up and do things to him," said Mona Perch, the literary theorist. "Like in the letters to the skin magazines."

"No! Don't do that!" I said.

"Mona! You read letters in skin magazines?"

"Epistemologically. Typically, this kid's big sister is having a pajama party and the girls slip into his room and—"

"Noooo, don't do that!" I said. "Don't slip into my room and—what?"

"Wait a minute!" said Esther Newberg, who is still pissed off that she is not Bobby Kennedy's chief of staff.

"Yes?"

"Wait, I'm thinking."

"Wait, I'm Thinking? WIT? I don't get it."

"What*ever* you do, dooonnn't slip into my room and—"

"No, I'm saying wait a minute because I'm thinking."

"And the rest of us can't, while you are?"

"I've got it!" Esther said. "Women On Top."

"It doesn't spell anything."

"It spells WOT."

"What?"

"WOT."

"WOT!"

"WOT's happening!"

"WOT's the story!"

"Slip into my room and do WOT, exactly?" I said.

"Pound you till you're tender," Dancy said. Dancy. I don't know.

"WOT it is!"

"WOT do women want!"

"The only thing is, Women On Top—the . . . sexual connotation . . ." said Patricia (The Only Person in the World Who Pronounces It Pa-triss-i-a) Twombly.

"Pa-triss-i-a, your mind is in the *gut*-tah," said Gyrene Bace. I love Gyrene Bace.

"But I mean, won't that put off Ms. Middle America?"

"Patricia, have you watched any sitcoms lately? WOT. WOT in the world. I like it."

"A garden is a lovesome thing, God wot," I said.

"What?"

"It's poetry."

"To you, maybe."

"To me? WOTta you mean, to me? A woman doesn't like a poem unless it's about killing the poet's daddy."

"Ohhh, WOT'sa matter, baby?"

"WOT'll you have?"

"Come WOT may."

"WOT's your name? Do I stand a chance with you?" someone sang, and then people started singing one thing after another.

"WOT kind of fool am I?"

". . . do WOT you do to me. . . ."

"WOT's go-in' aw-awn?"

"WOT is this thing called love?"

"Uh, I just had a thought," I said.

"If it's about us slipping into your room and—"

"No, no, I'm going to put that right out of my mind, until you actually loom above me in shorty nightgowns."

"Don't hold your breath, dicknose," said Gyrene, who probably sleeps in a motorcycle jacket. "Or, on second thought, do."

"Okay, Guy. Let's hear from the common porker."

"With WOT you run the risk," I said, "that certain people whose sensibilities are less advanced than mine . . ."

"Name one."

"Sandra Day O'Connor," said C in my behalf. That was nice of her. She used to do that kind of thing more often.

"Di-*viiii*-sive."

". . . are going to call it Terrible Women on Top," I said. "Or Trashy Women on Top. Or even Terrific . . ."

"Guy," C said, "we get your drift. Ladies?"

"WOT I say is," said Gyrene, "fuck us if we can't take a joke."

So WOT it was, and it caught on all over the country, upscale and down. Because it was serious, but fun:

The Top of the Moms doo-wop group that kept popping up at solemn assemblages of men.

The Wild Women supporto-competitive sports meets.

The *Do It Yourself, Charlie* housework-and-cookbook (I contributed my meat loaf).

The Happy Babies for Freedom of Choice demonstration.

The Assertive Shopping campaign, which brought down women's clothing prices nationally.

The surrounding of the Pentagon with roses (which seemed profligate until the price of 24,653 dozen roses was compared to the cost of one nonflying bomber, and then too the flowers were all personally delivered to people in wretchedly administered old folks' homes by the next morning, which got WOT on all three network newses two nights in a row).

I was proud to be married to the president of WOT. I marched in the R-E-S-P-E-C-T Parade for two miles with Clementine on my shoulders. (The kids came along too, Jackson dressed as a bee at his insistence. I made the costume, out of crepe paper, an old fishing rod, Ping-Pong balls and pajamas.) Milam and Leonard were instrumental in the organizing and the media handling, and Milam met his bemused-looking, seldom-seen wife-of-convenience, Paula, at a WOT gathering, but they weren't almost one of the girls, like I was. And did I hit on any of the girls? No. Though as a matter of fact Pa-triss-i-a Twombly once came out of a Portosan and asked me if I could tell that she'd taken off her panty hose.

"Well, your voice sounds a little lower," I said.

"How about in back?" she said.

"Pa-triss-i-a, I'm not going to lie," I said. "If it weren't for that pleated skirt, I would feel obliged, as a married gentleman, to throw a raincoat over you. It's a good thing I never lose my head over Republicans." She made a just-barely-inhibited *ooo* noise. She wasn't such a bad old girl.

I miss seeing Gyrene, who declined a post in the administration. "I can kick more ass on the outside," she said. I never did find out her real name. Dolores, somebody told me, but surely not. Why don't butch women get along with straight men the way femme men do with straight women? We could crush beer cans together and sing "Give Me Some Men Who Are Stout-hearted Men" with exaggerated mannerisms—and nobody running a risk of any more heartache than he or she feels already. It would be good for our perspectives.

When the Republicans spread rumors about Gyrene and C—now, here's an example of the way C used to be. The *Time* interviewer, working on the story that put C on the cover ("Womanwit: WOT's What"), hemmed and hawed and then brought up the "loose talk" about her and Gyrene. C smiled and said, "I could never be sexually involved with someone I can't beat in tennis.

"Oh, Guy, you're here. I should say, someone I can't *take a set off of* in tennis." And she rolled her eyes.

And that didn't bother me. Even though I could take C in tennis love-love. I bet I could beat Gyrene if she would play me. "Sorry," Gyrene says, "my calendar is full. I did not get involved in this outfit to pick up boys." But hey I'm not touchy. In fact, in the WOT days, C always made jokes about our marriage, and we were *happy*. She was sure of herself, she was sure of me, she was sure of everything. She didn't care what reactionaries thought. Now that she's the Leader of the Free World, she makes recurrent public allusions to how solid our union is—a bad sign.

My fault, probably.

No, no, I learned during marriage counseling not to talk about fault.

My contribution.

As in, the turd on the rug is the dog's contribution.

W H A T   A   P I E C E of work is another person. I'm not saying oneself is a bargain either, but: Often I think of criticisms of myself which if another person were to raise I would have to answer, "Yes. Yes. You're right. I take your point. But . . ." But they don't raise *those* criticisms. They come up with off-the-wall things. This morning Jackson called (*he* called *me,* will wonders never cease) and said, "The trouble with you is, Dad, you feel like *you* have to make sense out of everything."

Right.

Sure.

That's why my wife is President of the United States, thanks to an act of, assuming there is a God, God: a God who seems to take this notion of mysterious ways, his wonders to perform, as license to do just any old thing.

And that's why I have a son who says to me, "The trouble with you is, Dad."

"The trouble with you is, Dad."

Not until you have a son who is a certain age do you realize why it is that old men start wars and send young men off to fight them. "The trouble with you is, Dad." Dad who got up every morning to make him breakfast so his mother (a female person, if I could just interject a sexist note which is not entirely uncalled for I think) could take on—not to mention over—the world. Wait till he gets married. I hope his wife becomes the first woman pope. I hope he marries God. "And who do you think you are?" he will always be just about to say, and then always having to think of some other rejoinder.

I remember when Jackson was running around the house all outgoing and fantastical:

"I wish I had eyes all over and ears all over. And everything—legs . . . There he goes, the Vicious Whizzery! *Blango!* I just shot his whole body off!"

Of course maybe he was secretly taking aim at me at the time. That's all right—I was willing for him to outdo me, *in some way I could understand.* He had such a sweet loopy smile.

Lucy was always the scrupulous one.

"If Jackson and I got married we might have a midget child, that's what Mom said," Lucy told me one day when I was going crazy trying to fix my typewriter so I could write something I didn't really want to write so we could have electricity and mortgage and heat.

"Well, I guess it wouldn't be such a good idea," I said.

"I *want* a midget child," said Jackson.

Jackson I figured was going to be a creative genius of some kind. Lucy, such a warm and concerned little person, was going to work with disadvantaged children, catch little souls before they went off the beam.

Peaches and Herb, I used to call them. We used to read stories aloud together and dance to records, two little ones and one big one but actually more on the same level of something crucial than I have ever been with two other people, I now realize, or ever will be again. It was easy to feel vexed at the trouble they entailed, but what I didn't appreciate was by what a long shot it was the best deal I ever had, tending one's own green constellations for a while. Little persons who loved and trusted me as absolutely as I would let them, and who would reach up and grab my thumb.

I remember when the time came that I stopped hearing "Daddy" every day. When I did hear it, occasionally, I would turn instinctively, but it would always be some little kid I never saw before in my life.

Now, as the world knows (the world thinks it knows more about me and my family than I do, and yet it's always trying to interview me about them), Jackson is majoring in business with an eye toward "becoming CEO of a major innovative corporation," and Lucy is alternately lead singer and backup cacophonist for the not particularly noted weird art-rock group, L'Animal Anonyme.

Whose music I don't understand. I hope. I trust that I don't understand it, because if I do, it is awful. All I know is that when you mention Little Anthony and the Imperials to Lucy she gives you a kind but condescending look.

I was listening to two guys talking at lunch at Spratt's today. This administration, like any other I guess, is forever getting outraged

about secrets that have been disclosed. The disclosure I most regret, from my own, selfish point of view, is the secret that I went
to this other place near Spratt's, Whitlow's.

One thing that can be said for living in the White House is that
you can walk a couple of blocks away from it, over around E and
F streets, and in that neighborhood there are still places a person
who doesn't give a shit about public affairs can hang out in peace.
Until recently, Mrs. Triesta, Reader and Spiritual Adviser, would
read your palm there, four or five blocks from the White House,
until she closed down. (The CIA suspected her of being a foreign
agent—I am not kidding.) And you can still go to places like Whitlow's or Spratt's where you can get fried croaker and whiting and
cornbread and okra and buttermilk or a beer and listen to people
who don't give a shit about public affairs. Hayes Cotton, now writing a syndicated column, saw me coming out of Whitlow's one day.
I met him back in the movement days. In fact he helped me get
started in free-lancing. I said, "Hayes, don't blow the whistle on
me, this is my one place I can get away." But he needed a column.

"Guy," he said, "professional courtesy. You know what it's like
to need a column."

The fact that back when I needed a column it was something light
and human-interest for *Country Monthly* did not escape either of us.
But what the hell, a press guy is a press guy, until he becomes a
prick, which is what I have now become but hadn't yet at that time.
I sat down with him in Whitlow's and managed to stay off child
abuse, but I did talk about how Love, the presidential dog, was
adapting to the White House (had started backing around corners
for some reason), and about acts of God, and capitalism (I do have
a few things to say about the state of the nation, and one of them
is that what is happening is that the rest of the world is learning how
to do capitalism and is appreciating it more and working on ways
to freeze us out of it because we've been devoting our energies to
running it into the ground, getting too hip for our own good), and
one thing and another. It came out in the papers three days later,
FIRST HUBBY CHEWS THE FAT, and the next time I went into Whitlow's people stopped talking and looked at me funny. I have never
liked getting unsolicited funny looks. One old boy who had been
drinking all morning came over and asked if I'd give him my autograph and I said I wouldn't, and he said Clementine never did

anything for anybody either and I said how the hell did he know and he said he was a citizen as much as I was. I said I guessed he probably was, for what that was worth, and then he said he was a citizen more than I was because he paid taxes, and I said what did he think I paid, and he said why the hell should I pay taxes, I had a free ride on my wife. I said no I didn't and he said yes I did, and that's the kind of argument that really pisses me off: an argument that has no tenable middle, and as hard as you try to find one, the further you push the other person away—the other person sees your sense of middle as a threat. (I realize I haven't rendered, here, that sense of middle, but I swear it was there.)

I said, what was he saying, was he saying that I didn't know what I was talking about, when I was talking about myself? And he said everybody in the country knew he was right, and a couple of people told me to calm down, and I said *me* calm down, and finally the Secret Service guy had to hustle me out of there because I was about to hit somebody.

I'll say this for Whitlow's, nobody in there apparently gave enough of a shit about public affairs to alert the media, because there were never any FIRST HUBBY NEARLY LOSES IT stories in the news. I'll tell you what, though. I think that when someone who is held up to be famous is quoted as hanging out in a place like Whitlow's and talking like people in a place like Whitlow's do, the people in a place like Whitlow's don't like it. It bothers them. They want a famous person to know his place and to talk like a famous person. Anyway, after that I had to wear disguises and go around the corner to Spratt's. There was still an open staff slot for First Lady hairdresser, so I got a makeup woman named Leda who I suspect has done work for the CIA but she won't say. She can apply disguises that work anywhere, outdoors in the heat, some of them I could swim in. There's no problem about them working in Spratt's because it is not overly bright in there (and neither is anybody) and nobody looks at anybody they don't know.

Of course I still have the Secret Service lurking around, but a Secret Service guy doesn't look out of place in Spratt's, and people in Spratt's, as I say, don't give a shit about public affairs. They give a shit about things like whether their car is currently running, and Scripture. I can listen to people in Spratt's argue Scripture all day:

"Times was different back then. It don't have to be literally a snake."

"It didn't have to be back then either."

"No, but I'm sayin'—"

"It might have. Then again it might haven't."

"Wail, all I know is, it don't have to be now."

"Yeah, but I'm stuck, past there."

Today I was in my bald-guy-with-a-beard disguise, and what I'm getting at is, I was listening to these two guys:

"My oldest son has a one-forty IQ."

" 'At right? My—"

"They give him this test—"

"My oldest boy wouldn't take one of those."

"—and uh—"

"He scored fifteen hundred, you know, on his college board."

"Well, now, my son didn't do wuth a damn on that. He wadn't motivated wuth a damn on that."

"My oldest boy was."

I never speak up in Spratt's, because I like to have some place where I can just listen, be a reporter (whether or not I ever report)—hear what life is like without me. But I almost spoke up and said to these two guys, "I guarantee you my boy, Jackson, is smarter than either of them."

And what does Jackson aspire to be? A guy in a suit. Whereas Lucy jiggles arrhythmically and goes *ang-ang-ang* atonically for a living (not much of a living) in a plastic dress. Her boyfriend is a Thai. A Thai who, if I have this straight, has devised a new electronic octave.

His name, he says, is Ng.

Just Ng.

People ask me, "Lucy got a boyfriend?"

"Yes. He's a Thai." Because it doesn't bother me that he's a Thai. That's not the problem. It's just—

"A what?" they say.

"A *Thai.*"

I can't even say, "He's Thailandese," or "Thailandish." Or Siamese, which isn't right anymore and anyway sounds like a cat. Thai is the noun and the adjective. I can't even say, "He's from Thailand," because as I understand it he was born in Delaware (which is strange enough in itself). He's Thai-American.

"What's his name?" they say when they finally get what I'm saying.

"Ng."

I don't even think Ng is a Thai name. It's Chinese or Vietnamese or something. I have nothing against Thais or Chinese or Vietnamese, but.

I say the group is L'Animal Anonyme. That's what it was last week. A few months before that it was Automatic Pilot.

★   ★   ★

But that's not what I'm trying to get at. What I'm trying to get at is, I became an object of scrutiny before I had a chance to get going on anything I wanted to be known for.

I am not saying that I was primarily the one who raised these children. The two of us—well, the three of us, including big sister Lucy—sort of played child-rearing by ear. I am saying that there is a type of person who always keeps track of where everybody else is, takes into account everybody's probable viewpoint, bears in mind whether everybody is squared away—this person's eye is on the sparrow, so to speak. And this person is not the type who gets to be president of the United States. Even by acts of God.

And yet C's mind could be miles away, reconciling macro- and microcosm with regard to some urgent matter she was taking an active part in, and one of the kids could emit a faint choking noise three rooms away, trying to swallow a bottle cap or something, and bingo, C was there with the Heimlich maneuver. If either kid had ever nearly choked to death when C was away, I'm sure I would have heard him or her eventually, but in time? I worried about it. C doesn't like to worry about things. (Maybe that's why she doesn't want me to get into child abuse, something that can't be sorted out briskly.) She assumed she would hear them and she did. And she always seemed to be there when they had won an award or—the only three of Jackson's Little League games she made it to, he hit a home run.

If Reagan was a Teflon guy, C's surface is some kind of as-yet-untrademarked substance that catches only what she can cope with, and she's been able to cope with everything she's needed to, so far.

Whereas I catch all kinds of shit. I worked at home, so I was stuck with a great deal of the inglorious household and parent stuff, *and* I kept us solvent writing ephemera. You don't write anything titled

Our Tree Surgeon Doesn't Make House Calls unless you are making the best of feeling stuck. But does anybody in family or media pick up on that so I don't have to bring it up myself? No. Even though they're bringing out a new edition now as a result of Clementine's elevation, and this time it may sell pretty well. I may not have a quarter of a million in salary, like Clementine now that we don't need it, but I'm still earning, although my full-time government position is First Hubby, for which I am not paid a dime.

Of course I didn't know what cabin fever was till I moved into the White House. But my point is it would have been worth it if, now, freed up, I could do *my* life's work. Instead I am even to my children an oddity, to be commented upon. Maybe we should have named Lucy something different. Maybe it's too old-fashioned. But I spent a lot of time on those kids' names. Now when people try to interview her she gives them a postmodern stare and says "L'Animal Anonyme." She doesn't want to be a professional daughter, she tells me. I hear that.

I *know* I'm whining now! But god damn.

It's as if there were a rope of heart, a cardiac rope, between me and them and on one end it still pulls as hard on me, and oh, I know it probably pulls on them, nostalgically at least, at their end, but between us these days there is a slack, missingness, that somehow or other can't be taken up. And that slack itself has an endless pull like a, what is it, a phantom limb. And how about C and me? I would never tell C all this. It would make her sad. She proceeds on the assumption that we did a great parenting job.

It doesn't seem to bother her, for instance, that she believes in reincarnation, that Lucy once told her that this was "a hoot," and that one of L'Animal Anonyme's songs is "A White Sport Coat and Reincarnation."

Lucy is good. A daughter is a consolation to a father. She calls me (on my charge card, but that's all right) to tell me, diplomatically, after saying she misses me, what the trouble with me is. I don't have to call her eight times and leave never-to-be-responded-to messages with stoned-sounding roommates till I finally catch her, like I have to with Jackson, so he can give me his critique crisply.

CEO. It's so *pointed.* No winding up like his father, the hand-maiden, for Jackson. Oh no. He intends to be a *player.* He's already developing the executive's knack of making it clear, when I digress onto an interesting point, that his schedule is tight. He is twenty. I am sending him through college—blind trust, already set up. So he can think he knows more about the bottom line than I do.

I think they're angry at me. Common enough. Maybe anger toward parents is the fount of all worldly energy. But I didn't see it coming. I still want to help them. And I think they still want to be helped. But not by me, per se. I take out my affection on the dog that backs around corners: Love is her name, for reasons lost in the mists of family history (which is itself somewhat lost in the mists of world history, I hurt to say). She is a nice dog, with always-surprised eyes. It must be hard being a dog or a cat (they would hate being lumped together of course and I do so only in haste), since they have no hands and people don't like to be chewed on or licked. There is a song that L'Animal Anonyme does, I don't think Lucy wrote it—she may have written it, I suspect she writes their songs but doesn't let on:

> Oh Daddy damn you, love you,
> Daddy love you, damn you,

I think is how it goes, but it's hard to hear. I didn't see anything coming, that came.

Just like President DaSilva didn't see that fish.

"Are you ready for the fish?" the butler said to me at dinner last night, when my mind was a thousand miles away.

We have a butler now. I rest my case.

★ AUG. 6, 1993

I SHOULD, after all, try to write *something* light and printable, to justify all the time I spend in here with Grover Cleveland and the Chester A. Arthur Iroquois half-foot.

Okay. So, I had a good time last night.

We had a few people over for dinner, which is the only kind of social function I can stand. Except when it's *formal.* One thing I have to swallow is that the seating isn't boy-girl-boy-girl. It's boy-girl-boy-girl-Clementine-me-boy-girl-boy-girl. Nobody has ever asked me whether this bothers me, but it does. Because it means I have to sit next to some governor or V. S. Naipaul or somebody, who is looking across me trying to catch C's eye, instead of some nice wife or date whom I could either flirt with or commune with about what a pain in the ass it is to be a leader's spouse, or both.

Tonight I sat next to Gorbachev. He was there with Susan Sarandon. My feeling going in was that I had nothing against Gorbachev, but I'd rather sit next to Susan Sarandon. She might not be expected to take much of an interest in me either, but at least I could look down her dress. I am not all that good at dinner parties. When they're formal.

But it turned out Gorbachev wanted to talk to me. He'd been reading as many different kinds of American books as he could since he came over here and, more or less following the precedent of Jackie O., took a publishing job. He'd read *Tree Surgeon,* he said (which probably meant he read a couple of pieces in it, but that's okay), and he liked it, he said.

But what he really wanted to talk about were the problems of being a First Spouse. You can tell the son of a bitch misses Raisa deeply. "Ahh, she wuss ullways"—well, I won't try to do his accent. "She was always so much more of an ideologue than me," he said, twice. But that wasn't what he meant. He meant, "I always loved her more than she did me." He's thriving over here, very popular, bringing out all kinds of great new Russian books, and he loves New York. He gave Russia his best shot, a shot heard all over Eastern Europe, at least. And he's out with Susan Sarandon for God's sake. But he doesn't look the same, in exile. And I'd say it's Raisa. Who may have helped to overthrow him. Who at any rate chose to stay home.

Or is it just me? Do I assume that everyone keeps his soul alive by keeping his wife's tone of voice adjusted? Because the one thing I can't stand is the sound of her voice with no feeling in it. It's a horrible sound. Whatever it takes, to avoid that sound.

My wife has the funniest, most serious, most beautiful voice I've ever heard. And face, ever seen.

Oh, God.

What I was saying is, Gorby wanted to talk about the difficulties of being a First Spouse. "I thought I was considerate," he said. "I let her speak out. I didn't complain when I was criticized because of her. I bought her dresses. But I didn't know, I must not have known, how hard it was for her. I thought . . . I thought I *had* her."

What he'd had I think were a few vodkas before dinner, but he wasn't showing it to anybody but me. As it happened I had had a few Jack Daniel'ses. All of a sudden I just blurted out:

"I like Russians."

He beamed. "Yes," he said. "We are . . . difficult. But she—they, we, Russians . . . will warm up again.

"I pushed them," he said. "I wanted to make them free. I love my people. They are myself. But, then, they are not. You cannot force people to be free, to be loved."

"When you think of someone as being a part of you," I said, "you think they . . ." I couldn't quite get straight what I thought.

"Yes, you think they are part of your heart," he said. "And they are, but they are not. We have an old Russian proverb, my friend:

"My elbow is near, but I cannot kiss it."

"Yes!" I said, and that night in bed I quoted it to Clementine. You know how something you hear when you've been drinking seems to say it all. And then when you pass it on to somebody later . . .

"Russians!" C said. "I wish he were still the one to talk to over there, though."

"Yes," I said, "but I mean . . . don't you see how it applies to you and me?" I realized that I couldn't quite see exactly how it did anymore, myself. It had seemed so clear at the time.

"What was it again?" C said.

"My elbow is near," I said, "but I cannot kiss it."

"Oh," she said. "When I was a girl, they said if you kissed your elbow you'd become a boy."

"Yeah, me too," I said, "but that's not—"

She rolled over against me. "My love-bowl is near," she said, "and you can kiss it."

Love-bowl! Where did she come up with that?

And who in the world can you tell about your love life with your wife?

Especially since—who would believe it? I don't think the marriage counselor believed it. "How about . . . sexual problems?" he said, and we looked taken aback.

No, we both said, no problems there. And he looked taken aback. Maybe there is something wrong with us.

When they were making the movie . . . How many other people have been able to play themselves in their life stories, by the way? Audie Murphy, Muhammad Ali, Clementine. I thought she was convincing as herself. But the guy who played me, Jesus. He took me aside and asked me what I thought held our marriage together. Sense of humor?

"That's it," I said hastily. I guess that does have something to do with it. She likes for me to bring her jokes. For instance, a country band finished up their gig and had a few drinks and looked around and couldn't find the bass player. They went out to the parking lot and saw their whole bus shaking. And they heard a woman inside moaning and hollering with passion. They stood there listening for a while, and then there was a pause, and they heard the woman say, "Kiss me."

"Nooo," they heard the bass player saying. "I'm married. I *ought* not to be doing *this.*"

But they couldn't use that in the movie, because it didn't seem credible that her character would like it.

But Clementine loved it. Now she tells jokes like that to congressmen. They're a little taken aback to hear them coming from a woman, which is just fine with her.

If I'd told the truth to that dipstick who played me, I would have just said, "Sugar."

That's an acronym C and I worked out. For Screw Until (we) Get All Rubbery.

She can still make me feel, in bed, like I've got a heart of gold, twelve dicks, the gift of tongues and fingertips of chamois. *Only* in bed does she make me feel like that, anymore. But who could stand to feel like that all the time?

Well, maybe Clementine feels like that—feels that intense I mean—all the time.

She won't *discuss* things intensely, though. I like the idea of thesis and antithesis forming synthesis. Clementine likes the idea of doing what she has in mind. I thought marriage counseling would bolster what I had in mind, but she was so forebearing and sweet that I came off as a crank. I kept saying, "Now, I'm not saying we have *deep* problems, or that I'm unhappy, it's just that—" and the counselor looked at me like he was willing to take our money, but he wondered why we were there.

I thought I would like marriage counseling better. Usually men don't even want to do it. (I remember Hayes Cotton griping that his wife was dragging him to counseling. "It's all right for *her,*" he said. "She can tell the *truth.*") But in our case it was my idea. I thought, with a third person, we might get a discussion going. Maybe I'm queer or something, but I like a good freewheeling critical discussion.

I had in mind that the counselor might tell us some things that I can't very well say about myself. "The problem with you, Guy," I could imagine him saying, "is that you aren't manipulative *enough.*"

But all counseling did for us was, well, three things: (1) it dashed forever any illusions I might have had that there is any such thing, in marriage especially, as objective truth; (2) it showed me that marital disjunction *polarizes,* that is if one partner wants to argue and the other one doesn't then the first one tends to get more and more argumentative as the second one gets more and more withdrawn and vice versa; (3) it left us with a book entitled *To Love Is to Be Happy With,* which seemed to me to beg the question.

And then C accepted the vice-presidential nomination and one thing led to another and that was that. Whoever heard of a President in marriage counseling?

★ AUG. 7, 1993

SHE NEVER TELLS ME anything secret anymore. I guess I overreact. Last night when she mentioned she was weighing the option of sending more troops into Panama now that Noriega has beat the drug rap and gone back down there and regained power, I got too exercised.

"What?" I said. "Great! Have yourself a merry little isthmus."

If puns could kill.

"I'm sorry," I said. "I'm not being supportive. But why would I be supportive about going to war with Panama again? I'm a peacenik! I thought you were!"

"Guy," she said, "the President can't be a peacenik."

"Why not? What's the point of anybody else being one, if the person who's supposed to keep the military in line can't be one?"

"Guy, the last thing in the world the military wants to do is fight. It's too hard. All the military wants to do is stockpile unusable weapons. It's a wonder the military didn't self-destruct trying to take Grenada."

"Oh, you're in favor of taking Grenada now."

"I'd've been in favor of taking it right, and not pretending it was anything to boast about."

"You *would've?*"

"Well, the people in Grenada seemed to welcome it."

"What did you expect the people of Grenada to do, chase America away with stalks of sugarcane? Grenada is not going to be a nation until it can take care of itself, and it's not ever going to be able to take care of itself until the United States leaves it alone. If we'd let them be Communist they'd have revolted and turned semicapitalist on their own by now, like everybody else except Albania. And I'll bet fewer people would've been blown up. For that matter, Noriega still hasn't killed as many Panamanians as our troops have."

"Okay, okay. I just said it was an option," she said.

"But I don't think it *ought* to be an option. Okay, okay. Let me guess: You can't cut the defense budget the way you want to unless you show you aren't afraid to use force. You notice I am not saying anything about a, uh, shall we say a, uh . . . *woman* needing to prove any such thing because of her being a, uh . . . woman."

"I'm glad to hear you aren't."

"I wouldn't say that. I'm not saying it. And I can see that it would be good for you to have some kind of coup—excuse me, success—with the Quayle thing dragging out."

"Guy . . ."

"Excuse me, the Quayle thing *taking time.* In fact a surgical military action that worked might *nudge* Qaddafi on the Quayle thing. Also it would boost the credibility of your leaner, meaner defense proposals. It would make it easier for your father to continue to support you, too. It must kill your father, to be perceived as a dove."

"Guy, you sound like the press."

"To the world, I am First Hubby. To me, I am an old newspaper guy."

"Okay," she said.

"Now you're not being supportive."

"Supportive of what?"

"Of who I am to myself." I *hate* saying things like that.

"I'm sorry," she said.

"It's all right, I'm just trying to put you into my shoes. And on this Panama thing, it seems to me—of course I didn't go to the War College, but it seems to me that if there's one thing we should have learned by now, it is that there is no such thing as a surgical strike. Unless you think of surgery as something that requires the patient to lose two or three extra organs and the surgeon his thumb. His or her thumb."

"I get your point. Thank you for playing devil's advocate."

Devil's advocate! Against bloodshed! But I let it go at that. We went to bed.

I shouldn't have said that isthmus thing. I have to tell myself over and over, I can't be sarcastic with her. Playful but not sarcastic. To her sarcastic is violent. It hurts her.

One reason she is so good in a crisis is that she is as *intent,* all the time, as most people are only when they're scared. When everybody has every reason to be scared, it's her cup of tea.

Something that would *not* be her cup of tea: if I were to ask her whether it might be possible that she was considering bringing on a crisis because she is good in them. Another thing: if I were to ask her whether it had occurred to her that a little of her father might be coming out in her.

We went to bed, as I say. Sometimes at night, in bed, I can feel her coming apart. We screw her back together, at a different level, where she can sleep.

I'm not boasting. Sometimes I'm just hanging on. Neither of us has ever been loath to keep on doing what we can (we can do a lot) when either of us is less than fully inflamed. As Dancy advised me once, out of the blue (well, I think we were talking about her favorite biblical figure, Mary Magdelene, and also about the Lord's aversion to the lukewarm—you don't have to be close to Dancy to have amazing conversations with her): "A secure girl don't mind a nice semi to hump and rub up against, if the feller's enthusiastic enough otherwise." But last night was different. I faked an orgasm.

★ **AUG. 8, 1993**

THE "NONNNN'T WANT TO KNOW" family story goes back to when Lucy and Jackson were six and three, roughly. One afternoon while I was working and it sounded like they were playing nicely in the next room, Lucy was in fact applying a great deal—a *great* deal—of rubber cement to Jackson and decorating him with leaves, play money, doll socks, feathers and crepe-paper streamers. I should say, applying a great deal of rubber cement to Jackson and to his surroundings. And they got it on the bottoms of their feet and spread it around that way quite a bit, and by the time Lucy brought Jackson in to show him to me (he was almost wholly obliterated but quietly proud), they had also turned over the large (about quart-size, I would say) dispenser of rubber cement.

Several issues arose. One was that it said on the rubber cement dispenser, "Avoid contact with skin." Another was that Jackson started feeling sick, I guess from the fumes. I got him to the bathroom almost in time.

Rubber cement, even by itself, is no fun to wash off.

Federal Express was due any moment to pick up what I hadn't quite finished writing, which was already three days late.

The dogs got involved.

Lucy met C at the door saying, "You nonnnn't want to know."

Jackson survived, and it didn't take more than three or four hours to clean up quite a bit of the mess. (The Federal Express man, Marty, helped de-cement Jackson for a few minutes while I frantically finished typing a paean to the rutabaga.) The kids were able to help by rolling up the rubber cement that was on hard surfaces into boogers. That's one of the reasons they enjoyed working in the medium of rubber cement so much, because you could make boogers. Jackson, always hardy, seemed to feel that the whole experience was a plus one, on balance, and I believe Lucy honestly couldn't see much of a downside to it at all, though she was commiserative with Jackson. "Look at his itty-bitty big blue eyes," she said. Her timing with such remarks was so good that I even kept my temper. And C surprised us with an apropos joke she'd heard from one of her WOT colleagues' kids:

"There were three hippies standing in a line. One said [C started snapping her fingers rhythmically], 'Got the *boog*-ie woogie *feel*-ing and I *want*-a get it *on.*'

"The second one said [finger-snapping again], 'Got the *boog*-ie woogie *feel*-ing and I *want*-a get it *on.*'

"And the third one said [same finger-snapping motion], 'Got a *boog*-er on my *fin*-ger and I *want*-a get it *off.*'"

We had a nice little family life back then.

★ AUG. 9, 1993

HERE IS SOMETHING about her: she never says "You wouldn't understand." If a woman says that . . .

No, back up. I'm resolved not to generalize about women. Leonard says that the only reason men profess such bafflement about women is that women are the only people we know that well. So.

If *another person* says "You wouldn't understand," it means your only decent response is to say, *"Sure* I would, come on, please" and coax her into some kind of cryptic statement that you don't understand at all and yet the burden is then on you to convince her you do. C isn't like that.

She just *assumes* I understand. And if I don't I've let her down.

We were driving back into Dingler. To see about getting E.B. out of jail. My heart sinking. I realize I had brought the matter up, but I hadn't brought it up with any idea that the next thing I knew we'd be heading back toward Dingler with the prospect of trafficking with Milam and probably the Reverend Dingler and his dog.

"But am I griping?" I was thinking to myself. "No. Here I am

with Clementine, whatsoever that entails." And I was thinking,
"How did this get to be the deal?"

OSTRICH BEAR GIFTS said a sign for Chico's Monkey Farm. SEE
OCELOTS PANTHERS STORKS CRANES FINE CANDY COYOTES OYSTER
STEW POSTCARDS DEER HOT SOUP EMUS PAPAYA JUICE FREE ADMISSION.
BABY MONKEYS FOR SALE. GAS UP.

With a wom—another person—the key is to stay ahead of the
curve. If you're going to keep her (we'll call the other person "her")
on a course that gives you some sway.

But how in the hell are you going to stay ahead of the curve if
she's Leader of the Free World? And you aren't even free to be a
critical observer? If you're a critical observer, you can stay ahead
of anything, after a fashion: that's why people crave to work in the
media. In the media, you're on top of things, looking down on the
way things are handled. Some fun.

But a hubby is not a critical observer. A hubby is supportive.

Of course, I wasn't a husband yet, this morning in South Carolina. We were together in our car. We were young and in love. She
was a long way from being president. And already I knew I wasn't
ahead of the curve with Clementine and never would be. On the
radio the Archies were singing their dumb hit, "Sugar Sugar."

We went into a curve. I like the feeling of a curve: leaning into
it, pulling through it, at a speed set jointly by yourself and by the
curve: you feel it in your hips. Driving one-handed, I felt kind of
sporty, or would have if we were heading the other direction. The
curve shifted her weight closer toward me; I had on shorts, her
dress was up high so she could get the good of the vent fan, and
our bare legs touched. She picked up an old grease pencil that
rolled out from under the seat and started to write on my cast with
it:

To My Sugar From His Sugar

Oh my God oh my God.

I looked over at her. If we'd been in bed I would have squeezed
her up against me, straining to get every give of her down to the
bone and spoken in tongues in her mouth and her legs would have
convolved around mine and my mind would not have minded. But
we were in an Oldsmobile.

I gave her a look that was, I dare say, both carnivorous and helpless, and she gave it back without the helpless and reached over and that was the first time she took her fingernail and scraped my nose.

"Our babies," she said, "will have your nose. When we woke up this morning I would have gone right down to a justice of the peace and married you. If you'd asked me, that is."

Uhhhhhhh?

"In high school there would always be some girl who'd had to drop out because she was pregnant and the other girls would talk about the names they were going to give their babies. I was always a new girl because of the army and I would always say 'Dawn' and 'Wade' to fit in but the other girls would always look at me funny anyway because I could never act dreamy about it because it wasn't what I was dreaming about and I didn't have a boyfriend."

"You didn't?"

"No."

"How come?" I was going to say but she was already saying, "Now I feel like flowers all inside. They'll be funny babies and they won't haph any phobias, they'll be brave and happy because they'll know we love them."

She patted my cast and smiled at me and then she smiled out into the overcast spring morning as if everything were clear, as if it made perfect sense to cut your ties and strike off boldly into a new romantic life and then turn back the next morning toward the same old nest of shithooks in order to get somebody you don't know out of jail. And start talking about *babies*?

I started wondering. Had I been overlooking something? When I looked at Clementine and was filled to the teeth with feelings of "Hot slicketty Jesus!" was I overlooking something, the way you look at a house and see its lines as classically perfect because your mind automatically edits out the huge TV aerial on the roof, which an objective person would see as spoiling the effect?

She's ready to get *married*?! And we haven't even talked about— she hasn't asked me—why I hit her father. Why *had* I hit her father?

Should I bring it up? Or let sleeping dogs lie? Had I had any inkling that he was her father? A big crusty son of a bitch, and fatherly-looking, in a largely negative sort of way. Why *had* I hit her father? Because he called her a floozy? Because I was jealous or just out of my senses? Because I couldn't hit my own father, he being dead? Somehow I didn't think this was an area that Clementine would enjoy exploring.

Probably the reason I hit her father was, I was trying to get ahead of the curve. Or latch on to it as I felt it slipping ahead of me. This new Clementinian curve that was sweeping me up. But why hadn't she asked me?

Her way of staying ahead of the curve. Holding on to sway. There was a turkey buzzard standing in the road. Next to a sign advertising HOME KILLED BEEF AND PORK.

What was the curve here, exactly? When you're in love the curve is a swell that fills your trunks and makes you feel you can do anything. When you're with Clementine you can feel the curve peeling off her prow like a wake. And then too, an undertow.

Those were my feelings. Another person will tell you, what we need to do is talk about our feelings. But when another person says that, it means she wants to talk about her feelings, and your feelings for her. And what I would rather do, anyway, is to compare views—to work out, through the give-and-take of logical analysis, a synthesis that we can both acknowledge as equitable. That's the kind of guy I am.

There was a sign saying E-Z ON, E-Z OFF. SEE LIVE BEAR. TAKE PICTURES OF MILDRED THE BEAR.

"Are we always going to do what you think we ought to do?" was what I said.

No, wait. That's guilt telling me that. Which goes to show how far I will lean toward the other person's point of view. What I said was—well, who knows what I said. That's one thing we learned in marriage counseling. Or I learned it. Because it was philosophically interesting: that one person will remember something one way and assume for years that the other person remembers it the same way and then you start comparing notes in marriage counseling and you say, "For instance, that time you said . . ." so and so. And you realize that the other person hasn't been remembering it that way at all. It is perfectly certain in the other person's mind that not only did the person never say such a thing, but that she never *would* say such a thing. And there isn't any point in arguing about it. You just have to accept that one person remembers one thing and the other remembers the other. It may be true, as Billy Graham was quoted as saying during the flap over the Nixon Watergate tapes, that "The

Lord has got his tape recorder going all the time," which stirred me
to write a little song:

> The Lord has got his tape recorder going all the time,
> Going all the time,
> Going all the time,
> The Lord has got his tape recorder going all the time,
> So watch out, how you rattle on.

Who knows what I said? That, in general, is probably what Clementine knows: Who knows? Move on.

But as best I remember it, I didn't say anything as harsh as I just
said I did. What happened was, she looked over at me and said,
"Guy, I feel so good with you."

And if she'd said it five minutes earlier, before I started thinking
about curves and hearing about babies, I'd've melted all over the
seat cover. But what I said was, just by way of trying to hold my own:

"Mmm. Doing what *you* want to do."

And that went over, as the expression goes, like a prick in a pickle
barrel. You'd have thought I had hit her. This terrible thing happened to her eyes; something went tight in them and wide in them
at the same time.

And she didn't say anything.

"I mean . . ." I said, and then I went into a pretty even-handed
explanation of what I meant, I thought. She didn't say anything.
And her expression didn't change.

I worked hard on that explanation of what I meant and of what
it meant, it seemed to me, to us. I had never tried to explain myself
wholeheartedly to anybody before—I had always resisted the notion of talking about any *us* before—and I thought I was doing a
pretty good job of it, maybe a little too forcefully, but like I say I
was trying to hold my own, and I was put off that she wouldn't
answer me.

"Ooooo, I feel something now," said a preacher on the radio. "I
feel like I want to get up and run all over this studio."

"I mean . . ." I said. "What's wrong with what I said? Can't I say
what I think?" No answer. "Huh?"

"The Lord is in this radio station in a magnificent way. And he's got me in the palm of his hand. And he opens it up every now and then and says, 'Buddy, how you doin'?' And I say, 'All right, Lord,' and then he closes it up again."

"Yes," she said in a little voice. A little voice! Oh, that little voice. I'd rather be beat over the head than hear that little voice. In fact, I think I may have told her that.

And then I said, "That little voice is a killer."

It was getting cloudy. Maybe I am just touching up the picture by remembering clouds, but no. I remember clouds coming up, and lightning; because when the lightning flashed the radio went *Sxkj!* like the explosive noises we boys used to make after throwing pretend hand grenades. *Sxkj!*

"You know, it seems to me," I said. I realize now that I say "It seems to me" too much, or I say it in the wrong tone of voice or something, I don't know. I *don't* know. What's *wrong* with saying "It seems to me"? Clementine never says it, which is part of my point about her.

But anyway what I said was, "It seems to me . . . You know, yesterday, you were saying that people look at you funny, that you don't have a way with them?"

She didn't say anything.

"Trade with Brother Broadhurst's service station," said the voice of adoration. "He's a fine man, he loves the Lord and he sponsors this program." *Sxkj!*

"Have you ever considered that it might be because . . . they're afraid of what your reaction is going to be? Afraid you might just take off running ninety miles an hour with whatever they said in whatever direction you want to take it before they have a chance to think?"

"And may his business increase a hundredfold times. It costs money [*Sxkj!*] run a service station, so y'all go by there."

And she didn't say anything. Just looked out through the windshield as if I'd hit her.

"And you know Brother Broad [*Sxkj!*] also has the Washateria there, and live crickets." I switched the radio off.

"Well?" I said. Sharply, I guess. But damn. "I don't understand your reaction," I said. "What bothers you about what I've said?"

"I thought . . ." she said, "you *understood.*"

And that made me mad. "I just *said,*" I said, "that I *don't understand.* That's the whole point of what I'm saying, that I'm asking . . ."

And she started to cry. Oh, Lord, Clementine crying. It is the worst sight in the world. This awful *dry* crying. Crying like that at *nineteen.* My mother maybe before she died, but Clementine! Parched crying. Crying like the wrenching of a person who's dying of thirst.

And it made me mad.

It did. It just did. Send me to emotional prison for it, but it did.

"Why are you crying?" I said. She wouldn't say anything.

"You're scaring me," she said.

How did she think that made me feel? *"Scaring* you? *Scaring* you. I don't want to *scare* you. I'm just trying . . . scared of *what*? What do you think I would *do*?"

Did she think I would *hit* her? I would never *hit* her. It made me feel like shit, to think that she maybe thought that I maybe would hit her. She didn't have any grounds to make me feel like that!

We were speeding into town: blacktop, telephone poles, raggedy-ass roadside grass and a sign that said, WELCOME TO DIN-GLER, THE MAGIC CITY. Into rain curving out of the vertical straight at the windshield like heat-seeking rat-a-tat. Windshield wipers flapping time. I reached out to her awkwardly with, well, hell, my cast.

★ AUG. 10, 1993

THE SECRET SERVICE. Is too much with me.

It is hard to think like an American, when you know that you are being guarded all the time.

One thing Jo DaSilva told me when she passed me the First Spouse torch, she said, "Don't try to evade the Secret Service. It's like Mother Nature—don't mess around with the Secret Service." I've already been in this situation longer than she was, and I still resent the Secret Service.

I get along with people. But the Secret Service—they have an

enlisted-man mentality. And so do I. Actually I have the mentality
of an enlisted man who wants to desert. Whereas they want me to
act like an officer, show a little common humanity every now and
then but not *all the time.* Well, by common humanity I don't mean
I want to pal around with them. They're like guards. Who wants to
pal around with guards?

The one who is on duty right now, standing outside the door, is
my least favorite. Because he is so impassive.

"What would you really like to be doing?" I asked him this
morning.

He blinked. As if that were an improper, a sacrilegious question.

"This," he said.

"Watching a man?" I said. "You wouldn't rather be a race-car
driver?"

"Oh, sure."

"Well."

"But I do really like this."

He's lying. They love C, but with First Ladies they were used to
taking a kind of gruff-brotherly tone. Fuck a lot of gruff-brotherly.

Guard isn't quite right. Baby-sitter. It's like having male baby-
sitters. I used to hate it, when I was a kid, when my mother would
go out with my uncle Gene and aunt Martha and leave me with
some male youth. Female youths were scarier, actually, but they
also had allure. Sometimes they would sit on the rug with you with
their skirts hiked up and play canasta. Or they would teach you
dance steps. Male youths just belched and looked at you as if to say
that you would never be able to belch that loud as long as you lived.

Which is why the only Secret Service person I like is Wulf. Eliza-
beth Wulf. Her hair is a little like C's. My whole childhood—well,
the whole last part of it—I tried to work up the nerve to ask a female
baby-sitter to play strip canasta with me, and finally I asked Wulf
to the other day. She didn't know what canasta was. "All the better," I said, but she just laughed.

"Set the Wulf to watch the henhouse," I say to her, things like
that, and she laughs. I have never been unfaithful to C, but I hate
being in a position where how in the hell am I ever even going to
be *able* to, for the rest of my life?

Sometimes Wulf and I watch television together, to improve her
sense of history. We watched some kind of awful Van-Johnson-in-

the-navy movie (I don't think Van Johnson *liked* being in movies) in which this exchange occurred:

VAN JOHNSON: Any scuttlebutt about where this scow is taking us?

SOME SWABBY: I was just going to ask you, Lieutenant.

So whenever I see her I sidle up and do the Van Johnson line and she does the other one.

Actually I wonder whether the Secret Service *does* know things I don't. One reason I don't get along with them is that they seem edgy over having lost the last president to a fish. And nearly losing his predecessor to Marilyn Quayle. I played softball with the White House staff team against a Secret Service team yesterday afternoon. I wasn't in the mood for it. I was thinking about what I'd written the day before. Nobody on base, I grounded sharply to the third baseman.

And do you know what he did with it? He went around the horn with it. Threw it to the shortstop, who threw it to the second baseman, who threw it to first. And they *still* got me out by a step.

Hey, I'm forty-eight years old. Even at their age, I wasn't Bo Jackson. But I can still play. I started to run around the horn myself until I could get to the third baseman and clean his clock. But he probably knew martial arts. More like cleaning a computer. Also it would have taken me too long to run all the way over there. What I did was, I yelled: "Bush! Bush! [As in bush-league.] And speaking of which, if you're so smart how come you couldn't protect George from that woman?"

Which was not in good taste. I realize that. When I came back to the bench, Leonard said, "You know, you're making it hard for the rest of us."

That's Leonard, today. Back when he was fun to be around, he and I made up an entire family of minor malefactors, the Whites, and wrote a new two-paragraph story every couple of weeks about their offenses, which always involved collard greens—theft of, disagreement over, assault with, et cetera. That was not in good taste either, but the moral as we saw it was that since whites assumed the Whites to be black (we worked out an artfully ambiguous address for them, which also enabled blacks to assume they were white), the question of whether the Whites were real never occurred to anyone at the *Beacon* or even the police station. And how else were you going to attract public notice to White-collard crime?

Leonard no longer shares my sense of unreality. But, then, he isn't guarded night and day, either.

How the hell did Marilyn get as far as she did? The Secret Service's internal investigation turned up no inside involvement. And C says none of the intelligence services could figure out how she managed it either. We'll never know, unless C can get her back from Libya.

Maybe I should offer myself in exchange. Billy Carter had some fun with Libyans, maybe I would. I'm not having much fun here. Leonard never kids around anymore, he's getting to be more and more like Milam though he and Milam seem to like each other even less, if anything. E.B. can't afford to be traveling up here from South Carolina. Actually he used to pop up fairly often when we were living in the country, but then he could drive up to the front door and walk in. He showed up at the vice-presidential residence once unannounced, assuming he could bullshit his way in like he does everywhere else he wants to go, and I think it hurt his feelings—though he denies it—when the guards treated him like an interloper.

"I told them, didn't they see the *movie*?" he said when I found out about it. "I was the only one besides Clementine who played himself. My brother had to have Danny Glover do him, he couldn't handle it himself." Which is true, but it is also true that E.B.'s part wasn't much more than a walk-on and none of his lines survive because he improved so much on what he was given to say. Some people would be philosophical about learning that they play themselves too well to work as themselves in a movie, but it never set right with E.B.

So who is my social set now? Aside from the Secret Service and the parade floats who come to state dinners?

Maybe I should call Jackie O. up, invite her to lunch. Nah, she flinched when Jimmy Carter tried to give her a presidential kiss on the cheek at the Kennedy Library dedication. A Georgian never forgets a snub. We may not have good taste, but we don't hold with snubbing.

So maybe I should call up Rosalynn? She would fault me for not being active enough.

★ **AUG. 11–13, 1993**

BREAKING UP is hard to do by yourself.

She talked to me, sort of, there in the car, but it was like I was trying to sell her life insurance. On someone who had just that moment died before her eyes.

Why should the burden all be on me? And here is what I think is the worst thing I can confess: an element of me was thinking, "Well, if she's this changeable, hell, I'm well out of this."

If she's this hypersensitive, this intolerant of dissent.

It's a free country.

What did she want to do, I asked her.

I'd tried to talk to her.

She'd suddenly gone all hunched and angular and utterly unconducive to being hugged. Might as well have had quills out. Sitting there handling those pearls.

I didn't even feel like hugging her.

I was mad.

She must be crazy.

What did she want to do, I asked her.

She asked me if I would drop her off at an address that turned out to be, you guessed it, there was his fucking shingle: Milam's jackleg law office.

"Where can I reach you?" I asked her as she opened the door into the rain. She looked back, already wet in the face and rain coming in past her onto the seat, and said she didn't know. And met my eyes with eyes that weren't the same. And dashed off to that little ramshackle house where Milam and, apparently, some guys named Peet and Wormsig practiced.

"Wait," I said and jumped out on my side, wanting to escort her or something, do the gracious thing, but the door to the building was unlocked and she scooted right on in, hunched over, looking more defenseless than was called for. With her little suitcase that I'd snuck some flowers and a note into while she was in the bathroom that morning. The bathroom! The sound of her tinkle.

I stood there and got wet for a minute, hoping she was watching, but I was damned if I was going to run behind her.

I was going to drive west. To Puyallup, Wash.

Where we'd said we were headed together.

I lost my job for her! Okay, it was a bad newspaper, but it was a newspaper. How many other jobs are there whose purpose is to tell the unvarnished truth? Even if management wouldn't let us tell any *controversial* unvarnished truth, we knew that we *would,* by God, if they would only let us. The only thing more American than a job like that is the open road.

If she'd just said something like, "Oh, I know you've got your heart set on traveling, but wouldn't it be more exciting if we made history and love together," or something.

"I know you've got your heart set." That's all.

I made a big loud U-ie in the street and set off into the free country.

Fifteen miles down the highway—JIM'S BAIT. JUST GOOD BAIT. AND ORANGE DRINKS. AND SINKERS AND FLOATS. AND MOTHER'S OATS—I was thinking, "Oh, Jeeesus."

I called Milam's number and Milam answered and I hung up.

Fifty miles down the highway—WELCOME TO BEATTIESVILLE. SEE THE BIGGEST CHAIR IN THE WORLD—I called again and no one answered.

I could see, rationally, that we weren't meant for each other. Anybody that cold.

Sixty miles down the road I got the number of the only lawyer in Dingler named Peet and called him. No answer. Probably didn't exist. What kind of asshole would practice law with people named Wormsig and Peet?

Eighty miles down the road I had lunch.

The waitress said to a woman at one of the tables, "Did I think he was good-looking? I could eat his face."

"Ooo, Zalie," said the woman the waitress was talking to.

"But he ain't ever going to be anything but passing through," Zalie added.

"Well, now, how about Linton? Linton is around."

"Around is right. But he is so *needy*-acting. Makes you want to go, *ew.*"

"Oh, I know. Lalina come in like that all the time?"

"Yeyuh. She don't know what to do withersef now. She'll come in sevvle times a day. If she wants something she'll nod when she comes in the door. If she don't she'll shake her head."

"I didn't hardly see no misery at all before I lost Luther. If I had to go through all that again, Zalie, I think I'd just completely go down."

I called Wormsig. Milam's voice answered. Milam probably *was* Wormsig and Peet.

"I'm trying to get ahold of Clementine Searcy," I said.

"Who is this?" he asked.

"You know who the fuck this is, asshole," I said.

"I'll tell her that," he said, and hung up.

On down the road on the radio Porter Waggoner and Dolly Parton were rendering "Her and the Car and the Mobile Home," which is about a man who "came home to a vacant lot."

Before, I would have thought that was a funny song.

I woke up that night in a motel bed alone shuddering. I couldn't remember *shuddering* since I was five.

This wasn't any way to go through life, meeting her naked, hitting her father, boom in love, boom broken up. Shuddering.

America and all her people lay ahead of me to be delved into. West up into the hills I sped, the ground swelling more and more voluptuously under the caress of my tires. No other traffic, just me and the country. A pair of deer ran, starting with a lurching scramble and then flowing swiftly and briefly into an abrupt but seemingly brakeless stop; stopped to feed in someone's garden, cropping for a moment perfectly camouflaged except for the twitch of their tails, then lurched again and flowed into the woods as I flowed around a bend and could see a lake, soft-looking and luxuriously smooth. Its surface, only faintly and sparsely rippled, clung to the water level like a soft dark-green muslin gown to a woman's flank.

I had my typewriter. I recorded my observations. I wrote her letters. Explaining my position further. Telling her I didn't think it ought to end this way. I didn't tell her about shuddering. I wrote her a poem, which said in part,

I poured my heart a glass of wine.
It burned and said "Where's Clementine?"

Burma Shave. I didn't send it. I didn't want to be needy-acting.
"Here is my projected itinerary," I wrote her. "You could write me
general delivery, these towns, and I would be sure to get it."

★   ★   ★

No mail for me in Lovelady, Arkansas. I waited around a day in case.

★   ★   ★

In the *Snake County New Era,* a weekly paper, Mrs. Zinnia Appling
(her byline includes the Mrs.) begins her report on the week's
goings-on in the locality of Poltsville as follows:
    "The hills so green and the sky so blue, I can hardly think to
write."
    I want to show that to Clementine so bad. But then I think, she
probably wouldn't want to be shown anything, even anything that
nice, coming from me. My midsection contracts. I remember my
uncle Gene telling me about being out in the woods hunting with
a man who had heartburn and no water so he swallowed an Alka-
Seltzer right down dry.
    "He bowed up like a cut worm," Uncle Gene said.

★   ★   ★

Lumpy's Bait and Gifts, couple miles west of Lovelady.
    Two old ladies seem to be in charge.
    "Is somebody . . . named Lumpy?"
    "That was my late husband," says one of the old ladies. "He died
of a fox bite."
    Don't know what to say exactly. "I'm sorry to hear it."
    "Well, it was so many years ago."
    Long rectangular box on the floor, front half screened so you can
see some cedar chips and a shed snakeskin, back half wood so you
can't see what's up in there. A sign on it says LIVE HARECOON.
    "What's a harecoon?"
    "Just a little old ammal down in there," says the lady behind the
counter. "She'll let it out for you. I don't like to mess with it much.
Something they found when they were clearing some land."

Other lady finds me a "Razorbacks For Peace" T-shirt, extra large, to send to C, and then bends down to let the harecoon out. She flips a latch on the box and WANGO! something furry jumps three feet through the air and lands where my feet were when the Wango started.

"Good godomity," I yell, and I move a good two steps toward the door.

"Noisemaker didn't work," says the lady. "That'd'a really got you." The harecoon is two coon tails tied together with a piece of black velvet. The old lady fusses about with the box, resetting its mechanism.

"Somebody's going to have a heart attack and sue you," I say.

"I know it it's the truth. We've had it for two years though and nobody has yet. Some people are so touchy, though, that it's a wonder."

★   ★   ★

Something I didn't mention is what I said just before Clementine got out of the car.

"*I . . . love . . . you,*" I said, and the way I said it was, "*I* [I don't know about you] *love* [if you even know the meaning of that word] *you* [even if you don't have the simple decency to love me back]."

I guess that was pretty shitty, to say that to her like that. After she'd offered her life to me. But at the time . . . god damn.

"All this *feeling* can't just go to *waste,*" I thought to myself. Just then the tailgate on the truck in front of me fell open and I drove for the next two or three minutes through bursting watermelons.

★   ★   ★

No mail for me in Yellow Dress, Oklahoma. I left a forwarding address. Sometimes I wished the writing on my cast would fade faster and sometimes that it wouldn't fade so fast.

★   ★   ★

Driving along on U.S. 183 west of Yellow Dress through the dark when I notice a white floppy shape by the side of the road. What looks like a head goes *vwoop* as I pass.

"A turkey," I think. "A big old hurt white turkey."

I have a lot of things in the car—postcards, three different kinds of hats, firecrackers, a bottle of moonshine I had scored somewhere—and it's all getting so messy that the last thing in the world I need to throw in on top of it is an injured turkey. Don't have the facilities for a turkey. But I keep thinking about that turkey lying by the side of the cold road in the pitch-black dark out in the middle of Oklahoma. How do you know that a turkey isn't really suffering, or that there's nothing you can do for him. You don't.

The least I can do is put him out of his misery in some way. So I turn around and drive back three or four miles to where he is and just as I see him again I also see a pickup with a trailer on behind, pulling up. I stop, get out, and when I emerge from the pickup's headlights I see an old man in a cowboy hat run across the road through the wind and grab the turkey up. It flaps a little but he has it in hand. I run back to him. A younger man in a red cap with earflaps is with him. The wind is whipping us all around.

"Hey," I yell. "I saw that turkey too."

It may have passed through the old man's head that I am trying to establish a prior claim. He and the younger man are scurrying around trying to secure the turkey in the back of the truck. The turkey resisting.

"Where you from?" the old man asks. The turkey gets away from the younger man, off onto the shoulder.

I tell him I'm from Georgia originally, but driving to Washington State now and seeing little bit of the country along the way.

Meanwhile he is yelling at the younger man, "Grab him under the legs. Grab him under the legs!"

"I guess you got a place to keep a turkey!" I shout.

"That's right," the old man says.

"What you reckon you'll do with him?"

He looks at me a little funny and I think for a minute he's going to say sarcastically, "Name him Eddie and keep him around for my grandkids," but he just says to the younger man, "Here, put him in the trailer."

"If nothing else you can eat him," I say.

"If nothing else," the old man says.

"Well, I'm glad someone came along who can use him," I say. They get back in their truck and drive off into the night, to where they live.

Wind still whipping.

I wouldn't know what to do with an unprepared turkey. I also don't know a soul within miles and miles and miles.

★   ★   ★

Beer-pool hall, just west of Caress, Okla. Serving "red beer"— tomato juice in Coors. Graffiti in men's room: "In case of an air raid, Jump in Stool. It's Never Been Hit Yet." And "We Don't Piss In Your Ash Trays So Please Don't Put Your Butts in Our Urnil."

On the jukebox, "Daddy Was a Preacher, But Mama Was a Go-go Girl."

One young gap-toothed bar girl (people used the word *girl* more back in those days, so sue me), Linda. Older blond married one, Emmer Lou. Emmer Lou, two middle-aged women and middle-aged man talking: "It'll take all the hair off your tongue now, but it's the best thing in the world for toothache." Then they get to talking about how sick it makes them to have to put their bridge-work back in in the morning, which is a bit too much for me.

The gap-toothed bar girl, who's big in the beam but amiable- and sensuous-looking, is talking to one of two youngish guys. "You mean a triangular?" she asks him. "Okay, you run get us a motel room in Greenup. And hurry back!"

Then the local beautician comes in. I say local beautician because when the gap-toothed girl says something to her she says "I got a seven, a seven-thirty and an eight o'clock. I'll do you at night, though." Beautician looks like a Hollywood version of a too-much small-town girl. Big sweeping shock of black hair, great big high boobs and as tight a pair of pale-blue Levi's as could be molded to and halfway up inside a figuratively but by no means literally out-of-sight behind. (Prurient? Okay, prurient.) She's come in with her husband, who has slightly thinning blond hair frizzed up in front and a yellow-ribbed cardigan sweater and bell-bottom pants on, and looks overmatched (as though there's no way of his ever dissembling his wanting her every minute whether she wants him or not and he's worried about whether he can live up to her demands whenever they come) and their roughly eight- and nine-year-old son and daughter, who keep picking on each other. The husband is the one who keeps telling them to stop. The whole family goes to shooting pool, and she seems full of herself but also content (but, then, why does he look so fazed?).

★ ★ ★

The guy who went off to get a motel room in Greenup returns. He and his friend (who's been talking to the gap-toothed girl) play two games of pool, then the g-t girl announces, "I'm going to go get drunk," and they all three leave.

Emmer Lou's telling the other end of the bar that she bought a little girl's dress the other day. "You can't wear no little girl's dress," one of the middle-aged women says. "As a top over slacks," she explains.

I don't meet any of these people.

★ ★ ★

No mail in Grand Wash, Texas. Hard of her. Mean of her. I pulled my cast off. My hand was shriveled. I hadn't ever made love to her with the use of it. I called the law offices and got Wormsig.

"Listen, Wormsig," I said. "Do you like Milam?"

"Do I *like* . . . Milam?"

"Okay, listen. Does Clementine come in there?"

"Yep."

"Look. Would you talk to her for me? Would you ask her how I can get in touch with her?"

"You would like me to represent you in this matter?"

"Repre*sent* . . . Okay, okay."

"My fee is fifty dollars an hour. So far you owe me for five minutes."

So, hell, I wired him fifty, which was half a week's pay at the *Beacon,* and waited there in Grand Wash for a phone call. The next afternoon. Collect—I'd had to put down a deposit with the motel-keeper, who said, "There's so many rogues around. There's more rogues than good people."

Wormsig: "Her attorney says she doesn't want to have any more communications with you because they are just getting worse and worse, to the point of involving lawyers."

"Great work, Wormsig. How many minutes did that take?"

"You have three more."

"Go shit in your hat, give it a careful flip, and put it on."

★ ★ ★

Bar in Pye, New Mexico, where also no mail.

Talking to another guy who's passing through. He used to run a bar of his own:

"Where I live you got to not only sweeten the po-lice but you got to sweeten the po-lice on time. I got a little behind with 'em and first spot of trouble I had in my place, people selling pills, they come and throwed me in *jail*, I mean.

"Now, you don't want to go to jail in a iron suit, much less shower shoes and running shorts. Which I was at the time. So I picked the first medium-sized old boy I saw in the tank there and went to hit him just as hard as I could in the face so as to show people, you know, but before I could do it he hit me! *Flam.*

"I said why'd you do that. He said, 'I knew to do it. 'Cause you're the third old boy tonight to come in looking straight at me. The first one hit me right in the face as hard as he could.'

"So anyway I had made an acquaintance. He said he was in for simple battery and pointing a pistol at another. He said he didn't want to go into it. But he said, 'I'll tell you one thing, if you knew the whole thing of it, there wadden a thing *simple* about it.'

"Idden anything simple about anything."

If I set all this down, maybe something will add up.

★ ★ ★

I tried Dingler information. E.B. was listed—to my surprise, which I guess was racist of me. I called him, wondering if he'd remember me, which I guess was also racist of me.

"My man from the hoosegow!" E.B. said. "What you off into these days?"

"Driving around the country."

"Say you are. What for?"

"I'm going to write a book."

"Write a book! Come back here and write a book about me! I'm out of jail! And about to be the most famous Nigro in South Carolina! It's gettin' good down here. Boycottin' every white mercantile operation in town. Cept Vereen Fant's, who ain't ever cheated the peoples and carries Champale. Damn Champale distributor won't distribute to but white stores—you talk about got more meanness than sense—and is about to cut off Fant's but we gon' stick with him anyway cause he with us. How come you not down here with us? You told me in jail you was a crusader."

"Is Clementine around?"

"Is she *around*? She around ninety-nine miles an hour in all directions and beginnin' to pick up speed. She and that lawyer be organizin' Roto-Rooters, them two. If nobody of the deep bukra suwasion shoots 'em, they ought to turn out right worthwhile."

"Shoot?"

"Aw, don't worry about her, she don't sit still long enough. Worry about *me.*"

"Does she—she ever mention me?"

"You know, I asked her. 'Cause I wondered. She didn't allow much. I said, 'That boy when I met him seemed like he wouldn't ever have let anything drag him away from yo' face but bears and tigers.' "

"You did?"

"Said I did."

"Hey, E.B. Thanks, E.B."

"Ain't no thanks to it."

"What did she say, when you said that?"

"She said—huh, said you *scared* her, man."

"She . . . did?"

"What you want to scare her for?"

"I didn't. Shit. That's the last thing . . ."

"And what I can't see is, *how* did you?"

★ ★ ★

Another thing I didn't mention is that I started hitting myself in the head with my cast, there, in the car, when she wouldn't *discuss* things.

Crazy thing to do.

And I yelled I guess.

It scared her I guess.

But god damn.
She scared me.

★   ★   ★

"E.B.," I said, "I don't know. Uh, has she said anything about me
hitting her daddy?"

"Not to me. Not to me. I heard that, though—that that *was* her
daddy you hit."

"Doesn't that seem funny to you, that she wouldn't say anything about me hitting her daddy? I mean, she never mentioned it
to *me*."

"Well, I don't think that is a thing I have been involved in myself,
hitting anybody's daddy, or anybody hitting mine. Usually what I've
run into is one person's daddy hitting another one's, or somebody
getting hit *by* their daddy. Or maybe somebody hitting his *own*
daddy, time and again. You know. I don't know. I had a woman's
daddy to throw her mama's iron at me once, and I caught it. You
ever caught a iron? One that had just been snatched out of the wall
from being plugged in? Woo. I might've thrown it back if it wadn't
so hot, but it was."

"Yeah, but—"

"Man, if she don't mention you hitting her daddy, I'd say
that that'd be something you could live with probly. I have got
along with harder things to get along with than that, with a
woman."

"Yeah, but I don't understand—"

"Don't try to *under*stand things, man. Come back here with us
and stand in *amongst* 'em."

★   ★   ★

Well, I humped it all the way to Puyallup, by God. No mail.

Sitting in a coffee shop there, I begin to pick up some remarks
about Shakespeare. Two seats down from me is a heavyset man in
prominent white socks and a short blond crew cut, talking to a
smaller dark-haired man (who never says a word) in glasses sitting
next to him:

". . . went through *Hamlet,* choosing parts and adding my interpretations, typed the whole thing out and sent it to the queen of England. Not a word. Not a damn word. So I sent it to the American Shakespeare Society. Not a word from them! It wunn've mattered if it was pro or con, if they had just acknowledged my effort. But *nobody* replied. It dunn make sense.

"You know my book is going to be out in two months. Had to publish it at my own expense.

"And if anybody intelligent picks it up and reads it, and talks about it, and rumors start flying around, people will be going to the educated people with questions about it, and these people are going to have to read it. Because to understand the problem, you have to read the problem. And then if any man who's recognized as a notable, in any major field, picks that book up and reads it, that starts the line of questioning. Reads it and wants the opinions of his damn colleagues, that's enough to start the fire."

Friend silent through all this, as they eat their salads with Roquefort.

"Did I hear you say you've got a book coming out?" I ask him.

Friend looks away a little uneasily. The writer turns to me. Senses a kindred spirit perhaps. "Yes. Mostly philosophy. It's taken me a long time, I started on it in 1961, but whenever you get into that controversial an area, it's hard to get something accepted."

"How is it controversial?"

"Well, the title of it is *Censor Twain*. It means censor two. I'm cutting away both the Old Testament and the New Testament. Censoring both of them. Except for two small remanents. In the Old Testament, the first and greatest commandment. New Testament, all of Christ's teachings in the future tense. I'm taking those as the present American law."

"How you find out these things?"

"It's hard. There's no way you can do it unless you have contact with angels."

★   ★   ★

There, but for the lack of any very distinct idea of the grace of God, go I.

★ ★ ★

I never did write my book about driving around the country. Maybe
I should have.

But it would have been about C.

★ ★ ★

I didn't meet any women, to speak of, except one.

In Chihuahua, Ariz., where no mail awaits me, I take a look at Old
Lon's Trading Post.

In the window, cuspidors, with a sign: WILL OUTLAST 10 PLUGS OF
STAR CHEWING TOBACCO—OLD LON WILL BET $25 YOU CAN'T HIT THIS
DEAD CENTER AT 20 PACES (NO SWEDES PLEASE); pillboxes; camel
bells (300 YEAR OLD CAMEL BELLS—PLAY THE GIRL CAMELS' FAVORITE
LOVE SONG—"ALTHO THEY CALL YOU ONE HUMP HARRY, YOU'RE STILL
MY FAVORITE DROMEDARY").

Another sign: DOESN'T OUR PRICES MAKE YOU FEEL GOOD ALL
OVER? AND EVERYWHERE ELSE.

Inside, old Victrola with thick records, commodes, chifforobes,
old shoes, harness hames, and the most alarming sight in some
time:

A dress dummy, from the knees up, dressed in a policeman's
uniform with a card saying DON'T SAY "OINK" TO ME stuck to the
shirt. He is staring straight ahead, but with one of his skinny,
jerry-built arms (the other is hanging limply down) he is poised to
hit over the head, with a billy stick, this creature:

A dress form clothed in a long pinkish gauzy-skirted tutu and
around the neck a red bandanna, and above that one of those
monkey's heads carved out of a coconut, and on top of the head—at
about the point the club, if it ever descended, would strike—sits a
bunchy raggedy voluminous blue bow-ribbon. And jammed on top
of that is a coonskin cap. American humor!

I hear some odd breathing-habit noises. And then I see, con-
cealed by this assemblage, in a small circle of light cast by a reading
lamp, at a round table, intently working the jumble puzzle in the
Arizona Republic: a roundish man with short white hair. Presumably,
Old Lon.

To me, when I finally locate him, he says only, *"Good*-morning, nnnng-hm. *Wolley?"*

"Excuse me?"

"There a word, *Wolley? Lowley,* with a *e*? Six letters. P-toop'toop'-too. *Leyowl?"*

"Yellow," I say after a minute. You meet all kinds of people on the road. I never knew anybody to work the jumble aloud.

"Awwwwm."

The policeman dummy and the monkey-head dummy are both looking straight ahead out into the store, not even noticing each other apparently, but covered by the same amount of dust.

A tired-looking but attractive woman in her twenties comes in. She's carrying a big case with a handle. When Old Lon says *"Good-*morning, mmmmmn-hng," she looks at me. I point toward him. She sees the cop and the demon and is taken aback, and looks back at me—why does she need this?

"No, no," I say, still pointing. Then she sees Old Lon.

"Verorf?" he says.

"He's working the jumble," I say. Why do I always feel that I have to explain things?

She sets the case on the table and opens it to reveal a big set of silver, looks like a service for eight or ten, with all the big serving spoons. Folds the case out into three velvet-lined racks. The silver has all slid down out of the slots and she begins to slip each piece back into place. Smooth silver into smooth velvet, slip slip slip.

Old Lon looks over from his table. "That's nice silver, rrrr-nga," he says. *"Frover?"*

"Yes, and it's never been used," she says. "Needless to say I'm desperate for money."

"Ain't none of us set to retire right away," says Old Lon. "Nnnnnng-nmf, mf, mf. *Verorf?"*

"I know it's the truth," she says. "I'm trying to get my marriage back together and make a go of it, and I'm having a time of it." Still slipping silver back into slots.

"Looks like they'd make those so the silver would stay in place," I say.

She gives me an even look. "Well, I guess they didn't count on people carr'n it around much."

"Vorfer. Wonder how much you'd need to realize," Old Lon says. "Rrrn-nf."

"Fervor," I say.

"I'm asking one-fifty." Finishes slipping last piece in. Smoothly, with feeling.

"Well, that looks like the nicest silver I've ever had brought in here, a-hnnnng."

"Thank you."

"But I just can't handle it. Nf. Nf. I'm known pr'marily for furncher and guns. People know I don't deal in this and they don't come in for it. Fffff."

"I'd even take one-twenty-five for it."

"If you had time to advertise it on the radio you could get more for it," he says. "Nn'n'nie. *Sherto.*"

"I know I could. But I just don't have that time right now."

"Ethros. N'rff, you try the pawnshop down the street?"

"Well, he sounded crooked over the phone."

"Horset. Say nn'y'what?"

"Throes."

"I talked to him on the phone, and he sounded kind of . . ."

"Wellll, nnng, either the pawnshop or Roe's Trading Post down the street."

"I tried Roe, and he sent me down here."

"Well, that's Roe for you, pt'f."

"Well, okay," she says equably, with some unforced spirit. She closes the case and as she carries it out you can hear all the silver sliding to the bottom again. She leaves.

I head for the door myself and the policeman's limp arm gives a jerk! This weird lifeless appendage *dances.*

Old Lon is pulling a string that leads from his chair to this slack, stupid, abjectly undirected limb. "Ufff *that's* what makes a body's heart jump," he says. "Hoooon'g see you might 'spect to see the *club* arm . . ."

★   ★   ★

The thing is, she walked a little like Clementine. Untentative but with a kind of give to her gait, a roll but a tight roll, like the spin on a major-league curveball. Well, hell, everybody in the world has seen Clementine walk, now. But I doubt it means as much to any of them as it does to me. Something sui generis in her stride. I use the word *stride* partly in the old-fashioned tailor's sense, meaning, well, crotch. "Let out a little in the stride."

Nothing bobbly about it, or hitchy, but something *funny*. And with it all, her father's bearing. It's almost like an original dance step. I have in fact seen young professional women in Washington adopting Clementine's walk.

★   ★   ★

I catch up with her in the dusty street.

" 'Scuse me, it's none of my business—that's your wedding silver?"

Stops. "Yes, it is."

"I couldn't help overhearing you in Old Lon's. He wasn't too helpful, was he?"

"Course he's got a business to run."

"That terrible dummy thing, there, that he sits behind." I can't think what to say about it.

"Don't rilly encourage you to appeal to his finer side, does it?"

"I just wanted you to know—if I had the money I'd lend it to you."

"Well, thank you."

"I mean—not that it does you any good, but."

"What are *you* doing in Chihuahua without any money?"

"I broke up with somebody. In South Carolina."

"Well, if I had any hearts and flowers, I'd play 'em for you."

Ooooo, a woman's smile. Directed at me. I can't go for long without one of those. "I *scared* her," I blurt. Oh, great.

A blink and an even nicer, though tougher, smile. "Well I guess she knows you better'n I do, then."

"Would you like to get a beer—a cup of coffee or something, I'd—"

"I've got a valentine to get home to."

We're standing out in the middle of the street. In the middle of Arizona. We start walking along together.

"I heard you say—you're fighting to keep it together. I admire that."

"Thank you."

"Can I carry your silver?"

"Thanks just the same, you might be a highwayman."

A highwayman! People come up with words! "You look a little like her."

"Thank you."

"I got mad at her."

"That'll happen."

"That's what *I* thought. That's what *I* thought. But it made her just go completely cold. Just rigid. She got this little voice . . ."

"You must've dragged over an old wound in her."

"Oh. Does that happen to you?"

"I don't have any old wounds. My husband does. He says. So I take it that it's true. My daddy grew up on a farm in Mississippi. He says, 'When you come to a stump you can't pull up, plow around it.' "

"That's what you recommend?"

"It's what I'm trying to do."

"How did you drag over his old wound?"

"Asked him whether he had read the 'Jobs Offered' yet."

"Seems like a reasonable question."

"Don't matter how it seems to you, though. And I must've asked it *hard,* you know."

"Hard."

"Hard or sharp, or snide. Don't say anything snide or sharp or hard to one you love, I realize now. It just hurts or frightens, and then you either have to turn away, or be hurt or frightened back, or make up for it. My parents would talk to each other sharp and hard, it is bred into my voice, but I remember now how it made me feel to hear them do it. It made me feel scared. And they talked to me that way too, sometimes. Although they loved me. I am going to ream it out of my voice. I ain't going to live like that. I just am not. I am going to improve in my generation. I am."

"What's his name?"

"Cody."

"Hers is Clementine."

We have reached the pawnshop. Which *looks* crooked, even on the outside.

"Want me to go in there with you?"

"It wouldn't look right."

"Oh, okay, uh-huh. What's your name?"

"Bonita."

"Bonita. Could I—I just need, could I say something to you?"

"What's your name?"

"Guy."

"Guy. Okay."

"I mean, just—out here in the middle of Arizona. She won't—I can't call her and she won't answer my letters."

"You want to tell me, 'You bitch you bitch you *bitch*'?"

"No. I'm sorry. Never mind."

"Tell me. If it scares me I'll just scream and clonk you on the head with my wedding silver."

"I love you."

Nicely.

"You a *ro-*mantic son of a bitch. I see why somebody let you *at* her old wounds." And she wrinkles her nose in a way that I still remember and hauls her silver through the pawnshop door.

★ ★ ★

That's the thing that gave me heart.

★ **AUG. 14, 1993**

''I'M IN a huntin'-and-gatherin' frame of mind this morning, sugarfoot," I said to the President. I was watching her shave her legs. I like to watch her do any little thing to herself. "I believe I will go out and rustle up some hard intelligence data for you, as to what is actually on your constituents' minds. Get disguised, pop over to Spratt's for eggs and grits, and then to Lafayette Park to sample people's actual vital concerns. From the media you would think that America was a hotbed of disapproval of me, their disaffected First Gentleman. However, I find that when I get out there amongst 'em, in disguise, people—perhaps only the people I

choose to chat with, but still—don't even bring me up. Quite often
they mention that they don't have any place to live or anything to
eat, except what the wagon brings around there to the park, but I
know you're working on those problems. I often say so in the park,
in fact, and, to your credit, they *believe* me. I don't know that they
would if they knew who I was, though. Anything else in particular
you want me to sound them out about?"

"NATO."

"Ah. Well, now, I find that NATO doesn't come up very often
either. I know I should probably have a position on NATO myself,
but. Nice ring to it, *NATO,* I've always thought. Has anyone written
a theme song? Let's see . . . Plato . . . tomato . . .

> *"Meat and potatoes*
> *Have never been NATO's*
> *Primary concerns.*
> *Whatever our fate owes*
> *To armaments, NATO's*
> *Deterrency earns.*

"Not bad, hey, for spur of the moment? Have I got a hit on my
hands, do you think? Can I feel to see if you missed a spot? Hmmm.
How about way up here toward the top?"

"Guy, that's nice, but don't."

"You used to have more time for me, of a morning."

"I know. I wish I still did."

"We used to be flexible together. Make things up as we went
along. And now with the kids grown, we could—"

"Don't make me sad, Guy."

★　★　★

In Spratt's I heard a man say, "He *does* bleeve in an afterlife, now,
but he runs around sinning anyway. Says he assumes that God does
care about what we do, but he says he's humble enough to realize
God probably has a hard time telling one of us from another."

"That's what I thought," another man at his table said, "about
the IRS."

It rained during the night last night. After breakfast the heat of

Washington was not quite bad enough yet to make you want to pitch over forward on your face.

I sat down on a bench and wool-gathered.

Within moments I was wool-gathering to the point of indulging in a quirk of introspection which I realize—perhaps I don't realize fully enough, but I do realize—is that of a dipshit: I was thinking of an answer to an interviewer who, years before when I was making an ill-fated book publicity tour, had asked me, "How would you categorize yourself?"

(It never ceases to amaze me, how crudely the great majority of interviewers operate. Say you were an amorous man trying to get a decent woman to open up to you? If you said something comparable to "How would you categorize yourself?" she would slap your face. Or maybe she wouldn't. Maybe the great majority of amorous men operate that crudely too.)

"I would categorize myself, offhand," I was thinking to myself, "as a sage. A kind of wise man of the moderns—well, postmoderns, now. I know more than I let on. That is, I used to. But I started letting on more and more and at the same time forgetting some of what I knew, and, well, you know how it is."

And suddenly my reverie was broken by an apparition: a tallish stooped woman in a crinkly beige dress and something broad-brimmed and droopy enough to be called a picture hat, except that this hat was not picturesque but undecorated, utilitarian—liver-spot protection. Her face was heavily made up, was my quick impression—I could barely stand to look at her, or to inhale while turned in her direction, because she was so *powdery*. Little poofs of powder, face powder and maybe several other kinds, came off her as she took a seat at the other end of the bench, more heavily than I would have expected—bending herself into a preparatory posture and then, as if normal polite lowering were too difficult for her, just turning loose and going *blap* onto the bench. It made you think how much we take for granted, those of us who are still flexible enough to spiral down casually when we take a load off our feet.

"*Lord*ylordylordy," she said. "*Lord*ylordylordy."

She was having trouble getting her breath. Sitting down had winded her. And she wasn't what you could call entirely seated yet, either; as soon as she'd hit the bench she'd transferred some of her

weight back onto her feet, and she seemed to be keeping yet another percentage of herself up off of full commitment to the inter-
face of bench and bottom (a word I feel embarrassed to use, with
regard to her) by effort of will.

"Are you all right?" I asked her, keeping my nostrils averted as
best I could without giving the impression that she smelled—for
she didn't, she just gave off powder.

"Noooooo," she assured me.

She shifted her poundage—which you wouldn't have thought
was that considerable—around in various small ways back and
forth.

"Can I do something to make you more comfortable?" I asked
her. She was making me more aware of my own bones than I
wanted to be.

She gave me a sidelong glance. Startlingly pale—almost as if
blind—blue eyes. Cataracts? The eyes returned to the straight-
ahead, leaving me feeling abashed. *Comfortable,* I was left to infer,
was something she had long since given up on and might not even
approve of. No comfort for the afflicted. And no one, including her,
need look further than her for a prime example.

"I had a doctor tell me take lots of walks to save my legs and
another one tell me stay sitting down to keep from losing my
feet," she said in a strained but somehow almost enthusiastic
voice while staring in front of her. "I've had one doctor say, go
ahead, let it out, cry, emotions; *pffuh* [a puff of powder accompa-
nied this dismissive sound]; and an eye doctor say crying was bad
for my glaucoma."

I tried to think of something comforting.

"Well," I said, "the doctors don't know everything."

"*Pffuh,*" she said, in a way that seemed to express agreement and
yet to lump me in with the doctors.

"Maybe things will get better," I said. (I was wearing long stringy
hair and something I have always wanted to wear just for a day out
of morbid fascination: one of those little tufts of hair on the *lower*
lip that look like a mustache that's slipped. I resolved to be disguised in the future as someone from whom you would be more
likely to welcome reassurance.)

"I wish life was different, some kind of way," she said, "but it's
not."

"You got that right," I said. "But how about this new President? You think she's going to do some good?"

"How is she going to?"

"Well, now, I don't want to presume, but say you, or somebody you know, needs better health insurance or maybe even some free eyeglasses or—say you know somebody who is quadriplegic. I was talking to a man here in the park the other day who gets around in a wheelchair that he drives by means of blowing air into a tube with his mouth. And he gets around fine on his own, but he does need some governmental assistance just to keep up his chair, which is an expensive proposition when it breaks down. He said that under the Carter administration, say his universal drive broke down—under the Carter administration, he could go to a governmental agency and get it replaced pretty quickly. But under the Republicans, with all their economizing on social services, he was sucking wind, so to speak. Now that man deserves some help, and this President says she's going to set things up so that he'll start getting it again."

"Tweet, tweet, tweet," said the powdery lady, with only a quick, nasty, cloudy-blue look at me. "Tweet, tweet, tweet. What do you know about suffering. With your little old mustache on the wrong lip. What do you know about what anybody feels? What do you know about what has happened before that nobody can ever change? Nobody can ever make *suffering* better. And if *anybody* could, it *wouldn't* be the *guvvuhmunt.*"

"Wait a minute, now," I said, but the powdery lady arose in a cloud, without a word—unh, unh, lurch, a moment devoted to balance restoration—and shuffled off in a gait that *surely* was more agonized than necessary.

I'll have to admit, this encounter gave me some perspective. I returned to my institutional home, had myself dis-disguised and went so far as to pop in on my East Wing office.

Nobody looked up.

FROM CHIHUAHUA to Puyallup to Dingler is 4,492 miles. I did it in three days, sleeping in the car. Got into Dingler early in the evening and my first stop was the Dingler Country Club, whose name was humorous. It wasn't a country club in any real sense of the word except that it didn't let black people in. It had a pool table and tables to drink beer and liquor at. *Beacon* reporters were always welcome, since *Beacon* reporters were well known for discretion. I figured somebody from the paper would come in and tell me where to find somebody connected with the local movement, although I noticed there was no mention of it in the *Beacon* when I picked up a copy. That figured. Responsible elements wouldn't want to be stirring up any trouble.

Two responsible elements were sitting at the next table discussing "the situation." Actually the people who came into the C.C. were more responsible than some; actually I liked the C.C. The only special social event it ever had was that occasionally somebody would get drunk enough to announce a hat burning. Everybody would go outside and stand on the tops of their cars or the backs of their trucks and burn a hat. If they didn't have a hat they had to go find one. Somebody else's, sometimes, which meant they might not get back till late, and everybody else would be through burning hats, and there might be a fight over that. But no shooting or cutting, it was a country club.

One of the two at the next table was Gip, the local game warden. He was a great hunter, actually, highly respected for his knowledge of the Congaree River bottom. He took me out coon hunting one night, so I could write a feature story for the *Beacon,* and he and I were lying out under a tree looking up at the moon about two A.M. having just a little bit of whiskey waiting for his dog Belinda to sound, and he was telling me about a huge coon he had shot a few nights before. I was enjoying myself so much, I was thinking I might be able to write something about this for a national magazine.

"I wish you coulda seen it, Guy," he said. "That coon was big as a nigger. Hell, his old *foot* was big as a nigger."

I thought oh shit.

"I took that thing by to old Tooley's house and woke him up to show him that thing, it was so big. Just to see old Tooley's eyes light up. He said, 'Mist' Gip, thatair is a big coooon Lawd heppus.'

"A nigger appreciates an animal, you know. I went out West one time and saw prairie dogs. I said I wish I could take one of these things back and show it to the niggers back home. Because a nigger—something he hasn't ever seen before? He'll jump right off the ground.

"Tooley nibbout jumped when I showed him that old boar coon the other night. It was that big. And you know Tooley has seen his share of coons. I left it with him to clean for me, told him go on back to bed and he could do it in the morning, but he said, 'Nawsuh, Mist' Gip, coon that big deserve for me to clean it *now.'*

"Tooley *appreciated* that coon."

I was thinking, how in the world am I going to write this up— I mean it was to *some* extent kind of *warm,* but—and then Gip said:

"I hate niggers."

He said that. I wish he hadn't, but he did. Just sort of flatly. *Almost pensively.*

I said, "You *do?*"

He reacted with surprise. I guess nobody had ever reacted with surprise to his saying that before.

"Well, I mean, I don't *hate* 'em so much, as . . ." His voice trailed off. I guess it was like one man saying to another, *"Women!"* and the other man responding, *"Huh?"*

It depressed the shit out of me, I tell you that.

Old Belinda started to go *baroooo-ooo-ooo* just then, and we headed off through the brush to find her and her quarry.

I *don't* hate my people. I have met *lots* of completely oblivious northeastern rich people that I disliked more than any bigot I ever knew back home. But god damn.

Why didn't my people understand how bad they sounded, back in that historic time? Why couldn't they make allowances? Of course I've been making allowances and going the liberal way all my life and where has it got me? Doing something I can't stand and can't complain about. Got no ground to stand on. Maybe it's better to have low ground than no ground.

That just occurred to me. Jesus.

But it didn't at the time.

And it doesn't make me any less depressed, now that it does. If anything, it may make me more.

I never did write that coon-hunting story, which may be why Gip just nodded at me and sat down at the next table, with somebody more reliable whose nickname was evidently "Turd," because that is how Gip addressed him in a far more heated tone than I had heard him use in the woods:

"Listen, Turd, sunabitch, the limit is one mallard and two woodies, but see if I give a damn. Listen here, you're a goddam lie if you say I said it, but if I catch you with a hundred ducks it's cause you are a fool, cause I won't catch you if you move in the other direction. Just take one step, and I won't say a word.

"Listen, I got a wife and five kids that I am sure are mine, and I had to take them to the school today to associate with the Cocoas. Now they been doing that. They been going to school with 'em, since the trouble back in sixty-four. But now the Cocoas want something else, who knows what all. I pushed one of 'em right off the sidewalk and the city officer saw me and didn't say a word, because he knew I meant it.

"Listen, you are a goddam lie if you say I said it, but listen here, Turd, I will protect the rabbits, the possums, the squirrels, the raccoons, the deer, the boar, and all of the little animals that live around here, but when them goddamn federl interstate migertory birds come through, you can blast the hell out of 'em.

"All of these rules; and having to go to the post office and pay for duck stamps, and then these crazy rules about one mallard and two woodies made in Washington.

"Listen, Turd, you can kill all of them birds you want to and I'll bet anything I don't catch you, and I'll bet even more that if I do see you I won't ask you how many of them birds you have killed.

"They come down here, and the state pays me more than half my salary, but the goddamn federls try to tell me everything to do about their goddamn flyway, and there ain't no freedom of speech, and you're a goddamn lie if you say I said it, but I hope somebody kills ever goddamn migertory federl goose and duck that fly over this year, and this ain't no whiskey talk either.

"I have had enough. I have flat spang squat goddamn it Turd had enough."

"Oh, I know it," Turd replied. "You know the niggers is having another hoohaw tonight. On the cotehouse steps."

"Well, I ain't goin'. What time?"

"Hell, they announced nine, but you know niggers."

"I ain't goin'. Some sorry butthole is going to shoot one of 'em and then we goin' to have twice the TV cameras in town as last time, and twice the feds and twice the carryin' on."

"What do they want? We already give 'em ever'thing."

★   ★   ★

That was all I needed to know. Except—what should I do? Find C in the midst of a historic struggle and tell her I wanted her to be in love with me again?

I drove over into the black side of town, which anybody progressive called the Negro side back then. And who did I see coming out of the Asbury A.M.E. Church but E.B. and Leonard!

That was the first I knew that Leonard was back. They were both glad to see me, I was relieved to see.

Actually Leonard was already beginning to sound just a leeetle bit official and full of collective purpose, but he still wasn't anywhere near as much like that as he is now. It was good to see the relish he had for his work—he was just ahoppin', darting happy looks all around as if he loved Dingler. "You got here in time for some history," he said. "This is *it*. I call up the *Beacon* today. Brownie. I tell him, 'Well, I just thought you old boys ought to know you're going to miss a story tonight that is going to make national news.'

" 'Niggah business,' Brownie says."

(Leonard, being of northern liberal extraction, never did learn to pronounce *nigger* naturally. On the other hand, I never would have said it in front of E.B. But E.B. knew that that was just Leonard. I was glad to see E.B. and Leonard were tight.)

"If only we could get somebody to say that on television," Leonard said. "But no. The networks—I'm talking to the networks every day, Guy. But so far the networks are waiting for white Dingler to do something dumb. White Dingler has been doing dumb things with pride since this town was founded, but now that we need them to, they won't. They aren't even arresting anybody. They even turned E.B. loose, for Chrissake. Guy, you're good at getting arrested. Think. I can't do everything."

"You look *skinny,*" E.B. said. "You been pining?"

"Yeah, E.B., I'm not going to lie to you. As a matter of fact. It's good to see y'all, and it does my heart good to believe that you are bringing the forces of Dingler to their knees and all. But what I need is to find out about Clementine."

"Oh, Lord," E.B. said. "This boy all whipped up again. Take cover!"

"I've been calling her, and writing long letters . . ."

"Ah," Leonard said. "See, you shouldn't do that. You should have talked to me."

"Yeah, well, I tried to call you in Chicago but your mother was unlisted. I didn't know you'd come down here."

"Writing long letters. When you've fallen out. Write them, but don't send them. Writing long letters at that stage is trying to control the other person, with anger."

"It is?" I said.

See, I will listen to things. I will try to take things on board. If C had just told me something like that, even, I would have appreciated it. "I didn't think I wanted to control her. I'm a writer. It's what I do." But what I was realizing, not for the first time, was that I didn't know anything. Not that Leonard did either necessarily, but when he said what he said, it made sense, and it never would have occurred to me if he hadn't said it. Something frozen in me began to melt. All the good of which, at the moment, was a feeling like cold water in my socks.

"Has she said anything about me?"

"She won't talk about you, *at all,*" said Leonard. "Which *may* not be the worst possible sign."

"Where is she?"

"Don't go see her now, man," said E.B. "She be organizing. We'll tell her you're in town. We'll work on it for you."

★ **AUG. 16, 1993**

I DROVE OVER to the Dingler campus, which was just a little
ways up the road from the courthouse, and took a stroll. There was
a tree C and I leaned up against and—

Shit.

I went back to the car and started cleaning it up inside. If by any
chance I could get C to consent to ride in it with me again, it ought
not to look so slept-in. Wouldn't have mattered before, but now I
guessed I needed to mind my impression. I was wadding up a sheet
that I'd spread over the scratchy seat cover, and there were some
dirty shirts and underwear, and I thought, "Well, maybe I'll just
take these to the Wishy-Wash and sit there and think."

So there I was walking across campus with laundry again, and
there was our bush. I went and climbed up under it. Trying to pick
up the thread. To this day I couldn't tell you what kind of bush it
was. For a writer about country life, I don't know all that many
plants. I know the ones I need to know. Tomato, salmonella (I
believe bacteria are in the plant kingdom), marigold (keeps bugs off
the tomatoes), poison ivy, maple, one or two others; and the rest
I make up. People ask me what that bush is and I say, "Anhedonia."
What's that tree: "That's a pisco tree. Didn't get any berries this
year hardly, what with the bugs and the birds, and what we did get
were sour."

So say this was a rueberry bush. I was sitting there in it, rueing.
It was getting dark.

I heard voices.

"Dis pull one leg off, then."

"Turtle, what in the world?"

"Dis pull down one leg, an'—"

"Turtle, no, stop."

"You nin ever promise y'mama you wun take off dis one leg."

"Turtle, that's silly. I can't—"

"An' 'en you kin git 'em back on in a hurry, you wun run any
hazard of losin 'em, an—"

She interrupted his argument with a sigh full of wisdom and sadness. It was womanly. It was eloquent. It set even Turtle back some.

All he could think to say was, "Mm, mm, *mm.* I bet my peter is braaaat red."

"Turtle, the Lord has told us not to think about that."

"He has? Why?"

"Turtle, anyway we have to go meet the klavern."

My ears perked up.

"Awright. What's he going to say?" asked Turtle.

"The klavern is the group. One of them will come up to us and say . . . 'Croochy Sanctus' or something like that. What you have to remember is, you say 'Corpus Christi.' "

"I wonder why iddud be that. I got a cousin moved to Corpus Christi. My daddy's sister Gypsy's girl Tara. I kissed her once, before she got maard and moved. You womie show you where I kissed her?"

"Turtle, you don't know what to *say.* You don't have any *idea* what to say. How would you ever imagine that I would want to hear about you . . . kissing anybody named Tara? Anywhere on her at all."

"Nawwww. Nawwwww. She's maard and moved. She's my cousin."

And they started arguing.

But I wasn't listening, I was thinking. And when they came out of that bush with their sheets on, I wasn't two minutes behind them in mine.

(They figured Dingler security wouldn't bother them, I guess. What a college! Ku Klux sheets didn't violate the dress code.)

And when they met up with the other Klanfolk I was right behind them with the password.

"Oh, y'all the sem'nary students," said the Klansman who had challenged us. (There was no way Dingler could be described as a seminary, but never mind.) "We pleased to have y'all wuffus."

"I'm Lonelle Searle and this is Turtle Sparks. And . . ."—she said, turning to me—"*Oh,* I know who *you* are I bet, you're Dr. Bomar Salmon. I heard you wadden gon' be able to come."

She had her sheet just around her shoulders, and I noticed a twinkle in her eye.

"Naw, I was able to," I said. "At the last minute."

"Well I suuure am glad," she said to me, in a far more provoca-tive manner than seemed in order. Turtle, as you can imagine, gave me a hard look. "Dr. Salmon is wunna the new *puffessors* on cam-pus," Lonelle said. "I have heard awlllll about him. But I didn't know he's gon' be s' *younnngg*-lookin'. And all. He just came from Mis'sippi to get ready for the summer term, and he is ve'y po-*lit*ical f'm whut ah heah."

Her accent was *thickening*. For me. *Dr.* Bomar Salmon. What was I getting into?

"We did our sheets the best we could," Lonelle told the Klans-man in a more straightforward tone. "I couldn't figure out the head of mine."

"No, I couldn't either," I said.

Lonelle gave me a funny look, to go with the bad one Turtle was giving me. "Forgot to pack mine, bachelor, can't sew," I babbled, and Lonelle not only took me at my word but *batted her eyes.*

"Don't you worry," said the kleagle, or whatever he was, "we got ladies who can fix you up. The main thing is, you're standing up for yo' Creator and yo' race."

I didn't like it. I didn't like it. It wasn't so much that I didn't like being with those people, though Lord knows I didn't want anybody to think I was in their camp. I don't like pretending. I don't have the . . . I don't know, the *something* for it. I don't like to deceive. Anybody. I like to explain.

But I was in no position to.

We marched, as I perhaps do not need to explain, to the court-house. And you know, there were some awful-looking old boys in that procession, worse-looking than Turtle even, and weedy-look-ing bad-teethed people who you figured had to belong to a hate organization because no other organization would have them, and women so fat you couldn't see their eyes. But there were also folks Norman Rockwell might have drawn as salt of the earth, if they hadn't been robed the way they were; and they were chatting like at a church social. Lonelle introduced me to a quick-eyed man with glasses who said he was in sales, for a company that made "caulks, dies, putties, sealants and finishes. We have the finest selection in probly this whole part of the state. You know, Dr. Salmon, I didn't used to be in sales. I felt I lacked the education. But one day I went

into a small store run by a no-legged old man named Fordyce
Knott, who can sell better in pinned-up overalls sitting down than
I can, today, in a new suit and Buick. I went in there to see about
some relish and came out with fifty dollars' worth of patriotic
T-shirts. I thought, 'My soul, if selling can work like that, I want
some of it.' "

I asked him what he liked about the Klan.

"Well, Dr. Salmon, I have to give it a lot of my time. But it was
Fordyce Knott who first convinced me of this: we have to make a
stand. Dr. Dingler can't do it, or he'll be crucified. The people in
office can't do it. The police can't do it. We know that. They would
like to, but the way the Supreme Court is, they are just not free to.
They thank us privately, though. And I don't mind telling you, my
association with Fordyce Knott means county business thrown my
way. Dr. Salmon, I'll tell you the truth, it's not the niggers so much
themselves. I've known colored people all my life. It's the communism. There is a little Jewish man running this thing. He first tried
to infiltrate our newspaper, but they caught on to him. You don't
see him out front, but he is a Communist, it's documented. What
business does he have in this town?"

My people, my people! I'd done a feature story for the *Beacon* on
Fordyce Knott! Scroungy old peckerhead, but handicapped, and
sharp, quotable. Claimed his cousin had invented an electric hat—
"It heats the top of your head in the winter and it also can light up
your face and flash a message. 'HIDY.' It'll light up and go 'HIDY.'
Useful if you're shy. If you're inter-ested, could see if he's got an
extra one." I didn't buy a hat, but I wrote Fordyce Knott up as
inspiredly cranky and good-natured. Got me a chance to do more
features. In fact I took *Leonard* out to talk to Fordyce Knott, and
they got along nice as pie. Hell, he sold Leonard some cowboy
boots. Maybe Fordyce Knott wasn't a bigot, by conviction; he just
had a sense for what any given person would buy. I would have to
warn Leonard he might be in danger, even though it would please
him no end.

As we marched, Lonelle . . . I'm going to tell you something
terrible. The truth is, if I had run into Lonelle a week or so before
when I was driving through the Southwest, and she had been as
friendly as she was being on that march, I would have been in as
many legs of her panties as I could decently ease her loose of.

Because Lonelle was comely. In a way. She was not even all that dumb. In a way. If she had been exposed to, say, New York reform Democrats all her childhood instead of redneck Christians . . .

Well, I say that, but then I realize that the latter was exactly what Clementine was exposed to all *her* childhood. Well, no, of course here's the difference: Clementine was an army brat. Soon as her father was out of prison camp, she was out from under the guardianship of his buddy the Reverend Dingler and moving around the country and, for that matter, Taiwan and Paris. And even Dingler wasn't unlettered.

Lonelle wasn't dim, let's leave it at that. And she had roundness and heat, and there was something about her prejudice that was flouncy instead of pinched. I think you could have spent a little time with Lonelle and just *showed* her that there was something more benignly funky than hate-mongering religiosity, and she would have gone for it.

Which just made me all the more eager not to have her bumping up against me. Because I was not horny or crazy enough to get involved with a Klanswoman even if I weren't already in love— however forlornly—with a Maid of Orleans whose cause I believed in. And a woman who—you couldn't compare the two, I don't mean to suggest that you could compare the two.

All I am saying is, I don't want to put Lonelle down. She was doing her best to be appealing to me, and I would be lying if I said her best was all that bad (maybe I was identifying with her, worrying about how good mine was going to be), and she didn't know any better.

That's all I'm saying. What I was saying at the time was, Ohhh, shit.

Because I didn't have any idea what I was going to do.

And of course the first face I saw when we got to the courthouse was C's.

Oh Lord she looked good. Oh, Lord, she looked good. I saw her and I remembered how her lips felt. And I was proud of her.

She wasn't confused. She gave her head a quick unselfconscious toss like a horse almost, bouncing her hair—which had grown out some, a blossom of unforced curls. She had some kind of *gleam* she was following. I had to prove I belonged up there with her.

Lonelle was whispering in my ear. "Can I call you Bomar?"

I didn't see how I could object.

She said, "You look a little like Darrin, in *Bewitched.*"

LONELLE HAD MANEUVERED around to where I was be-
tween her and Turtle. "I *loooved* your book *Darwin's Lies,*" she told
me.

"Lo-nelle," Turtle said in a hurt voice.

"Now, Turtle, you ought to preeeshate Dr. Salmon," she said,
giving me a look that said it was our secret, for now, that to her I
was Bomar. "F'm what *ah* hear, Dr. Salmon was the one, at the Ole
Miss riots? Shot that French repotuh."

"At right?" said Turtle, trying not to sound impressed. "French
sumbitch needed shootin'. Anybody'd done that."

"No!" I insisted.

"Aw, come on," Lonelle said, "you among friends."

"I *didn't,* though."

"Well, you just being modest. Turtle, Dr. Salmon had to *leave*
Ole Miss? Cause the faculty was gettin' a little too *lib*'ral for him?
Dudden that just *show* you?"

And do you know what my instinct was? My instinct was to confess who I was and try to broaden Lonelle's sense of the political
spectrum. I would never make a good spy, or actor. (Or *novelist.* I've
tried it. I hate to get people in trouble.) I like to explain things. I
don't want to give people the wrong impression. But on the way
over to the rally, I had worked out a plan. I was determined to do
something dramatic, to reintroduce myself to Clementine.

There she was, the only woman or white person standing up
there on the steps with the leaders, with an I'm-in-my-element air.
She was attending respectfully but independently to the Reverend
Micah (it had to be him, he looked like a leaner and taller E.B., with
an air of grandeur instead of amplitude), who was holding sonor-
ously forth about brotherly love.

"We are *all* his chil-dren. He holds us *all* in his ahrrums, and
there we shall know *peace* that passethhhh *all* understandin'."

"Do you know what they have out now?" said Lonelle. "A nigger model on the cover of *Seventeen.* I thought I would die."

I don't remember what the specific issue for this rally was; by then the cause had gone well beyond justice for E.B., who however was standing there next to C with his hands on his hips, smiling down on us all as if to say, "Well, isn't this fine, all these nice black people and white-sheeted people assembled to celebrate my charges being dropped."

"Look at that *white* girl," Lonelle hissed.

"White nigger girl," said Turtle. "I bet she eat that nigger dick like it a *ahce-*cream cone."

Oh, God.

"Turtle," Lonelle said. "Is that all you can think of to say? Honestly. You know what you are doin'? You are sinkin' to those people's level. What I treasure about Klan get-togethers is meeting nice *Christian* people. No drinkin', no filthy language. I know that girl. She idden a thing but just a hippie. She used to be in my Christ Through the Ages class? And she didn't do a thing all semester but innerup the professor and act snide. You realize them hippies run stark bare nekkid? You wouldn't catch *me* runnin' stark bare nekkid without a stitch of clothes on at all, like the day *I* was bawun. Even in the dawmito'y halls, I nearly always have on thin little cotton p-j's."

"Uhf," said Turtle.

"I am in college to *study?* Please? And *read?* Please?" she said. She took my arm, up under the sheet. "You have a big muscle," she whispered. That was because I was holding back from hitting Turtle, which wasn't my plan.

Four or five other black men stood on the steps. Milam and Leonard were barely visible in the background, looking concerned. Milam's lips were moving into a walkie-talkie. A staunch black-community contingent was gathered around, studiously not looking at us Ku Kluxes. We stood on a little rise off to the left, just ten yards from the steps. Milam and Leonard were eyeing us. I saw Leonard blink and stare harder in my direction. He shook his head and poked Milam.

"There idden any TV cameras," said Lonelle. "Awwwww."

"Tell you summelse they ain't," said Turtle. "The first sign of po-lice."

Uh-oh.

"And *you . . .*" said the Reverend Micah, directing his gaze upon us sheeted ones; and then he paused, taking us in.

Turtle went rigid. The pause stretched out. Lonelle pressed closer to me. E.B. caught sight of me, and then C did, and I still remember the expression on her face. Fresh-eyed (the way she still makes me feel, out of nowhere, about three times a week) with surprise, and glad to see me.

Glad to see me, C glad, to see me. It gave me heart to fling myself out of myself, into my plan—I'm going to do it now, I told myself, going to . . . do it . . .

"*. . . you! Too!*" pronounced the Reverend Micah. "Seek as you will to deny it! You, *too,* are our brothers and sisters! We are *one* in the Lord! *We . . . love . . . you . . . too!*"

That was too much for Turtle. He pulled a gun.

Just as Lonelle put her hand down the back of my pants.

They were loose on me and riding low. I hadn't been eating much.

I just flailed out. Swung around away from Lonelle and at Turtle in one ill-coordinated vault. Which wasn't my plan.

Here was my plan. I had read that when James Thurber and John McNulty, the humorists, were newspapermen in Columbus, Ohio, back in the twenties, they had destroyed the credibility of the Klan in that city by coming up to each other in the street, when crowds were around, and shouting ludicrous things while pretending to be Klansmen themselves. My plan was to shout ludicrous things. Somehow I was going to work in haphephobia—the extreme ticklishness C and I had read about in the Wishy-Wash—as a private joke to her. I mean, a Klansman yelling, lashing out with his arms, jumping and exclaiming that he couldn't stand to be touched anywhere around the ribs and needed some relief for his . . . condition . . . of . . . extreme . . . ticklishness.

Well. It might have been completely out of line. I don't know.

I jumped all right. The only other time I have made such a virtually-out-of-the-body leap was one Christmas Eve night when C and I were setting up Santa Claus for the kids and Jackson wandered out of his bedroom rubbing his eyes, and I cleared two couches in a single bound to get to him before he could catch his parents creating an illusion. Because Santa Claus is a *beneficent* wrong impression. I guess. Maybe it isn't. Maybe it gives kids the wrong idea of what life is going to be like. I don't know.

Lonelle lent stimulus, but she also added drag, because her hand got caught. Mine flailed right into the point of Turtle's .22 pistol (thank God it was not a more powerful gun), and just before I slapped the barrel head-on and shoved it back at him I felt a hot jolt in the meat between my thumb and forefinger. I wound up on top of Turtle with Lonelle on top of me. Confusion followed. I had Turtle's pistol but there was another shot. Streetlights out. Yelling and hollering. E.B. was flinging people off me and hauling me up, saying, "My Lord, if *you* ain't trouble. Let's *go* from here. Don't worry. She gon' be all right."

The last face I saw was Lonelle's, looking hurt. I had felt her getting her hand extracted, and hey, you can sure feel the difference between a hand slipping in and a hand being jerked away.

Then I realized E.B. meant Clementine.

★ AUG. 18, 1993

"WHAT HAPPENED?" I yelled as E.B. was pushing me into about a '62 Mercury. We sped away. Relatively speaking. Black people generally drove at five miles an hour under the limit in the South in those days, so as to eliminate at least one pretext for being pulled over.

"You asking *me* what happened? You was down there in the trenches. Why?"

"What happened to Clementine? Is she *hurt*?"

"Well, she got shot. In the leg. But it don't seem bad. She on her way to the hospital. Uhh."

I was in the back seat, E.B. was looking over the seat at me from the shotgun position, and the driver was a person whose face I never saw. His shoulders were hunched up close to his ears and he was intent on the road. "This is B-29 Cheeks driving," E.B. said. "B-29, this is Guy Fox in the back. Who, uhhh."

He was looking at my hand. Which, I realized on inspection, was holding Turtle's pistol and bleeding all over it.

"Clementine is fine, my man. She the sprucest shot white lady I ever saw. Now I will ask you, what happened?"

I told him. Even with Lonelle and all. (I never told Clementine about Lonelle. I thought she was going to say, "Who was that *woman* with you?" and I'd reassure her that the woman meant nothing to me, but she never brought her up. I could never figure out why. I almost brought her up myself, but I am not that dumb.)

"Well. If that ain't a story. And the *thing* of it is, I believe it."

"Why wouldn't you believe it? Hey, I'm bleeding here."

"Just 'cause it's true, and you bleedin', don't mean people gon' believe it. Here, gimme that gun. Shit, I don't *want* it. But somebody got to think, here."

"Where is Leonard? I need to talk to him. And I want to see Clementine."

"He with Clementine, and Milam. Taking her to the hospital. Where you better not go. Lord, it sho is a good thing I got more organizing aptitude than I want to admit. B-29, let's hightail it to Doc Stockley's."

"Who's Doc Stockley?" I didn't know where the hell we were.

"Here, gimme that shot hand. Wrap my man up with my hankercher here. You mind being wrapped up with a old colored-man jailbird's hankercher? Catch my cooties, start losing IQ?"

"E.B. you are so full of shit. Are you sure—listen, I've got to see Clementine. Jesus, she got *shot*?"

"Well, you both got shot. Same bullet, must have been. Ain't that romantic? You ever hear of the bullet-borne baby?"

"E.B. . . ."

"Story from the old war times. A soldier got shot through his bizness with a musket ball that took on his seed and happen to pass into a lady on her po'ch swing, who was watching the war."

"E.B. . . ."

"And nine months later she had a chile. What they say. I don' *know*."

"E.B. . . ."

"Well, listen now. I ain't in on the policy-making level, you hear what I'm saying? I'm jus' in on the formerly victim of injustice currently findin' hisself wadin' into the middle a bunch of Ku Kluxes to save a old cellmate's ass from being stomped into the cotehouse lawn level. And the reason I am on that level is because yo' lady friend—you know what her first words was, on being shot?''

"What?"

"Lemme think now, exackly. It was on the order of, 'That's Guy. I want him!' "

"Really?"

"I'mon tell you, now, the truth. I *probly* would've risked my black ass stridin' in 'mongst a whole bunch of armed shit-fer-sense rednecks just out of friendship one dude to another. Unh-hunh. That is, I would ovva felt kind of bad, the next day, that I didn't. But the lady—the lady, man. I see why you hit her daddy or whatever you did. And infiltrate the Ku Klux. I mean, it ain't any *pussy* that strong, but the lady got me doing shit *I* wouldn't do. And pussy make a body do a lot of things. So I figure if you got *both* things working on you—I'm glad it ain't me got to live with it, frankly."

"Yeah, well."

"But my hat is off. She a take-to-able woman. She don't seem like *comp'ny,* you know. Droppin'-in comp'ny. She seem like she feel at home amongst the cheerfully grievous."

"I have to see her."

"You gon' see her. I'll fix it up. Because she want me to. So just don't worry 'bout it. Now, here is Doc Stockley's."

We went up to a little frame house whose door was opened by a big-faced brown stern-looking woman. She wore dark paisley pedal-pusher pants and an outsized white jacket with the sleeves rolled up. "E.B., what I tell you?" she said.

"Doc, I got you a patient. Friend of Clementine's. Sustained a misaventure to his hand."

"How come this the first I heard of it, or him?" she said.

"Well, Doc, it just now *happened.* "

"Was this at that rally? I told y'all don't have that rally tonight."

A phone rang.

"Come on in and take him to the examining room," she said. She went to the phone.

"She be hearing about it now," said E.B.

"I sure didn't know there was a black woman doctor in Dingler," I said.

"They *vay*-rous things in Dingler," said E.B. "Sit on the table, there."

It was a regular doctor's-office table, and there were cabinets and a jar full of cotton swabs and a calendar with a picture of an Alp. There was also a half-empty can (E.B. shook it, and we each had a swallow) of Country Club Malt Liquor.

"E.B., it's not that I—I mean I'm sure she's a good doctor, but if we went to the hospital I could see Clementine."

"Man, you talk like you ain't involved in social unrest."

Doc Stockley reappeared. "Well, now. I have heard of you. Will you tell me a thing or two more?"

I told her, except about Lonelle.

"Let me see that hand. Mmm-huh. Now tell me this. Did you take a course of the *Latin* language in school?"

"Yes'm."

"Then you know the word *stig-ma-ta.* Such as our Savior's marks of the nails of the cross. And you can tell me what the word would be, for just one of them."

"I think *stigmatum.*"

"Yes, the neutral case. You may count on arriving to your Maker with one stig-ma-tum. Don't be feeling vain about it now, cause it is outside all the bones, here—wouldn't bear much weight. Now, I understand people to say that when last taken note of by the local authoritizzz, you had a broken hand. Well, I am cleaning this wound here, and then I am fixing to give you a cast, make it so we can slip it off to change the dressing, and then what we must do is make that cast look like it is old."

"Huh?"

"In your schooling, did you take any French?"

"Some."

"Well, then, you know the term *agent,* excuse my accent, *provocateur.* It would disadvance the effort your friend Clementine is in-*vovv*ed in, if you were recognized as being shot while pretending to be of the persuasion of parading in a sheet. Do you hear what I'm saying?"

"I—"

"Now hear this, too. E.B., go out and wait in the car. Hear this about that Clementine. I believe that while she has been laboring in the vineyards here, you have been . . . *driving.* In a car. A-way."

"Well, that's—"

"You drive away from that chile again, you a fool!"

"I'm not going to."

"What are you?"

"Huh? What do you mean?"

"White boy on this side of town."

"Well, I'm a liberal."

"What I thought. You going to love somebody, you better not be bein' no liberal. You got to be *prejudiced. On the side of her.* Hear what I'm saying? You got any medical inshunce?"

"No, I lost my job, and—"

"You been driving around with no medical inshunce? That is *not* the kind of unwhite thing to do. You got any money? Let me have half of it."

And she fixed me up and ushered me out. "Take him to yo' hincty brother's," she called to E.B. as I was getting back in the car. To me she said, "You find who you looking for there. And you better be glad enough."

As we pulled away, she added, "And look out *yusself,* too."

"I never would've thought there was a black woman doctor in Dingler," I said to E.B.

"Well, what she *was,* was a white doctor's maid. And then kinda more than a maid. And then kinda his nurse. And then kinda more than a nurse. And then he died. Willed her his stuff. And she can use it."

"Oh. But, no . . . license."

"Oh, she tight with the white power. They happy to have her doing what she does. Keep us folks from clutterin' the hospital."

"Speaking of the white power, did you know that Fordyce Knott—"

"She tight with him."

"Is he—I thought Dingler ran things."

"Oh, Dingler just money and the radio, nationwide. Old Knott know people *here.*"

"Well, I think he's telling people that Leonard is a Communist, and—"

"Man, you got to catch up! We organized here. Leonard tight with old Knott."

"He is?"

"It's wheels within deals, man. The white power learned a little *something* back in sixty-four. And times is nearbout booming—they *hiring* at the mill. We aingon have no blood in Dingler, no more'n usual, if you just quit stirrin' up the white trash."

"Me? I didn't—"

"Man, we got *contented* peckerwoods here. White power don't want them stirred up either. Thass all I want to know about it and if I was you thass how I would feel too. Juss a good thing you didn't get televised. B-29, you can go faster than this."

★ AUG. 19, 1993

THAT ESSENTIALLY is what I know about the Crowe County Movement, except that Dr. Dingler got a hospital contract out of it. And black people got better hospital care—it embarrassed the town that Clementine refused to spend the night in the old Dingler Memorial because there were no black patients registered. Dr. Stockley continued to have a place in the economy, however. Blacks also got more jobs and more respectful treatment in commercial establishments, as a result of the boycott. The Reverend Micah was elected to the board of commissioners. And E.B. not only stayed out of jail but got into the beer business. Clementine started to get famous, thanks in no small portion to her being shot—by someone never identified.

Turtle's name never came up publicly. I understand, however, that Gip the game warden took him out hunting and told him a thing or two about the new racism and its constraints. Lonelle (hell hath no fury) insisted on fingering Dr. Bomar Salmon as the gun-man, but when he turned out to be a twitchy hairless man who had spent the evening in question reveling in the Dingler College Library's unique collection of bizarre right-wing tracts, and who looked nothing at all like Darrin on *Bewitched,* he was in the clear. My scar is officially from a childhood hunting accident (I never went hunting in my childhood), and Clementine and I met after the shooting, when I walked into movement headquarters and relieved a tense moment by saying something that the scriptwriter conceived of as winningly comic.

That's more than I know about what goes on in the White House. And a lot more than I would be able to tell if I did know it.

I like to slide my right hand up the inside of her leg, though, till we both know our wounds are touching.

★   ★   ★

She was in the Reverend Micah's upstairs bedroom, which his elderly aunt had let her have for the duration. Nice old double bed with a sampler framed over it: A BACHELOR IS LIKE DETERGENT: WORKS FAST AND LEAVES NO RING. Lying there with the covers to her chin. Sleepy-looking but smiling.

It had been six weeks since we'd parted. For me six weeks of wandering, for her six weeks of getting on with things.

"Guy," she said, to my—well, *relief* is hardly the word—"you protected me."

"Pure instinct," I said. (Whether it was Clementine that Turtle was *trying* to shoot, and whether I changed the course of the bullet—who knows, who knows?) "Are you okay?"

"Mmm. Just woozy from a pain pill. How about you?"

"I'm fine. I'm sorry I got mad at you."

"You look skinny."

"You look so good."

"I'm enjoying my work, Guy."

"Did you hear, what happened exactly?"

"Doc Stockley called."

Outside a man was playing a blues song on a guitar and singing:

> *"Baby you prutty . . .*
> *But you gonna die someday.*
> *Baby you prutty . . ."*

"C, you know, everybody acts like things are under control here, but you could've . . ."

> *"I want some of yo' lovin'*
> *Befo' you pass away."*

"Guy, I'm meeting such interesting people. And I'm good with them. And now you're meeting them too. Doc Stockley said you were very polite. And had nice hands."

"She *did*? Well. I'm glad."

"She said she didn't know about good sense. She told us what you told her. And I saw you, Guy. You're a fast jumper. What exactly did you have in mind, though, being in that sheet?"

"I was—I don't know. I wanted to prove . . ."

"You don't have to prove anything to me, Guy."

"I don't, huh? Didn't Milam give you any of my messages?"

"Yes."

> *"Baby, skin,*
> *Baby, skin to skin."*

"I wish you'd answered. I wanted to talk to you. I tried to explain."

> *"Ain't but two things workin'.*
> *Ain't but one thing goin' in."*

"Explaining's no good, Guy. Letters and the phone is only good when people still enjoy each other's faith. People can't talk about getting back together unless they can see each other's eyes. I could tell you wanted me. But I couldn't tell whether you were *with* me."

"*With* you? How could I be *with* you if—"

"Guy, don't twist my words."

"I'm not twisting them, I'm quoting them."

"Guy, put yourself in my place." And she pulled back the covers. So I did.

It took a while to work out how to, without putting pressure on her leg. A lovely unanxious slow-motion flush breathing-underwater-feeling period of time.

"This mattress is kind of hard but spongy in a nice way, isn't it? What do you think it's stuffed with?" she said.

"I don't know. Feels like ham."

> *"toon tonky too tooooon tong*
> *p'tung*
> *toon tonky too tooooon tang*
> *p'taing*
> *p'tong poon tayy-poooon*
> *toonky toon toona tooonaah*
> *da d'doooomble ahh doon.*

Good mawnin lil schoool gull.
toon tonky too tooooon tong

Good mawnin lil schoool gull.
p'tong poon toona poon

Kin I go ho-o-o-ome
p'tong tooong p'tung tooong'ta

Kin I go ho-o-o-ome

Wit choo?
tooon tonky toon tonky tonk toon

Tell yo muthu'n yo faaaa-thuh
tooon-a toontoon tooon-ta

I am a schooooool boy, too.
p'tang a tang tanga tanga,
atang atang atang a doon
                    d'doooomble doondoon."

"C, I can't hold . . . I . . ."
"Guy, ooo it's all right it's good Guy here put here put your here put"

"Lil schoool gull"

"HUH-uh Mffff Mfffff."
"FWOO."
*"Ooo-*laaaaaaah."

"toooon tonky toon toooon-ta"

"Oh. Precious Savior. And we're *new* at it!"

★   ★   ★

"C, will you marry me?" I said a few minutes later.
"You started calling me C. No one ever called me that. That's sweet, Guy."
"C. C. C. C."

"You said in one of your letters you loved me desperately. You don't have to love me *desperately*. See?"

"Now you're twisting *my* words."

"No, I'm not. Guy, I'm glad you came back."

"You didn't say whether you'd marry me," I said.

"Well. I want to be *courted*."

That made me start to laugh.

"What? What?" she said.

I heaved up and looked down at her and grinned. Well, you know, *grinned* isn't a good enough word. It's kind of a tight-sounding word. I don't know what my expression was, but I said, "You make me smile in a way that I never have before, and have always wanted to. You make my face feel like a ripe peach tastes. You have permanently expanded my heart. You make my heart do flips like Cheetah in the Tarzan movies. Every movie I see is about you and me. The difference for me between you and any other woman is the difference between a made-from-scratch biscuit right out of the oven with butter melting golden all over and a canned biscuit that's cold. Can you make biscuits from scratch?"

"No."

"And see? See? I hear that and am not dismayed. You are a deep well of bosomlovely plus something new I didn't know there was any of. You make me feel not only ravenous but also friendly. When I was driving I saw a woman walking down the street, kind of a completely unfluttery determined spunky no-airs trucking-right-along walk. I've always liked girls like that. Only they're not musky. You're like that, and musky with it."

"Well. I guess that's kind of courtly."

"Courtly. Courtly is like ladylike." ("Fuck a lot of courtly," was what I wanted to say, but I didn't.)

"You're not a courtier, are you, Guy?"

"No. I love you deeper than that." (I was wondering: "Are we talking about the same thing?")

"Well. I guess you do."

"So will you marry me, even though it's crazy because we don't have any income and you're not even half finished with college yet? What are you living on, since I saw you last?"

"Leonard's family has hundreds of millions of dollars. And they put lots of it into liberal causes." (C has always assumed that ravens would feed her, like Elijah in the Bible.) "Well, I'll support us now. Don't get shot anymore, C."

"I won't. I was scared."

But somehow I don't believe she was scared, when she was shot—not the way she had been scared of me in the car.

"I won't ever scare you again," I said. "I promise. It made me feel ashamed."

"Guy, you were, literally, beside yourself."

"I was? You'd think if I was, literally, beside myself, I'd have been in a position to notice. Now, come on, don't . . . I'm just—"

"Guy. Don't listen to words. Listen to me."

"Ah. Well. Hm. The melody." (I'm not very good at carrying a tune.)

"And hold me."

"I will. *Will* you marry me?"

"Yes! Guy?"

"*Hot* dog! What?"

"We're going to have a baby."

★ AUG. 20, 1993

WELL, HEY, it happened to the Reagans. But I always assumed they hadn't been as careful as I thought we had been. When Doc Stockley gave her the news, five weeks after our first night of love (Clementine stays on top of things), C checked that diaphragm she'd been keeping in her dorm room, and it leaked. And her thoughts turned to Merrilee Buckle—Clementine's roommate's friend, who had access, and who disapproved of Clementine and of contraception. I am tempted at this point, though I know I shouldn't be, to mutter: "Women." There is almost nothing I would put past a given male Christian human being, but I do not believe that one old boy, however vile, would punch a hole in another old boy's birth control. But C says she has heard women talk about doing it, she just never thought it would happen to her.

That was the origin of our Lucy, who does have my nose, to her chagrin I believe, although it is my nose in cute, reduced, feminine form. When she was little I would do that thing that children do to little children, "I got your nose," and show her my thumb, and she would say, "Nooooooo, you ham't." Our Lucy, the deconstructive chanteuse, who called last night to sing me her new song, that is to say the new song of her group, which has changed its name to Majestic Meat:

> *"Wanta whoop wanta weep,*
> *Uh . . . don't know which,*
> *Oo-oo-ooo ain't . . . love*
> *A son of a bitch."*

Pretty good, actually, that part, which was the only part I could get straight. But does it have to be my daughter singing it? Does she even have to *know* that? She gets her voice, which is sweeter than chicken when it wants to be, from her mother's side of the family. C's mother, I understand, had a beautiful voice. Then, of course, there is Dancy. When Lucy was little she and her mother and Dancy would sometimes sing hymns together in harmony— something I have never been able to do with anybody. It is a sweet mystery to me: voices harmonizing together, merging and twining around one another, changing places back and forth, now one ascendant, now the other, like the *g* and the *n* in *mignon*. Now, singing is Lucy's work, but harmony is not its strong suit so far as I can hear. Here's probably the most blatant example: one night at an arts center I listened to Lucy go through the entire lyrics of the national anthem with each word beginning in *bl.* The way little kids will sometimes drive you crazy going "Blinkle blinkle, blittle blar, blow bli blonder blat blou blar"?

> *"Blo-oh, blay blan blou blee*
> *Bly ble blawn's blearly blight?*
> *Blat blo bloud-bly ble blail*
> *Bly ble bli-blight's blast bleaming."*

And on and on and on. Every verse. A woman in the audience actually stood up and moaned, "Ohhhh, *please* stop. *Please.*" Which

Lucy found blatifying. Gratifying. Well, I guess it was pretty droll, actually, in an excruciating way.

My daughter. I have a daughter. O Merrilee Buckle, horrible person though you must have been and still undoubtedly are somewhere, I cannot think of you but fondly.

Those were fine days, C blooming inwardly with Lucy and outwardly in activist bonhomie. This wasn't running-around-nekkid college-girl activism, either. She was finding out what she was especially good at: saying "Why not?"

"Why not?" A great American question.

I remember when Ronald Reagan was debating Walter Mondale, and Mondale asked Reagan semiscornfully whether he actually intended to share Star Wars development technology with the Russians, as Reagan had airily suggested. And Reagan said, "Why not?" And an unplayable ball was in Mondale's court.

Unplayable because to Reagan, "Why not?" meant "Why not just smile and say any damn thing that has a nice ring to it, whether it has any relation to reality or not?"

And there is *alll . . . most* just a smidgen of that in Clementine's optimism too. But there's a smidgen of that in all American buoyance. And in Clementine's "Why not?" there is fiber. She doesn't organize things, she sets up that buoyant fiber for somebody to latch on to, and where the fiber goes, so goes she.

Here's an example from our marriage. Just before WOT arose, at a momentary lull in C's career, I said to her, "What we ought to do is a book called *Around the World in Eighty Ways:* hopping, gliding, pedaling, hitching, trains, planes, somersaulting . . ."

And C said, "Okay, let's do it." And I was nonplussed. Because I knew she *would* do it. But I had to say, "Well, of course there'd be enormous logistical problems, and we couldn't very well take the kids . . ."

So we didn't do it.

But in the Crowe County Movement, there were people who would say, "What we ought to do is not just walk around in the street with signs but go knock on Dingler's door and say, 'Hey, here's what *we* want. What *you* want?' "

And instead of chuckling and slapping hands, C would say, "Okay, let's do it," and people would look at her and blink, and then they would say, "Yeah." And they and C would do it. She wouldn't jump out in front and take the play away from the local people whose livelihoods were at stake, but she would smile at them and make them feel, "Why not?" And she would be right there in the forefront of the door-knocking and the dealing.

She knew Dingler. Dingler had been her guardian. She seemed to have a hold on him. But she clearly liked him no more—she maybe liked him less—than anybody in town. She wasn't blithe about him. She didn't like to talk about him. You could tell she had to grit her teeth to talk to him. But with those local people with her she would talk to him, and talk to him not as one white person to another but as someone who knew how to put in a word or two here and there in such a way as to help the movement move. (When it came time to negotiate the movie deal, by the way, C gave up a lot of money—hey, I could always make money, right?—in exchange for script approval, which wasn't easy to get, but it was her life story, and the only thing she insisted on—for instance, she didn't insist that her husband not be portrayed as a dipshit—was that the script keep the local black movers up in the forefront. In that regard it was a much more tolerable movement movie than *Mississippi Burning*.)

The wedding—three weeks after we got back together—was good. She was still slim—C not only has the great hair required for her presidency, she has the body. I don't know what it's made of, but it seems to be bulge-resistant. She didn't start looking pregnant until the boycott negotiations reached a point where if she revealed one more bit of irresistibility . . . and she did. How is even the most squinch-hearted reactionary going to say no to a radiant mother-to-be? That is, if the mother-to-be is C.

The wedding *itself* was good. The Reverend Micah presided, Leonard was best man, and no one gave Clementine away. She said she didn't believe in being given away. She didn't even *invite* her father. I told her she had to. I told her if she didn't it would break his heart. In fact, I invited him. He was in Vietnam. He took emergency compassionate leave and showed up the night before.

Dancy had been there for a week already. Dancy. Lord, Lord. I had heard about Dancy, but. She came through the door of the Asbury A.M.E. Church with Clementine, who had met her at the airport personally (a bit of an honor—by that time most people either came to C or were fetched to her by someone else). I saw very big red hair, a blue velour jumpsuit and a profusion of beads. "That's him!" she cried. "I knew him immediately!" Of all of us there on the floor painting a banner, I was the only one who was male and over twelve. Still it's nice to be recognized with gusto, and never before had anyone strutted hip-first like Tina Turner across a room into my arms while belting several bars of a New Orleans soul song: "Burrother-i'in-law, brother-in-law" (to the tune of "Mother-in-Law," the early sixties Ernie K-Doe hit). Dancy sang well, and when she hugged she skuweeeezed.

"And he's *white,*" she whispered, just *barely* discreetly, in my ear. "I have nevah see-un so many cul-lud *pee*-pull. Our muthuh is whirlin' in her grave. Let 'er whirl. I know I hope to whirl some in mine. You're kind of inward-seeming. Are you a good lover? Sissy wouldn't say."

All of which got my guard up a bit, but I was also, at least tentatively, refreshed by it, because I had been around a lot of earnestness lately. E.B. had some kind of money-making scheme he was working on involving shrimp (he has always had shrimp connections—after my book with compost in the title came out, he showed up at our house in Maryland with a truckload of shrimp hulls, which he dumped on our compost heap as a kind of hostess gift). Leonard was being grumpy about having to lie resourcefully to the press (he still hasn't *entirely* gotten over that feeling) about the facts of the shooting. The press themselves had pretty much come and gone for the nonce. (That would be a good name for a newspaper: *The New York Nonce.*) So I was ready for some ironic company. It was hard for me to figure exactly where Dancy's irony was coming from, but I figured I would try to go with it. My fiancée had left us together.

"No," I said, "but I can make meat loaf."

"I declare. You know, you *look* lak you can," she said. I was walking her outside, where we sat under a big hickory-nut tree.

I said, "You talk mo' Suhthun than C."

"You call Sissy 'C'? That's *nice.* That's *nice.* Well, I *like* having an accent. I *ch'yooose* to have one. I lived for a whall in Paris too, you know, Mistuh Fox, and could if I chose put on dandified ways. *Va t'en. Espèce de bête.* That means 'Go away, some kind of animal.' So this will, at least, be a religious service? But no bridesmaids' dresses! Well, the cullud ones wouldn't be able to afford them, I suppose, as if I could."

She smiled at me, in a not wholly artificial way, and I smiled back, in a way that I hoped was at least as natural.

"I've been *strictly* instructed," Dancy said, "not to tell you the family secrets. You know owuh parents *had to*—though I'm sure they wawnted to—get married too. Yes. They did." She put her fingers to her breast and fluttered her eyes. "That was me. I was awlllways trouble."

She was six years older than C, twenty-five, my age. But in a way she seemed a generation older. In another way she seemed no age at all.

"Guy, you are very handsome sort of, how do you find me? Pretty as my baby sister? Oh, you think I'm *testing* yooouuu. I'm not *testing* yooouuu. Why, you're part of the fam'leh, my gurracious me. I believe I am going to go ovuh to some othuh tree and pout, till you stop suspecting me of *testing* yoouuu.

"Sissy's never been mayrid befo'. No. Not at all. *I* have been. But nothin' could puhsuade me to tell you about *that.* Wild *horses* couldn't. No. He used to *hit* me. With very fine old antique figurines. Breaking the few things I had from my momma, on *me.* That man hit me with a delft baby so hahhhd one night. . . . Well, you cannot *chayynge* people. You know that yourself, Mistuh Fox. I hope."

She gave me a significant look, though what it signified was beyond me and also, I believe, beyond Dancy. She had C's sad eyes, only at bottom fearful. That's what passed through my mind, and Dancy saw it, with those same eyes. We haven't come so close to being friends since.

Then, as I was saying, there was Dad. The poor son of a bitch came all that way, and neither of his daughters was very sweet to him. Jesus. If your *daughters* aren't very sweet to you.

And should you marry a woman who isn't very sweet to her dad? She wasn't nasty to him. She gave him a little hug. But Jesus. If all your *daughter* gives you is a little hug. She also gave him such a *sad* look. And Dancy gave him her look.

I don't know. As I say, C doesn't like talking about him. And now they are strange bedfellows, politically. She and her dad and even, God help us, the Reverend B. Vaughn Dingler, Sr.

The Colonel (he wasn't the General yet then) didn't know I was the one who had made sure he was invited. Actually, Leonard and I and Milam talked it over, but I brought it up. Milam arranged it. There was no denying, even then, that Milam had a knack for what works for Clementine the public figure. Maybe he was already running her for president in his mind, I don't know. I just thought she would regret it later if her father didn't get a chance, at least, to come to her wedding. And I suppose I still felt bad about hitting him. But the main thing, probably, I was already beginning to feel like a father myself. I feel bad that I haven't gotten to know him at all, even after all these years. But he gets my back up so bad. And C's. I made a point to keep the kids in touch with him when they were little. They needed a grandfather, and he's pretty good with them in a gruff way. Jackson went fishing with him every summer for years. For all I know, he told Jackson all about what it is like to have North Koreans trying to brainwash you. I know this is a terrible thing to say, but I sympathize with the North Koreans.

★   ★   ★

I met his plane. He gave me a look like a punch, which I took. There was a little dinner for the people in the wedding and I drove him there.

I couldn't expect him to warm right away to a guy who had hit him at first sight and who was now presumably sleeping with his daughter (I don't think he knew about the baby coming at least). To my relief, he did not initiate a belated "Well, you've got quite a right hand there" conversation.

What he did say, though, was, "Brief me."

Which put me off. I filled him in on the wedding arrangements.

"You were in the army, I understand," he barked. He did, he barked. No doubt he was used to barking. He was about five-ten but looked bigger because he sat so straight. His face looked like it was hacked with an entrenching tool out of hard ground, except that his eyes were keen. I knew good and well he'd already checked out my personnel records.

"I was," I said. "Clerically, at Fort Bragg. So I could go to college on the GI Bill. Colonel, I didn't take to the service. The only thing

I remember from it is map reading and something an instructor
told us one day in the course of a lecture on nutrition:

" 'Two thirds of the world's peoples have never known solid
stool!' "

The Colonel didn't find that amusing. It was the sixties, a polar-
ized time in American history. The story of My Lai wouldn't come
out until a couple of months later, but it was already in the wind.
I may have felt a solidarity with him before he showed up, but.

"Your father in the service?" he said.

I'll bet he knew the answer to that too.

"I never knew my father. He was a columnist for the *Atlanta
Constitution* who finally talked them into sending him to cover the
war in the Pacific. On Iwo Jima a mortar shell went off behind him
and threw him facedown on the keys of his typewriter. The last
words he'd written were, 'This island is ours. A deathly calm . . .'
And he had x-ed out *calm* and replaced it with *silence*. Odds are his
next word was going to be *prevails*. I was born three days later.
My mother died eighteen years later singing to Jesus. She never
remarried."

And what did the Colonel need with that? Lord, Lord, the blind
head-bumpings of male succession. We never mentioned our previous fisticuffs. Women would have, I imagine. Women would have
talked it out, I guess. You'd think anybody would have. Hey, men.
Listen, I don't hold any brief for men.

E.B. got on with the Colonel, by sort of barking back at him.
When the Colonel said, "You ever in the service?" to E.B., E.B.
said, "Colonel, you see this scar under my eye? I got that scar
defending my country. Well, not the whole country but the spot of
it I was standing on. Which was right up at the head of the line for
the pay phone. I defended it so hard until the man I was defending
it against bit me right there. And a few days later it was swole up
to where they had to operate. And when they did they found a piece
of potato chip in there."

"What post?" the Colonel said.

"Fort Hood, Texas, Colonel."

Then they started talking divisions and sergeant majors and
shit.

And Dancy and Leonard hit it off. "Maybe you'd like to be con-
verted," she suggested.

"No, thanks," Leonard said. "I'm an atheist."

"Awwwwww. I could have you up to agnostic in half an hour. Episcopal by midnight. And after that—did you ever hear of talking in tonnnngues, Leonard?" She didn't use her big accent with Leonard. At C's urging I had warned Leonard that Dancy was liable to work her will on him and then give a general testimonial, or freak out, or something; but he succumbed anyway and then was peeved that I'd advised him against it. "She talked about Jesus a lot," he said, "but it was interesting. She told me the parable of the shepherd leaving the ninety-and-nine sheep to find the little lost one, which I pointed out was consistent with the ACLU. The only really ethnic thing she did was wash my feet—"

"Leonard, I wouldn't call that *ethnic.*"

"—and that was actually very pleasant. I talked to her about hysteria."

"You *did?*"

"Yes, Freud's fixation on it, and the Greeks' belief that it had to do with a free-floating womb. She was very—"

"You're a better man than I am, Leonard."

"We found the concept of the womb had a great fascination for both of us. She—"

"Could we talk about this later?" I said, it being time to proceed to the altar.

The wedding itself, as I say, was good. The music. The soul. People beaming at Clementine. "Ma'am, I sure like that name Clementine," I whispered to her.

She answered, "I like that name Fox."

"Beats the hell out of Earp," I said, and my darling C went down the aisle wed, expectant and laughing. All three of which, I was proud of.

She and Dancy were edgy around each other. "Dancy used to dress me up in her clothes like a doll or the dog and then tell me not only that I was adopted but also that I would never get to be her size because I had an incurable disease," C told me, but that's what all big sisters do. (Except Lucy. Lucy was good.) Somehow there seemed to be more to it than that. There was always the possibility that Dancy would do something to disrupt the wedding, of course, but she knew better than to do anything to offend the folks whose church it was. I don't think anybody has ever heard such a sultry rendering of "Whispering Hope" as Dancy favored us with, especially from a matron of honor, but it came across as good-hearted.

So, hey, Dancy. So her own nuptials are upcoming. In the Rose Garden. Why should that fill us with apprehension? Dancy's okay, I think. I wish she trusted me.

Leonard was best man. I thought about asking E.B., but I'd known Leonard longer and he was more likely to get his feelings hurt.

And here's a really weird thing. Milam hung back, didn't get into the spirit of the occasion at all, but that didn't surprise me. What did was this: C informed me that Milam was put out because *he* wasn't best man.

"What?" I said. *"What?* If there were such a thing as *worst* man, he would have been my first choice. How can he *possibly*—"

"Well, you know Milam," she said.

"No," I said, "I don't." Milam can organize anything, but he doesn't *understand* anything. How can that be? I gather he knows, now, all about how to massage politicians' egos—no, maybe he just knows which ones need it, and C does it—and threaten them, make deals, all that. How can he not *get* anything? "Does he think I *like* him?"

"I don't think he thinks about that. He just thought he was in line for it. He outranks Leonard."

"Jesus. *You* didn't want him to be best man, did you?"

"Well, I owe him a lot."

I let the matter drop.

Owe Milam a lot.

I guess she did owe Milam a lot, already. C is the spark, and if you'll hold a torch to the spark then she'll also be the torch-bearer. What Milam is—Milam doesn't fit into the torch metaphor very clearly, but Milam is the detail guy. Tell him what you want worked out and he will work it. If you told Milam you had decided to go around the world in eighty ways, he would work it all out for you. I do not intend, however, to have my ways worked out by Milam. C, however, does not see Milam as intrusive. This is a gender thing, I think. When we were living in the country and there was some basic carpentry needed around the house, C would be for calling a carpenter. I would be for doing it myself. Maybe I wouldn't get around to doing it, but I wouldn't want somebody else doing something in the house that I was capable of doing.

I don't like having Milam around. I don't even like for C to like having him around. But I wasn't going to get pissed off at C there on the eve of our wedding. In fact, I intended to avoid getting pissed off at Clementine like I intended to avoid the plague.

The Colonel—you have to give him credit. He long-sufferingly squired around my only living relative, Aunt Big Sybil, who showed up against all expectations and said things like, "Now, your mother was a Porter? *Carol* Parker? Hmmm. Cheryl Parker. No, no, I don't believe I *know* a *Cheryl* Powell. Now, I knew a *Carol* Perkins." When I wasn't trying to talk to the Colonel myself, I felt for the son of a bitch.

"Sissy looks happy," he told me after the ceremony. "You're to be commended for that." His handshake reminded me of Dancy's hug, only less personal. Then he went back to Saigon.

The North Koreans tortured him, when he was a prisoner. Cut open the bottoms of his feet and sewed gravel and shit up in there, and tied him so he couldn't sit down. But he didn't break.

And then you come home and—what could happen, that fifteen years later your daughters wouldn't be very sweet to you?

Dingler was there. Nobody invited Dingler. Unless Milam did. When she saw Dingler, Dancy went rigid the way C did when I was angry in the car. You could hear Dingler's ve'y ve'y creepy and unignorable voice weaving its way into our reception like a shiny durable acrylic thread. If he'd had his little dog with him, I'd've smothered him with it.

Clementine, of course, was wheeling and dealing with Dingler by then. She gave him a look, when he fat-weaseled his way through the receiving line, that was like fuck you, only man to man.

★ AUG. 21, 1993

I HAD AN IDEA this morning. "Hey, C," I said. "Why don't you get disguised with me and we'll walk around the Ellipse like real people and then have lunch at Spratt's?"

"Guy," she said, "I have to jawbone thirty-six congressmen this morning."

"Oh, well," I said. "Lah-di-dah. One at a time, or all at once?"

"One at a time."

"I see. Well, don't worry that you might cause me to feel like the odd man out. Remember when all I wanted to do was collaborate with *one* exotic dancer, and you had to establish right away that you might walk through the door any moment? No, no, you don't need to answer. I am not one to hold anything from the past, or the present, over a loved one's head. You don't even need to thank the God who made you that he also made me so enormously secure in my own manhood that I of course—"

"See you at dinner, Guy," she said.

"You should know," I said, "that I have never yet gone out into the real world in disguise without coming back having scored at least one hot chick's number—if not, indeed, a hum job. Oh, there's all kinds of new stuff going on out there in the real world. Do you know what a hum job *is,* even?" I shouted, but she was out the door. The S.S. man on portal patrol gave me a look.

I asked Leda, the makeup woman, if she had disguised any other White House residents over the years. She said that was classified.

I said, "*What?* You mean to tell me that if, for instance, Nancy Reagan ever got dressed up like a little match girl so she could wander among her subjects you wouldn't be able to tell me, *I,* who hold the same post she once held? So to speak?"

"Ooo, I didn't want any part of doing her. They say she bit somebody's arm once that was waxing her legs."

"You do not surprise me. I am perfectly willing to believe that. But how come you'll tell me that, but you won't tell me whether anybody else has employed your services so as to enable her or him to do what I'm doing? For instance whether George Bush sometimes tired of being George Bush and had himself done up as a . . . potentate or something."

"Anything on that order would fall under the head of classified, Mr. F." (She won't call me Guy, so we agreed on Mr. F., which could stand for either Mr. First Whatever or Mr. Fox.)

That's all I could get out of her. I cherish her conversation, but she gives me precious little of it. I suppose people don't tend to trust people whom they are disguising.

I have never been able to give good directions to a barber, much less a cosmetologist, so I gave Leda her head, carte blanche, as long as she didn't repeat the lower-lip mustache thing. When she held up the mirror, I was a Bessarabian. I say Bessarabian though I don't even know where Bessarabia is. But I was swarthy (Arabian), and epicene (Bess). I decided not to give Leda her head again. But *she* seemed pleased, and I didn't want to hurt her feelings, so what I said was, "*Anh.* Fine. Yes. Fine. The kind of look that a person would never think to give himself." But then I added, nicely, "Could I be a *little* less sloe-eyed? Contacts a couple of shades lighter, maybe, and a little less of the, what do you call that stuff, kohl?"

What is this job doing to me, I asked myself.

She sighed in a way she never would have, had I been Nancy.

"Leda," I said, "do you know, about your name, that there's a Greek myth—"

"I know awlllll about it," she snapped. But she toned me down some. Almost too much. I looked drab. Oh well.

All kinds come into Spratt's, so no one shrank away from me a couple of hours later as I made my way along the steam-table line and chose the chicken-livers-and-onions-and-peppers on rice, iced tea (sweetened) and a side of fried squash.

Carrying my tray, looking for a table, I saw the powdery lady. She was dressed about the same as before, only with small polka dots, and she must have already walked around and shaken down some, because she wasn't *giving off* so much powder, was just thickly coated with it. Still those strange almost-dead pale eyes, what I could see of them.

"Do you mind . . . if I join you, meddom?" I said, realizing in midstream that Bessarabians, even toned-down ones, never sound like they are from Georgia. So the *i* in my *mind* and the one of my *I* were entirely different vowels. I would never make a spy. She didn't say anything, so I sat.

She was having some dry toast and a cup of tea.

"Are you minding if I ask you," I asked her, "in this land of plenteee, is that all you are eating?"

She did not respond directly. Instead she looked at what I had before me and said, "That wouldn't stay on a camel's stomach."

Aha! I had apparently passed for a person of the sand.

"Why indeed no," I said, striving to sound un-American in a hard-to-pin-down way, "for a camel, he eat . . . grains."

Maybe I *could* do espionage. It is probably far easier to fool people than an honest person thinks.

"I em an Hemmerican, bye the weh," I said. What the hell; this woman had never been anywhere near Bessarabia. Frankly I wished I'd gone with Leda's original concept.

"That's your business," the powdery lady said with a kind of tremulous rigidity. She did put off some exhaust with that remark, and I suppressed a cough.

"And in this city of poley-teek," I said. "How is your imprission of the Prizzidant?"

"She does not protect me from just such as you," she said.

"As *ah*-eee?" I said. "Who do you theenk of me as, may ah-ee esk, gressious meddom."

"You know what I mean," she said.

"Becoss of my complexion," I said sadly, "you think of me as a terroreest. But, *ah,* let me say! I am a listener daily of the Dr. Deengler brodecast by ray-jo, and I hear him say, the Prizzadont, she is turning the swordeh into the plowwasherr."

She took a sip of tea and squared her shoulders painfully. "Dr. Dingler," she said, "has changed his message. Dr. Dingler has gone back on the Word."

She arose in sections, puffed twice and departed.

★ **SUN., AUG. 22, 1993**

OUR HONEYMOON consisted of us staying in bed till noon for a week. Playing peepeye, in honor of the peepeye lady, and Little Brown Church in the Vale (talk about a fusion of the sacred and the flesh), and one thing and another. Sometimes C would speak French. We tried everything we could think of that we thought we might like. My it was good.

The rest of the day C devoted to the struggle. And I set about finding a way of making a living that I could live with and that would fit in with her vocation. A writer can work anywhere, anytime, right? What I say now is: right, right. What I said then was, *yes.* Some young men set out to see the world or to make a fortune. I set out to fit in with her.

I didn't consider that an embarrassing purpose in life. Now, I have met embarrassing male spouses. Whose main vigorous activity in life seems to be jogging with her and caricaturing the role of her wife. Once C and I were having breakfast with a female college president and her spouse, in their house, and the third time he jumped up to go get more coffee C felt so over-fussed-over that she said, "No, let me," and got up, and that irritated the college president, who was humorlessly boomy in a way that would have seemed deplorably predictable in a male exec. She said to her husband (who had said he was a consultant), "No, you do it."

"It's okay if she wants to," he said.

She said, "Why not just do it?"

By this time C was in the kitchen, and I was with her, and we were looking at each other, in agreement that that was not the way that either of us wanted either of us to be.

What I did, during the twenty-four years of our marriage before this presidency thing came up, I contrived to stay afloat in honest self-employment. Inconsequential work, maybe, but never cheesy. Work that paid most of the bills. (The movie money, which all together was a little over $100,000, gave us a bit in the bank and helped buy the house and land we don't get a chance to use anymore, but we still have a sizable mortgage. C quit her TV job at about the time it became lucrative, to work full-time for WOT at $18,000 a year. Milam and Leonard, WOT's only male employees, have family money.) Work that didn't get in the way of C's heroism or our family life. And now I'm a figure of fun. Like a male Miss America but without the sense of achievement.

★   ★   ★

Back when I was talking to the press, they kept asking me how it felt to be First Hubby. I always told them a story from my first newspaper job. It was in Elba, Alabama, on a paper that was even smaller than the *Beacon.* One of my first assignments was to do a little feature story on the new mayor's first day in office. My first question was going to be, "How does it feel to be the mayor?"

Only I was nervous, and said it wrong: "How does it be to feel the mayor?"

The mayor looked at me, and blinked. And I looked away hurriedly, embarrassed, saying, "What I mean is . . ." and not being able somehow to say what I did mean, and I found myself looking right in the eyes of his wife, who was sitting over in a corner of his office, fanning herself and fluffing her hair up off her neck. She smiled.

"It be right nice, of an evening," she said.

Nobody ever used that story. What they always wanted to know was, how I felt to be a man in the shadow of his wife. And I would tell them the truth: I don't think anybody can tell anybody how anything feels, but I have always liked not being noticed by people I don't know. And I would give them other true-enough but essentially unresponsive and vaguely hard-to-follow answers; and before long they would start asking me how Clementine felt about things, and I would say I *knew* nobody could tell anybody how anything felt to anybody else; and pretty soon they would go away.

It is true enough that I like the background. You can watch and think back there. I am not by nature a maker of appearances. I was reading Betty Ford's autobiography. She quotes Pat Nixon as saying, "Oh, I never watch the news." You read that and you think to yourself, that *can't* be true, you would surely watch the news if your spouse were on it every night and some nights you could even see yourself. But no you wouldn't. Not if you hate the way you appear on television as much as I do.

Last night there was a big reception. Which I hated. But I was bearing up, I told myself. I was being gracious.

May I say that it is not very realistic, let alone fair, to expect the person who doesn't want to be there to be the one who "makes an effort" without seeming to? If you go into a social function and nobody knows you or wants to, or if they do know you they don't want to know you any better or perhaps wish they didn't know you at all so they could ignore you more thoroughly, then it doesn't feel like a social *swim* to you. It feels like a social sink. It is hard to help make things go swimmingly for one and all if you are fighting to be casual about finding a way to avoid standing in the middle of a crowd alone. (Especially if what you *want* to do is be alone, but not in this setting.) People to whom other people gravitate at a party don't understand this. Maybe C felt awkward around people before we met, as she said, but I haven't seen any sign of it since.

Milam, just bulldozes right on in and buttonholes people and impresses them with how serenely he doesn't realize or care that he has no sense of how to say the right thing. And they know that he can convey things to C. Whereas they know that I *disapprove* of influence.

This didn't used to be a problem in our life. At a WOT gathering, even to some extent at a Three-D function, there were always people I could identify with, who were barefoot or disaffected or just odd in the head or drunk, who wanted to talk about anything *but* whatever we were supposed to be there for. But at a Washington gathering it's as if it's immoral to chew the rag; everybody is always cutting to the chase. If you won't cut with them, they give you a glazed look.

Anyway, as I say, there was this big reception last night, and afterward C said, "I wish you'd had a better time."

Not as in: Oh, I'm sorry you didn't have a good time, these things must be hard for you.

More like: It sure would be easier for me if I had a husband who would have a better time.

So now I've got to—instead of complaining about what a shitty time I had—I've got to convince her that it isn't true, that I did have a better time. Than I did. That I was bearing up.

Then I happen to turn on the television tonight and there I am at the reception, scowling. *Plainly* having a terrible time. Which I was. But I had been sure in my own mind that I was graciously not looking like it. I still think I was bearing up, most of the time; the news just picked out a moment of emotional candor. But I guess none of us knows what face we present to the world. It would clear up a lot of confusion in life, if we did.

Actually I think Clementine does.

She could have been an actress. I think she knows what she looks like when she looks at people. She even knows how the light is striking her, natural or artificial, how it is cast on her features. From working on that movie and in television. She is aware of the light, in that way. I'm not.

Here's something I never told anybody about C: she sometimes gets confused for a moment, while giving directions (not that she ever has to do anything that mundane anymore), about which way is left and which right. I always used to tell her, "Just remember, your *right* hand is the one you *write* with," but that didn't focus things for her as clearly as it always does for me.

People have told me my father was funny. I don't know. In pictures he mostly looks skinny (the Depression) and moony over my mother. I've read some of his old columns and they were all pretty straight. Maybe he was like me, he had found work that enabled him to have his marriage.

But then he went off to the war. He died a funny sort of death, I guess, facedown in his work.

My mother could be pretty *wry*. "Blessed are they who expecteth nothing," she told me once when my homework assignment was proverbs, "because they shall not be disappointed."

Or she would say, " 'I see,' said the blind man, to his deaf daughter."

Anyway, at the age when C was getting off on *The Grapes of Wrath* I was reading American humorists. Benchley, Thurber, Perelman and so on. And I wrote funny things in school papers. There in Dingler, trying to shape myself around Clementine, I couldn't see any reason why I couldn't write humor for money.

It just didn't do for anybody, particularly anybody white, to be writing funny things about the civil rights movement, so I bought a forty-dollar used Royal standard typewriter and sat in the movement headquarters and wrote about the things I'd written about for the *Beacon:* enormous vegetables that people had grown (often in shapes that resembled rabbit heads or the state of Florida), chickens, possum cooking, coon hunting, watermelon-seed-spitting contests.

Believe it or not, the town went ahead and held its annual okra festival right in the middle of the "situation." The boycott was suspended for the day, competitions were integrated and E.B. won the eating contest, edging out a three-hundred-pound white man named Finis Culp, who wasn't feeling like himself and threw up. (In the movie, this was transformed into a kind of biracial hoedown, which was all wrong but did make for a prettier scene than Finis Culp's collapse.) C pushed for black cooperation in the festival—the Reverend Micah was against it. C went so far as to persuade the black community not to put up a candidate for Okra Queen, which would have been sticky. If you ask me, the okra festival was the Crowe County Compromise's turning point (Finis Culp wasn't at all popular in town), but Leonard was leery of publicizing it, and in the long run I guess he was right, because I doubt that it would have played too well with black voters in 1992. So I was the only person who wrote it up. But I didn't know where to sell it. I didn't know where to sell any of the things I was writing.

Another thing I would do was acculturate the visiting press. I was under wraps—never told anybody the true story of the shooting, of course, nor even about the cruciality of Fordyce Knott—but I was able to point reporters in directions that put Dr. Dingler in an embarrassing light, and I now knew where all the good black and white places to eat and drink were, and I was too young and quiet to be portrayable as a character, so I enjoyed it.

When Hayes Cotton came to town for *Rolling Stone* (back when *Rolling Stone* was countercultural), I drank beer with him all one afternoon in Ora's, where the brothers hung out (I didn't go to the Country Club anymore, since a redneck shot my wife), and smoked dope with him up in the bell tower of the Asbury A.M.E. Church (we had to be careful about that), and ate barbecue with him at Mama Vera's, and took him out to Schoolboy's Melody Room for the "Sexy Cute Dancing," and then we swung by the white music place, Woody's, to hear Soup Rawls and All the Availables do Webb Pierce and Lefty Frizzell and Floyd Tillman songs (they were into a period where that's all they would do), and then I asked him if he would read my okra-festival piece.

"Aw hell," he said. "Could I do something *else* with it for you besides read it? Could I eat it in my sandwich here? I ain't going to tell you I like it if I don't. I won't tell you how *much* I *don't* like it, but I ain't going to lie to you to the extent of saying I *do* like it, because then you'll work on it some more and make me read it again."

But he did read it and liked it, although he pointed out that "anything that turns on okra vomit is going to be hard to place," and he sent it to Willie Morris at *Harper's,* who finally said he couldn't quite figure out whether it was behind or ahead of its time, but another editor there liked it enough that when he left to go to *Country Monthly* he engaged me to write for him every month.

Which led to the income that sustained us while C was finishing college at Johns Hopkins and pursuing her career. It wasn't thrilling work, partly because I was professional enough to keep bearing in mind what Hayes Cotton had said about placeability, but we were a happy little family. For a number of years C wasn't famous enough to be recognizable at cafeterias—even after she became Darlin' Clementine the ombudsperson on local TV, going to bat for people who couldn't get a fair shake, she could still circulate more or less like a normal person because she has always been able to look several different ways by tying her hair up differently or just sort of scooting around in different ways. She even does different walks when she wants to.

I guess that's the actress in her too—the ability to look unlike herself. She can do voices, too. One night after we rewatched *The Lady Eve* she started saying "Oh, Hopsie" in that Barbara Stanwyck voice and then in that same voice saying *dirty* things. Lord.

Sometimes I wish she weren't so wonderful. I have internal conversations with C, which I don't share with her, in which I say to her, "You're wonderful. It's wonderful that you're wonderful. But sometimes I wish you weren't *so wonderful.* I love it when you're wonderful. But I love it more when we're lying quietly side by side listening to each other relax. And I would like it I think if we *griped* at each other more, without bringing each other down." But you can't ask somebody to be less wonderful.

Well. We had fun back then. Lots of family jokes. Which reminds me.

Two weeks ago I posted the following letter to Clementine at her Oval Office address, including the secret code number that family and friends use so that their mail goes directly to the President's desk without being opened:

Dear Miss President Fox:
  Have you ever been a "bikers' mama"?
  Tattoos?
  I am writing to you and other prominent American women, and I believe I will add Mexicans, asking these and other questions, in case I would meet them.

Do you have a funny feeling ever you are a part of the entire universe? I do.

Is there any money you could give me?

What is your favorite unguent? Where?

Your hair been used/featured in certain ceremonies? Has this been possible without your knowledge?

Do you have any identifying tricks such as chewing/whistling same time, throwing small pebbles and able to hit birds with them?

Tattoos?

You must get many requests as these, and so, hoping to see you!

Yours ever in my many high regards,
(signed) Dearborn Asseghai

She must have received it by now. And not a word from her. When she began to be a public figure she started to bring home all her least explicable mail, and it made me feel good when I learned that her staff, as she accumulated one, was instructed to be on the lookout for such mail so that she and I and (when it wasn't salacious) the kids could enjoy it and even sometimes answer it together. When she was ombudsing on TV, a woman wrote her:

I was writing my dreams down in a book for seven months for my therapy. My husband "lost" it. He threw away seven months of my dreams!

That's all the woman's letter said. Apparently she just had to tell somebody. But she enclosed a return address. Clementine brought the letter home and the kids and I spent a whole evening making up dreams—what great dreams the kids made up, as natural as rain—and then we sent them to the woman as partial replacements. She wrote back:

Thank you. These are nicer than mine were. I showed them to my husband. Before you wrote, I threw away one of every pair of his shoes. And we have made up.

That got the kids and me to thinking, and the next night when Clementine got home I was at the imaginary piano and the kids and I were singing:

"Threw away one of ev'ry pair of your shoes.
That's what I call collecting my dues.

I don't care how tempting it seems,
Baby don't you mess with my dreams—
Two can . . . play those . . . tooth-for-tooth blues.
One *of*
             ev*'ry*
                    pair
                        of
                           yooooour
                                     shooooes."

She liked it.

Then I started to make up letters, and names to go with them (sometimes the kids would help, but they got busier and busier with their own activities, which I usually drove them to until they got their own cars—there went the last of the movie money—and all I had to do was worry about them not being home yet and the roads getting wetter and wetter), and mailing them to Clementine, and she would always bring these home. Although she must have known that they were ringers, she never let on.

Actually that's one of her strengths: you never quite know whether she is sharing all of a joke with you or not. Her straight face. That's what first caught my eye and continues to hold it, her wonderfully mobile straight face. I loved it when Barbara Walters came to the house, in the WOT years, and asked her what her favorite joke was (what kind of question is that to ask for network TV?). C said what I thought she would say:

"When I was seven and eight and nine, and my father was stationed in San Antonio, Texas, we went to a little church where a man named Mr. Rice Loudy handed out the bulletins as people went in every Sunday. He had white hair that stuck up around the part and big, bent fingers. The bulletins—the little printed folded-over sheets that told you the order of service, and the numbers of the hymns, and announcements? Well, the first Sunday we showed up for church—it was the third or fourth time we'd changed addresses since I was born, and I was adjusting again—Mr. Rice Loudy looked at me. I guess I must have thought he was trying to decide whether to let me in or not, so I said, 'It's okay, I'm new.' He gave me a long look, and without changing expression, he handed me a bulletin. And when I sat down I saw it was blank.

"Every Sunday after that, for three years, Mr. Rice Loudy would always look at me, and never say anything, and hand me a bulletin. It was always blank. There were always some that didn't get printed, you know, that slipped by the machine, and he would always look through and find one like that and save it for me.

"We never exchanged a word. Just looks. Then one day he wasn't there. The man who took his place at the door gave me a bulletin that had all the printing in it, and there was the announcement of Mr. Rice Loudy's funeral. And I begged and begged my mother till she gave in and took me to it. And—"

"But your favorite joke . . . ?"

"Was those blank bulletins."

You have never seen a blanker look than Barbara Walters gave Clementine then. In fact, when the interview was aired, that story wasn't included. Ah, mass communications. Yet Clementine is great at mass communications. Someday I will figure her out.

But. Either someone steams open the letters with the special code number on them and reads them before Clementine does and throws some of them out, or being President has changed my wife. Or I've lost my touch. Jesus Christ, when you start worrying about whether you've given offense in a joke with your wife—what is there in that letter that could have put her off?—there's something wrong somewhere. I spent a lot of time on that letter. I thought it would give her a lift.

★ AUG. 23, 1993

I FIRST HEARD C, Leonard and Milam talking about a third party back in '90. "That dog won't even get up off the couch," I said.

Who knew?

Especially, the Three-D party—Democracy, Decency and Daring?

C and Leonard tended to agree with me, actually, and for some time WOT took a wait-and-see attitude. Milam thought the thing was doable, but Milam always thought everything was doable. He never had any sense of what the right thing to do was, but when C unleashed him on anything, he would get it done; I give him credit. Gradually C began thinking that the party was at least a good thing for WOT to have a hand in. I never did understand DaSilva's notion of a complete releveraging of the Defense Department, and neither did anybody else but DaSilva. The premise died with him, really—C has had to recouch it in her terms. But it was just crazy enough to appeal to her, and she and I both liked DaSilva when we met him. He was a corporate-raider Robin Hood, arbitrageurizing more than half a billion dollars into his pocket, then giving 8o percent of it to the poor. I know, there was something dubious about the whole thing to me, too. But the guy was, after all, managing to give $100 million a year to the Coalition for the Homeless, Catholic Charities, the Southern Poverty Law Fund, United Jewish Appeal and various other good works, and in the process building up a certain amount of political friendship. He was also managing to save enough to help bankroll this party. He had even read Flann O'Brien. "I felt my wallet in my pocket, like the hand of an old friend," DaSilva quoted from *The Third Policeman*—misquoted, but still—when he asked me who some of my favorite writers were and I tossed out the name of O'Brien, which with most people was enough to get us off the subject of who some of my favorite writers were.

A lot of people found DaSilva hard to take, up close. Milam couldn't stand him. (It goes without saying that he couldn't stand Milam; Milam was used to that.) DaSilva said a lot of great things:

"The Democrats are hanging back waiting for hard times. Meanwhile a certain level of Republicans are getting fat on these times, and other people are *voting* Republican the way they write fan letters to TV stars. I *am* rich, and I'm telling you that the rich are getting a free ride.

"People ask me whether I'm not put off by some of the panhandling tactics of the urban homeless. Well, you know it's not only homelessness that's up, it's also shamelessness. If Donald Trump can behave the way he does, then why shouldn't people go up to strangers in the street, get right up in their face and ask for money?

"We are running enormous deficits. And the people who are

profiting by these deficits tell us that they don't mean anything. Okay, in that case we're prosperous. Let's spend some money. On ourselves. Let's repair our bridges that are falling down, let's provide medical care for the aged who *can't* pay for it, and let's begin the long process of building an economy in our inner cities that isn't based on robbery and begging and drugs.

"Are we afraid of communism now? No. Whether we want to admit it or not, what traditional hard-working Americans are afraid of now is being caught between the rapacious rich and the rapacious poor. We need a middle-class revolt, which forces the rich to pay for programs that help the poor aspire to that old-fashioned goal, a decent living. People complain about the poor. But it's the *rich* who drive up prices and make us all try, in vain, to keep up with them."

As clever a speaker and financier as DaSilva was, the political smart money was taken aback when the party got itself together enough to have a convention, and even attracted considerable media coverage.

★   ★   ★

I went along with C to the Three-D Nominating Convention because I had liked the looks of Seattle (nice rock gardens and waterfront) when I passed through it driving to Puyallup. I figured the goings-on would either transcend or fall short of real politics and I could get a nice light country column out of the trip. My mother used to have a rock garden when I was little. I spent a lot of time lifting the rocks to find roly-poly bugs and sometimes little snakes.

It was an interesting crowd on the convention floor, cutting across ideological grounds. There were whole-earth folks with children in Snuglis, white working people who just couldn't stomach the Democrats anymore, black entrepreneurs who just never could stomach the Republicans, a disproportionate representation of Asian-Americans for some reason, and retired folks in motorcycle leathers. I saw one young woman delegate from Maine in a T-shirt that said "RESIST AUTHORITY" and, just beneath that, "If You Want To." But since they were even more charmed and astonished—as well they might have been—than most people to find themselves potentially on live television, you'd see half of them sitting there in their delegations huddled around little portable TVs, hoping to see themselves pop up.

"You know if you're *watching* television you're not too likely to see your face on it, live," I told the delegate from Guam, who was wearing a (fake, politically correct) silver fox hat, holding up a sign that said DEMOCRACY-*SI-SI*, DECENCY-*SI-SI*, DARING-*RING-RING* and staring fixedly at the set in his lap.

"I will look up quick," he said.

I decided to go find a rock garden. But on the way out I saw Hayes Cotton waving at me from the press bar. He'd written some pretty good stuff about WOT, but it didn't have the panache of his work in the sixties. I hadn't seen him since back then.

"Guy Fox!" he said when I joined him. "Here is a man," he informed the beautiful, detached-looking young woman standing next to him, "who made a very convincing case that a notable chapter in the civil rights movement turned on a three-hundred-pound redneck man vomiting okra. Okra power! Not the white power, not the black power, but a third power: green power! Okra vomit! What would that look like on a flag? 'Don't Tread on Me.' "

"Well, it was fried okra," I said.

"That's right. I'd forgotten. So it must have been more of a brownish green. Still kind of a low-rent image, Guy. Listen, if it had been some particular tony East Side of Manhattan shop's special spinach-quiche vomit, you'd be where Tom Wolfe is now. As it is, what are you doing?"

I started telling him, but *Country Monthly* didn't register. The woman he was with—or, more precisely, the woman he was standing beside—had black curly hair like C's. She was also angularly, foalishly lissome like C when I had met her, and she had a similar look in her eyes. Only a more musing look, more reflective. She was wearing a cowgirl blouse with pretend-pearly snaps, just enough of which were unsnapped at the top to make her look unbrazen but . . . open.

"Those were the days, Guy," Cotton said. "These guys covering politics today, they don't know any stories! Except what's fit to print or—preferably, *very* preferably—to put on the damn idiot screen. Sound bites, man."

"Whereas what would really be news would be Man Bites Sound," I said, but that didn't register either.

"They've got it all turned around backwards! They're in it for the boring stuff! All that crap about impact groups and image-adjusting that they ought to just halfway cover so they can be in the business of staying up late and telling real stories about okra vomit. They think what the candidates say and look like on television is the *point*! They don't drink! They work their ass off and go to bed early and wake up fresh and keep their hair trimmed so they can hustle their way onto television and then, in time, get their own weekly TV magazine show where they interview Cher by live remote and she says she likes fucking twenty-six-year-old drummers and what are you going to say back? If you're a fifty-year-old man? It ain't fair. Guy . . ." He leaned close and whispered: "They don't even chase no pussy."

★　★　★

But that wasn't what was depressing me as I walked back to our hotel. (For one thing, I liked it that the young woman in the cowboy blouse—I never caught her name—didn't look like she was about to *be* pussy either, in Cotton-chaseable terms. In fact, she looked almost as though she were interested in me.)

What depressed me was that I wasn't far from being a fifty-year-old man myself, already. And nobody who was anybody—or even who *ever* was anybody—read my stuff. Maybe Cotton was past his prime, but he had *had* one—he'd won a Pulitzer uncovering civil rights abuses in the early sixties. Whereas the only scandal I'd ever uncovered was when I learned (from our postmistress, in the country) that the head of a small-town Maryland arts council, Clyde Verge, had made up several artists and their projects (Verna Passevant, "The Songs of Mosquitoes and Flies"; T.P. Fullilove, "Criticizing Clouds"; Foley Bigelow, "Carrots in the Shapes of States: An Attempt to Grow These Root Vegetables So as to Resemble Vermont, New Hampshire, Illinois, Idaho, Virginia, Kentucky and Tennessee on Purpose") and then pocketed, himself, the state arts-council funds he allocated to these fictional projects. (Four hundred fifty dollars, all together.) I wrote a column exposing him, but my editor at *Country Monthly* assumed that I had made up Clyde

Verge *and* the projects *he* had made up. When the magazine learned that I had not written a spoof but was actually exposing a living person, the lawyers got all worried, and then Clyde Verge died of a heart attack during a dispute with his next-door neighbor over whose dog was shitting on whose property. So my only exposé got killed, and I had to write another column in a hurry about—well, about the songs of mosquitoes and flies.

★   ★   ★

I went up to our hotel room and got out my old notes from the Dingler-to-Puyallup ride.

★   ★   ★

Walla Walla, Wash. Locals often seem to accent the first *Walla*.

McFeely Tavern. RELAX FREELY AT MCFEELY. THIS BAR WILL BE TENDED BY THE PARTY BEHIND THE BAR. ANYONE NOT AGREEING WITH THE METHOD OF BARTENDING WILL PLEASE NOTE THE MISTLETOE ON THE BARTENDER'S COAT TAIL.

Centerpiece behind bar a small sculpture: a nut with legs running from a bolt with legs, over the caption "No! Not Without a Washer!" Above that on mirror, cartoon of an elk looking around a tree at his own behind and saying, "That's funny, I thought I knew every elk in town." Just above eye level, a stained-glass panel depicting two monks tapping a keg. Above that, a color photograph of John Kennedy. Above *that,* a red helicopter with the rotor going around, a bear pilot, a banner saying TAKE HOME HAMM'S, and dangling from the helicopter, on a long spring so that it bounces from monk level to JFK level, a bear in a cowboy suit with a six-pack of Hamm's under his arm and a baby bear hanging on to his gun belt so that the gun belt's pulled down around his ankles. And over all, a real elk's head with a red Christmas-tree light on every antler point.

American humor!

★   ★   ★

Playing on the jukebox, "Bonaparte's Retreat." And Les Paul and Mary Ford singing "Vaya con Dios."

Elderly couple at bar talking about a shriveled old guy who is playing bar shuffleboard with a white-haired woman: "You notice he's already calling her Mama?"

One middle-aged woman to another: "So many people, they marry and then build a life, and die.

"And then what is that really?"

On the next page, Seattle. And I remembered the epiphany I had beheld on the corner of Pacific and Aloha streets: The Fuzzy-Wuzzy Rug Company sign.

Little red carpet, and seated on carpet, little white bear, and on the bear, flashing, one after another, these words:

FUZZY . . .

WUZZY . . .

FUZZY . . .

WUZZY . . .

Seems highly evocative somehow. Then remember Aunt Big Sybil, when I was a kid, picking up white kitten and saying, "I wondah what it feeeels like to be fuzzy." And me thinking something not quite right about that.

The things we remember. What is not quite right about it?

Kittens can't know how it feels to be "fuzzy."

They can't have the concept we have of fuzziness, which is conditioned by the skin we use to stroke kittens. They encounter their own fuzz with a raspy tongue.

Compare: How does it feel to be the mayor? His wife *can* describe how it be's to feel the mayor, because she's felt him as an object. But a person can't feel himself as an object—certainly not as the object we think of him as. When we ask the mayor how it feels to be the mayor, we are asking him how it feels to be what we think of as a mayor. He has to try to think of something that we will recognize as mayoral, which in fact probably falsifies his feelings.

"Mm, you feel good."

"No, I don't, not tonight."

How does it feel to be black?

How does it feel to be you?

Got to remember not only how she feels to me, but how she feels to her.

There's the fuzzy, and then there's the wuzzy.

Remember sign in Arkansas petting zoo: DON'T LOVE BUNNIES TO DEATH.

★   ★   ★

The room phone rang.

It was C.

"Guy?" she said. When she says it with a question mark—goes so far as to be that softening—I know it means trouble.

"They may want me to run for vice-president," she said.

Uhhh. Happy for you, dear. Supportive answer, come on. Angry tone, get back.

"Well, that sure is an honor. But . . . I thought you said, now that the kids are grown, you'd drive across the country with me."

"Guy, we can *campaign* across the country."

"Not me," I said.

Shouldn't've said that, shouldn't've said that. But god damn.

Silent on the other end.

I know her silences.

"Hey," I said, "whither thou goest. It just came as a surprise. I mean, I was born in a log cabin, and now my wife has a thousand-to-one chance of being vice-president of the United States? What a country!"

"Come on back over here," she said.

"I can't," I said, "I've got to write a column." What I was thinking was, "Wheeling-dealing is one thing, and sitting around watching wheeling-dealing, when you can't report any of it, is another." "Whatever you do, don't settle for ambassador to Guam," I said.

She hung up in good spirits and then the phone rang again.

"Hey, I just got wind of something. Your wife offer to buy you a new suit, by any chance?"

"Hayes, I ain't telling you shit!" I said.

The phone rang again. What if it was C, or one of the kids? I answered it.

"Guyyy?" said a soft female voice.

Hmm.

"I just met you in the press bar, with Hayes Cotton? And there's a rumor going around . . ."

"I ain't telling you shit either."

I realized, with a heavy heart, that I was going to have to consider developing a better telephone manner.

I also realized that C and I were going to have to talk. I wasn't in fact resigned to her becoming a national politico, and there was no point in pretending that I was. I paced around the room, thought about what I was going to say.

What if the roles were reversed, I wondered.

That didn't really track, because I was no more likely to run for vice-president of the United States, even on a kind of fun ticket, than—well, than C was likely to be pacing a hotel room trying to figure out how to register her reservations about my running for vice-president of the United States.

But say, for the sake of argument, the roles were reversed.

What would she say?

Not anything gripy.

She would maybe come up with some alternative more compelling than running for vice-president of the United States.

To me, driving around the country was more compelling. By my standards.

There was the rub. Different standards. And her standards were the world's standards, by and large. Or were they? Wouldn't most people rather drive around the country than run for vice-president of the United States? I was the normal one.

On the other hand, most people would probably say that if one person wanted to run for vice-president of the United States and another person wanted her to drive around the country with him, the one who wanted to run for vice-president of the United States had the edge.

Why?

I wasn't getting anywhere.

I paced some more.

I called up Lucy.

Miraculously, she was in.

"Lucy," I said, "your mama wants to run for vice-president of the United States."

"Awwwwwwww," Lucy said ironically.

"That doesn't help me," I said. "The thing is I want us to drive around the country. That seems to me a normal aspiration. Deserves to have weight."

"That's a good name for a group, Dad," Lucy said. "Deserving Weight."

"No, it isn't a good name for a group. You're just saying that. That's the kind of thing I would say, to get out of taking sides between you and Jackson. Not that I'm asking you to take sides. I'm just saying . . . Oh, never mind."

"That's another good name for a group, Dad. Never Mind."

"Lucy, are you okay?"

"I am. I am sort of."

"What do you mean you are sort of?"

"I'm just in a lull."

"Well, I hear that. I guess you take after me, having lulls. Your mama don't have no lulls. Lucy? You're not in a drug lull, are you?"

"No, I'm in a love lull."

"Do I want to hear about this?"

"Do I want to hear about yours?"

"Well, I would've thought you used to would've."

"I used to try to help people understand things, Dad. But I don't anymore."

"You don't?"

"No. I try to do things."

"Well, uh, hm. What are we talking about here?"

"I love you, Dad."

"I love you too, Luce. Are you eating your vegetables?"

"That's another good name for a group. Eating Your Vegetables."

"Lucy, everything is not a good name for a group."

"I know, but sometimes people be naming groups, and sometimes people be running for vice-president."

"Yeah, well, don't worry about anything on this end."

"Thanks, Dad."

Lord, Lord. It's hard being two people's daughter at once.

It was raining outside. Clementine came back to the room damp and beaming. What was I going to say, in the face of that beam? Even if an element of my makeup was saying, "Wait a minute, wait a minute." She beams like *that*, god damn me if I don't beam.

"They picked me," she said.

She looked—this is a terrible thing to say, in a way, but: she looked like a bride.

Whose? was a question that a certain element raised. On the other hand, that element goes for a moist rosy woman who is

kicking off her shoes like a young girl dancing. That element and
I could have stood there together and watched C kick off two or
three dozen pairs of shoes like that. She was hopping, having a little
trouble getting the left one off, trying to push the heel of it free with
her right stockinged foot, using her hands to pull off her suit jacket.
Her hair was damp and loose around her eyes and she was looking
at me, looking through me, looking a little bashful and brazen
both—knowing I wanted her, knowing the world wanted her, knowing what she wanted; and something in my breast actually said to
her, "Damn you, damn you," but to the rhythm of Thumpa
Thumpa. After all, it was nobody but Lucy's parents, and Jackson's,
who went to bed.

★   ★   ★

And then . . .

★   ★   ★

Maybe it was predictable that Cuomo and Bradley and the other
Democratic big guns (no doubt assuming that Bush was unbeat-
able, the electorate firmly mired in Oh-What-The-Hell conserva-
tism) would fink out again. But who would have believed that the
Democrats would somehow manage to come out of their forlornly
wishful convention with "The New Dukakis" as their standard-
bearer?

It helped of course that the Republicans (whose purpose if you
ask me was to keep Dukakis in the public eye as an example of what
Democrats were like) had appointed him and Kitty to a bipartisan
drug-war panel; that the Medellín cartel had kidnapped them while
they were on a fact-finding tour; and that the unexpectedly feisty
couple had seized their captors' Uzis and shot their way to freedom
in an episode that so aroused public outrage that the cartel's profits
dipped by 9 percent (the price of Uzi stock, on the other hand, rose)
. . . But still.

And who'da thunk—until it happened two weeks before Election
Day—that Marilyn Quayle and her family's spiritual adviser would
defect to Libya as evidence surfaced that the feisty Second Lady had
first seduced and then attempted to poison George Bush and *then*

(to give the President credit, he apparently didn't learn of the poison-attempt part until the public did) successfully blackmailed him into keeping her husband on the ticket. Or that Dan Quayle, left in the lurch, would be found in a fetal position with his head under the vice-presidential desk. Or that Bush's reaction would be to say, "Read my lips: there was no quid pro quo," and then to make vague references to "the disloyalty thing" while holding up yet another batch of White House puppies. Or that in the middle of that press conference Barbara Bush would suddenly appear at the podium, snatch the puppies away from her husband and stomp angrily away without a word.

All I can say is, you had to love it.

Unless it meant that a very real possibility had suddenly arisen that your wife might become vice-president, hence that you might become the vice-president's husband. I actually could not entirely enjoy the look on the abruptly de-puppied Bush's face, because I was thinking of myself.

Even with all that, of course (and although both Clementine and DaSilva had already kicked a little ass in the debates, and although Dukakis had made the mistake of posing on the back of a horse, which reared), let us not forget that the DaSilva-Fox ticket beat Dukakis-Jackson by only three electoral votes and Bush-Dole by eighteen. (For one thing, hastily taken polls showed that many voters were troubled by the presence on the Three-D ticket of a woman who had her own family spiritual adviser of sorts—Dr. Dingler having mysteriously endorsed her on the radio.) But beat them DaSilva-Fox did, handily outdrawing Ms. Dole among women and taking quite a few black votes away from the Reverend Jackson.

It is all a blur to me now, nine months after the election.

Damn your eyes, Marilyn! But, then, so many people have helped make it possible for me to be where I am today.

★ AUG. 24, 1993

"HOW COME WE never start conversations with you asking me a question?" I said last night.

She was wearing these little half-glasses she uses for reading now, I think because she thinks they make her look more like Lyndon Johnson. She has a soft spot for Lyndon Johnson, which bears watching.

"Because I'm the President *and* you're always trying to get into my panties," she said.

"I like it when you say *panties*," I said frankly.

"Mm."

"Would you say *panties* again?"

"Panties."

"You know exactly what you're doing, don't you?"

"Mm."

"What are you doing?"

"Trying to read something that I have received here from my Council of Economic Advisers regarding run-amuck capitalism, which I have to talk to Milam about tomorrow and sound like I know what it's all about so he won't lose interest. As soon as he gets the impression that I don't care about something he stops caring about it, which means I stop hearing about it altogether and the next thing I know, the nation is being repossessed."

"I never have liked people who knew exactly what they were doing."

She gave me a look. "I know you don't mean that, that's just one of your little humorisms."

"You know, if I were a woman, you'd have to say supportive things to me all the time, and send me flowers and shit."

" 'Flowers and shit.' "

"Well, you would."

"I purposely married a man, for that reason."

"How come you wanted to marry me?"

She gave me a longer look.

"Guys aren't supposed to ask things like that, are they?"

"No," she said frankly.

"Well, I've put it off for twenty-four years."

"Next year, I'll give you an answer. As a silver-anniversary present."

"What are your Council of Economic Advisers like? Would I like them? Do they ever ask about me?"

She smiled at me over her glasses. I mean she looked at me over her glasses and smiled under them.

"You don't look anything like Lyndon Johnson," I said, "and you never will. There. I've said it."

"You know how to hurt a woman."

I bit her on the neck. "Say *panties* again," I said.

"Guy, I really do have to read this."

"Well, hell. C?"

"Guy . . ."

"Just answer me one thing. Will you answer me one thing?"

"*Guy* . . ."

"How come you never asked me why I hit your father?"

She blinked, and looked up. She didn't say anything.

"Were you sorry that I hit your father?"

She still didn't say anything.

"Your father, now, you *do* look a little like."

She looked away.

"How do you *feel* about your father?"

"I always looked up to him. He cut a broad swath."

"C! That's the same thing you told Barbara Walters. Word for word. This is *me.*"

She swallowed. "Guy," she said, "don't poke at me."

"Poke at you?"

"Guy, I'm going into the Lincoln Room for a while."

"What? Hey."

"I'll be back. Panties."

And she was back, late, snuffling just a little, silky in the dark.

I CAMPAIGNED SOME. People coming up to me and saying, "So. You a humorist." And waiting for me to say something funny. When strangers meet Kim Basinger out in public, do they expect her to get naked? No. They probably don't even hold out much hope. So why do they expect me to say something funny?

I would say, "Yes."

"Do you feel a lot of pressure, to be funny all the time?"

I would say, "No."

"Well," they would say, after a moment, "Lord knows we need all of it we can get, these days."

Even the kids showed up for a couple of obligatory family appearances. The seven DaSilva siblings were demon campaigners, wearing hats, leading cheers. But Jackson is about as dynamic a glad-hander as I am, in fact worse. I at least make an effort. "Damn it, you don't need to *snap* at voters," I told him. He looked at me as if I were an old worn-out wasp telling a young wasp he didn't need to sting.

"So what do your hotshot professors of the business arts think of DaSilva's theories?" I asked him.

"Crackpot," he said.

I live with a father's direst fear for his son: that someday this supposed chip off the old block will announce to us what we have suspected for years without quite admitting it even to ourselves, what he himself has known since ten or twelve: he is Republican.

Lucy, for her part, couldn't believe DaSilva's hair. She kept staring at that enormous black-and-silver wave up front that he thought of as his trademark. "Dad," she told me, "you have to get me away from that hair. I *want* it too much. I want a hat of it. I want a whole *outfit* of it. It makes me feel faint. Seriously—"

"Hey, that's a slip. You better hurry up and change the name of your group to Seriously. I mean it. Seriously."

"Dad. I don't like campaigning. It's like the opposite of what I do. I was just talking to a girl who said, 'You either put yourself first or DaSilva/Fox first. I suspect there are people in this campaign who are putting themselves first. *I* slept with the hard count last night.' 'Bless your heart' was all I could think of to say. What *is* the hard count?"

"It's a tally of votes or something, Luce. I guess she was sleeping with it to keep the opposition from seeing it. Don't worry your pretty little postmodern head about it."

"But I don't want to hurt Mom's feelings. Can't you give her some excuse?"

"I can't just make something up," I said.

"When we were little you used to make things up," she said.

"Aw. Yeah. We all used to make things up together," I said. "Remember the threw-away-my-dreams song?" I floated off into nostalgia. What kind of man is it who won't lie to his wife for his own daughter?

Lucy took things into her own hands. She went to Leonard. At this point her group was calling itself Get Technical. "Leonard," Lucy said, "we don't want it to look like we're exploiting Mom for publicity, we just want to help. Why don't we sing at one of your rallies. Have you heard our new song?" And she sang a few lines, more melodically than the group as a whole would have rendered them:

> *"You got big old hair and a little bitty heart.*
> *I should've known about you from the start.*
> *Your pompadour is a work of aaaaart—*
> *You got big old hair and a little bitty heart."*

That got Lucy off the hook, and Jackson was already long gone back to his case studies. Hey, they're kids, they have their own lives to lead.

Actually the campaign didn't overwhelm my life all that much. America evinced no very burning desire to know all about the husband of the second name on a third ticket, especially one who was as boring as I was in interviews. I had a nice-sounding occupation and no dubious business entanglements (no business entanglements at all), so I didn't attract much attention. C didn't need me around all the time to hold her hand. She had Leonard and of course Milam, and E.B. took off from his business interests ("I got an all-night E-Z Off the Interstate, man—I'm making money while I *sleep*") to pump DaSilva for investment tips and serve as driver, bodyguard and highly visible sign of ethnic diversity. (E.B., now, *was* a glad-hander.) I wrote introductions to *Country Monthly*'s series of books on vegetables, caught up with the campaign often enough to keep the marital bed warm, said encouraging things on the phone and figured this wouldn't last past November.

There was a regrettable incident in Idaho. C and DaSilva were having a high-level dinner with Ralph Nader (he was making a speech nearby), and not even Milam was included. Milam was pouting, and he and Leonard were ragging on each other about something.

"Hey," E.B. said, "this is *cowboy* country. Let's go check it out."

"They drink tomato juice and beer," I said.

"Damn, I got to see that," E.B. said. "Let's hit some spots."

So we all got into a car. "I might remind you," Milam said, "we are running for vice-president of the United States. And it's late and this is a rough part of the country." On the radio, a strange religious station was playing a song that included this verse, which Lucy would have liked:

> The boys who go to church, they all seem homely,
> The boys who get me going all seem wild.
> Oh, which is better? Me being lonely,
> Or running the risk that I'll have Satan's child?

"I tell you, rough," said E.B. "You know, it's a wonder to *me* why white music ain't caught on more widely."

"I passed a place this morning called Jayroe's that looked good," I said. "Cold Beer, Live Bait, Dancing, Billiards, Video Rentals and Barbecue Links: 'You Can Find Better Prices But You Can't Beat Our Meat.' Looked like it used to be a gas station that caught fire."

"I don't like the sound of it," said Milam. "There's a G. Williker's out on the Interstate loop."

"A what?"

"A G. Williker's. It's a chain."

"Milam, shit."

"What's wrong with that?"

"Milam, do you think cowboys go into a place called G. Williker's? It's probably got fake stained glass, ferns, drinks with little umbrellas in them and Willikerburgers."

"That's right. You know what you're getting."

"Be a mensch, Milam," said Leonard. "Let's fucking go to Jayroe's. Take off your campaign button, Milam."

Jayroe's was good. No decor to speak of except a sign in the men's room that said, SHE OFFERED HER HONOR, I HONORED HER OFFER, AND ALL THROUGH THE NIGHT I WAS OFF 'ER AND ON 'ER. We had several beers and I started talking to two old men sitting at my end of the bar. Asked them what there was to see around there.

One of them said, "That mountain you pass between here and Montrose, they say it's the biggest flat mountain in the world. It lacks a lot of being flat, though, when you get up on it. So I just don't know."

"Yep," said the second one.

"I used to know how many lakes there are on that mountain."

"Yep."

"They told just last week how many years ago it was they first started the ski business up there."

"*Oh,* yeah."

I heard a voice being raised down at Milam's end of the bar, so I missed the connection between the above and this:

"My sister told me how many hundred hogs they use a day, just for those little chunks of fat in the can."

"Yep."

Now we were getting into my area of expertise. I've written several columns on grease and lard and shortening. I love that word, *shortening.*

But I heard the voice being raised again. E.B. and Leonard were over at the jukebox talking amicably with a man who had a squirrel climbing around on his shoulders and head.

Probably somebody had got pissed off just looking at Milam. I was feeling good about America. I went to see what I could do.

"Said *don't* touch my hat," a cowboy two stools down from Milam was saying. The cowboy's hat was on the bar between them.

"I don't intend to, believe me," said Milam.

"No, see, don't even *think* about touching my hat."

"I'm not," said Milam.

"Hey," I said, "nice hat."

"Oh," said the cowboy. "You think it's a nice hat, but your friend here don't want to touch it."

"Let me buy you a beer," I said.

"What's your friend's name?" the cowboy said.

"Milam."

"Kinda name's that."

"He's from Atlanta."

"Lanna! Hell he doin' in here lookin' my hat?"

"He probly admires it," I said. "Bartender, another one of what our friend here is having."

"What's his other name?"

"Beau!" Milam said. As if he didn't need any help from me. You know, first names affect a person's whole life. I think one of the problems with Milam is that his just isn't usable. He doesn't look like a Bo, and when you find out how to spell it, it sort of halfway pisses you off somehow. He probably ought to go by his initials, except they're B.M.

"You don't look like no Bo to me," the cowboy said, and I could see that the next step was the spelling.

"Well, he did when he was born, maybe," I said.

"You lookin' at my hat?" the cowboy said to me. "Look away from my hat."

"Hey," I said. What I tend to do, I go along and make allowances, take people at their own estimate, take an interest in their own terms, and then I get fed up—wait a minute, this guy isn't taking *me* on board in *my* terms—and I sound meaner than I mean to.

"I got no interest in your hat," I told the cowboy. He hit me and it was like a cinder block. Don't sound meaner than you mean to to somebody who punches cows. I went staggering back.

Not many people know that Leonard fought in the Golden Gloves. At 127 pounds, and he's the only person I know who fought in the Golden Gloves because his mother made him, but still. Leonard was right there, popped the cowboy three times *bimbimbim* and then threw up on him. Leonard can fight, but he can't drink.

"Wawwrrr," said the cowboy, trying to see.

"Aw shit, I don't want to hit him now," said E.B. "Hey, y'all, evybody in here, we coolin' down now."

And Milam Maced the cowboy.

Had this little spray thing in his pocket.

Maced him *twice*. And then Maced the bartender.

Well, it's a good thing there weren't many other able-bodied patrons in there because those who were were coming. E.B. shoved the only really pressing one—the one with the squirrel—back up against the pool table and we bolted through the door, Leonard still retching while he ran.

"That was cold-blooded," E.B. said to Milam when we jumped in the car.

"*Back* out," Milam said. "*Back* down the shoulder a ways, *that* way, and then turn around."

"What?"

"So they can't see the license. Now here, take this side road. If they call the police they'll give a description of the car."

"Ouuuugh, you better do it," Leonard said. "Ouuugh."

"Yeah, shit, he's right," I said. My head was still ringing.

E.B. did it, but he didn't like it. "We'd've sorted that out. I had to shove that man, he mighta fell on his squirrel. What you carryin' that spray shit for?" he said.

"I told you we should go to G. Williker's," Milam said.

★ AUG. 26, 1993

"SUBORDINATES soon learn to waste no words in confabs with her," I read aloud to her this morning from *Newsweek*.

"Mm."

"Do I waste words?"

"Mm."

"Am I beginning to sound like a wife?"

"Mm."

She was doing her yoga.

Phone rang, I answered.

"Ms. President, your call from Colonel Qaddafi."

"Mm," I said.

"Cleeemeen-tine, I am ti-yurred of that woe-man."
"Just a minute," I said. "C, I believe this is for you."
"Who?"
I mouthed the syllables silently: Mo-am-mar.
She came down from her headstand.
"Guy . . ."
"I was just leaving," I said.
Hmmmm.

★   ★   ★

C and the flaky colonel, cooking something up. That's the difference. I am not cooking anything up. I just chat with stiffs. That is
my social set now, stiffs. Except Gorbachev. Gorbachev was good.
But, then, he is out of power.

★   ★   ★

I could have a better attitude. My behavior during the inauguration,
for instance, was not impeccable. I realize that. But I had a solemn
covenant to uphold: I had promised my children that at the moment of the accession of the first male Second Lady (that is to say,
at the moment President DaSilva finished his oath of office), I
would do something befitting the moment. And I happen to have
mastered the art of making a lonnnnng, thinnnnn, untraceable, just-
audible-enough-that-everyone-within-twenty-feet-can-hear-it-but-
just-soft-enough-that-no-one-ever-quite-need-mention-it fart
noise without seeming to move a muscle. All that happened was
that the assembled notables all flicked tiny little glances around at
each other in a certain surreptitious way that only my children
appreciated—Jackson unbent enough to admit that he enjoyed it
too.
    "Guy," C said after the ceremony, "it didn't occur to me to make
you promise not to do that."

★   ★   ★

I suppose it was even more awkward for the DaSilvas, having to
pass the time of day with the Bushes, under the circumstances—

except I dare say George was chipper enough. When isn't he? But neither C nor I can make small talk with military men, and there we were with her opposite number, General Colin Powell. To me it was a hollow gesture on Bush's part, chucking Powell into Quayle's abdicated slot just so the Republicans could claim they'd appointed the first black veep. But Powell was quite pleasant, mentioned C's father, and we both liked his wife.

And I'll have to admit it was inspired of C to reappoint Powell to her vacated veepship after she became President. Who better than the former chairman of the Joint Chiefs of Staff to help push through the radical leaner-meanerization of the defense budget? And Mrs. Powell is very good at presiding over White House teas. I just wasn't up to White House teas. Actually I proposed to C that I might rethink the whole tea concept, deformalize it, introduce some levity. . . . But after the inaugural fart noise, she didn't trust me.

"Guy," C said, "there are going to be ladies from Wichita Falls and Terre Haute and Spartanburg who have been dreaming of attending a proper White House tea all their lives, and I do not choose to have them reduced to tears on the East Lawn during the administration of the first woman President."

So the Second Lady, Mrs. Powell (with experience as a general's wife), has taken over that sort of thing and is very good at it.

As a matter of fact, the veep question was the last one (aside from my urging of a Medal of Freedom for Bo Diddley) that I tried to put any real input into.

"We're not running for reelection, right?" I said.

"Right," C said—though you can trust an elected official's answer to that question about as far as you can trust a reporter's to "You're not going to print this, are you?"

"So we're not balancing the ticket, are we? We're not trying to appeal to people we don't find appealing ourselves."

"Right," she said, but I could sense I was already losing her.

"And we want somebody who will be working with you closely, will in effect be your mate."

"Um-hm."

"And, you'll excuse me, but two women in the same kitchen doesn't work, right?"

She looked at me levelly.

"Now. You're not going to be able to turn the Reagan economic legacy around in three years. What you can do is do some things that haven't been done before. In this case, appoint a kind of vice-president we haven't had before.

"Okay. We haven't had a black vice-president. I spoke with E.B. today on the phone. I like to keep in touch with the soul of our movement. Because you remember if I hadn't met E.B. in jail . . . And I brought this matter of the vice-president up to him, and he first wanted to know whether it was by any chance going to be him, and I said no, he didn't like office work. Then he wondered whether it was by any chance going to be his brother the Reverend Micah, and I said no, maybe UN rep or something but not vice-president, because that is what you told me you had already told the Reverend Micah. Okay? And then E.B. said he felt that the truth was that he felt black men weren't ready to be second in command to women. Liable to be leaning too far in the direction of proving that they weren't taking any shit from her, next thing you know there's another coup attempt. 'And we'd fuck it up,' he said, 'and that would look bad. Then too, white people fuck it up,' he said. 'That last bunch was very white as I recall, and they fucked it up.'

"So E.B. was tending back toward the feasibility of a black veep, but in a speculative vein that you might not find particularly helpful.

"So let's focus on my personal bias here. We are talking about a man who will be your mate. So, as your husband, I suggest a man who is liberal, good company and gay. Barney Frank."

"Guy," she said, "that's kind of funny, but it is not all that funny to someone who is actually a politician. Barney Frank doesn't want to be some kind of symbolic vice-president, he's a legislator. And I'm—I actually have to *do* this, you know? I have to be President."

When did she get to be actually a politician?

And why didn't I ask her that question?

Because—you would think you would feel free to ask your wife a question like that, but would you?

No.

Suddenly she's actually a politician, and that makes sense to the newsmagazines or something, but how about me? But if I were to put it to her like that, it would push us further apart. Me the wienie, she the *macher*.

I take her point, about Barney Frank and all. She's right, of course. But where's our camaraderie?

"C," I said to her, "this has just happened to us. It's happened to both of us." And I came up short for a moment, because that is not the way I talk. I regrouped and pressed on:

"I don't want to sound silly to you, but I feel silly. Don't you feel silly at all?"

She started to smile but then god damn, she said no.

★   ★   ★

Hey. If she can be in cahoots with Qaddafi, why can't I make a fart noise?

And if what happened at the moment of *Clementine's* accession to the presidency was an act of God, then surely he will forgive me the vulgarity of my small gesture at the inauguration.

★   ★   ★

That conversation with E.B., though. He was forcing it, like when we first met in jail. I had already asked C what kind of job we could offer him. The Secret Service provided driving and body-guarding.

"He could be your personal aide," C had said.

"What would he do?" I said. But toward the end of that phone conversation, I put it to him: "You want to be my personal aide?"

"Naw, man. I went to Orangeburg a couple years, you know. Played ball."

"Huh? Yeah, you told me, quite a few times. 'E.B. around end, forget it my friend. Feet gettin' busy, *whoof* where is he?' "

"That's right. But I did go to *class,* too, some."

"E.B. What do you think I'm offering you, a job where you go around in a white jacket? I don't know what you *would* do exactly, but—"

"Not what I'm talking about. You ever studied *Huckleberry Finn* at a *black* college? I did. I ain't interested in being old Jim on the raft, man."

"E.B., get off my case."

"I ain't on it. I'm on mine."

"Hey, you know C trusts you."

"I know that. She *love* me, man. I'm going to miss working with
y'all. But I've got binnis to tend to. Come down see us down here."

"Okay. I don't really want a personal aide anyway."

"Didn't think you did."

"But, I mean . . . I'll give you my secret number here. We can
confer frequently by phone."

"Yeah. That'd be good. Listen, Guy. The way President DaSilva
got killed, man—you know, people ain't even *joking* about it. Just
saying, 'Just one of those things, I guess.' 'Just go to show you.' Just
go to show you *what*? It bothered people, man."

"Yeah. It was so *funny*, I mean *dumb*, I mean *ridiculous*, that it was
horrible in a new kind of way. But . . . I guess it *was* just one of those
things."

"Onh-honh. Well. But. All these modern weapons today. Send
a laser beam cross the light-years. You don't think somebody could
ballisticize a fish?"

★ **AUG. 27, 1993**

THE UPSIDE OF DaSilva was his sense of how money ought to
be spent. The downside was his lack of compunction as to how it
should be made. It was he after all who engineered the acquisition
of Disney by McDonald's—*which meant that McDonald's owned the
Muppets.* When Disney bought the Muppets, to begin with, I ranted
around the house for days, dismayed that neither of the kids shared
my outrage. Jackson had already come to think of the Muppets as
capital assets, Lucy had already dismissed them as sentimental.

All those hours the three of us had spent with Fozzy Bear and
Kermit and Miss Piggy and Gonzo and the Swedish Chef and "Pigs
. . . in . . . Spaaaaace"! The Muppets weren't a marketing strategy!
Which is what everything becomes when corporations swallow each
other in the name of "efficiency." What corporate efficiency means
is nothing odd, no loose ends, no sparks—everything reduced to
the blandest common denominator. If corporate marketing had
designed Clementine's hair (or DaSilva's, for that matter), it would
be constituted of some laser-flocked, immutable material originally

developed for spacecraft insulation: as fused and gistless a perfect mop as Snow White's. (The Disney version. Is there any other version now?)

So it did not thrill me to hear the details of the first major event of the DaSilva-Fox administration. That ill-fated joint venture with the Chinese.

"We're going to China!" C informed me.

Sounded good so far. I had even been pleasantly surprised to learn that the new head of the Communist party over there was not only youth-oriented but an admirer of multinational corporations. I figured if anybody could throw some real kinks into megabusiness, the Chinese could. I adopted an attitude of guarded optimism.

"What will we have to do over there?" I said. "Do I have to wear a suit?"

"We're going to be the honored guests at a banquet on the Wall of China, hosted by Li Pung himself."

"Li Pung lizards! I'm game. Bird's-nest soup—no, no, *fried whole baby birds*—and monkey brains warmed in the skull. Don't worry, you know me, I like to try strange food. I ate armadillo once. Okay, maybe I'll be on the verge of gagging a couple of times, but there'll surely be sesame noodles or rice vodka or something to chase the fish eyes with. I'll do the American appetite proud."

"Well, it's not going to be Chinese *food.* Not at the Chinese end. The dinner that the President is hosting over here, on the South Face of the Capitol, will be Chinese food, and my Chinese counterpart will be the guest."

"And we, on the Wall of China, will be eating . . . ?"

"There's a McDonald's-Disney tie-in. No taxpayers' money will be spent. I know, I know, but you know DaSilva, and—"

"Oh, no! Not me! I may be a writer of facetiae, but at least they've never had a *sponsor.* I wouldn't even write for the L.L. Bean catalog. And may I remind you that McDonald's-Disney is the same corporation that just bought *Country Monthly* and slick-upscaled it to the point that no honest American could ever stomach going back to writing for it? I refuse to take part in a McDonald's promotion. Wait a minute. Does that mean the *food* . . . ?"

It did.

Two weeks later, there we sat at that huge banquet table on the

Great Wall, eating suet burgers and those skinless, absurdly uniform French fries, and posing for pictures with Mickey, Minnie and the first family of China. We had flown for 43,000 hours, waved hello to 43 billion people, climbed into a Mercedes, popped into a hotel for a few hours' sleep . . .

Yes, we had been intimate. We had done it in China. And it had been good. "You want to rock and roll, Ms. Veep?" I asked her. "Or do you prefer 'Veepiatrix'? It is time we worked this out, because I want to pay you the respect of your office. Maybe you would respond to 'Your Heartbeatawayess?' " (Little did I realize.)

Well, on the way over in Air Force Two (which we had also did it in, which was why my mood was as good as it was), we had viewed my favorite Chinese movie, *The Shanghai Gesture*. C gave me a wonderful impression of Gene Tierney as the doing-her-darnedest-to-be-damned white girl in that movie, saying:

"You can call me what you like, as long as you give me something with a cherry in it."

C knows I like that movie stuff. She likes it too. She could have been a movie star I bet, if she'd gotten into that business earlier. Maybe she's a little too gawky in a full-length shot, but so were Dietrich (well, let's forget that comparison, though C does a wonderful rendition of "The Laziest Girl in Town") and Garbo. That would have been an even crazier life, though.

I guess.

"Oh . . . Guy," she said, squeezing me fiercely with her arms and at the same time giving me gentle, rhythmic soft-lipped kisses on the side of the neck as we bent all our middle weight into each other, bristle gristle skin and juice, "I'm . . . doing . . . what . . . I . . . want . . . to . . . do."

"So . . . am . . . I," I said, which was true right then.

But not the next morning.

Like I say, there we were on the Wall with the Li Pungs and the Mouses. We hadn't had a chance to see much of China—traveling like that is worse than being on a package tour. Well, we did drive past two people in a park with badminton rackets keeping twenty or thirty shuttlecocks aloft between them at once, which was impressive. But our sightseeing was scheduled for the next day, so we never had it.

Oh, I saw an old man sitting in the park with a covered bird cage in his lap, and I asked about that.

"He keeps it covered," the escort said, "so not to embarrass his neighbor, whose bird may not sing so sweet."

If it had been my country, I would have asked whether it weren't possible that the old man was bluffing, that his bird was dead in there, that he didn't have a bird at all; but I was determined to be diplomatic.

Which wasn't easy when the first man I met on the Wall shook my hand and said, "You are Southern humorist. I am Tung Lo [or something], Chinese humorist." Oh, shit, I thought. And then he welcomed me with a nigger joke:

"Two old boys [more like *o'rd boyees,* actually, but I won't try to render the accent] standing on overpass look down. Pickup truck going by underneath. A black person sleeping in back—"

"Yes, yes, I've heard it!" I said as convivially as I could. There are limits.

As I say, there we were on that extraordinary structure about which Richard Nixon is alleged to have remarked, on his first sight of it, "Gee, that's a great wall"; there we were scarfing Big Macs, in the company of a Mickey and a Minnie who spoke in Chinese accents and a man who was taking the peril back out of Cathay . . .

Oh, shit, it was horrible. I guess it was better than being at the Capitol—no, it was worse. Because god damn, there we were so far from home, and suddenly such a mess was in my sweet wife's lap.

Prime time in the States, ten A.M. in Beijing (which may be prime time over there for all I know), the world is watching. I hate being on television. I would have sold a lot more books in my day if it weren't for the fact that TV drives me into a shell. I tend to keep glancing at the monitor and trying to change my expression, always a split second too late. But being beamed into the homes of countless who-knows-whoms makes Clementine feel, if anything, more live. Thank God.

And we're sitting there on the Wall of China, eating schlocky takeout, watching television. I looked around, and there was China. As far as the eye could see. China. It's amazing how all you have to do is fly forever, and you can just *be* somewhere. Like *China.* And this . . . wall, stretching off into the distance (whatever distance means, in this day and age, it still means something when you see that wall) like a dragon. And we were all sitting there watching ourselves watching ourselves, for a while, and then watching the other banquet watching itself for a while, and back and forth, on television.

I don't remember what DaSilva was saying from his end of the simultaneous hookup. Going on about money bringing people together, common purpose, so on, and then—straying blithely from his script into inelegance as was the poor likable son of a bitch's wont—he took it upon himself to quote from musical comedy.

"There's a great American show being revived in Washington right now, Mr. First Secretary, called *Hello, Dolly!* I attended that show last night. I was struck by something that the star of that show says:

" 'As my late husband Horace Vandergelder always said, "Money is like manure—" ' "

And that's when the fish hit him.

The last word of the forty-second president of the United States was *manure*. (Nobody ever mentions this, just as nobody ever remarks upon the fact that the commander of the American ship that shot down a civilian airliner in 1988 was named Will Rogers and the news came in on the Fourth of July.)

He never even got to finish the quotation: "—it doesn't do any good unless you spread it around."

Hey, manure is good stuff, in its place, but it didn't make this particular act of God any easier to take.

It was C who made it seem like a part of real life. We were watching the monitor, but we of course couldn't tell, any more than anybody else could, that the President had been hit by a fish—as if that would have clarified the situation. All we could see was, he'd been hit violently by something and had gone down.

I was thinking, "What th'????" With maybe some faint thread of speculation along the lines of, "He said *manure* at the dinner table and somebody threw something at him?"

Clementine started talking. She knew she was miked; she took charge. She was the Hindenburg radio guy and America's instantly-on-alert second-in-command rolled into one.

"Jo," she said. Poor Jo had leaped to her husband's side like me toward Turtle's pistol, quicker than the Secret Service. "Jo DaSilva. Can you hear me? Is the President hurt?"

And, well. It was the greatest television of all time, of course. Like most great television, it was deeply regrettable; but there it was, live—Jo looking into the camera as if into Clementine's eyes and saying, "Clementine, oh my God, I think he's dead."

They liked each other, those two women. Still do. That helped. But it hardly redeemed the situation.

What can I say? It was awful.

And C was great. From China. Not knowing what in the fuck, or I should say heaven's name, had gone down. Talking the nation, the world even, gravely but somehow lightly up out of dread and travesty, like an air controller talking a blinded pilot down. But sounding like one of us, one of us viewers, which indeed was all she was at the moment, we were all in the same boat; but she was a viewer with presence—the first TV-generation President at last. While we watched people on the scene scrambling and casting about, she went on for what seemed like ten minutes, but I guess was two minutes, talking calmly, never coming anywhere near an Alexander Haig "I am in charge" number, just making it plain that the first woman president of the United States, whatever you might think of her politics, had the heart of a mother elephant, the we'll-see-about-this edge of a dance-hall gal, and a voice that could make almost anything better. As other faces started to appear on the screen, she continued to hold things together. I would watch her in person for a while, and then—I couldn't help it—I'd watch her for a while on the screen. It was a little like watching a great-faced woman tennis player in close-up, rooting for her to pull this thing out against the odds and trusting that she would. (Why hadn't presidents ever been as convincing-looking as athletes before?) Only she wasn't looking at an opponent, with those eyes that were reassuringly (if maybe a little startlingly) deeper than whatever this was that was happening to us—she was looking at us. Or at people on the scene in Washington, officials and newspeople, asking them calmly pointed questions as if she were the international anchor. I felt like Ingrid Bergman in *Casablanca* when she said to Bogie, "You're going to have to do the thinking for all of us now." I was not, however, moved to agree with Bogart that "The problems of three people don't amount to a hill of beans in this crazy world." I never will believe that. In the course of it all she gave me two or three quick little looks that were almost winks.

I started to cry, she was so great.

I'm crying now.

★ AUG. 28, 1993

J O D A S I L V A , at her one big moment in the world's awareness, had been splattered with blood and fish. *Lordy*lordylordy. How must it be, to feel that.

Neither of us brought up that point as she passed the torch to me, but we both knew nobody would ever look at her again without remembering the way she looked cradling her husband.

Unexplained phenomena is what they call them, things like that. Toads raining down on a Texas highway is the only other example I can think of at the moment. Scientists cannot account. There were reports of three or four other fish falling in the Washington area at about the same time as the one that killed the President, but at least two of those turned out to have been planted by hoaxers—not people who were out to mess with people's minds or, conversely, to reassure people (by trying to make it look like the fish who hit the President wasn't an isolated incident, or whatever), just people sincerely seeking publicity.

Otherwise—as E.B. said, there weren't even any jokes. It was reported, in fact, that people who had SHIT HAPPENS stickers on their bumpers were scraping them off.

C showed me the classified Secret Service report the other night, I guess because she knows I am interested in fish. A porgy, or scup, approximate weight thirteen pounds (unusually big for a porgy, I'd say—the ones I've caught were three, four pounds at most), male. It was very fresh, though probably not alive after falling an estimated 330 feet in the vertical. The nearest habitat of the porgy is the mouth of the Delaware Bay, 105 miles from the Capitol. No evidence of any aircraft anywhere in the area carrying whole fresh fish, or of any aircraft at all overhead at the time. The conclusion of the Secret Service report is that there is nothing the Secret Service could have done.

No new food for thought there. Only item of lurid interest is that tests were made, porgies of various weights dropped from various heights onto simulations of the human head. I don't suppose the simulations had pompadours.

It's been awkward for all the commentators, electronic and print, none of whom can be said to have come up with any real angle, with regard to the death, itself. It would've been interesting to see Cronkite and Sevareid handle it. In the remarks of leading Democrats and Republicans, you could detect a hint of "That's about the kind of presidential death a third party would have," but just the faintest, almost subliminal hint. That's as close as anyone except C has come to anything but hollow rhetoric, publicly, with regard to the death, itself.

Everyone just proclaimed that C had shown greatness. And the people agreed. In the first polls to appear, her approval ratings were in the *nineties*.

Then that story appeared in some Iranian paper, purportedly an interview with Marilyn Quayle. Who purportedly claimed that the fish was part of a plot. That C was part of a cabal that had first overthrown the Bush administration—using Mrs. Q as scapegoat—and then DaSilva.

Nobody took that very seriously, of course. What were the odds?

The main thing is, C was magnificent. Almost as if prepared? No. Nobody could have been prepared for that exchange between her and Jo DaSilva.

Jo received me in the East Wing office. She had quit smoking, with great difficulty, after the election. America didn't want a smoking First Lady. She'd started again right after the tragedy.

She stubbed out a Virginia Slim.

"Anyway, it's a feminist brand," she said. She is more wry than her husband was.

"Guess it's unfattening, too," I said. I was referring to the *Slim* in the name, but she looked down at her thighs or somewhere.

"I haven't been eating much," she said.

"No, of course," I said, and I told her lamely how sorry I was. Well, not *how* sorry. I didn't share with her the rough analogy I had

worked up—that in this untimely succession I felt myself to be in
the position of a woman who happened to be handed the job of
center fielder for the Yankees, and didn't really want the job, and
was chatting with the man she was prematurely succeeding, who
had dreamed of this job all his life. One reason I didn't share it with
her is that there are no male-female equivalents. Any woman who
found herself in that position would probably shrug and not feel
guilty, would feel entitled, for what it was worth, after all her sex
had been through. I didn't feel entitled.

Jo, undoubtedly, didn't feel that I was either. I hadn't even campaigned hard. I hadn't wanted us to win.

But Jo was good. "I loved the little time I had as First Lady, Guy,"
she said. "I don't know how it will be for you. I'll pass on what Lady
Bird Johnson told me. Barbara Bush didn't tell me anything much,
but you couldn't blame her. She was still thinking of more things
to tell poor George. But Lady Bird came up to me at the gala and
said, 'Just remember, one: Your life is no longer your own. And
two: It never was.' "

"Was that a kind of religious statement, do you think?" I said.

"Maybe you feel it's different for a man."

I didn't want to pursue that. "All I know is," I said, "you and
Lady Bird are okay in my book. I'm sure I'll make you both look
even better by comparison." That wasn't bad, was it? Whew.

She gave me a tolerant look. I know in my soul, women are fine
people, basically. If they feel you're on their side. What if I'd had
to have this conversation with Nancy Reagan?

"Lady Bird told me one other thing," Jo said. "Girl to girl. I
guess you'll have to figure out how to apply it to your situation."

She looked at me for a moment, sort of the way family cats look
at family dogs.

"A Texas expression, I guess. She said, 'You can always tally-
whacker, but you can't tell it much.' "

I wasn't sure I entirely saw the point, to tell the truth, but I acted
like I did.

Then Jo pulled out one of those big brown accordion-file folders,
the kind that have a flap and tie with a string. "You are the first
man in history to see this," she said. "But my last official decision
is this: let the chain not be broken." She pushed it across her desk
to me.

"First Lady File," it said. "For First Ladies' Eyes ONLY. Especially not Presidents'."

Then she cried. I came around her desk and patted her; we weren't really close enough for anything else. I am not the type of person to say, "He would have been a great president," though he would have been an interesting one. His hair came to mind—I couldn't say anything about that. His and my shared interest in Flann O'Brien? Jo was better educated than her husband, but she wasn't much of a recreational reader. As a matter of fact, it occurred to me as I stood there trying to think of something to say, Leonard may have slipped DaSilva the O'Brien quote, in an effort to make me feel involved in the campaign (before the fight in Jayroe's). You never know in this business.

"You never know in this business," I said. Fortunately I don't think she was listening for words, and I think my tone was okay.

"He *loved* being President!" she said. Angry. Not at me though, I think. "He *loved* it!"

★   ★   ★

I am not going to reproduce anything from the First Lady File. Who knows, somebody might eventually read this. (Well, here's one little item I will quote without attribution: "Do not invite Esquimaux into the Conservatory.") Mary Todd Lincoln is disappointing, I am afraid: nothing hallucinatory or even indignant. The last few ladies are all pretty guarded, except Mrs. Bush in her last entry. But here and there a passage jumps out. I've brought the whole file up here to my writing room, and I thumb through it from time to time. It always leaves me thinking:

Why would people live like this?

With a few exceptions—for instance, Rosalynn Carter (and why more modern American women didn't take to her, I don't know, unless it was because she was from Georgia)—I gather they put up with it because, as Jo DaSilva said, "He loved it."

Not that they let him forget what they were putting up with for him.

★ **SUN., AUG. 29, 1993**

''G U Y ,   M A R I L Y N   Q U A Y L E is coming back. Not only that, we've worked out a formal *extradition* agreement with Libya.''

"Deal went through, huh?"

"Like shit through a silver horn."

"Ms. President! Where do you get these expressions?"

"Jealous that I don't get all my coarse sayings from you anymore?"

"Just jealous of Qaddafi. I still say I preferred him as a devil figure. Not that we should drop bombs on his little girl, but America *needs* a popinjay figure. I'd think it would be more fun for Qaddafi too. Remember how much we used to enjoy going to wrestling?"

It's true that we *said* we enjoyed wrestling because the crowds were the most integrated in America—all races, ages and genders thoroughly intermingled. But *why* was the turnout so all-American? Good guys and bad guys flailing away at each other. An alternative to war. I remember the first night we went, it was the most primal thing I'd ever seen thirty thousand people involved in together. Blood flying, tremendous thumps of body-slammed flesh, and what shouting! At one point the crowd started chanting, in thunderous unison:

"E-*GO*! E-*GO*! E-*GO*!"

And I thought for a moment, "My God, they've boiled things down to the point where the good guy is understood to be the ego, the bad guy the id—but no, that doesn't work out, because surely we are *hearing* a lot of id here, but come to think of it this sounds like a largely *derisive* chant, and yet not entirely unaffectionate, so what we are hearing must be a kind of roiling mass subconscious. . . ." It was scary, actually, and yet somehow not really hateful—and then we realized that what the crowd was doing was taunting the supposed manager of one of the wrestlers. This manager, a pencil-thin-mustached bantam with fidgety-flouncy ways, was nicknamed Ego, and he had jumped intrusively into the ring. You will never get C to admit that she studied wrestling in the interests of applied political science, but. We used to do holds in bed, full nelsons. . . .

"Guy. This isn't wrestling. Wrestling's fixed."

Oh. "When is Marilyn arriving?"

"Sunday, week from today."

"Aha! Of course. *That's* what you were waiting for. Sunday. The Monday papers will be full of Marilyn in chains—she will be coming back manacled I suppose."

"She'll be under arrest for high treason, Guy."

"Poor old Marilyn."

"Guy! Guy, you can't be on everybody's side."

"I'm not on her side. I'm just sympathizing with her for having to hang around in Libya so long while you were deciding when you needed her. The fix was in, wasn't it?"

"Guy, can't you be happy with me?"

"The Monday papers will be full of Marilyn, so there won't be much room for Dancy, if she pulls a Dancy at the wedding. You're sure Qaddafi won't double-cross you?"

"Yes."

"I am happy. Happy as a husband who has such a clever wife, happy as an American who has such a clever President."

"Guy, are you jealous of Qaddafi?"

"No, no, I'm sorry. You should be married to somebody in your business, who would appreciate your work more. I just didn't know this was going to be your business. I also didn't know Muammar Qaddafi would ever be talking to my wife while she's in bed with me."

The phone rang.

"Shall I get it?" I said. "Or would it be awkward if a man answers? You know he's probably bisexual, don't you?"

"You get it. Then we can at least be *jealous* together."

It was Jackson! Actually calling me, unsolicited!

"Dad. Hi."

"Hey, Jackson! How's school? Did you see Texas has talked Nolan Ryan into unretiring for the stretch run?"

"Yeah. His arm's too old."

"Too old? It's three years younger than either of mine. That arm

can give 'em a couple of innings of heat two or three times a week,
you mark my words."

"I guess. Dad?"

"Hm?"

"You're still not giving any interviews, right?"

"That's right. Me and Darryl Strawberry."

"Well, I wondered if you would."

"You mean—what do you mean?"

"I have a friend. And I was going to bring her to Dancy's wedding—"

"You do? C! Jackson's got a friend! *Bring* her to the wedding.
We'd like to meet her."

"No, I—Mom said I couldn't."

"Why not? C, you knew Jackson had a friend? Why can't she
come to the wedding? What's wrong with her, Jackson, is she a
. . . She's not a Republican, is she, son?"

"No. I don't know."

"You don't *know?*"

"Mom said no press."

"Your girlfriend is a reporter? What for, the *Kiplinger Newsletter?*"

"She says she knows you."

"Yeah? What's her name?"

"Sue Wicks."

"Doesn't ring a bell."

"Well, I was just wondering. I invited her to the wedding, and
now . . . If she could interview you, I thought it would make up for
me having to tell her she can't come to the wedding. I thought. But
if you don't want to . . ."

My son wants me to do something for him. How about that?

"School paper, huh? Well, that might not be bad. Even J. D.
Salinger indulged the odd schoolgirl. What's her position on older
men's arms, do you think?"

"No, actually, Dad, she's—"

"Never mind, never mind. I'll do it. If you'll promise to smile at
the wedding, and talk to your Aunt Big Sybil."

"Aunt Big Sybil is coming? What will I say to her?"

"Just ask her to name all the people in the world, living and dead,
that you're related to, and then don't expect her to make any
sense."

"Okay."

Why did I agree to do that? I wondered.

"Why did you agree to do that?" C asked.

"It's a free country," I said. "School paper, what the hell. You knew Jackson had a girlfriend?"

"I told you he did."

"You didn't; I would have remembered it. You don't even tell me family things anymore. He doesn't even know whether she's a Republican. He says she says she knows me. How would she know me? Jackson's never brought anybody to meet us before. Sue Wicks. She must not be a Thai, anyway. Not that I object to Thais, as such. But *two* Thais, I'd begin to wonder. Why do you think Lucy likes that Thai?"

"It's not the school paper, Guy."

"It's not?"

"She works for the *New York Post.*"

"Jackson is going out with an older . . . The *New York Post*!?"

"That's right. I just found that out today, I was going to tell you—we couldn't let her get ahold of Dancy. Now she's got ahold of you."

"Well, thanks a lot for keeping me abreast of things!"

"If you'd talk to your staff, they'd keep you abreast of things."

"Talk to my staff about my son. Right. Jesus. The *New York Post.* Well, I just won't tell her anything she can use. Give me credit, C, I know how to be boring. Jackson's going out with a working woman? Why didn't you tell me?"

"I did. But he was vague about her."

"As long as I avoid the lurid, the *Post* won't find any of it fit to print. The *Post* needs a decapitated divorcee or something, or it's no story. I will avoid the lurid. I am less of a problem than Dancy, in that small regard. Why are you trying to scratch your own back?"

"Mm. You know that place just under my right shoulder blade, that itches?"

"Yes, I know that place just under your right shoulder blade that itches. That place just under your right shoulder blade that has been itching since 1969, at least. I am more intimate with you than Qaddafi, in that small regard. Speaking of back-scratching."

"Mmm. Unph. That's it, thanks."

" 'That's it, thanks'? Whatever happened to 'That's it, that's it, *that's it*—ohhhhh, sugar, ohhhhhh'?"

"Mm."

"An extradition agreement, huh? Bringing Libya into international law. Well that *is* something."

"Mm."

"C, I am going to ask you something that I doubt Josephine ever had to ask Napoleon, but these are different times. Do you think I don't appreciate your achievements enough or something?"

She gave me a look that could have been an "as if you didn't know" look, but no, C's looks always have more spin on them than that. Intimacy is like a yo-yo; you have to keep some spin at the bottom, or it stops going back and forth. But you have to keep some slack at the bottom, too, so you have that little hesitation, in which the possibility of unwinding lurks. There's no savor in what's too snappy. On the other hand, when somebody just gives you a look, doesn't say anything at all . . .

"I was thinking of presenting you with a plaque," I said. "If only I were better at woodwork." No! That wasn't the way to go! Soften up! I *tried:* "You're better at gestures than I am," I said. "Remember the banquet in New York, when you were named Woman of the Year? Just before you went up to accept the award you reached down and shifted a little and handed me your panties under the table? That was nice. How'd you do it? You must have rolled them partway down just by moving around in your seat."

"When I looked at you from the dais," she said, "you gave me such a sweet smile."

Ah. "Well, hell, yes. Not only was I the only person in the room who knew you had no panties on, but I knew you couldn't have slipped them off like that unless your stockings were the mid-thigh ones with the red garters I gave you."

"And I was relieved," she said.

Huh? "Relieved?" I said.

"That you had restrained your natural impulse. I looked down, and you weren't wearing my panties over your head."

Uhh. "You noticed that, huh?" I said, smiling.

But she wasn't smiling. There was something hard in her look. I tried to soften it with my look, but a hard look kills my smile, it summons my hard look. Something went tight in me. When there is a lot of kidding in a marriage, and the kidding goes off a little bit . . .

"C," I said, "did you get a letter I sent you a while back?"

"Bikers' mama? Tattoos?"

"You didn't like it?"

"No."

"Oh. Well, I thought it . . . How come?"

"It scared me."

"It *scared* you? Why?"

"It sounded mean."

"Mean? I'm sorry, I was just—*mean*? Clementine! You're dealing with an insane terrorist and you don't turn a hair! But when I try—"

"I don't *love* Qaddafi, Guy. I don't expect him to love me."

So. I'm the overshadowed spouse *and* the one who doesn't give enough. Life is not fair.

"Uhhbbblblbluh," I said, something like that.

"Guy," she said, "be funny with me. Don't be . . . *goony.*"

That hurt.

"Goony!" I said. "What else can I be? I tried to get you to appoint Barney Frank vice-president, and you didn't listen. I tried to be myself, and America didn't like it."

"Guy, you *haven't* been yourself."

"I haven't?"

"No."

"I'm nicer than this?"

"Yes."

"Oh."

"Guy, I'm trying to *do* something. I don't want to just float along like Bush, I want to . . . make things better. I think the world is *twisted,* and when I talk on television or to Qaddafi or even make *deals* and things, I feel like I'm untwisting it a little, slowly. But when I talk to you . . . you make me feel like *I'm* twisted."

"I do?"

"Yes."

Hey. I assume that everyone is twisted. That's what I'm interested in, is twists. I want to *know* about twists.

On the other hand, I have always been interested in not being goony. Especially to C.

So I didn't say, "And you don't think you *are* twisted?"

I said, *"Do* you have any tattoos that I don't know about? Do you *want* a tattoo, one that says 'Mom,' or—"

"One that says 'Mom,' " she said in an odd soft voice, and I held her, loosely.

★ MON., AUG. 30, 1993

SITTING HERE in my workroom staring at the Washington Monument. Staring at the Washington Monument has never done much for me. Or even at the Jefferson Memorial, which looks like a breast. Jefferson was a widower. Dolley Madison handled ceremonial First Lady duties for him. "A fine, portly, buxom dame," Washington Irving called her. She did both Jefferson and Madison a world of good. Jefferson was single, and she made up for it. Madison was shy, and she made up for it.

She used snuff. But she wasn't goony.

I've been thinking. Maybe C is not as strong as everybody, including me, thinks. There's a knot in her. Everybody's got a knot, right? And can it ever be untangled? Probably not. Probably the best we can do is keep it loose. And if anybody can do that for her, I can.

C looked in.

"Yo, Ms. Prez," I said.

"Mmm," she answered. She came in and looked at my Chester A. Arthur Iroquois half-foot.

"What *is* this thing?" she said.

"My researches, so far, do not tell us much. As to Chester A. Arthur, he was widely regarded as corrupt when he took office. There was even newspaper speculation that he had a hand in the shooting of his predecessor, James Garfield. However, he instituted civil-service reform and became known as 'Elegant Arthur.' The White House was so shabby he wanted to tear it down and build a new one, but Congress wouldn't approve, so he brought Louis Tiffany in to redecorate. He also had someone replace the plumbing, which was leaking 'foul matters.' He had nearly everything in the house auctioned off. Perhaps he hated to part with this half-foot here, or it just fell through the cracks."

"Or nobody wanted it."

"Oh, no, it's too nice a piece. As to the Iroquois Confederacy, it was a league of Indian nations that had pretty much broken up—perhaps owing to nonstandard spelling, more likely to pale-face rapacity—by the time Arthur was elected. One of the principles on which the confederacy was based, when it was founded in the sixteenth century, was cessation of cannibalism. Can the half-foot symbolize a tidbit uneaten? Yet Arthur himself brought in a French chef, and—"

"Is *that* what you're writing?" she said.

"No," I said. "Maybe a footnote. Can I have a little tidbit of you? Come on. I shouldn't bring up assassination. I think about it, though. I'm sorry."

"Nobody still believes Arthur had anything to do with it, do they?"

"Oh, no, no. Arthur seems to have been a pretty good guy for a Republican. He wanted to restore the nation's peace of mind, so he made a point of being chipper—bouncy, even, in a dignified way—although he suffered from Bright's disease. Kidney pain. I know about that, from when I had that stone. Nothing worse. And wasn't very cheerful, was I?"

"You weren't, no."

"Yeah. Listen. I'm going to be more positive. I promise. You know what Chester A. Arthur did? He set up a little easel in the transverse hall, where visitors could see it, with a photograph of a beautiful woman on it, with fresh roses always laid before it. People gossiped, until someone realized that the woman in the picture was: Nell, his late wife. If *that* doesn't make you feel romantic—"

"Mm. Guy—"

"Here, let me pull up your blouse here—just for a minute, I'll tuck it back, I just want to—What?"

"Nothing. I just—I've got to go."

"*What?* I give you all this fascinating Chester A. Arthur lore, and you won't even—"

"Was he reelected?"

"He left office on a wave of popularity. He was too sick to run again, as it happened, but I think he had the sense to quit while he . . . uh. C, is *that* what you want to talk about? That, I couldn't stand. *Running, begging for votes, pleading* for the *privilege* of being *kept* in this hellhole till the *next century*? Do you realize we would be here until 2001? And what are the kids and I going to say, on the stump? 'We're not as bad as the Ferraros would have been'? C, you know what *I'd* like to do? I'd like to have more kids. I bet we could do it. C'mere. I want to make a noise on your stomach."

"I can't."

"You *can't*? You don't have to do anything, just give me access to your stomach. Hey. What's the matter?"

"Nothing."

Does everybody, in the world, say that when you ask them what's the matter and something is? If C does, then everybody does. It's not like her. I'm the one who mopes. But not anymore! I've given up moping! Chester A. Arthur didn't mope.

"Are you worried about me doing that interview?" I said. "I'll tell her about Chester Arthur. I wonder if he was a forebear of Jean Arthur."

"I'm not worried about your interview."

"What, then? Marilyn deal still okay?"

"Mm-hm. I better run."

"What then? The wedding? Anything I can do, in my capacity as brother-in-law of the bride? Your father's coming, right?"

"Mm-hm."

"Listen. I'm going to have a nice talk with the old man, finally. You and he are allies now, right? You and he and Dingler. Who'da thunk. Hey, *Dingler's* not coming to the wedding, is he?"

"Mm."

"He *is*? My Lord. Why in the world does Dancy want Dingler at her wedding? Is his Chihuahua still alive? He'll probably bring it in mummified form. Dancy *invited* him?"

"She agreed to it."

"Ah. Politics. Well, what the hell. *I want to make a noise on your stomach.*"

"Not now."

"It won't take a minute. What can be so important?"

"One of my many headaches."

"One of your *what*? You never have headaches!"

"Not *that* kind of headache. I've got to go fire the secretary of defense."

"Oh."

I guess I'm the first husband in American history to hear that one.

More to the point, that's the first time she ever pulled away when I tried to make a noise on her stomach, *f'm'PLPLP,* like you do with babies. She has always welcomed it before. You've got your lips all pooched out to go *f'm'PLPLP* against your sweet wife's still-firm stomach, and . . .

But I didn't say to her what I started to say as she left: "Next you'll be firing me."

Chester A. Arthur didn't whine.

★ TUES., AUG. 31, 1993

SHE AND MILAM and Leonard are working late on something.

So I'm typing here.

I watched C in her afternoon press conference, slick as a whistle. To see her on TV, you'd think she loved to talk over knotty questions. Not that anybody asked her any tough ones.

"Yesterday you fired the secretary of defense. Can you tell us why? And does this mean that all of President DaSilva's appointees are in jeopardy?"

"As President DaSilva said during the campaign, as I said when I became President, we need a leaner, meaner military. My daddy was career army and I know that much of what the military establishment wants Americans to believe is hogwash. Yes, we need a strong defense, but 'throwing money at the problem' does not build strength. What we have had in this country since the Vietnam buildup is an enormously bloated defense establishment which is incapable of waging effective modern warfare. In 1981 Ronald Reagan said this about domestic spending: 'Well, you know, we can lecture our children about extravagance until we run out of voice and breath. Or we can cure their extravagance by simply reducing their allowance.' I say that now about defense spending. During the Bush administration, there was much talk of defense cuts, and no action. During this administration there will be action. The American Revolution was won by smart, economical, sharpshooting men of action. Since then we have become the redcoats. Colonel Blimps. We will change that. We will have nuclear defenses, but only such nuclear defenses as we require. We will have technologically up-to-date tanks, but we will have technologically up-to-date tanks that work. As a step in that direction I am announcing to you now that the new secretary of defense on the Fox-Powell cabinet is a man with years of experience running a tough, economical, sharpshooting operation. Mr. Ralph Nader. Mr. Nader, will you come out and say a few words?"

And before the media could swallow good, Nader had said about fifteen words and Clementine had stepped back in and announced that she had no specifics yet on the defense cuts she would propose but that she would be submitting a plan that would divert however-many billion dollars from defense to a comprehensive national health-care plan.

And she's got a shot at pushing some version of it all through, too, if she can maintain this popularity. She's got no party. So both parties are vying with each other, like suitors, over which can be more supportive. Ever since that TV performance from China, she's hotter than money. When she walked off to "Hail to the Chief" you could see her hips twitch juuuuust a little bit. Hell, if she weren't my wife I'd be all for her.

But I'm going to be positive.

★   ★   ★

After the press conference I decided to don disguise and sit in Lafayette Park for a while. Maybe I could help by testing the public pulse.

Not much going on in Lafayette Park. Talked to a retired man whose project, he said, was "looking through the dictionary finding all the words meaning *involvement.*"

"Like what are some?"

"*Love* is a one-syllable example. *Friendship* is a two-syllable example. *Cooperate* is a four-syllable example."

"You skipped three-syllable," I said.

"Well, *involvement,*" he said.

"Oh, right. Got any five-syllable ones?"

"Not yet, no."

"Cunnilingually," I suggested.

"Well, now, that's a new one on me."

"Check it out," I said. "Listen, what do you think of this President we've got?"

"She's involved," he said. "I don't watch it all that much anymore, to tell you the honest truth; I'm saving my eyes for the dictionary. But if these last few men could be president, why can't she? I don't believe men with any wits about 'em want to have that job anymore. I don't. I don't want to have any job. I told my wife, I've distributed GM parts for forty-two years, I'll fix supper and leave the working world to you. She sells wordless, cordless information. Worked out some kind of computerized deal that bypasses words altogether, some way, and you don't even have to plug it in the wall. I can't begin to understand it. She's a little skinny Filipino woman with a lazy eye, but *smart?* I met her at a Rotary gathering. She's not but forty-two years *old.*"

"C-U-N-N-I-L-I-N-G-U-A-L-L-Y," I said.

★   ★   ★

Whether that view is representative, I don't know. I didn't see anybody else I wanted to talk to. Aside from the eternal protester, no familiar faces. No sign of the powdery lady or Redick. Haven't heard from him since our parting of ways. No ego-massager, Redick. Took a walk all the way down around the south side of the White House. Squirrels stick their heads out through the bars as you pass, to see if you're a squirrel-feeding type of tourist, then jump back inside. They have a *good* deal.

★   ★   ★

If it had been C instead of me in the park this afternoon, it would be Fox Park by now. "Crazy like a Fox," they're saying. My name. The wedding's in five days, and what has all this writing-for-myself amounted to?

★   ★   ★

Dinner alone, C having a working sandwich in the Oval Office. I watched our tape of *Jezebel.* Bette Davis (as convention-flouting antebellum belle Julie Bogardus) wants Henry Fonda (as her reasonably progressive-thinking Southern gentleman fiancé, Preston Dillard) to go with her to pick out her dress for the Memphis Ball. But he won't leave the conference room at the bank, where he is in "the fight of his life," something to do with investing in railroads. She gets more and more willful. He goes to her family manse and stalks up to her boudoir with a walking stick in his hand.

"Why, Pres. Banging on a lady's door. I'm scandalized at you."

He puts his stick down. Henry Fonda wouldn't hit a woman with a stick! And Bette Davis knows that. "Julie," he says, "how long must we go on like this?"

Peeved because he wouldn't go with her to the dressmaker's, she has decided to wear a *red* dress to the ball. He tells her she will wear white or else. She gives him a little kiss and shows him to the door.

"Preston," she says, "you forgot your stick."

"So I did. I forgot to use it too."

"So you did."

He leaves. And she looks . . . *disappointed?*

She sends a note to roistering, dueling Buck Cantrell, played by George Brent. He shows up on the evening of the ball, and says that seeing her in that red dress "makes me feel kind of all over." But Buck won't take her to the *ball* like that—tells her he won't "help you do something you'll regret."

Buck leaves and Preston arrives. He says they will absolutely not take one step out of Halcyon Plantation, there, until she's properly dressed. But she says, "Are you sure you aren't afraid somebody will insult me and you'll have to defend me?"

So he does take her—lets her spite herself—and of course it's a social disaster. He even makes her stay and whirl about with him on an empty dance floor, which everyone else has left in protest.

And their engagement is off, and he goes north and brings back some pasty Yankee wife he doesn't love, and he gets the yellow fever, and it's a bad business all around.

The central issue is summed up in this exchange between Preston, who hopes the Civil War can be avoided, and Buck, ready to take arm in defense of the old ways:

PRESTON: "I think it was Voltaire who said, 'I disagree with
           everything you say, but I will defend to the death
           your right to say it.'"
BUCK: "Pres, that don't make sense!"

★   ★   ★

The phone just rang and it was Dancy. She was downright convers-
able-with.

"Hi, Dancy. Your world-leading sister is still downstairs bearing
her awesome burden."

"I bet she is. You see that little swish of hers to the president
song?"

"I did. If it'd been you, Dancy, you'd've given 'em a lot more
motion than that."

"Looord, I'da been all over that stage. But I don't want to be
president, I just want to be a bride."

"I can't wait. You going to change your name?"

"*Hyyy*-phenate, darlin'. You think I could pass up Dancy Searcy-
Fitch?"

"Searcy-Fitch. Almost rhymes with *crucifix.*"

"*Guy-wyy.* You don't think I know it?"

"He's an agronomist, right?"

"From the top of his head to the soles of his feet, honey. He willlll
talk to you about improving yields."

"Improving yields of what?"

"Most anything. Soybeans. Groats. I think groats. Maybe I'm
running two things together. Oh, but especially alfalfa. He
loooooooves alfalfa."

"He a good lover?"

"Well, now, Guy, it's sweet of you to ask. He's . . . You don't rilly
want to know, do you?"

"Well, yes or no would be enough of an answer. I was just—you
asked me if I was one when we met, you remember. Knowing you,
I assume it's yes."

"You do kind of know me, don't you? You actually kind of like
me, don't you?"

"Dancy, I do."

"Guy, I'm gonna tell you. If I wasn't in the kitchen on the phone here and him out back doing *somethin'* with *sevvul hundud* pounds of peat moss, that big old soil exputt would be all over me right now, with evuh ounce of strength. And keeping an ear out to make shooah I like it. He hasn't had a *wide range* of opportunity in the past, and if I was a coconut he would enjoy husk, shell and all."

"And he's a Christian? Is he a faith agronomist?"

"No, he is not. He is accredited. He teaches at the University of Tennessee. He is a Baptist, is all. But he is a Baptist to the point that that's the main reason he hasn't had a wide range of opportunity in the past. He and I had to pray together every night for a *month* before he'd let me come across. Those were some prayers, I'm telling you, I wish I had 'em on tape. Video. Speshly todes the *eeyund.* I tell you. I was pray-*innnn, unh.* Once he saw the light, though, it was here come the bulldogs. He's sweet to me, Guy. If I was just a dear friend of mine I'd be so happy for me I'd be crying like a baby. Since I'm myself, though, I don't know. I wonder whether I'm going to hurt him. Is the God's honest truth."

"Aww, Dancy, how come?"

"It goes way back, Guy."

"You know I never have talked to you about y'all's childhood."

"Oh. Guy. You better talk to Sissy about that."

"Well, sure. But she doesn't like to. She likes to look ahead."

"She does. She does. And she has got a lot to look ahead to, too. Toot-toot. How are y'all getting along?"

"Oh, good, fine."

"You don't sound too thrilled to say so."

"Well, you know, this job she's got."

"Think she's going Washington on you?"

"Nah. Washington's going her. Dancy? You know how, you can't *ever* get angry with her? Like she's *allergic* to anger? Did something happen, when y'all were girls, that I don't know about?"

"Guy! I want to talk about mah *weddin'.*"

"Dancy! Listen! I'm going to have a party Saturday night! You and your agronomist man and—he got any family coming? Invite them. And Lucy and Jackson and E.B. and Leonard and your daddy and Aunt Big Sybil and . . . Uh, Dancy? I believe our old friend the

Reverend B. Vaughn Dingler, Sr., is coming up for your wedding, with your daddy. Now, I don't know what you—"

"Guy, I'm going to tell you something. I'm going to tell you something."

"What? Listen, Dancy, whatever you want—you know I don't want the son of a bitch around, and I'll just take it upon myself to not invite him on those grounds. I want it to be people *you* want to be there. But I thought I ought to run it by you."

"Thank you, Guy. Guy? I like you, too, Brother-in-law. And I don't mind him. I don't mind him. Anymore. I want you to invite him."

"All right. And Dancy, don't worry that we'll give your Baptist a hard time. We'll—"

"That, I'm not worried about."

★ **WED., SEPT. 1, 1993**

WE MADE LOVE late last night when she came up, but lately it's beginning to make me think of JFK and how he needed to do it every day or he'd get a headache.

Listen to this shit! What am I

★   ★   ★

Well.

★   ★   ★

Well.

★   ★   ★

What I ought to do now is—what?

★   ★   ★

Write. Right? Write.

★   ★   ★

So here's what just happened. I was sitting here writing the first paragraph above, and C came in. Put her arms quietly around me like she used to. And I flinched.

I didn't want her to read what I'd written.

I don't think I've ever *flinched* before when she put her arms around me.

Hell, I'm going out.

★   ★   ★

No, that means submitting to makeup for an hour.

What a life.

★   ★   ★

I didn't want her to read what I'd written. Though why not? I should have wanted to talk to her about it. But that's no way to broach it, by having her read what's on the word-processor screen.

Anyway I surprised her by flinching. Surprised myself. Suddenly that's the issue—why'd I flinch? I'm on the defensive.

★   ★   ★

So I said, "You surprised me." And I stood up, moving away from the screen, and held her for a moment; she not quite herself to the touch.

"What's the matter?" I said.

Second day in a row for that question.

Once when she was little Lucy asked me what was the matter and I said, "Nothing."

"Oh," she said. There was a pause.

"Is there something the matter with you?" I asked.

"*I* have a brother who has a penis. And my *father* won't let me tell."

"No," I said, "I just didn't think you ought to write it on the envelope of your Christmas card to Granddaddy."

"Welllll, bye-bye," she said.

★   ★   ★

The thing is, I've been thinking that I'd like to have little children around again. I wasn't ready for them when we had them, and they were great anyway. Now that they're grown, I'm ready for some more. I would just be in my early fifties when it was time to start teaching them to throw a ball; I'll still be able to throw then.

And I would be able to do *right* by these.

★   ★   ★

Here's what happened. "Night before last, I had a dream," C said.

"You *did*?" I said.

Because that's a first. We talked about this once. She said she never remembered dreaming anything.

"Never?" I said.

"Only sometimes that I'm—no, never."

"Only sometimes that you're what?"

"Why are you mad at me?"

"I'm not *mad* at you, I just—you *said* . . ."

By then I *was* mad at her, so we changed the subject. That was years ago.

But just now, for the first time, she told me a dream she'd had.

"I had a little baby in my arms. And rocks . . . it was like I was in an avalanche. I was covering the baby, protecting it, and rocks were falling on us. Then the whole ground under us started to come loose, but I held on. Rocks were pounding down on us and we were sliding . . . there was a cliff. The cliff was getting closer and closer because the ground was falling away. And I couldn't grab anything to keep us from going off the cliff because I couldn't turn the baby loose, and all these rocks were falling on the baby and me, and I held on to the baby and held on to the baby and the baby and I were both going to the cliff, and I tried to grab something with one arm but then the baby was exposed and I had to put both arms around the little baby again and I thought . . . I thought I had done all I could but we were *both*—if I didn't . . . And I thought to myself in the dream . . . I thought:

"I have to let the baby die."

I hugged her. "Aww," I said. "What an awful dream. Have you ever dreamed that before?"

"No," she said.

"Was I in the dream at all?"

"No, but . . . Guy?"

Uh-oh.

"Hmm?" I said. And she switched gears on me.

"You remember in the country when we only had Lucy and she was little and we'd get her to sleep early in the evening and eat out on the picnic table and spend the rest of the evening on it? That blue tablecloth? And I'd have my yellow dress on and nothing on under it and I'd be tan all over from being able to take it off and lie out during the day in the sun that way, out in the country?"

"Yes, dear, I do. *Of course,* I do."

"And we had that big huge half a watermelon one time and I sat in it and mushed down in it while you put your face down in it and ate through it all the way to me, and ate, and ate, and handed me up some chunks?"

"That was some goooood eatin'," I said.

"And then when we were making love we made all kinds of terrible jokes about seeds?"

"That was Jackson," I said. "I know in my soul that was Jackson. Not the kind of thing I can share with him, though. That's one of the things about fathers trying to talk to sons—I look at him and think about that watermelon. It's been a relief to me, that he's grown up not looking at all like a watermelon. But—"

"Guy?"

"Hmm?"

"Your vasectomy?"

"C! You want to have another *baby?* You were thinking about that last night, weren't you, after I mentioned it yesterday. What did the doctor say the chances were, if we reversed it—eighty percent? I like the hell out of them odds, sugar. Let's do it! Let's go practice now."

"Guy. I don't—I'm President. There are a million things building up. It's not a good time to be pregnant."

"Well, but if we wait till '96—You *aren't* going to run for reelection, are you?"

"No, we agreed."

"Mm-hm. But anyway, if we wait till '96, you'll be getting kind of close—it might be too late. Come on, we can work it out. The nation will love it! I've got time, I'll be the primary nurturer. It'll give me a reason not to do all this other shit."

"Guy?"

"What?" *Don't sound mad.* "What is all this about, C?"

"What I was going to say is, you need to get revasected."

"*Re—?*"

"It must've opened back up. And I need to get an abortion."

★   ★   ★

I guess that's how she does it. That, and her popularity. It's how she gets congressmen and so on to do what she wants. Springs things on them in ways that . . . what are you going to say? The dream, the watermelon . . . And then the bottom line. The way she figures it.

What if I ever laid anything like that on her like that? Forget it. There are no male-female equivalents.

★   ★   ★

And the way she was looking at me! Like a fuzzy kitten who's chewing her way through a brick wall. You surely wouldn't speak harshly to a kitten, and you surely wouldn't add one more element of difficulty to somebody who's chewing through a brick wall. *But what kind of kitten chews through brick walls?*

The kind I married.

★   ★   ★

Well, I got mad. I did. And so that became the issue.

★   ★   ★

She is bewildered.

★   ★   ★

I'm grotesquely unsympathetic to her, is the way she looks at it, when she needs me to support her in this crisis—she's in favor of the right to abortion, but she can't very well announce to a loving nation that's she's going to have one.

★   ★   ★

Just to a loving husband.
  Who got mad.

★   ★   ★

"Where will you—how will you?"
  "Here. In the White House. It doesn't have to come out that I'm having one. Women have . . . D and C's."
  "And you've already made up your mind? This is not a decision that I have a right to—"
  "Guy, I *want* to have your baby. Don't you think I do? It's not about *you,* it's—"
  "*It's not about me!? Who says it's not about me!? If it hurts my feelings, to begin with, and if it means I'll never have a baby again, then it's partly about me!*"

★   ★   ★

Her words again, I'm picking up her words and throwing them back at her. Well? What else do I have to throw?

★   ★   ★

"Don't you see what I mean, C? Don't you see my point?"
  "Guy, you didn't even let me finish my sentence."
  "*How the hell could you be going to finish it in any way that—how can you say it isn't about me?*"

★   ★   ★

She thought I would understand.

   She certainly never thought I would start banging myself on the head again like I did that time in the car going back into Dingler.

★   ★   ★

But god damn.

★   ★   ★

And then she flew to London. Economic minisummit, all-business Maggie deal, no spouses. She won't be back until Sunday morning before the wedding.

★ THURS., SEPT. 2, 1993

IT'S NOT AS BAD as when we broke up. She can't afford to break up now, of course. Except who knows, the nation might like it if she dumped me.

★   ★   ★

She hasn't called from London.

★   ★   ★

I've been chewing over our argument.

★   ★   ★

"It's not about you."

★   ★   ★

"Don't you see," I said, "that's an *arrogant* thing to say."

"I don't mean it that way, you know that."

"How do I know that? All I have to go on is what you *say."*

"I'm not a writer, I can't talk as well as you."

"Bull . . . shit. You're one of the best talkers in the Western Hemisphere."

"Guy—"

"You outdebated Jesse Jackson!"

"I was coached."

"So was he."

"I was coached better."

"Clementine! Why do you put yourself down like that? Do you realize . . . In the very process of contending that you aren't good at talking without being coached, you're outarguing me without being coached, and I'm the one who's trying to tell you that— you're *wrong,* but you're . . ."

"Okay, you're right, I'm wrong, you're the smartest person in the world."

"What? That's the dumbest . . . you're insulting my in*tel*—Wait. Wait. That's not what we're arg—what we're discussing. What we're discussing is that you said, 'This is not about you.' If *I* ever said anything like that to you . . . But I *wouldn't."*

"You are now."

"I am now what?"

"Arrogant."

"Oh, no, you don't. Don't shift the blame on me. Remember that time you insisted on playing basketball with Jackson and me and you just came flailing in after the ball and took about a nine-inch strip of skin off my arm with your fingernail and I said 'Ouch' too loud, you thought, and the upshot was that you got *your* feelings hurt?"

"No, but I didn't *mean* to—"

"You keep *saying* that! I *know* you didn't mean to scratch my arm. I *know* you didn't decide to get an abortion to hurt me. I'm not so dumb as to think that you're trying to work out ways to make me say 'Ouch'! I just want to be able to say 'Ouch'!"

"Okay, okay, nothing I say is right."

"Oh, no. Not this time. Don't you realize that all these little responses—'nothing I say is right'—don't you know that's a *weapon*? While you're cutting the defense budget, why don't you cut down on your own arsenal?"

"Guy, what does this have to do with the defense budget?"

"If you don't get my point, just never mind. Just never mind."

"I just don't understand."

"What?"

"Why you can't see that it would be hard for me to have a baby now."

"Clementine! God *damn*! I *do* understand that. I didn't *say* I didn't understand that. I said I *did* understand that. I'm trying to tell you that I'm taking your point of view into account. I'm not saying you have to have the baby on account of me! I'm just saying—"

"Guy, I'd love to have a baby for you. But I can't."

"What did I just *say*? I just *said* I realized . . . I don't expect you to have a baby *for me*. You keep saying, in effect, the same thing, that it isn't about me and you don't mean it! And all I keep trying to—C! Don't get like that! C! *Stop being such an asshole!*"

★   ★   ★.

It went something or other along those lines.

★   ★   ★

Anyway, I said that. I did. I called my sweet wife, the Leader of the Free World, an asshole.

Well?

Well, that is the bottom line.

Why?

Because I feel like such an asshole about it.

★   ★   ★

Also in there, somewhere, when I was trying to convince her that she was a good talker uncoached, I said, "How about on the Wall of China? That was uncoached. . . . Or was Marilyn Quayle right?"

Silence.

"I don't mean that," I said, "I'm just trying to make a point."
And she said, "That's a killer."

★　★　★

She just decided it without asking me. It must have been hard for
her, and she didn't trust me enough to talk it over with me. That's
how I should have responded to her, of course, if I'd been thinking about her: "Oh, I realize this must have been a hard decision,
I

feel bad that you didn't feel you could talk to me about it before
you—"

Why the fuck does that have to be my immediate reaction? Granted, it
would have been nice of me, but is that a *normal* reaction? Somebody lays a fait accompli on you and you're supposed to say, "Oh,
I realize this must have been hard for you and I wish you had
let me be more supportive while you were making this unilateral
decision"?

★　★　★

We never even got around to the question that was lurking in the
back of my small-enough-to-think-of-it-but-too-large-to-bring-it-
up mind:

Who ever heard of a vasectomy opening up on its own?

★ FRI., SEPT. 3, 1993, 8 A.M.

W H A T   A M   I supposed to do? Call up the White House physician,
who happens to be a woman—hey, I'm not saying anything, it's just
that she does. Happen to be one. Call up the White House physician and say, "Uh, just out of academic interest, what are the
chances of a—say a person had a friend who had a vasectomy eight

or ten years ago. What are the chances that it would just, by itself, at this late date . . . open back up and grow together?"?

Forget the White House physician. For one thing, she of course is in London with the President. For another thing, if the White House physician is willing to call an abortion a D and C—and hey, I'm not being antichoice, I'm just saying—then the White House physician would lie.

So. What? Well, let's see. The obvious, though extremely awkward, thing to do would be to call the doctor who performed it. But the only way I was going to go through with having anybody waving microscopic knives down there was to block out every detail, including the name of the operating physician. We never had a family doctor; neither C nor I ever got sick. She had a gynecologist. Dr. Adele Fitzer. Who is now . . . the White House physician. I could call the kids' pediatrician. "Dr. Koenig. Just, you know, hadn't talked to you in five or six years—fine, White House life is fine. Thank you, thank you, well, as you can imagine, I'm very proud of her. Yes, I *am* actually calling from the White House itself. But don't, don't—no, actually, Dr. Koenig, I wish you *wouldn't* tell everybody in the office, okay? Say, uh, just in passing, Dr. Koenig. You know anything about a vasectomy?"

★   ★   ★

Meanwhile I'm thinking things like:

I didn't *call* her an asshole, really, I said, "Stop *being* such an asshole." Which implies that she is not basically an asshole, it's an aberration. And anyway, people call each other assholes in *romantic comedies* now. I refused to go to see *On Golden Pond,* but it seems to me entirely possible that Henry Fonda called Katherine Hepburn an asshole in it. People just don't say "ya cockeyed lug" anymore.

On the other hand, when you think about it, what a thing to call your wife! On the other hand, what *are* you going to call your wife when you're mad at her? *Bitch* is kind of pale somehow. And it's invidious, in a flinchy kind of way, like *ball-breaker.* At least *asshole* isn't sexist. I refuse to call anyone *cunt.* All those hard consonants, it's the least appropriate-sounding word in the language. A *cunt* is something you drive into the ground. "One of the tent pegs is missing, honeypie, can I make use of your *cunt* for the night?"

Maybe people *should* go back to thirties and forties movie epithets. "Say, ya big palooka." From coprology to Capralogy. Also thirties and forties movie endearments: "You're swell."

But you can't call a woman a lug or a palooka. Floozy. Her father called her a floozy.

And now I have to go be interviewed by my superstraight son's girlfriend, who works for an organ of communication whose front-page headline today (Leonard was kind enough to see that I got a copy) was this:

TIE TOP COP

TO SHOT TOT

★ SAME DAY, 4 P.M.

I THINK IT WENT all right.

Hell, I shouldn't do interviews, I don't have any idea how it went.

It didn't go in any way that I expected.

I'm going to listen to the tape now. I'm in the Family Quarters by myself.

Don't suppose C is having much fun—economics with Mrs. T. Seems a bit much, though, no spouses. I could have been having a pint or two or three with Denis Thatcher. Or maybe he's the wrong class for pints. Suppose it's whiskeys, with Denis. All right. And C could be pleased with how well I get on with the other husbands.

It's going to be four nights in all, apart. We haven't been away from each other that long since before we were shot together.

God damn, I sound like a wife.

★   ★   ★

I bet Denis wouldn't call Maggie an asshole if she sat on his face wrong. Knows his place, old Denis.

★   ★   ★

That's disgusting. Okay, I'm going to cut back on my swearing. I did it with my drinking (except tonight), I can do it with my trash-mouthing.

If I *hadn't* called her an asshole I could have said to her, "Fer corn sakes, Punkin', it seems to me that old Sawbones told me he didn't just sew up my little old *vas,* in all *deferens,* he also cut it. Now, I know Mother Nature is clever, but I'd kinda like to see the *fucking X rays* on this one."

★   ★   ★

Called Lucy but she was out.
  Called Jackson but he was out.
  Called E.B. but he was out.
  Hey, it's Friday night.
  Went to my office this morning for the interview. It was like going to school after being out sick for a couple of weeks, everybody looking at you funny, had forgotten you were alive, figure you've been goofing off. Only worse, because I'm supposed to be more or less in the role of the teacher.

★   ★   ★

I should mention that Leonard, on his way to London, had somebody in his office send me a little memo. Wouldn't say this to me face-to-face, hey, we were on a newspaper together. All I get from Leonard is a copy of the SHOT TOT headline and a note, "To the *Washington* Post, you won't talk." But from one of his staffers I get this:

1. Get your "quotable quote" in.
2. You don't have to answer the question that's asked.
3. You are addressing the *public.* Don't engage in a dialogue with the interviewer.

"This may be your idea of a dialogue," C said during our argument, "but it's not."

"It's not *what*?" I said too loudly.

She didn't respond.

"It's not *your* idea of a dialogue, or you're saying unilaterally that it's not a dialogue? Because . . . Never mind."

Also, when we were arguing about whether she was good with words or not, she said, "I'm just not good at talking about what things *mean.* Why do you think you have to know what everything means? Your Iroquois half-foot there doesn't mean *anything,* and you like it. Why can't you just *accept* me?"

"But C," I said, "you just explained what the half-foot *does* mean. Which means that you're extremely good at explaining what things mean. It also means that the half-foot means—"

"Guy!" she said. "I don't have time for this."

"Well, I do," I said. I have to have *some* advantage.

She was throwing some things into a little bag. Even a president has to throw a few things into a little bag, when she's going on a trip.

"C," I said. "What if *you* were First Lady?"

"Guy," she said. "I just *wouldn't* be."

★   ★   ★

I go in, sit down at my desk. *Buzz.* I don't know how to work the damn buzzer. Punch a couple of buttons, finally holler, "COME THE FU— FOR HEAVEN'S SAKE IN!"

Woman comes in.

I try to remember who she is. I've seen her before. Some kind of aide.

"I thought you might want to tape it," she says. "The interview. Just hit this button, and then it's voice-activated."

"Yes, okay," I say. Actually no, I don't want to. Seems Nixonian. But I guess I ought to go along with the program to this extent.

"Can I get you anything?"

Is it okay to ask for coffee? No idea what this woman's job description is. Best not risk it.

"No, thanks. Just, when she gets here, send her in."

"She's here now."

"Ah. Okay. Send her in." Decisive.

She comes in.

It's the woman from the convention! The one I met with Hayes

Cotton. The beautiful one. I was too busy looking at her hair and face and cowboy blouse to catch her name. So this is Sue Wicks. She has a tape recorder of her own.

★   ★   ★

So. Let's go to the tape. My aide said she would have a transcript made of it, but I don't trust her. So now I'll just do it myself, and I will add some notes:

G: We've met before.

S: I know we have, Mr. . . . People don't actually call you Mr. First Spouse, do they?

G: People call me Guy. And this is my quotable quote. Say you asked me how I like life in the White House. Which is what everybody else asks me, so of course you probably won't. But here is my answer, anyway, which is my quotable quote: "One thing is, we get a lot better TV reception than we got in the country. But now that we get it, it's always us on it." I also have my recipe for a happy marriage to fall back on, if you want a fall-back quotable quote. There. Now the rest is all obfuscation, so far as I am concerned. You want my recipe for a happy marriage? Here it is:

   To respond to every degree of anger with just that much hurt. To every degree of hurt with just that much concern. To every degree of concern with just that much apprecia-tion. To every degree of appreciation with just that much generosity. To every degree of generosity, with just that much gratitude.

   But who can agree on the degrees? That marriage ought to be a fifty-fifty proposition, who can deny? But in practice who will ever admit that it is fifty-fifty except (sometimes, maybe) the partner who, according to the other, is getting the better of it? Perhaps the best we can hope for is a union in which each partner is able to behave publicly as if it were fifty-fifty while arguing privately that it is forty-sixty and believing secretly that it is sixty-forty.

S: That sounds canned. We met at the convention, and then I called you at your hotel and you wouldn't talk.

G :   I was in a bad mood. The President doesn't believe in
      moods, so I have to share mine with others.
S :   I hear you don't like being interviewed.
G :   That's right.
S :   Why not?
G :   It makes me feel like fodder. The fodder of our country.
      When somebody asks me a question that I'm interested in,
      I tend to want to pitch in and thrash around as hard as I can
      trying to get to the bottom of it. When somebody asks me
      a question I'm not interested in, I tend to want to say,
      "Blehh." What interviewers want is something they can use.
      They want to get a quick take on how they think I think it
      feels to be who they think I am.
S :   So, who are you?
G :   That's too deep a question for a guy like me.
S :   Are you happy?
G :   No. I'm being interviewed. What I want to know is, what are
      your intentions toward my son? [*She looked startled. As if,
      uh-oh, this is a little too serious for her to joke about.*] Excuse me.
      I'm just being silly.
[*Then she smiled a lively smile.*]
S :   I like your son a lot.
G :   Really? I mean, why wouldn't you, right? Let me tell you
      something. Shit. Shoot. I've got this tape recorder going
      and I don't know how to turn it off.
[*What I was going to tell her was something like—well, what I wanted
to tell her, in some nonreprehensible form . . . I just wanted to say some
kind of fatherly thing. My thoughts were: that when I first saw her, I
wanted to open her cowboy blouse (that part, which I believe she knew
already, I would have shared by means of just a little twinkle or something),
and this time when I saw her I wanted to say, "Good for Jackson!" I could
see now that she didn't resemble C as much as I'd thought before, but she
was striking in a similarly dark, spacey and dignified way. She made me
feel nervous and expansive, a bad combination.*]
      Well, I'll tell you this, about Jackson. When he was about
      ten or twelve, he was already a good athlete, and we were
      at a big WOT family picnic. There was a big volleyball game
      that had boiled down over the afternoon to the *serious* play-
      ers. And Jackson was good enough, he could play with us.

But several little kids trailed him into the game. And guys—
including women guys—started saying, "No, no little kids."
Because they didn't want to be stepping on them and watching them miss the ball. Jackson said if the little kids couldn't
play, he wouldn't play. And he left the game. He *wanted* to
play. He was *welcome* to play. And you know, most kids
would be eager to be accepted over the little kids. But
Jackson has this purity, which he gets no doubt from his
mother. I've never told him I was proud of him for it.
Seemed like it would spoil it in some way. But I am. He
could have played pro baseball, you know. His coaches in
school said so. But he got to a point where he didn't seem
to want to play anymore. Not just play baseball—he didn't
seem to want to *play*. Maybe he took playing too seriously.
Maybe having a father who was professionally humorous
depressed him. I don't know. He was such a crazy little kid.
Then came the eighties. Money. Anyway—I just want to say
this: Jackson might get moody. He might just kind of grunt
a lot and think to himself about debentures or whatever
business majors think to themselves about. He might say
the wrong thing or get mad or something—I don't know.
But Jackson has got a good heart. Give him the benefit of
the doubt. That's all. I just wanted to say that. I don't even
know whether you—

S: I know what you mean. But Guy . . . he does like to play.

G: Heh. Good. Have you met Lucy, by any chance?

S: I talked to her on the phone once. She's one of my culture
heroes.

G: You did? She is?

S: *She* likes to play.

G: But couldn't she play something I *understand*?

S: Get hip, Mr. Hub.

G: Yeah, I guess so. But I thought she was going to work with
children.

S: What were you like as a child?

G: Immature. I don't know. What was your childhood like?

S: Hell.

G: Heh. Um? Really?

S: Yes.

G : Well, gosh, I'm sorry. Where'd you grow up?

s : Who says I have?

G : Hm! You know, you are an amazing color. What are you ethnically?

s : Oglala-Flemish.

G : Excuse me?

s : My mother was an Oglala Sioux, she was a dancer; and my father was Flemish. He was an artist.

G : Wicks is Flemish?

s : No, Iycxx. I-Y-C-X-X. And my first name is S-I-O-U-X.

G : Well, I be damn. Sioux Iycxx.

[*This name threw me off stride. I kept turning it over and over—could this possibly be her real name? It was too strange not to be real. I learned to read at my mother's breast, with her telling me to* sound out *the words and if they didn't sound out the way you'd think they would, then that was always an opportunity to learn something odd about the language. A prickly-*looking *damn name, all those* x's, *but such a likable-looking young woman.*]

Well, that's some combination. An Ind—a Native American, and a . . . what's Flemish? Belgian?

s : It means from Flanders, which is now partly in Belgium and partly in France. The language is a dialect of Dutch. Distinguished by weird-looking words.

G : Well, I've learned something here today. Got enough for your story, have you? Maybe we could go have some lunch.

s : It's nine-forty-five. And no, I don't have enough for my story. You know, I interviewed the President at the convention. She was easier than you are.

G : Yes, she knows how to be interviewed, all right.

s : She told me about the peepeye lady. She said that's when she knew she loved you. When you pretended to be a photographer so the peepeye lady could do her stuff.

G : Oh, yeah? That's nice. In the Wishy-Wash. I'm surprised she told you that story. While I was *courting* her, you mean?

s : Yes, after you came into the headquarters there and—

G : Just like in the movie. You know the peepeye lady was in the movie, but they cut her out. It didn't work visually. How the hell could a peepeye lady not work *visually*? Hard to do her justice, of course. We couldn't find the real peepeye lady, didn't know her name. I'm kind of glad she wasn't in the movie, actually. So you interviewed the President, huh? She didn't tell me that.

s : It was before anybody knew she was going to be on the ticket. I talked to her about WOT. She probably doesn't remember talking to me—I was working for an independent weekly in North Carolina. Then we got off into girl talk. About our childhoods.

G : Really? She never talks to me about her childhood. Her mother, hymns, those pearls, but that's about all. I've always wondered about her childhood. She thinks I'm obsessed with people's childhoods.

s : Actually I guess we talked more about mine.

G : Which was hell. What was hell about it?

s : First you tell me about yours.

G : Oh, that's the way you work.

s : No, it's just that mine is kind of a conversation-stopper. My mother hit me a lot. Because my stepfather . . . my mother told me I was leading my stepfather on. That's what he told me too. He said he couldn't help himself. He said I played on his nature. "You play on my nature," he said. I didn't know what that could mean, but he made it clear that it was wicked of me, and he did things to me that I hated. He hit me too, sometimes, but usually she did that. That was considered her role. I ran away when I was fifteen.

G : Oh. I'm sorry, Sioux. [*Lord, Lord.*]

s : Well, *they didn't make me believe I was wicked.* Now yours.

G : You know, I wanted to make child abuse my pet project. But everybody said it didn't fit me. A humorist. I guess I should have taken on some project like Why Most People Look Sad. Maybe that *is* why most people look sad: child abuse is nightmarish, and yet evidently *common.* Something you'd think was utterly unnatural and abnormal, evidently *isn't,* utterly. If people commonly beat and molest little children in their care, it makes you wonder what is natural. You wonder whether it might have happened to you, even, and you've blocked it out, or whether you're married to someone, or whether it's happened to your own kids—an uncle or something, and they're afraid to tell. My kids never had any uncles, by the way. And people in history: I'll bet Joan of Arc was an abused child. I mean, even before the stake. And there's all this Freud stuff. It is my theory—actually this is Leonard Shore's theory, but I agree with it—you know, that all that stuff about Freud deciding that women who claimed to have been molested as children were fantasizing?

[*And then I went on to tell her at great length about my theories of child abuse and the culture's defense of Freud, the explicatory father. Or ugly stepfather? Jesus, me telling her.*]

And you can quote me. As long as you blame it on Leonard. His mother will love that.

s: Excuse me, uhh, speaking of defenses.

g: My father was killed on Iwo Jima just before I was born, and my mother and I never mar—my mother never remarried. We lived with my Uncle Gene and my aunt Big Martha. I don't know why my mother never remarried. She was beautiful; in her wedding pictures she looks like Vivien Leigh. She was very religious. She said she just wanted to get me raised and then she wanted . . . then she just wanted to die. She would get so unhappy. Somehow, I developed an early antipathy to Sunday school. I wish now I had just gone along with it for my mother's sake, you know, but I didn't like feeling *obliged* to go learn about perfect love. I could tell you that I withdrew from Sunday school out of premature liberalism: we were sitting there singing, "Red and yellow black and white, we are precious in his sight, Jesus loves the little children of the world," and I looked around and noticed that all us little children were white. But that just struck me as strange—why would they teach us that song, if they didn't mean it? Of course they would have said that they *did* love little black children, in their place. What got to me was, I didn't like Sunday school clothes. Also, I didn't think an American should to have to be governed by the prospect of damnation.

s: My mother used to tell me I was going to hell.

g: Really? With my mother . . . My poor mother, she told me once: "You have made my life a double-jointed hell!" An-

other time it was "a pluperfect hell." The words that pop
out sometimes. She wasn't *like* that, though. She was a loving woman, she liked to smile, and I could make her do that,
too. It made me feel good, to make her smile. She and my
uncle Gene died in a car wreck right after I graduated from
college.

Okay?

[*Another abused child—an orphan, buffeted around: my mother.*]

S: Okay.

G: I had a good childhood. Played baseball, you know.

S: Huntin' and fishin'?

G: Well, not really. Little bit of fishing, but I never went hunting. Didn't like the idea of hurting an animal.

S: I thought I'd read that your scar on your hand, there, was—

G: Oh, well, yeah, there was that one time. I dropped the gun
and it went off.

S: Not much of a sharpshooter, then.

G: Well, now, Sioux . . . I guess you're right. Though that may
not have been a bad formative experience to have with a
[*almost said a pistol*]—with a gun. Now. I'm going to tell you
what I think.

[*I think that the only time I was anything approaching a hero—deflected
an assassin's bullet, maybe—was a time nobody can know about. I also
think I was a bad son and now I'm a bad husband, but I knew better than
to tell a reporter that. And have I driven her, as they say in the thirties
and forties movies, into the arms of another man? But, then, if she's not
going to have the baby, why would she tell me about it? Is she trying to
drive me somewhere?*]

I think that child abuse is part of a broader phenomenon
that *everybody* is guilty of. Let me think of an example.
Well, this is an odd one, but I thought about it when I
read the front-page headline in your paper yesterday. TIE
TOP COP TO SHOT TOT. I couldn't bring myself to read the
story.

S: Oh, the chief of police apparently goes on caribou-shooting
expeditions or something with the father of a little child
whose body was found riddled . . . I couldn't read it either.
I don't cover things like that. I do longer thought pieces for
the Sunday paper.

G : Like the day after tomorrow.

s : Uh-huh. You were telling me about an example of a broader phenomenon.

G : You know the President loves Henry Fonda movies.

s : You know, when I met you I thought you *looked* like somebody. And that's who it is: Henry Fonda.

G : Aha. You break the tie.

s : What?

G : The President once told me the same thing. But somebody else said I looked like Darrin on *Bewitched.*

s : No way.

G : Thank you. You know, one time when Jackson was a little kid, he came up to me out of the blue and said, "Nobody likes Darrin on *Bewitched* but Samantha. And sometimes Larry." That's something I remember. I don't know why. Samantha was Darrin's wife, and she was a witch. His mother-in-law was also a witch. So were his children. Darrin represented workadaddy values in the midst of women and children who could turn him into a midget or give him amnesia at any moment. Larry was his boss. Another time, when Jackson was a little older, he came up to me and said, "Is there any job you can have where you can be home with your children, besides a writer?" I was in fact writing in my head at the time, and I said, "No. Well, sculptor." What a shi—a cockeyed thing that was to say. I should have said, "Oh, I'm glad to hear you want to be able to stay home with your children. And who knows, by the time you get to be old enough to be a father, as smart as you are and with new electronic stuff and all, you could probably be anything you want to be at home." But I didn't.

s : I'll bet he's forgiven you.

G : You know why my kids are so fascinated with early sitcoms? Same reason C and I watch thirties and forties movies—to get a sense of what our parents were like before we were born. Seeing what kinds of looks were considered beautiful then—what kinds of faces and what kinds of expressions. Was this what *life* was like, or just movies and TV? It half gives us the creeps and half charms us.

s : What about Henry Fonda movies?

G: Well, C—the President—loves Henry Fonda. The first time
    we tried out the White House movie theater—

S: I hear you'd rather watch your old tapes.

G: That's right. That was one of my gaffes, admitting that.
    Okay, I'll tell you what—you want a story? I hereby declare
    that I am not repentant about illegally copying videotapes
    for my own home use, and if there is a public outcry about
    it, why I will just go to Allenwood Prison and take my
    medicine like Haldeman and John Mitchell. Go ahead! Print
    it! The FBI knows where it can find me! Come and get me,
    coppers!

[*I can see the headline now.*

HUBBY TO FEDS:

EAT HOT TAPES!]

S: Uh-oh, I'll *never* get invited to any of your family's wed-
    dings.

G: That's all right, neither will I. You can come and visit me
    in the joint. Maybe they'll let me out of the hole for the
    afternoon and one of the squash courts will be open. Actu-
    ally, I don't play squash. Do you?

S: No.

G: Good.

S: But you saw a Henry Fonda movie in the White House
    theater?

G: Right. I'm a little hard to follow, aren't I? Well, I never said
    I was the Leader of the Free World. Actually, the Leader of
    the Free World probably *ought* to be hard to follow.

[*You know who else could have been an abused child? Jesus. Of Nazareth.
Obsession with the disembodied perfect Father, on the one hand, and on the
other, "Suffer the little children to come unto me, for theirs is the Kingdom
of Heaven." Joseph, a kind of stepfather, couldn't buy the Virgin Birth and
took it out on the child? Who preached love too pure for anybody to live
with. "Jesus thown everything off balance," says the Misfit in "A Good
Man Is Hard to Find."*]

Sorry. White House theater. We had some friends in. *Once
Upon a Time in the West,* directed by Sergio Leone. A movie
of the sixties. And lo and behold, Henry Fonda is a bad guy!

A *rotten* guy. The first scene he's in, he is gunning down kids in cold blood! Henry Fonda—*Young Mr. Lincoln, Mister Roberts, The Male Animal,* the very emblem of liberal American decency—shooting tots. (Incidentally, this movie came out in 1969, the year of My Lai.) Well, Clementine walked out. She wasn't sitting still for that—she knew Henry Fonda better than that. But the rest of us stayed. The rest of us—I can't tell you their names. But one of them was black [*E.B.*] and one of them was Jewish [*Leonard*] and one of them [*Milam*] was, you know, nothing, Wasp. Afterwards, the four of us were arguing over the movie. For some reason—listen, this is off the record. Okay?

s: Okay. [*She turned off her machine.*]

g: For some reason, I kind of liked it that Henry Fonda was a bad guy. Though I never told Clementine that. I even kind of liked it when it came out that in real life Henry Fonda was mean to his wife and kids. I certainly never told Clementine *that.* Okay, you can turn your recorder back on. So I found the movie interesting, on those grounds, though I thought it was pretty much overblown, and we were all discussing it back and forth and then the Jewish person said something like, "Gimme a break—an *Italian* western?"

   And I was just about to say, "Yeah, it's just about the kind of western a Western European would make," or something, when the Wasp guy—now, you'd have to know the Wasp guy. He has a way of saying the wrong thing. He said, "It's like Jewish opera."

   Now. You could understand why the Jewish guy would be offended, maybe. "Offenbach and Meyerbeer," he snapped. Jewish opera composers. Actually, I was surprised that he was so touchy. I'd've thought he might say, *A Night at the Opera.* I mean, it wasn't necessarily anti-Semitic for somebody to suggest that there's no such thing as Jewish opera, especially somebody who probably doesn't *like* opera. It's not any more derogatory than "an *Italian* western," actually. Okay, there's something unpleasant about it. I keep thinking about it for some reason: Jewish opera. I mean, it's not like saying "Where are all the great black tennis players," it's less obviously illiberal than that. But there is some-

thing unpleasant about it. But you'd have to know the guy
who said it. He's always saying unpleasant things. Once
when somebody quoted Cactus Jack Garner as comparing
the vice-presidency to a pitcher of warm spit, this guy
pointed out that there really shouldn't be anything disgusting about the thought of drinking spit, one's own at least,
because spit is what is in our mouths all the time. That's the
kind of thing this guy says. He doesn't *know* any better. But
what I'm getting at is, here's what I did: I leaped at the
chance to join in with the Jewish guy in going for this other
guy's throat. Like he'd revealed some particularly unspeak-
able kind of essential bigotry. And this guy, believe me, this
guy—if he doesn't have political correctness, he's got no
moral justification at all. And we went after that shred he's
got. It was, "I don't believe I'da said *that,*" only heavier. We
were *nasty* to him. Until finally the black guy said, "I'm glad
Clementine ain't here to see this. Y'all acting as hateful as
Henry Fonda."

   And then the Jewish guy and the black guy started arguing. These two are my best friends in the world [*not that I
get to talk to them much anymore*]. Aside from my wife of course.
And here they are going at it tooth and nail over Jewish
opera. And now the third guy, the guy we picked on, is
standing there looking *smug.*

[*So I hit him. I didn't tell her that. I had always wanted to hit Milam,
of course, but everybody Milam has ever met has always wanted to hit him.
Somehow or another it is one of his strengths. While you're wasting energy
wanting to hit him and knowing it won't do any good, he's making moves.
In this case E.B. and Leonard turned on me now, because I hit Milam.
E.B. sat on him until we were sure he didn't have Mace on him—even
Milam doesn't take Mace to a Henry Fonda movie in the White House—
and meanwhile both E.B. and Leonard were yelling at me. By the way, I
never hit anybody before I met Clementine. And now I have hit her father
and her, so to speak, right hand. Who will I hit next?*]

   This guy that we picked on was not a likable guy, but we
knew that already. It was something about the way he said
it, "Jewish opera." He didn't say it like an insult, or even like
a wisecrack. He said it so innocently. That was the thing. As
if he'd come up with an interesting analogy, for a change:

his defenses were down. You would never think of this guy as innocent. Maybe we didn't *want* to think of him as innocent. Or maybe it bothered us, deep down inside, that Henry Fonda had slaughtered little children, and we had to take it out on somebody. But I don't think so. I think we were liberals hungry, like everybody else, for an innocent victim. Maybe it stimulated us that we'd just seen Henry Fonda shooting little children.

[*And ever since then Milam has looked at me as if to say that I don't have any more friends, or moral justification, than he does.*]

I don't know what I'm saying.

s : A broader phenomenon.

G : Right. A broader phenomenon, a broader can of worms: *innocence abuse.* There's something about innocence that fascinates people and that people can't stand. People poke at it to see if it's real, *hurt* it to see if it's real. Destroy it to see if it was real. Innocence *attracts* people and *scares* people. Innocence invites abuse.

Because innocence is also power. Innocence abuse works both ways. Innocent people take advantage of their own innocence. Not only don't they know better, they don't *want* to know better. Ronald Reagan, for instance. Sometimes other people are charmed by that, and sometimes they lash out at it. Why is it so sweet to watch two little children playing nicely together? Because we know how strongly little children are inclined to pick on each other, take advantage of each other, pretend to know more than each other, tell each other there's no Santa Claus. Meanwhile struggling to hold on to their own innocences—to the extent that those innocences are to their advantage—by hook or crook. And parents! The other day [*in disguise*] I saw a grown woman, her face contorted with rage, staring down at a little two-year-old kid with dirt all over his mouth. She was *screaming* at the kid, "What in the *hell* do you think you're doing?" The kid probably hadn't given it much thought, actually, but now he was, he was trying to come up with some kind of lie to stop her screaming.

Some people lash out at their own innocence. Clementine doesn't. She takes good care of hers. She has partly inherited and partly worked out for herself a combination of military innocence, fundamentalist Christian innocence and sixties innocence that is one powerful combination. How it is that she *holds on to* it, keeps it from being crushed—I don't know. I've known her twenty-four years or so, and I believe she had worked out how to hold on to it some time before that. I believe it was treasured and threatened early, and she dug in her heels.

s :   Well. Hm. I'll have to play that back and think it over.

g :   I will too. It probably doesn't make any sense. You've got me talking out beyond where I know whether I'm making any sense or not. Anyway, she's a great woman. And after twenty-four years with her, I still wish I could grasp what it is about her that *makes* her . . . Hm.

[*The sinking feeling struck me that what I wanted to do, maybe, was to lash out at it, explain it away.*]

s :   That combination you mention. People have been surprised that the President has been able to appeal to the military, and the Christian Right, as well as what you might call sixties idealism.

g :   That's right.

s :   That she's been able to rally her father's support, and even B. Vaughn Dingler's. Behind programs that you would have thought they'd oppose.

g :   That's right.

s :   How do you think she's been able to do that?

g :   Mystery to me. Well, I think Dingler probably saw some advantages to moving a bit to the left—climate changing, for one thing, and he's been doing all he could to distinguish himself from those reactionary televangelists who got in trouble back in the eighties. Probably been lucky for him that he's not a pretty face—that radio following, day in and day out, is less volatile than TV. And he's never been connected with any scandal at all. He saw that going along with the Crowe County Compromise was good for him in the long run. He ain't dumb, Dingler. And nobody ever got hurt being on this President's side. You'll be surprised, some of the people Clementine can get the support of.

The General, I don't know. Giving his daughter a hand.

And he probably has no use for all those Pentagon whipper-snappers.

[*Leonard's theory is, "Hell hath no high horse like a general retired. Especially a general pushed into retirement without that third star he thought he had coming."*]

The General and I aren't exactly confidants.

s: Well, I guess I've asked you everything except whether you've stopped beating your wife.

G: Huh. I have a friend [*E.B.*] who told me once, "I have sometimes felt almost like hitting a woman, but there never was any *place* on any of them that I could bear to hit." A sexist remark, no doubt. I believe I can say that this President is unbeaten since *I've* known her. Unbeaten and untied.

What did she tell you about her childhood?

s: It was off the record.

G: And you abided by that?

s: Yes, I did. She made it clear up front. And she'd already given me plenty to write.

G: You're not even going to tell *me*?

s: No.

G: Like I say, she knows how to be interviewed. She told you about the peepeye lady, eh?

s: No innocence abuse in that story.

G: No. No.

Unhh. What a lot of . . . malarkey. How did C get mixed up with a person like me?

But god damn, I mean Gee Whiz. I was just *thinking*. A little Freudian half-slip there, "my mother and I never mar—." But I guess that's normal enough.

Sioux. When I was a kid there was a brand of honey, Sioux Bee honey. The trademark was a little Indian girl bee.

And I was telling *her* about child abuse. She could have jumped on me like Leonard and I did on Milam.

"They never made me believe I was wicked." I wonder if that's entirely true. Hold on to your hat, Jackson.

I figure, let her have some fun with the video-crime thing. Not even the *New York Post* can make any sense out of "Jewish opera."

And I got through the whole thing without a word about Qaddafi or Marilyn. Or pregnancy.

We'll find out Sunday morning. I wonder what C told her, aside from the peepeye lady. The peepeye lady. Lord, Lord.

★　　★　　★

I called her in London, before I sat down to write this.

She hasn't called back.

★ SAT. AFTERNOON, SEPT. 4, 1993

SHE STILL HASN'T CALLED. Well, the time difference and all.

E.B. called back. He's coming in tomorrow for the wedding. But it hasn't been the same.

Hell, it's *going* to be the same. At the party tonight. Lucy and Jackson are coming, and Leonard is going to be back early from London, and we'll all get to meet Dancy's faith agronomist. I hope he can stand to watch people drink.

The General is coming and he may even bring Dingler. I told him, whatever you think, General.

Hell, I wish even Milam would be there, but he's not coming back till tomorrow morning with C.

I be god da—I be switched if I'll be jealous of Milam.

We wondered whether Milam even had sex till he got married, and even then we couldn't be sure.

Anyway, C and *Milam*?

And it couldn't be anybody else, if it isn't me.

When would she—anyway, she's not two-faced, she wouldn't—I mean it's just been since she realized she was pregnant, or since that dream, that she's not been herself with me physically. I can't believe—

She left her earring on the bedside table. You'd think she'd've missed it and called about that.

No, here's what she did: she left it for me.

★ SUN., SEPT. 5, 1993, 12:30 A.M.

I WOULD LOVE to sit here all night and write about the party.
What a party!

But what an end to it.

I guess I will sit here all night and write, write right up until it's
time to get dressed for the wedding. I don't want to see anybody
between now and then.

★   ★   ★

It was E.B. who said C felt at home with the grievously cheerful. So.
That's what I'll try to be.

★   ★   ★

I rented out Spratt's. Usually Spratt's closes at six-thirty. Old man
Spratt—I didn't even know there was an old man Spratt until I
called—didn't want to stay open for a private party, but I talked him
into it. Although I hate talking people into things.

"It ain't safe this part of town after dark," Spratt said. "Only
people around here then up to no good. I'll be here till all hours
cleaning up. I got to be ready for the breakfast crowd. Now, if the
President was coming, I'd make the effort for her."

"Mr. Spratt," I said, "the President won't be there, but this is
for her, and me. And the President's sister. And there'll be—the
President's press secretary will be there, and the President's father,
General Searcy, you know? And the President's—our kids."

"Let me tell you something, Mr. Fox. You going to be there?"

"Well, sure. I'm giving the party."

"You going to be in disguise?"

Uh-oh.

"I hear you been coming to my place sitting around here in
disguises. You don't want to be seen here before dark, that it?"

"No, Mr. Spratt, no. I just can't enjoy going out when people recognize me, they—"

"Who else coming? Photographers, TV?"

"No, no, definitely not. Nobody from the media. Well, uh, maybe one; that is, you know Reverend Dingler on the radio?"

"Dr. B. Vaughn Dingler, Senior?"

Uh-oh. "Yes, but he probably won't—"

"Now, if Dr. Dingler comes, I'd be proud to meet him. I listen to his progum every day of my life."

★   ★   ★

Dingler showed. He and the General together. You'd call it a drop-by, I guess. The General standing there like a thick-bark tree, Dingler a little more wrinkled but basically still as little, pink, plump, unfelicitously mustached and ungodly-looking as he was when I first saw him outside the Dingler jail. To think that C was reared, more or less, by those two guys! Also, for a few crucial years, by her mother, of course. Well, I was the host, and I was determined to see that everybody mixed nicely. Knit the wedding party together so that maybe when C got back people would be telling her, "You know, Guy's party got this whole thing off on the right foot." I was determined, for one thing, not to let Dingler's voice penetrate the atmosphere the way it had at our wedding reception.

But before I could get over to the odd couple, Holman Fitch, Dancy's agronomist, planted himself right in front of them.

Holman stood like a tree too, but like a tree lifting its leafy arms to pray. I don't know how Holman can keep his arms in the air so much. As soon as he starts to talk he has them up and out, wide, forty-five degrees above the horizontal, and he's waving his hands at the end of them. He'll pause and they'll begin to drift downward and then he'll start talking again and they'll go back up. There is something engaging about it. Doesn't seem as though there would be, but there is. Something *almost* flouncy about him, but not really.

Dingler stepped forward (disengaging himself from the fulsome Spratt) to shake Holman's hand. In that fluid-whiny voice that caused people's heads to turn, Dingler: "Well, now, I understand you are ve'y much a follower of our Lord and Savior Jesus Christ. Now, we all feel ve'y—" Holman looked Dingler square in the eye, lifted his arms and said, without the slightest hint of sarcasm but with no oily elision of consonants either, "Verily verily."

It reminded me of Milam looking pointedly at Mabry Packard's booger. And yet I liked it. For these reasons:

1. I liked Mabry Packard and I don't like Dingler.
2. It wasn't innocent. That is, it was artful enough to seem artless.
3. It worked. I don't think Dingler's voice will ever sound so creepily powerful to me (or to Dancy, whose face lit up) again.

It left Dingler with his mouth hanging open. Not a pretty sight, but not one for the party to linger over, because Holman's priority was the General. He looked away from Dingler, took the General's hand and squeezed it with both of his, which were as big as the General's, and said:

"Sir, I am glad to meet you and to shake your hand. Sir, I ask you for your daughter's hand. I should have done it sooner but I wanted to do it in person. Sir, I cherish your daughter Dancy and I intend to see that she is safe and happy. And General, I hope you will come visit us in Knoxville as often as you can."

All the while looking the General right spang in the eye. Dancy stood close against Holman's side, and Holman lowered his right arm and gave her a squeeze. I believe the General liked the cut of his jib.

"Dancy looks happy," the General said. "You're to be commended for that." He didn't say it grudgingly, the way he said it twenty-four years ago to me. Holman brought his left arm down and, good Lord, gave *the General* a squeeze. The General actually looked into Dancy's eyes and both of them smiled. I thought: "What does Holman have that I don't have?"

And then—I missed the transition—Holman had his arms up and was waving his hands and telling the General about alfalfa.

"You see, we don't need winter-hardiness in the South, so we can use nonhardy cultivars and concentrate on resistance to root rot, rust and downy mildew. You see, they can get eight, nine, some-

times ten cuttings a season in California, and my thinking has
been . . .''

The General and Dancy smiled at each other *again*. I was glad to
see it. I missed C. Lucy arrived with Ng, Jackson with Aunt Big
Sybil, Leonard with a fax machine; and Holman was the life and
soul of the party. Telling everybody how happy he was to meet
them and how happy he was to be in love with Dancy. It would have
been embarrassing if it hadn't sounded just as heartfelt as, and no
more heartfelt than, his disquisitions on ''the world's most valuable
forage legume—it goes back two thousand years before Christ!
And if we could find a way to cross it with timothy, which . . .''

What Holman had was a line of talk and a perfect willingness to
use it. Manure is no good unless you spread it around.

Meanwhile Dancy was off on her own saying, ''Isn't he su-
weeeeet?'' Sounding like herself only unfrantic.

''Holman is good, Dancy,'' I told her. ''I believe you have met
your match.''

''See?'' she said. ''All these years I *hoped* I wasn't crazy.''

''You still think you might hurt him?''

''Hunh-unh, no. After I talked to you on the phone the other
night, Guy? I decided to talk to Holman about it. I went into
eh-yuvrythang—about how I had been kind of wiiild? And that I was
afraid I was a crazy and hurtful person? And his big old ahhhhms
kept edging up, but I kept talking—and he listened, he did, he
looked right at me and listened and his ahhhhms would edge back
down. But then they'd start edging back up again. And then I
finished, and they shot up into the air and then he wrapped them
around meeee, Lawud . . . have . . . mercy. And he just told me he
loved me and quoted me a Bible verse: 'Oh Lord, how manifold are
thy works! In wisdom hast thou made them all: the earth is full of
thy riches.' And then he told me he loved me forever and was
hungry. So I rustled him up some supper. He chopped, and told
me about how cucumbers are related to the loofah.''

''That's good. That's *good*, Dancy. Are you going to keep on
being a Christian performance artist?''

''Yes, but not so much in art circles anymore. More locally, in
churches. And probably . . . I don't think I'll be s' earthy with it?
I'll save that for Holman. I just wish I could give him a baby. But
I'm afraid I'm past it, Brother-in-law. Holman's late wife couldn't

have them. He could've married a little young fertile girl, Guy, but he loves me. Maybe we'll adopt some babies. Do you think Lucy and Jackson will come visit me more if I'm settled down?"

"I wouldn't be surprised." Jackson was being really nice to Aunt Big Sybil, taking her around and introducing her to everybody. Lucy and Ng were laughing with Leonard. "And you and Holman come to the White House."

I felt good for Dancy, but my heart wasn't as light as I wanted it to be.

If I were more like Holman, I was thinking, I could handle First Hubbyhood maybe. Holman knows what he is about.

And so, I guess, does Lucy. She came over and hugged me and she was wearing an outfit that I would spend more time describing if I were feeling as good, now, as Lucy made me feel a few hours ago. It had spangles on it, and little bouncy . . . coil things. She had these loose vwoopy coil things on her dress that vwoooped slowly up and down.

"What are those things on your dress, Lucy babe?" I asked her.

"Sproings," she said. "Slowww sproings."

And I remembered when she was a little bitty girl she swirled around in a new dress and said, "This dress woos out great."

"Woos?" I said.

"Yes, when you twirl around it goes *zeeee.*"

I also remembered Jackson coming up to me and saying, "I want a cowboy shirt with floodsh on the back."

"Floodsh? What's floodsh?"

"They hang down in the back to keep you company so you won't die," he said.

"You mean fringe?"

"Yes," he said. The things that people come out with.

"You look better in sproings than anybody in the whole wide world," I told Lucy. She kind of juked up and down to put them into action and then swept back into the midst of the party. My party. I love the idea of getting different people you know together. But it seems like they so often have nothing in common.

If C were here, of course, they'd have her in common. But she's thousands of miles away and dealing with foreigners and probably upset about me. I called her an asshole!

Leonard had gotten stuck with Aunt Big Sybil. I went over to them.

On the way I crossed paths with Ng. "Hello, Guy," he said. "How's the book coming?"

"Ng," I said, "that is the worst question you can ask a writer. Do I ask you whether you've learned to tune your guitar yet? Just kidding. Did you and Lucy listen to that John Lee Hooker tape I sent you?"

"Actually, Guy, I've been listening to a lot of Barry Manilow lately. It blows me away."

"I see. Ng, come with me for a minute."

"She was my mother's wife's father-in-law," Aunt Big Sybil was saying, "or is that right? Now, she was a Naseworthy, and the Naseworkers were all—"

"Aunt Big Sybil," I said, "I think you and Ng would have a lot to talk about. His Barry was a Manilow."

"The *Nawth* Ca'lina Mandevilles, or the Munsons around Charlotte?" she asked Ng, and I eased Leonard away. He had on what I would say was probably an Armani jacket. He frowns whenever he sees me now, because I get on him for dating a TV weatherwoman, which he says is not a conflict of interest because she doesn't cover politics. He used to fall in love with wary-looking art critics and sociologists, for their personal problems, but now he doesn't have time.

"So," Leonard said a little wistfully, "it looks like this thing is going to work out okay with Brother Soil Scientist."

"Dancy seems like a different person."

"All she ever wanted was for somebody to see through *part* of her but not all—see through her defenses and settle on her self. I keep seeing better-and-better-looking women, and if just one of them would say to me, 'Leonard, I see you,' with *bright* eyes . . . it would give me such a lift."

"See you and raise you," I said. "How's C? I haven't talked to her."

"I think Maggie would like her much better as a thick Republican man, but they're getting down to cases. And everybody else over there thinks she's the best thing since Marmite. Last night she was in a pub teaching the flower of the British press corps—as bloody-minded a crew as I ever want to meet—the words to 'Oklahoma'! I met your counterpart over there, by the way, Denis. He's a joke."

"Yeah, well . . . 'Oklahoma'!"

"You know, '*Ohhhhk*-la—' "

"I know. How's Milam?"

"The last thing I remember, she was raising a pint and crying, 'Up the Welfare State! Up, womb-to-tomb!' "

" 'Up, womb-to-tomb,'?" I said.

"Yes. I dare say Maggie had some thoughts to share with her today after the tabloids hit the stands, and I dare say C didn't turn a hair. She's getting to be almost scary, she's so hot. I wish there were some way for her to cross-examine Marilyn Quayle personally on TV, it would be the best thing since Perry Mason. How's *Milam*? He's no different in London than anywhere else. Old Milam, the Jew-hating self."

"Oh, come on. You know, I was just thinking, there's a lot of pressure on Milam. And nobody ever acts like they *like* him, at all, and that's bound to—"

"*Like* him?"

"Does . . . anybody?"

"Well, you know C, she sort of likes him I guess."

"I know he's always been in love with her."

"*Milam*? Nahhh. Milam's got just what he wants in the romance department—a cowed wife and kiddies to come home to every now and then for half an hour. C's too controlling for Milam."

"She is?"

"Sure. It's like he's advertising and she's editorial. I think they regard each other as necessary evils. So, speaking of tabloids, how was your session with the *New York* For Crissake *Post*?"

"Well, you'd better be prepared for a bit of a flap about video copying," I said.

"What? Ah . . ." He waved a hand dismissively.

"Well. But you've seen the way Milam looks at her. And she can be so soft-hearted."

"Huh. She didn't get where she is by being soft-hearted. Now, *Dancy* is soft-hearted. I think Dancy got to be the way she is—was—from absorbing a lot of shit as a kid, protecting her baby sister. C demands protection. She has that obvious ambivalence about it, though—a guy like Holman, she'd run from. But, I'm telling you?"

"I've got to take a leak, I'll catch you in a minute."

Does C talk to Leonard about her childhood? It may be that I just don't know anything about anything. I probably don't even know what *my* life is like, much less my wife's. And if not Milam, then who . . . ? Leonard? And now, the British press corps. I can't go through life wondering stuff like that.

I went into the men's room. Holman's brother Lloyd, tomorrow's best man, was in there at the next urinal. I had met him just briefly.

"What line of business you in, Lloyd?" I was looking at the graffiti: THE NEW WOMAN IS THE OLD MAN, and under that, THE NEW MAN IS AN OLD WOMAN.

Lloyd zipped up and went to the sink. "I'm in the healing game," he said. I thought, uh-oh, maybe Dancy has fallen in with a weird crowd after all, but then he added, "Urologist."

And my plumbing seized up. "Uh-oh," I said. "I'm not going to be able to pass a drop. I swear, Lloyd, that my stream is usually quite strong for my age and I even still sleep through the night. There's kidney trouble in my family, but don't get the idea, from my performance here right now, that it has kicked in with me yet; I've never had any trouble with ur . . ."

Then I realized my opportunity.

"Uh, Lloyd," I said. "So that entails, what? Like vasectomies?"

"That's my specialty," he said. "I've done about six thousand of them. Yep, microsurgery, you know—get in there working with instruments you can hardly see."

"That so? Well, I . . . know a guy who had a vasectomy quite a few years back and he was wondering the other day—I was just wondering, have you ever had any of your vasectomies . . . open up again?"

"Nahhhhh," he said. He didn't seem to be at all the same kind of guy as Holman. "Sure, if it's not done *properly,* if you miss a vas or something, then those little boogers will make their way through. But if your friend's been sterile for quite a few years, then he doesn't have a thing in the world to worry about."

"Oh," I said. Oh. "No chance at all."

"You can't say *that.* Never say *never.* But the odds of both ends of a properly closed vas working their way open and then joining up again are, oh, a hundred thousand to one."

"What? *Yeah?* A hundred—it *has* happened?"

"Most anything can happen. Yes, there are cases in the literature. But there are cases in the literature, also, of kidneys growing hair and teeth—woops, forget I said that."

A hundred thousand to one! Short odds, compared to the likelihood of a peepeye lady showing up at just the right moment in a washateria, or of a fish killing a president! "Yaaaaay!" I said out loud. Lloyd gave me a clinical look. I began to pee like a horse.

★   ★   ★

"Jackson!" I said when I came out of the Men's. "That's some lady friend of yours, that Sioux. She's a pistol. I like her. When are you going to bring her around the house?"

"Ah, I don't know."

"Well, do."

"I will."

"Did you talk to her? Did she say I was a block off the old chip?"

"She said she thought it went well."

"Hey, Jackson. It's good to see you. You're good to be nice to Aunt Big Sybil. Old Holman Fitch is all right, isn't he? He must've been a heck of a defensive basketball player."

Jackson laughed a little. Anybody else, I'd've had to explain what I meant—you're supposed to keep your hands up in the air on defense. Jackson, Lucy, C—all of them get different jokes, all of them get jokes nobody else would. Jackson and I notice a lot of the same little things in the same ways. I looked across the room and saw Lucy and Ng giving each other a smack.

I said to Jackson, "A Thai is, like, kissing your sister."

"Dad," he said. He *got* it, and all, but he also said, "What is it with you and Ng? He's a good guy, and a good musician. You're down on him because he's a Thai?"

"I don't even think he *is* a Thai," I said. "Ng is not a Thai name."

"What does it *matter*?" Jackson said.

"I'm down on him," I said, "because he took Lucy."

"*Took* her. *Daaad*," Jackson said, disgusted. He looked at me with something of the glare that his grandfather has given me. The glare that I no doubt have given Jackson. In Jackson's eyes I could see that glare wrestling fiercely with sweetness. "Win," I said to the sweetness. "Win." But I couldn't say any of this to Jackson, aloud or even, it seemed, with my eyes. I am a guy. So is Jackson. Guys get gradually better over the generations, I believe, but only gradually. The previous generation feels an instinctive duty to make sure of that.

"Come on, gimme a break," I said. "Tell me about Sioux Iycxx."

But then E.B. arrived. "Jackson," he said, "I haven't seen you in a while, my man. You got taller than your daddy." They did some kind of handshake that made me feel better about Jackson. E.B., on the other hand, talks with less and less of an accent, which is to say he seems to have less and less fun talking. Well, he's a businessman now.

"Jackson can dunk," I told E.B.

"Dunk a what?"

"What do you mean, dunk a what? He can dunk a regulation basketball."

"Can," E.B. said. "Jus' *now*? Jus' now that he's six foot thirteen? My boy Junior could dunk when he was three."

"Feet or years?" said Jackson. Jackson's good. Jackson can talk shit.

"Both," E.B. said. "You think you smart as Junior, don't you? Course Junior doing them drugs now. Junior ain't so smart since he been doing them drugs. Probably can't jump neither. Don't you do them drugs, Jackson. Break yo' daddy 'n' momma's heart."

"E.B., I didn't know that," I said.

"Y'all got enough to worry about up here," he said, looking away. "Hey, Leonard. And there's that Dancy over there. You remember me? Yeah. You lookin' good. Lemme meet this 'gronomy man. I talk to you about it later, Guy."

"E.B.," I said, "if he starts talking about buckwheat, don't take it wrong."

"Heh. How come it's wrong the way I *take* it? Last time I was at a White House do, two different statesmen start telling me about catching browns. Go to China, catch them browns. Go to Arizona, catch them browns."

"Well, that's brown trout, I guess."

"Statesmen ever talk to you about catching browns?"

"Okay, E.B. If anybody says anything with the wrong color in it, just sing out and we'll call a special session of the Supreme Court."

"Yeah. Which got nobody black on it again."

"E.B. We've got a black vice-president. Well, Jamaican-American. What's got into you?"

"I'll talk to you later, man."

Why can't everybody be happy? At least for a while? Or at least when I'm on the upswing myself, as I was at that moment, although it wasn't as if I were out of the woods.

I was losing my upswing. But then Holman stood in a chair, shot up his arms, and did an angronomico-scriptural recital of some force:

> "From the Book of Mark:
> "Behold there went out a sower to sow:
> "And it came to pass, as he sowed, some fell by the wayside, and the fowls of the air came and devoured it up.
> "And some fell on stony ground, where it had not much earth; and immediately it sprang up, because it had no depth of earth:
> "But when the sun was up, it was scorched; and because it had no root, it withered away.
> "And some fell among thorns, and the thorns grew up, and choked it, and it yielded no fruit.
> "And other fell on good ground, and did yield fruit that sprang up and increased; and brought forth, some thirty, and some sixty, and some a hundred.
> "And he said unto them, He that hath ears to hear, let him hear."

Leonard leaned over to me and said, "Jewish opera."

"New Testament, though, Leonard," I said.

"Di-viiiii-sive," he said.

Then Lucy and Ng jumped up on a *table*. Ng with his guitar.

"Is *ev*'vih'buddy *hep*-pih?" Lucy sang out. I don't know why she couldn't just say it in a normal cheerful way, but anyway she was in good spirits.

"My Aunt Dancy's gettin' married!" Lucy sang out. "To a man whose motto is, 'Don't Treat Your Soil Like Dirt.' "

That was something Lucy had just made up, I feel sure, but everybody cheered.

"And now we of The Soft Spots," she said (I guess that's the group's name now), "want to do a little song for you about marriage. Here we go."

This is what she sang, in an exaggeratedly weepy way to a tune evocative of "Wildwood Flower" and Ng's I suppose adept but weird accompaniment:

"Dear, what did I do that so upset you
To cause you to attack me with a knife?
I'm just barely glad, now, I met you,
Knowing you have taken my life."

Uh-oh, I started thinking.

"Even underneath this mound of earth, it
Frequently occurs to me to say
That ev'rything considered it was worth it.
I'd marry you again any day.

Then again sometimes I wish we'd waited
Or that, instead of stabbing, you had cried.
I can't very well be elated
Now that it's sunk in that I have died.

Dear, what did I do. . . .

Live and learn, they say, but I don't know, dear,
That's easier for them and you to say.
Lying all alone six feet below here—
Never mind, I'm with you anyway.

But it would make me feel a good deal better
If I could rise and hold you, or at least
Find some way to tell you in a letter:
It's hard to be the one who is deceased.

Dear, what did I do. . . ."

And people somehow liked it! The same people who had just
finished liking the Bible! I would have been afraid they'd be offended, but not Lucy. She may have my nose, but she's got her
mother's nerve. And then. My girl got even better.

She's up there dancing on the table. Wearing sproings. She says,
"My Aunt Dancy is getting married! This is a dance to my Aunt
Dancy."

Ng went into some kind of downright tunelike thing that I must
admit had, for an Ng number, almost a kind of lilt to it, a strange
deep-structural lilt, and Lucy started moving, sproings a-sproing-
ing, and singing:

"My . . . Aunt . . . Dancy.
She . . . ain't . . . fancy.
Nooooo-o, o-o."

Those were the only lyrics, but Lucy did them over and over and never the same way twice somehow, and while she did them she did a dance.

It was Dancy. The exaggerated mannerisms—which had not been much in evidence tonight, but we all knew them—that were somehow compelling and somehow upsetting and . . . Lucy had turned her aunt into a dance. I wish I had it on videotape. It was amazing. Lucy up there doing her aunt. It had an aesthetic distance to it and yet it was fond.

And Dancy hopped up there with her. Unrehearsed. The two of them doing Dancy together. Dancy could do herself, all right. Nobody's ever said Dancy couldn't do herself. But doing herself on a table up there with Lucy, she was herself in her glory.

My girl. I had never cried while writing before in my life, until the other night when I wrote about C on the Wall, and now I'm close to doing it again. Partly because I know what is coming up next.

Just when I was thinking, "Well, I could watch Lucy and Dancy doing Dancy for another hour or so with pleasure" (which probably meant that I would have been ready for something else within half an hour), Lucy and Dancy together, with that instinct musicians have, decided to wrap it up, and they hugged each other and Dancy jumped down and Holman picked her up off the floor and *held her in the air* with those arms of his. Held her right up over his head.

Crowd goes wild. Everybody whooping. I gave a party where everybody whooped. E.B. too, which is a strange thing to say, because ordinarily E.B. would have been whooping before anybody else. Anyway he was whooping now.

"And I just want to say," Lucy said, "that I hope Dancy and Holman stay together as long and as nice as my mom—who I wish was here but she'll be here tomorrow—and my dad. Now I want to sing you a song that is traditional, except my dad wrote these words. You know what I mean, Dad. Come on up here and help us sing 'em. Jackson knows 'em too, come on up, Jackson."

"Nahhh," Jackson and I both said, but they talked us into it.

"Well," I said, from the table. "The thing is that the song 'My Darling Clementine' . . ."

Cheers went up.

". . . is a great tune, but the lyrics are about a Forty-niner miner's daughter going down to the water with some ducklings and falling into the foamy brine and drowning. Who needs that? And we all know that if the Clementine we know fell into foaming brine with some ducklings, she would turn the whole thing into a . . . This is your line, Jackson, if you recall."

"Pot of soup," he said.

Whoops from the assemblage.

"The only thing our Clementine has in common with the one in the song," I said, "is that they both have sizable feet. So, with that in mind, when the kids were younger and C was doing great things with WOT, I wrote these lyrics. And the three of us sang them for her one evening when she came home. All of y'all sing along on the 'Oh-my-darlings.' "

And Ng kicked into the tune—Ng can play a normal singable American tune!

"In the movement (see the movie)
Back in 1969,
Moved a lady demonstrator
By the name of Clementine.

> *Oh my darling, oh my darling,*
> *Oh my darling, Clementine.*
> *Disobedience forever—*
> *Civil always, Clementine.*

Light she was and like a feather,
Though her shoes were number nine.
In the fog she'd wear her frogfeet—
Very cagey, Clementine.

> *Oh my darling, oh my darling,*
> *Oh my darling, Clementine,*
> *You will stay afloat forever—*
> *Never worry, Clementine.*

Drove she Dingler to distraction—
Call for Dr. Frankenstein.

While involved in risky action,
She fell into foaming brine.

> *Oh my darling, oh my darling,*
> *Oh my darling, Clementine.*
> *Spunk and getup keep her head up,*
> *Hallelujah, Clementine.*

Ruby lips upon the water,
As she paddled, doing fine.
Just a-chuckling with the ducklings
Was our buoyant Clementine.

> *Oh my darling, oh my darling,*
> *Oh my darling, Clementine.*
> *Don't she have a lovely breaststroke—*
> *Lordamercy, Clementine.*

Got the Pentagon surrounded
With a blooming picket line
Made of roses—Holy Moses!
Onward peaceful Clementine.

> *Oh my darling, oh my darling,*
> *Oh my darling, Clementine,*
> *From the sands of Iwo Jima*
> *To the shores of Clementine.*

In my dreams she used to haunt me
Till she made her surname mine.
Now I'm right behind her panting—
Can't keep up with Clementine.

> *Oh my darling, oh my darling,*
> *Oh my darling, Clementine.*
> *I have lost my heart forever—*
> *I ain't sorry, Clementine.*

What a mover, and she'll never
Ever lose her special shine.
Thank the Lord she wore her flippers
When she slipped into that brine.

> *Oh my darling, oh my darling,*
> *Oh my darling, Clementine.*
> *WOT a joy you are forever,*
> *Thing of beauty, Clementine.*

We all had tears in our eyes up there. Fucking *Ng,* even, looked sort of halfway engaged.

I wish C had been there. Hell, I wish her father hadn't left early. We should have pressed him to stay. But he had to go somewhere with Dingler.

"If Lucy and Ng don't look out they're going to go mainstream," Leonard said. "I can see them being good campaigners."

Uh-oh.

The party went on for a while and was good.

Then Jackson was helping Aunt Big Sybil get herself together to leave, chatting her up very nicely, and he said, "Aunt Big Sybil, why do we call you Aunt *Big* Sybil?"

"Well son," she said, "you know your Great Aunt Little Sybil was your grandmother's cousin. Your daddy's mama's cousin. Now you never knew your daddy's mama, she was run away with by my husband, your Great Uncle Gene, when they had a car wreck and was killed."

I was only halfway listening to this, and then it registered.

Huh?

"Uh, Aunt Big Sybil . . . ," I said. "Did you say Great Uncle Gene and Mom were *running away* with each other when they died?"

Aunt Big Sybil blinked and looked at me, and said:

"Now dear you heard me, I was saying your Aunt Little Martha was your mother's cousin, and I didn't say one word about your Great Uncle Gene, I was talking to Jackson. Gene wasn't your great uncle, he was your uncle, you know that. Why that man taught you to throw a ball."

"Yes'm, I know that, but—"

"Don't make me talk any more, Little Guy," she said. Her lip quivered like a little girl's, only slack and wrinkled. She always called me Little Guy, because my father was Guy Senior. Her poor old lip quivered and I thought, Lord have mercy, I believe I knew something about this but never let it be conscious until now.

"Well," I said faintly, "this is a night for revelations."

"Ohhh, Land," Aunt Big Sybil said. "I haven't read the Bible for years. I don't think it applies right much to what happens." Then she looked away, buttoning up her coat.

Only Jackson and I heard all this. I didn't really quite look at him and he didn't really quite look at me, except a little bit, out of the corners of our eyes. I stood there feeling less like a father, which, though embarrassing, was good for both of us, I think.

Jackson went off with Aunt Big Sybil, and the young folks were going to meet at some club, and Dancy and Holman and his relatives were leaving, and Leonard was telling Dancy good night, and E.B. came up and I thought, "Maybe I could talk to E.B. about all the things I have learned tonight," but I looked at him and realized he had other things on his mind.

"I'm sorry about E.B., Junior," I said.

"Shouldn't've called the boy Junior," he said. "Or if I was gon' be a Senior I should've been a pusson of statue like my brother Micah instead of somebody who just has a fine time yassuh yassuh with one and all."

"E.B., this is not like you."

"Exackly what I mean. Like me is: here I is, bodacious and whoopty. Like me is ignoring what's wrong."

"That's not true. You were always the one who told me what was actually going down, wheels within wheels."

"Yeah and that's why I wadden the one doing anything about it. Me and you, Mistah Guy, we just grinned, we didn't struggle."

"Shit, E.B."

"Well, it's true. I see my boy getting sucked into the drugs. And I see lots of little black children in Dingler still got they navels pooched out from not enough of the right things to eat. And I see shit just like it was, only I got a beer business."

I was trying to think what to say.

"Well, I ain't going to go on being that way," E.B. said. "The drugs? The same old shit? You know who's still running things? Same old Fordyce Knott. And I'm going after him. Me and Doc Stockley. Tell President C I'm sorry I can't stay for the wedding. I ain't in a mood to party anymore."

"You mean you're—what are you saying, E.B.?" I started to follow him but Leonard came up. Looking grim. Something had come to him, over the fax machine he had brought or something: Leonard was hooked up all kinds of ways.

"Setback time," he said.

"Hey Leonard, listen," I said, "we got to talk to E.B. here," but E.B. was out the door. Well, then, maybe I could tell Leonard about . . . But Leonard wasn't listening.

"It was bound to start happening sometime. Your man Redick?" Leonard said to me. "His talk show tonight, by some kind of phone hookup which I have to give him credit for, his guest was Marilyn Quayle. She is *not* coming back. And she has repeated over National Public Radio the things she said in that Iranian rag before: that C, not she, plotted to overthrow Bush-Quayle and then DaSilva. And did you ever hear anybody on NPR who didn't sound perfectly rational?"

Then the fax machine started humming, and what it delivered to us was a facsimile of the front page of the bulldog edition of the Sunday *New York Post,* which consisted mostly of this headline:

> MS. PRES VICTIM
> OF CHILD ABUSE?
> HUBBY "WONDERS"

Then came the story, a clever tissue of half-quotes from me and allusions to things C must, for some reason, have let slip in that old off-the-record interview.

"By Sue Wicks."

★ SUN., SEPT. 5, 1993, 5:30 P.M.

WHEW.

★ MON., LABOR DAY, 1993

I BELIEVE I'm sufficiently rested now to wrap this up.

I got up from this chair Sunday morning—still no call from C—gave the old half-foot a pat for good luck, climbed into my tux and hoped for the best.

After we saw the story Saturday night I tried to explain the interview to Leonard, but the more I talked about it, the more I realized it was a hard interview to explain. It didn't help that I kept saying, "She told me it was spelled with all these *x*'s. Sioux Iycxx. Like the Indian. S-I-O-U-X, I-."

"What are you *talking* about?" Leonard said. I told him it was all on tape and yes, I had probably said literally all the things she had quoted me as saying but I certainly hadn't meant to hint what the story hinted—that C was blackmailing her father and Dingler into supporting her by concealing their involvement in some sort of child-abuse story in her past.

"Your office has a copy of the transcript?"

"No, but it's on my machine in the quarters. I'll print you out a copy. You'll see, I didn't—"

"Guy, when are you going to learn how to do things? Oh, fuck it," he said. "I'll send somebody to pick it up. I've got to see about the Marilyn story. Oyoyoy."

Which is what my mother used to say. Not "Oh, fuck it," but "Oyoyoy." She probably picked it up from the radio, Molly Goldberg or Mrs. Nussbaum. Mothers. Our Judeo-Christian heritage.

★   ★   ★

I was an usher.

Rose Garden.

I hate wearing a tux anyway.

No sleep.

I went out there before anybody else had arrived and poked around in the grass, digging up little spots where packed-in dead grass was keeping the green from coming in. I used to do that a lot in the country, dig around in the turf with my finger and think. A groundskeeper gave me a hurt look. My lawn is not my own.

I went back inside. I didn't want to hang around chatting with the rest of the wedding party any more than necessary.

The phone rang. C calling from the airport?

"Schmuck."

It was Leonard.

"Leonard," I said, "I was up all night."

"What do you think I was?" he said. "I read your transcript. With notes. And I would like to repeat something I said a little earlier: Schmuck."

"Yeah, well."

"Just tell everybody the story does not reflect your views. Thank God nobody believes anything in the *New York Post.* The transcript was interesting, though. All that innocence shit."

"Yeah? I just got started talking, and there was a lot on my mind—"

"Milam doesn't have any *innocence.*"

"Leonard, everybody's got some innocence."

"Maybe. It's a mystery. Did you hear about Tommy Hugh Cranch?"

"No."

"You *remember* Tommy Hugh Cranch? And the Mystery Object?"

I did.

The *Beacon* had a Mystery Object contest. A greatly blown-up photograph of some small aspect of some common object—could be any common object in the world—ran every day, until some reader guessed exactly *what* common object it was a greatly blown-up image of some small aspect of. Then there was a new Mystery Object.

The prize was fifty dollars' worth of men's or women's wear. In those days in Dingler you could get, say, six white shirts for that.

Could be any common object in the world.

When I left the *Beacon* for Clementine, the photograph that was running had been running for ninety-three days. Most people mailed in their guesses but some showed up in person, came right in the front door with a light in their eye and said, "Is it a pressure-cooker valve thang on the top that goes *flibbedy libbedy*?"

"Is it a dog's lip right through here with the picture turned sideways?"

"Somebody's little, you know, little line that goes from their lip to their nose, one of 'em? One of those . . . little lines?"

"You know the place on a Rototiller where the shaft meets the housing?"

"Pum-granate stalk."

And Tommy Hugh Cranch, the photo editor and the only person at the paper who knew what the Mystery Object was, and who resented having to come out in person to field every bad-eye Tom

Dick and Harry's speculation, would look at each of these hopeful readers as if any fool ought to be able to tell it wasn't that, and he'd say, "Nope."

"Nope."

"Hunh-unh."

"Naw."

And go back irritably to his office.

And the guesser would go away deflated.

And every time one of them would leave, Leonard and I would turn to each other and say—

What he and I said together then over the White House phone:

"Whut *ee*us that thang?"

And we'd holler back to Tommy Hugh Cranch what Leonard and I hollered together then over the White House phone:

"Don't die, Tommy Hugh!"

★   ★   ★

"So. Who ever knows what you're going to be nostalgic about someday. Right?"

My man Leonard. "Right," I said. "What did happen to Tommy Hugh Cranch?"

"He *did* die. He hit a fish."

"He hit a fish?"

"He's out in a motorboat off the Gulf Coast somewhere. He's going along forty miles an hour with his head up over the windshield, looking for a place that looks like fish, and he catches one. A flying fish. Between the eyes."

"Well, I be damn. Old Tommy Hugh. Is there going to be a *wave* of killer fish?"

"As to that, who can say?"

"And did the Mystery Object . . ."

"Yep. Died with him."

"Thank you for sharing that, Leonard. But I know who *my* Mystery Object is."

"Hey, last night—I didn't say she was *cold*-hearted."

"No, I know. I know that."

"Actually a setback or two may be good for her. She was getting awfully full of herself. Up the welfare state, for Chrissake. But Guy.

Schmuck. Don't give any more interviews. Unless it's to a licensed psychopathologist. Somewhere out there, there's a fish with your number on it."

"Huh. Leonard, listen. Confidentially, *is* there some kind of—"

"I'm not telling you shit confidentially. You got better access than I do. Are you still my best friend?"

"Yeah. Hey, Leonard. I was talking to E.B. last night—"

"I don't want to *know* now. I don't want to *know* now."

I felt a little better. I went back outside. Didn't want to be derelict in yet another regard.

Nobody said much to me. It was Dancy's day.

Lucy went by in a hurry, she was going to sing, but she stopped to be daughterly. "Is everything okay?"

"I think so. That story—it was all out of context, babe."

"I know, the press."

"Well, now, I wouldn't want you to generalize about the press. But in this case—"

"Just weird 'em out, Dad," she said. "That's what I do. And don't worry about Mom. Mom will deal."

Mom will. But with me? I kept looking for her to make her entrance. As it happened I was extending my arm to Aunt Big Sybil when Dingler arrived.

"You think you know ve'y many things, Mr. Fox," he hissed. "But you don't know *one thing.*"

I just didn't even answer him.

Whup-whup-whup we heard the chopper coming in.

Jackson was an usher too. "Dad. The interview, what . . . ?"

"She kind of sandbagged me, bud. She told me her name was Indian-Flemish. Why she did that, I . . ."

"It is. Oglala-Flemish. S-I-O-U-"

"It *is*? But her byline."

"She doesn't spell her byline that way. No one would believe she was real."

"Oh. Well." One little mystery down, thirty-three thousand to go. I felt tired.

"Dad, listen, I'm sorry if—"

"Hey, you didn't do anything wrong. Even she—I don't know, she's a reporter. . . ."

He looked relieved. My Lord. I still had the capacity to relieve someone. I felt better again. My boy and I ushered and ushered well.

Then I watched my wife the President come down the aisle as matron of honor. I caught her eye and she gave me an impenetrable look.

I didn't think she had to do that, frankly. I thought she could have given me a penetrable look. But maybe I had given her an impenetrable look. I sat there and thought:

"What I have to remember is that people look back at us the way we look at them."

And:

"We are essentially in public here (when aren't we anymore?). It is not the time for private looks."

And:

"Lord, Lord. I used to be an impious young reporter for the Dingler *Beacon*. My last salaried position."

Dancy was, like they say, radiant. Nobody had told her about my gaffe or the Marilyn contretemps. She and Holman looked at each other just exactly the way you would've wanted them to. Lucy took it upon herself to inject a little levity by singing "I Never Promised You a Rose Garden," but everybody knew that Dancy loved a joke, and then Lucy sang "Oh Promise Me" pretty as an angel of heaven.

The vows were exchanged. Nothing freakish happened.

And then both families got together for a picture. Something I was not at all up for. I was tired, tired. C probably was too. I wanted to take her up to bed. Just as I got within an arm's length of her, there was the General in my face.

He glared. He looked like he was about to bark. I could feel myself getting angry. C grabbed my arm.

"General," I said (for that is what I call my father-in-law), "that story does not accurately reflect—"

He said, *"Hunnhh,"* went red in the face and fell.

There he was, that distinguished thing, a dying father. He lay on the lawn for a moment not-quite-flat, near-quivering. He didn't want to kick, he didn't want to stiffen, he didn't want to stand, he didn't want to lie, he didn't want to be questioned, he didn't want to be abandoned, he didn't want to be still or to move, he didn't want to be silent or to cry. He didn't want to clench against the pain, that would be too painful, and he didn't want to ease into it for the same reason. He was so frustrated he couldn't even scream in frustration. There was nothing he could want except unconsciousness and he didn't dare relax enough for that or explode into it either. He couldn't stand even to tremble.

Or so it seemed to me in that moment before everybody moved toward him. "Lloyd, quick!" I said to Holman's brother, but Lloyd stood frozen. Some doctor! Afraid of malpractice, for Christ—

Jackson was adroitly loosening his grandfather's dress blues. Then blowing air into his grandfather's mouth.

Jackson.

"Jackson knows CPR," I said aloud. *I* didn't know he knew CPR.

Then Dr. Fitzer, never far from the President, took over and—

And then—everything happened quickly, but just about the time Dr. Fitzer took over from Jackson, Milam was standing next to C whispering in her ear, in the sort of excited voice kids get when they're saying, "Play like," play like he's saying so-and-so:

"His last words," Milam was suggesting, "were 'Remember what Ike said: Beware the military-industrial complex.' We'll have a Searcy Plan. . . ."

I swear. I looked at Milam for a split second, C and I looked at each other for a split second, and then we looked back at her father and there was a swirl of medical personnel. And I heard her saying to Milam, "Make sure *everything* is done." Milam went scurrying. She went to the General, leaned over him. He reached up and touched her pearls. The White House photographer got pictures.

"Just curious," I heard Holman say next to me. "Why'd you call on *Lloyd*?"

"He was the closest doctor," I said.

"Lloyd's not a doctor," Holman said.

"He's not? He told me he was a urologist."

"I don't know what put *that* in his mind. Lloyd *will tell* people things, though. I'd better have a talk with him."

Dancy called Holman away. So much for my spermatological solace.

The General was breathing again and relaxed, his color was better, they were wheeling him to an ambulance. C was walking beside him (the White House photographer got more pictures). Milam was at her ear and she was nodding. Leonard was at her ear and she was nodding. Dr. Fitzer was at her ear and she was nodding.

She accepted hugs from Jackson and Lucy and Dancy. Secret Service all about.

A bride was on hand, a man just snatched from the jaws of death was on hand, and C was the centerpiece. The White House photographer got more pictures.

And I was bleeding, actually kind of copiously, where C's red nails had slashed my wrist.

I'm bleeding now, in fact. I'd better go get my dressing changed and finish this tomorrow.

★ TUES., SEPT. 7, 1993

I HADN'T REALIZED I was bleeding until I tried to push into the crowd around C. Suddenly I felt a little faint. Great, just what was needed, a fainting husband—I slapped myself in the head and saw blood spurting. I started to call out to C but she was surrounded. Somebody had ahold of my arm, lifting it over my head.

Wulf of the Secret Service. Her day on First Hubby patrol. She grabbed one of the white-jacket guys who had materialized, and he ran to get bandages. I was feeling considerably faint now, but I wanted to catch the others.

"Stop!" Wulf said. "Lie down!" My head swam.

I woke up on the Rose Garden lawn, just Wulf and me.

"I better go to Walter F. Reed," I said. "That's where they'll be."

"No, don't," she said. She has a nice face, Wulf. "The President said to wait here. She'll be back soon and she wants to talk to you."

"Fuck the President," I thought. "Run away with me, Wulf," I thought.

"Wulf," I said, "we're going out."

★   ★   ★

I just had a quick makeup job, white hair and some wrinkles. I felt like I didn't need much help to look old. I instructed Wulf to take my arm and we walked around the Ellipse, checked out the monuments, checked out the afternoon. Weather was nice. We talked about that. Talked about how glad we were that August was over. Talked about the Orioles, going for their fourth straight pennant under Frank Robinson. We dawdled. I practiced my old-man act.

"I like wearing this old felt hat, here," I told Wulf. "I think I could enjoy old-manhood. Dirty old manhood." I gave her a little pat on the bottom. She jumped.

"Just kidding!" I said. "I know better than to mess around with the Secret Service. Say, Wulf. You don't *know* anything, do you? I mean about the fish and all, conspiracies."

She said I was talking foolish. So we talked about fish. I told her about Tommy Hugh and the Mystery Object. I felt kind of bad about Tommy Hugh, actually. We had come around the East Wing of the White House and were crossing Pennsylvania to Lafayette Park. She said she went fishing once with her father.

What's your father do, I asked her.

Urologist, she said.

"*Urologist?* He is? He *really* is? Listen, Wulf. Can you get ahold of your father now, on the phone?"

"I think probably so, Sunday afternoon."

"See that phone booth over there? You can watch me from there. Please go and call your father and ask him, does it ever happen that a vasectomy, after eight or ten years, will reverse itself. Everything grow back together. Will you do that for me? If you will, I'll sit down on that bench right there and promise not to faint."

Reluctantly, she agreed.

I sat down. And looked at where I lived. Where ah leeyuved. C and I used to have this thing we'd say to each other. I don't remember how it got started. Something about things hitting you where you lived. Anyway, if one of us asked the other how he or she was doing, the other would just make a vaguely emotive noise and say, "Where ah leeyuv." Neither of us had said it in a while.

That's what I was thinking about, when who to my wondering eyes should appear but the powdery old lady. Poof, poof, back up to the bench, bend and blap. And a big poof. She didn't say anything. Of course, I didn't look like any of the other people she had seen me as.

I was not much in the mood for the powdery old lady. I was in the mood for Wulf. I wanted to be with somebody who made *me* feel better. And her powder bothered my sinuses. Which made me think of Redick. Well, hell, was Redick my fault? He was doing his thing. And so was the powdery lady doing hers.

"How are you, madam?" I asked her in a creaky voice. I tipped my hat.

She wouldn't look at me.

"Isn't it a nice day?" I said.

"Hot," she said. She probably couldn't feel any breeze through that powder. "Too hot."

"Do you follow the Orioles?" I asked her.

"Never liked birds. They peck," she said. She was in an even worse mood than usual.

Wulf walked past, gave me a little "Oh, I see you've found a new girlfriend" look, and handed me a folded piece of paper. "Excuse me, madam," I said to the powdery lady. "A message has just reached me, of the highest importance."

I opened it. It said: "Happens in one of fourteen hundred cases."

I almost jumped straight up in the air. One in fourteen hundred! That was *better* than a hundred thousand to one. That was *much* better. That, in comparison with everything else in my life lately, was damn near *likely*.

"Well!" I said to the powdery lady. "Well. That, at least, is good news. Well! It *is* a nice day. Here we are, with a fine view of the White House, home of our President and her—"

"Fuck the President," said the powdery old lady. I turned, startled, and she looked me square in the eye. "The President," she said, "is an asshole."

"C!" I said.

She just looked at me. Through those rheumy powder-blue contacts.

"C," I said. "Hey, you shouldn't be out here, it's not safe! What in th—how's the General? It was always you?"

"Oh, Hopsie," she said.

"Here, I can't stand looking at you like that. Take off those contacts."

"Guy, somebody will see!"

"Come on, take them off. C. C. I *missed* you. Here, give me a little squeeze—*ack*. Here, get some of that powder off."

"No, Guy. Wait, I'll take the contacts off. Now."

"Ah. It *is* you down in there. You've been meeting me like this!"

"I thought you'd recognize me."

"I've been having trouble recognizing you *and* me lately. Hi. Aren't you something? How's your daddy?"

"He's going to be all right. What's wrong with your arm?" She took it in her hands as if it were her arm. Well, that doesn't make sense, does it? But it felt good.

"What's wrong with it? You clawed it. You opened an artery or something."

"Oh, Guy. When I saw Daddy—"

"It's okay. I didn't think you meant to kill me. But I couldn't get up with you to go to the hospital. I was spurting blood. Hey, Jackson knows CPR."

"He took a course at school."

"Well, he never told me."

"Yes, I think he did, he told me all about it."

"No, he didn't, I'd've remembered."

"Dr. Fitzer says his being so quick could've made the difference."

"Jackson. And Lucy—C, *damn* I wish you'd seen Lucy last night at the party. She was doing the Dancy dance."

"I heard about it. We've got good kids, Guy."

"Yeah. We do."

"You're not all that bad a father, you know. Fussy, but not all that bad."

"C. C. But not such a good hubby. Listen, C, that interview, I swear—"

"I talked to Leonard, and I talked to Jackson."

"Does Jackson feel bad about it?"

"Not as bad as I wish he did. I'm afraid he's serious about her. Just what I need."

"Well, listen, I'll say this. She's . . . well, I was going to say she was nice. I looked up *Sioux* in the dictionary last night. Did you know that *Sioux* is the Sioux word for *enemy*, or *little snake*? Figure that. She interests me."

"She would."

"Listen, if I can deal with Ng. Anyway, I think she really likes Jackson."

"Who is she not to? Guy, I wish you wouldn't go around talking about my innocences."

"Yeah, I know. I was just . . . I know."

"Lashing out at them."

"Oh. I forgot that was in there. Well. Listen. C. Tell me, now. What did happen when you were a little girl?"

"I hate to talk about it."

"I know, but—you told Leonard about it, didn't you?"

"Leonard and Dancy and I talked about it, a while back. Dancy and I agreed it was time to let it all go. She talked to Holman about it too."

"But you never told me about it."

"Guy, you'd've gotten all—you'd've wanted me to *delve into* it with you. You'd've wanted to get to the *bottom* of it. You'd've *explained* it. You'd've explained *me.* I don't want that, Guy."

"But why didn't you tell me *that,* and then tell me? So tell me, now."

"Daddy was in the prison camp, you know. Dancy and I—well, when Daddy came *back,* Dancy was just nine, and I was just *three.* So I don't even really remember any of this. I just remember being scared. Bertie Dingler . . ."

"Bertie?"

"B. Vaughn Dingler, Jr., Memorial Junior College? Bertie was B. Vaughn Dingler, Jr. He was, I don't know, eighteen. And I guess—well, you can imagine, Dingler's son. He was weird. And he did things to Dancy. And . . . oh, Guy."

"C, I'm sorry. You don't have to tell me. I'm sorry. Here, I've got an old man's handkerchief."

"No, I'm going to finish. Dancy . . . *fought* him, Guy. She couldn't stop him from doing things to her, but she stopped him from . . . me. She must have been so brave. She was mean to me, but she didn't want anybody *else* to be. And I couldn't help her, Guy, I was too *little.* That's all I—and we were too ashamed to tell anybody. Because, you can imagine, Bertie told us . . . Dancy has told me all this. He told us . . . religious things, and he told us he would do it to our mother. Dancy and I were even ashamed to talk to each *other* about it. We *still* are. We haven't been as close as we should be, because of it. Which is so stupid. And we probably should talk to a therapist but we—I can't really do that now. And—I should have talked to you, Guy. But I was still . . . I'm the President, Guy, and I'm proud of that. Ever since you've known me I've been doing things I was proud of. But that wasn't true before we met. And I was—I'm still—I know I shouldn't be, but I'm ashamed of the other thing. Oh, Guy, I *wish* I had seen Lucy dancing with Dancy. Oh, Guyyyyyyy."

"C. Sugar. They'll do it again. We'll have a command perform-ance. Please don't . . . No, *do* cry."

"I can't. The Secret Service is watching. Ah'm. There."

"Well, let's go . . . where we leeyuv. I'll walk you back."

"Wait, no. I'm going to tell you the rest. Daddy came home. And we—not we, I was too little to think. Dancy thought Daddy would protect us. So she told him."

"And he got so mad. It was a terrible time for him of course. He'd been tortured. He didn't want to hear that his friend's son . . . First he got mad at Dancy. He didn't want to believe her. And then . . . he got so mad. We wanted him to defend us, we didn't want him—he *scared us.* He made it worse. For our *daddy* to be so mad. And then he *did* believe Dancy, and—

"See, Guy, I've never even *known* for sure. I can't talk to Daddy about it. I can't talk to Daddy about anything."

"I can't either. Holman can."

"That's what Dancy says. I think Holman is good, Guy."

"Yeah. He's probably a knowing agent of the Southern Baptist conspiracy but . . ."

"No, I had him investigated. His family is kind of strange . . ."

"Everybody's is," I said.

"That's right, isn't it? Everybody's is. But Guy, Daddy . . . I don't *know.* Whether it was Daddy. Or Dingler. But one of them killed Bertie."

"Wooh. You don't know. . . ."

"Dancy doesn't either. But somehow—I mean, Bertie disap-peared right then, and his body was found. See, I was *three.* And I've never known how much to *believe* of what Dancy says, you know, details. Which I'm ashamed to say, because I know she didn't make the main part up, I remember Bertie and us fighting. It was terrible. And Mama was just so sweet to us, she cried, and held us so sweet. And Daddy was so mad. She was sort of like us—like Daddy too, I guess. Ashamed to talk. I think it probably killed Mama."

"Oh, Lord, C. But your father and Dingler are still friends?"

"Still . . . they feel linked in some way. It's sick, isn't it?"

"I don't think it's what Jesus had in mind."

"Now the family's got to talk about it, I guess."

"But you probably want to rest now. Let's go back."

"No, Guy. We'll go back in the house and you'll look at me with those eyes . . ."

"I'll what?"

"You remember when we'd just met, and we were driving away from Dingler. Guy, I would have done anything in the world you wanted me to. That's why I said being pregnant didn't have anything to do with you—I didn't *want* it to have anything to do with you. Because I would still do anything that I could tell from your eyes you really wanted me to do."

"Abdicate?"

"No."

"If you had to choose between the presidency and me you'd pick the presidency?"

"In a New York minute."

"So how can you say—"

"It wouldn't be *you* if you gave me that kind of ultimatum."

What a piece of work is woman.

"I see. And back there in the car—come on, C, you never wanted to drive around lackadaisically like me."

"No, I wouldn't have been happy doing it. But I would have *done* it. And we would've broken up. But when you mentioned your friend in jail—he was *your* friend. I didn't want to go back to Dingler either. But if we went back and helped your friend, and got involved in what was going on—I thought it was a way we could both be happy together. And then you got so *mad.*"

"And you overreacted so. You weren't reacting to me, you were reacting to your father."

"Guy, you're explaining me. It's not that simple. You can't *solve* life."

"No, but you can translate as much as you can into words."

"Into *something.* Not necessarily *words.* Guy, you're a writer. You have this little imaginary friend you talk to. And there's probably some solution for why you have that strange habit. But you don't want a solution. You don't want words about *why* you do it. You want to *do* it. And I want to do politics."

"Uh, C?"

"What."

"I don't know whether you've noticed, or not—don't let me offend you, now. But you've been doing pretty well here with words."

"Well, thank you. And now I want to go get all this stuff off and go fuck. I figured out what a half-foot represents, while I was in London."

"What?"

"A good six inches."

"C, I swear. You ought to be in a cage."

"You make a good-looking old man."

"You make a good-looking old woman. But wait a minute now. One. Can we talk like this more often? I don't mean like *this,* quite, but. Full and frank discussions. Wide-ranging exchanges of views. Hey, my childhood of course is pretty small potatoes compared to that story of yours, but there are some interesting . . . For instance, Aunt Big Sybil—"

"Okay, we'll talk like this more often."

"Okay. Two. The baby. The prospective baby, I mean."

"Oh, Guy, don't you know I've been thinking about the prospective baby?"

"He or she could play under your desk, like John-John Kennedy."

"Do you want a baby playing under *your* desk?"

"I've *had* babies playing under my desk."

"Yes, and you yelled at them."

"And they turned out great, right?"

"You don't want to have a baby, you want to have an argument about having a baby."

"That's something to talk about. So that folds back into One, above. We'll talk like this about having this baby? Weigh all the real advantages and disadvantages and all of our feelings and reach a decision we can share?"

"Guy. You're being almost *executive.*"

"Thank you. I guess. I've been suffering from agenda envy. Oh, something else—"

"Is this Three?"

"This is sort of Three. This is connected to Three. I'm talking about Milam. That was awful, making up last words for your father—"

"I know. But Guy, Milam loves what I *do*. Purely because it gives him a chance to do what he does. We don't need anything else from each other. Nothing hurts his feelings because he doesn't have any. What a comfort that is."

"You can't get along without him, can you?"

"I could so. There are other fish in the sea. But—"

"Don't say that! However, it brings me right into point Three. C, now, don't be offended: *are* you involved in a plot?"

"Guy. You are such a wanker sometimes."

"Now you're picking up coarse British expressions. Answer my question."

"Guy, I am involved in so many plots. . . . What do you think I do for a living?"

"C, you know what I'm talking about. I don't want to stir Dingler back up again, but why *is* he backing you? Is he afraid you'll blow the whistle on him?"

"Maybe."

"So maybe Sioux Iycxx's story is true."

"Guy, if you want to *explain* Dingler you can do it with demographics. Somehow or another he has developed a New Age following, and therefore he is going progressive. It doesn't matter to me what his reasons are. My reasons are, if there's some good to be gotten out of him, I deserve it—and Guy, *dealing* with him, I'm not afraid of him."

"But, uh, this conspiracy theory that Marilyn Quayle . . ."

"That bitch is in Qaddafi's pants, is I'll bet what happened. We'll see about her, and him."

"C! You're being coarse again, and you're avoiding my question! *Was there or was there not a conspiracy to overthrow Bush and then DaSilva so as to put you in power?*"

"By shooting DaSilva with a fish and so on?"

"Well, yes."

"Guy. Listen. There is something that we've got to get straight. Look at me. You have got to believe in something. I believe in God. That means there are a lot of things I don't have to worry about. One of them is the possibility that somehow without my knowledge some human cabal is using me as a pawn in this preposterous way."

"Okay. I believe in something. I believe in my wife's incredible eyes."

"No. That's not enough. You need to believe in something outside you and me."

"A Third Force."

"Mm."

"Okay. I believe in the fish. I believe that the fish was a fluke."

"Guy . . ."

"Huh? Huh? Little humor? Something we need as much of as we
can get these days?"

"Guy. What I need is for you to *love* me. Or else . . ."

"Love me or leave me?"

"That's right."

"I'd love you, even if I did leave you."

"No. I'm not talking about wandering around *feeling* like you love
me. I'm talking about, *love* me. It doesn't do me any good for you
to be driving down the road feeling bad."

"C, I'm on your side. I just need to be *myself* on your side."

"Guy, you don't have to *try* to be yourself. You are more yourself
than . . . *Dancy* is."

"Dancy loves you."

"Yes. She does. She's jealous of me but she loves me. She always
did. And I want to be with her more."

"I'm for that."

"So."

"So," I said. "If we talk more like this, give and take, freedom of
speech, then I've got being myself covered. So I can be somebody
else. I can be a conscientious First Hubby: a serious joke. For you
I can be a cheerful helpmate. Maybe I can even learn to lie in
interviews. Heh."

"What?"

"I was just remembering one time when Jackson was little. He
had just learned how to pump himself in the swing. And he was
sitting there in the swing and he said, 'Well. Now I can pump myself
in the swing. And I can pour my own milk. And I can tie my own
shoes.'

" 'Why do you sound so sad about it?' I said.

"He sighed. He said, 'Now I have to do it all the time.' "

"Your son is a serious person."

"If he would just call me every now and then, and talk about a
movie he's seen or—I'll call him. I won't be put off. I'm not going

to get mad, I'm going to get even! I'll make him start being glad
to hear my voice whether he likes it or not! He must still be a little
bit crazy or he wouldn't be involved with someone named Sioux.
I am grimly determined to be silly again with Jackson."

"You aren't going to lose your temper?"

"Nope. That's my plan. Have you noticed I've stopped using
cusswords? Well, I have. Will you do me a favor and not say *asshole*
anymore even in jest, even in disguise?"

"Presidents don't just give favors away. What's in it for me?"

"Decorum. People don't want their President to slip up and say
asshole on TV."

"Mm."

"And here's another little tip for you. I was just thinking—remember, when you were pregnant with Lucy, it helped you in
negotiations? Maybe you don't want to admit it, but it did. Don't
you think the nation would go for an expectant President? How is
anyone going to accuse you of plots if you stand before them as an
ever-growing example of Motherhood?"

"Why Guy! I believe that is what is called *realpolitik.*"

The powdery lady and I brushed each other's lips cloudily. We
enjoyed the park for a little while, and then, circuitously, we es-
corted each other back to the house.

★   ★   ★

So. That's it. Before the powdery lady showed up in the park there,
I was seriously considering sending this—take out the dirty bits
first, but then sending the rest of this—off to a publisher, it's a free
country, what the heck.

But no, not now. For one thing, the ending is too soppy. If
anybody else had written it, I'd say, "Yuck." Its only justification
is, it's what we said.

I've left out some other things we said as we were sitting there
enjoying the park. C said, "What is so *bad* about being First
Hubby?"

"You mean aside from the fact that everywhere I go, people rush
to shake my hand so that they can tell everybody what a jerk I am
for being frankly less excited to meet them than they are to meet
me?" I said. "Well, nothing, really, except that I have no freedom

of speech, no right to privacy, no freedom of assembly, I can't petition for grievances, I can't bear arms—"

"You don't like arms. You can't stand arms."

"No, but what if I could? What if I wanted an Uzi in my lap, of an evening, like any other law-abiding citizen? The Secret Service—who amount to troops quartered in my home without my consent—would have a fit. I'm afraid somebody's going to ask me what my religion is because I'd have to tell them it's none. I can't vote my own interests—"

"How's that?"

"The last time I voted, my overriding interest was staying out of the government, but I couldn't bring myself to pull a lever against my wife. I can't make a living, I can't jump in the car and drive off down the highway, I can't shoot the shit with weirdos and common drunks, I can't burn the flag—*I don't feel like an American.* I *miss* feeling like an American."

"Guy," she said, "nobody feels like an American in their marriage."

Which may be true. And in intimacy nobody talks literature, either. The language of marriage is embarrassing, one way or another. It might as well be embarrassingly soppy and accommodating. Nobody else but us is listening.

Maybe I took being an English major too much to heart, but it has taken me a long time to arrive at a conclusion that many people who don't get all caught up in the liberal arts, and many who do, reach at much younger ages: that on many if not most occasions, the person you are addressing—a woman, say—would *rather* hear something subliterary. She does not want someone straining beside her in the night to frame a bit of truth, suitable for showing to Flaubert. She would rather hear something mawkish, trite, even palpably (no, *deceptively*) mendacious, as long as it makes her feel that you are *on her side.*

So, Lord knows, would voters.

So why did C choose me?

Maybe because I am as terrible as her father in some different way that she can live with. Maybe she has conquered me now, as she did her father. Maybe as I convince her I am her partisan, the truth will emerge.

She is already telling me things she never did before.

I said to her last night: "I still feel bad that after all these years, we had never talked about what happened to you when you were little. Didn't you ever want to tell me?"

"Yes," she said, "but I was afraid I wouldn't be clever enough."

"Aw," I said, with real feeling. Thinking meanwhile, "You are so full of shit"—but also: "This is the way she is. Her defenses are part of her. This is the way she is going to be." And feeling a certain peace.

"I was afraid you wouldn't want me anymore," she went on—looking, as she said it, brave-vulnerable with her eyes and lips in a way that she knows good and well is ravishing. "Guy, nobody but you comes on to me."

"Aw," I said. "Hey, you're the President."

"But they never did. Not even the Reverend Micah."

"That's because they could tell that you loved me," I said. "Also, you're scary," I said, crossing my fingers.

"*Guy,*" she said. Whew. She liked it.

"Yes, you are, too. Even to me. Or you were. You're not so scary to me anymore." She liked that too.

"See," she said. "It's different."

"It's better," I said, and that was the truth. I've never felt free enough, before, to say any old thing that pops into my head, with feeling. Free speech of a kind. Freedom to be corny. Maybe I've sold out, I don't know. Before the powdery lady and I walked home, I said, "Let's eavesdrop a little," and we moved over to another bench where two old guys were talking.

"People be saying, 'Watch that shit,' " one of them said. "Too late now. Shoulda been watching it when the shit was *building.* The shit *live* here now. Too late to be hip to it."

"People know it's bad now but do it anyway," the second one said.

"You can be too hip for yo' own ass. Ass be sitting there smiling, nodding. You be styling right on by like you don't know whose it is. Yo' ass know, though. Yo' ass know *you* know."

"Slip by for a while. But the grease dry up."

"People don't know what they *want.* Don't like it when they get it."

"Saying, 'I saw Jesus in a dream last night.' "

"Ohmm-huh."

"Saying, 'I thought he was *taller* than that.' "

What the stuff is that those old guys had in mind, that "lives here," I don't know. But I've given up on being hip, it's too hard for a person in my position. I'm going to take things just as tall as they come. I will no longer dwell in the valley of the tongue-in-cheek. Anger, oblique anger, is what it is. The tongue-in-cheek sucks.

Last night C told me something else about her childhood:

"One day after they found Bertie Dingler dead, I started crying. I cried all day. They thought I was crazy. Mama would try to comfort me, then Daddy would yell at me because I wouldn't be comforted. Dingler came over to offer spiritual guidance. You can imagine how comforting that was. And then I went into my room and put on my Christmas pageant costume. Angel wings and a halo. And I came back out into the living room and smiled and recited my part from the pageant: 'Unto us this day a child is born.' And I smiled. I smiled and smiled. I decided just to be sweet and do whatever I wanted to.

"I think Daddy and Dingler have been afraid of me ever since. And that scares me. What if they ever *stopped* being scared? I don't *know* whether I was glad you hit Daddy, but it made me feel you were part of my pageant."

"Lord," I said. I couldn't think of anything to say about that. I just accepted it. You should have heard her recite that line, in an eerie child's voice. She was on a roll. She went on to tell me about girl talk with Mrs. Thatcher:

"We were having breakfast just the two of us, the morning after I was singing in the pub with the press, and Maggie said, 'My dear, Americans are meant to be outspoken. Tell me, do you still fancy your husband?'

"I was surprised. But I didn't let on. I told her I did.

" 'Jolly good thing, too,' she said. She actually said that: 'Jolly good thing, too.' And then she said, 'When one *does,* then it is so lovely to toy with other men.' "

"So," I said. "That's how you world-leading women talk. I never heard you do a British accent before. You could have been an actress, you know."

"Being an actress is helpful to people, Guy. If you just tell them what you think all the time, they don't know how to react. Plus the fact you might as well face up to it that you *aren't* telling the truth all the time, so you might as well put as much acting into it as you can."

I couldn't think of anything to say to that, either. "Maggie still has it for old Denis, then?"

"I gather she does."

"At least by the standards that obtain over there."

"We might be surprised."

"I bet that's true. I bet everybody's marriage might surprise everybody else."

I still haven't told C, or anybody else, about what Aunt Big Sybil said about how my mother and her husband died—whatever it was that Aunt Sybil *did* say, exactly. Maybe I don't want to know, exactly. Maybe I will be able to put my own spin on it, sometime. And lay it on C. To what end? Resonance? Sympathy? I just know there is leverage in what's held back.

★   ★   ★

My mother left me for *Uncle Gene?*
    Bitch!

★   ★   ★

Well, I won't go on and on. This (without the dirty bits) is for your eyes only, future First Spouses. For publication I'll write something more seemly, more consistent. This—well, you of all people can see why this can't be published. This is the only copy, except for the unexpurgated original, which I am too sentimental, or something, to destroy. I have it stashed somewhere safe, where I can get at it for nostalgia's sake. I have made arrangements, just in case, that if anything untoward happens to C (or me), it goes to Gorbachev at Villard.

Maybe you future First Ladies and Hubbies will have less trouble fitting into the job. But see if you can swell the First Lady folder this well. See if your President can be as good as mine is going to be. C is going to *do* some things. And I guess she will run for reelection. But if she starts thinking about that *instead* of doing things, I will be on her case. And she trusts what I say now, I have her ear.

One other thing I said to her as we were walking home:

"C? E.B.'s in trouble again."

ABOUT THE AUTHOR

Roy Blount, Jr., a contributing editor to *The Atlantic* and *Spy* who writes for many magazines and has performed a one-man show at the American Place Theatre, is a novelist.
    Now.